THE SLEEPER AWAKES
AND MEN LIKE GODS

THE SLEEPER AWAKES
AND MEN LIKE GODS

Dystopian and Utopian Fiction from the Father of Science Fiction

H.G. WELLS

Edited by

AMANDA MONTANDON

Afterword by

ERIC FLINT

WFP

WORDFIRE PRESS

CONTENTS

MEN LIKE GODS

EDITOR'S NOTE

"May you live in interesting times."

—Chamberlain curse

We are currently living in interesting times; whether that is a blessing or a curse remains to be seen. Yet, we are not the first to have lived through complex and interesting times. We will not be the last.

H.G. Wells lived in interesting times—he witnessed both World Wars in his lifetime, the Spanish Influenza, the invention of the airplane, women's suffrage, the atomic bomb, and so much more. His works are still widely read today and have influenced many modern authors. With current events bearing striking similarities to previous times in history where disillusionment and tensions have reached a boiling point, Wells's writings are even more relevant. Many social influencers and literary circles are referencing George Orwell's *1984* and *Animal Farm*. You might have recently heard quotes from Aldous Huxley's *A Brave New World*. But did you know that Wells inspired those authors with their dystopias and utopias? If so, you might presume that they were influenced by his most famous novels: *The Time Machine, The War of the Worlds*, or *The Invisible Man* ... but you would be mistaken.

While those novels are famous for a reason, H.G. Wells plumbed the depths of society and human nature in many of his other works; *The*

Sleeper Awakes and *Men Like Gods* are not commonplace titles or required reading for many educational programs, but they are shockingly applicable to our present times. I chose to marry these two novels in this volume so that you may readily see both sides of the same coin. I took painstaking care to preserve the original thoughts, intents, British spellings, and wordings. Keep in mind that these works are a window into a different time period and do not cater to modern sensibilities.

Will you be inspired as Huxley and Orwell were to write your own novel expanding on these ideas? Do you see our current society rising to the peak of a Utopian mountain? Or will you resonate with the idea that we are spiraling toward a drain through which humanity must be flushed? Turn the page, flip the coin, but don't forget to call it ... heads ... or tails?

—Amanda Montandon

THE SLEEPER AWAKES

PREFACE FROM THE 1910 EDITION

When the Sleeper Wakes, whose title I have now altered to *The Sleeper Awakes*, was first published as a book in 1899 after a serial appearance in the *Graphic* and one or two American and colonial periodicals. It is one of the most ambitious and least satisfactory of my books, and I have taken the opportunity afforded by this reprinting to make a number of excisions and alterations. Like most of my earlier work, it was written under considerable pressure; there are marks of haste not only in the writing of the latter part, but in the very construction of the story. Except for certain streaks of a slovenliness which seems to be an almost unavoidable defect in me, there is little to be ashamed of in the writing of the opening portion; but it will be fairly manifest to the critic that instead of being put aside and thought over through a leisurely interlude, the ill-conceived latter part was pushed to its end. I was at that time overworked, and badly in need of a holiday. In addition to various necessary journalistic tasks, I had in hand another book, *Love and Mr. Lewisham*, which had taken a very much stronger hold upon my affections than this present story. My circumstances demanded that one or other should be finished before I took any rest, and so I wound up the Sleeper sufficiently to make it a marketable work, hoping to be able to revise it before the book printers at any rate got hold of it. But fortune was against me. I came back to England from Italy only to fall dangerously ill, and I still remember the impotent rage and strain of my attempt to put some sort of finish to my story of Mr. Lewisham, with my temperature at a hundred and two. I couldn't endure the thought of leaving that book a fragment. I did afterwards contrive to save it from the consequences of that febrile spurt —*Love and Mr. Lewisham* is indeed one of my most carefully balanced books—but the Sleeper escaped me.

It is twelve years now since the Sleeper was written, and that young man of thirty-one is already too remote for me to attempt any very drastic reconstruction of his work. I have played now merely the part of an editorial elder brother: cut out relentlessly a number of long tiresome passages that showed all too plainly the fagged, toiling brain, the heavy sluggish *driven* pen, and straightened out certain indecisions at the end. Except for that, I have done no more than hack here and there at clumsy phrases and repetitions. The worst thing in the earlier version, and the thing that rankled most in my mind, was the treatment of the relations of Helen Wotton and Graham. Haste in art is almost always vulgarisation, and I slipped into the obvious vulgarity of making what the newspaper syndicates call a "love interest" out of Helen. There was even a clumsy intimation that instead of going up in the flying machine to fight, Graham might have given in to Ostrog, and married Helen. I have now removed the suggestion of these uncanny connubialities. Not the slightest intimation of any sexual interest could in truth have arisen between these two. They loved and kissed one another, but as a girl and her heroic grandfather might love, and in a crisis kiss. I have found it possible, without any very serious disarrangement, to clear all that objectionable stuff out of the story, and so a little ease my conscience on the score of this ungainly lapse. I have also, with a few strokes of the pen, eliminated certain dishonest and regrettable suggestions that the People beat Ostrog. My Graham dies, as all his kind must die, with no certainty of either victory or defeat.

Who will win—Ostrog or the People? A thousand years hence that will still be just the open question we leave to-day.

—H.G. Wells

This book, *The Sleeper Awakes*, was written in that remote and comparatively happy year, 1898. It is the first or a series of books which I have written at intervals since that time; *The World Set Free* is the latest; they are all "fantasias of possibility"; each one takes some great creative tendency, or group of tendencies, and develops its possible consequences in the future. *The War in the Air* did that for example with aviation, and is perhaps, as a forecast, the most successful of them all. The present volume takes up certain ideas already very much discussed in the concluding years of the last century, the idea of the growth of the towns and the depopulation of the country-side and the degradation of labour through the higher organisation of industrial production. "Suppose these forces to go on," that is the fundamental hypothesis of the story.

The "Sleeper" is of course the average man, who owns everything—did he but choose to take hold of his possessions—and who neglects everything. He wakes up to find himself the puppet of a conspiracy of highly intellectual men in a world which is a practical realisation of Mr. Belloc's nightmare of the Servile State. And the book resolves itself into as vigorous an imagination as the writer's quality permitted of this world of base servitude in hypertrophied cities.

Will such a world ever exist?

I will confess I doubt it. At the time when I wrote this story I had a considerable belief in its possibility, but later on, in *Anticipations* (1900), I made a very careful analysis of the causes of town aggregation and showed that a period of town dispersal was already beginning. And the thesis of a gradual systematic enslavement of organised labour, presupposes an intelligence, a power of combination, and a *wickedness* in the class of rich financiers and industrial organisers, such as this class certainly does not possess, and probably cannot possess. A body of men who had the character and the largeness of imagination necessary to combine and overcome the natural insubordination of the worker would have a character and largeness of imagination too fine and great for any such plot against humanity. I was young in those days, I was thirty-two, I had met few big businessmen, and I still thought of them as wicked, able men. It was only later that I realised that on the contrary they were, for the most part, rather foolish plungers, fortunate and energetic rather than capable, vulgar rather than wicked, and quite incapable of worldwide constructive plans or generous combined action. "Ostrog" in *The Sleeper Awakes*, gave way to reality when I drew Uncle Ponderevo in *Tono-Bungay*. The great city of this story is no more then than a nightmare of Capitalism triumphant, a nightmare that was dreamt nearly a quarter of a century ago. It is a fantastic possibility no longer possible. Much evil may be in store for mankind, but to this immense, grim organisation of servitude, our race will never come.

—H.G. Wells
Easton Glebe, Dunmow, 1921

INSOMNIA

ONE AFTERNOON, AT LOW WATER, MR. ISBISTER, A YOUNG ARTIST lodging at Boscastle, walked from that place to the picturesque cove of Pentargen, desiring to examine the caves there. Half-way down the precipitous path to the Pentargen beach he came suddenly upon a man sitting in an attitude of profound distress beneath a projecting mass of rock. The hands of this man hung limply over his knees, his eyes were red and staring before him, and his face was wet with tears.

He glanced round at Isbister's footfall. Both men were disconcerted, Isbister the more so, and, to override the awkwardness of his involuntary pause, he remarked, with an air of mature conviction, that the weather was hot for the time of year.

"Very," answered the stranger shortly, hesitated a second, and added in a colourless tone, "I can't sleep."

Isbister stopped abruptly. "No?" was all he said, but his bearing conveyed his helpful impulse.

"It may sound incredible," said the stranger, turning weary eyes to Isbister's face and emphasizing his words with a languid hand, "but I have had no sleep—no sleep at all for six nights."

"Had advice?"

"Yes. Bad advice for the most part. Drugs. My nervous system.... They are all very well for the run of people. It's hard to explain. I dare not take ... sufficiently powerful drugs."

"That makes it difficult," said Isbister.

He stood helplessly in the narrow path, perplexed what to do. Clearly the man wanted to talk. An idea natural enough under the circumstances, prompted him to keep the conversation going. "I've never suffered from sleeplessness myself," he said in a tone of commonplace gossip, "but in those cases I have known, people have usually found something—"

"I dare make no experiments."

He spoke wearily. He gave a gesture of rejection, and for a space both men were silent.

"Exercise?" suggested Isbister diffidently, with a glance from his interlocutor's face of wretchedness to the touring costume he wore.

"That is what I have tried. Unwisely perhaps. I have followed the coast, day after day—from New Quay. It has only added muscular fatigue to the mental. The cause of this unrest was overwork—trouble. There was something—"

He stopped as if from sheer fatigue. He rubbed his forehead with a lean hand. He resumed speech like one who talks to himself.

"I am a lone wolf, a solitary man, wandering through a world in which I have no part. I am wifeless—childless—who is it speaks of the childless as the dead twigs on the tree of life? I am wifeless, childless—I could find no duty to do. No desire even in my heart. One thing at last I set myself to do.

"I said, I *will* do this, and to do it, to overcome the inertia of this dull body, I resorted to drugs. Great God, I've had enough of drugs! I don't know if *you* feel the heavy inconvenience of the body, its exasperating demand of time from the mind—time—life! Live! We only live in patches. We have to eat, and then comes the dull digestive complacencies—or irritations. We have to take the air or else our thoughts grow sluggish, stupid, run into gulfs and blind alleys. A thousand distractions arise from within and without, and then comes drowsiness and sleep. Men seem to live for sleep. How little of a man's day is his own—even at the best! And then come those false friends, those Thug helpers, the alkaloids that stifle natural fatigue and kill rest—black coffee, cocaine—"

"I see," said Isbister.

"I did my work," said the sleepless man with a querulous intonation.

"And this is the price?"

"Yes."

For a little while the two remained without speaking.

"You cannot imagine the craving for rest that I feel—a hunger and thirst. For six long days, since my work was done, my mind has been a whirlpool, swift, unprogressive and incessant, a torrent of thoughts leading nowhere, spinning round swift and steady—" He paused. "Towards the gulf."

"You must sleep," said Isbister decisively, and with an air of a remedy discovered. "Certainly you must sleep."

"My mind is perfectly lucid. It was never clearer. But I know I am drawing towards the vortex. Presently—"

"Yes?"

"You have seen things go down an eddy? Out of the light of the day, out of this sweet world of sanity—down—"

"But," expostulated Isbister.

The man threw out a hand towards him, and his eyes were wild, and his voice suddenly high. "I shall kill myself. If in no other way—at the foot of yonder dark precipice there, where the waves are green, and the white surge lifts and falls, and that little thread of water trembles down. There at any rate is ... sleep."

"That's unreasonable," said Isbister, startled at the man's hysterical gust of emotion. "Drugs are better than that."

"There at any rate is sleep," repeated the stranger, not heeding him.

Isbister looked at him. "It's not a cert, you know," he remarked. "There's a cliff like that at Lulworth Cove—as high, anyhow—and a little girl fell from top to bottom. And lives to-day—sound and well."

"But those rocks there?"

"One might lie on them rather dismally through a cold night, broken bones grating as one shivered, chill water splashing over you. Eh?"

Their eyes met. "Sorry to upset your ideals," said Isbister with a sense of devil-may-careish brilliance. "But a suicide over that cliff (or any cliff for the matter of that), really, as an artist—" He laughed. "It's so damned amateurish."

"But the other thing," said the sleepless man irritably, "the other thing. No man can keep sane if night after night—"

"Have you been walking along this coast alone?"

"Yes."

"Silly sort of thing to do. If you'll excuse my saying so. Alone! As you say; body fag is no cure for brain fag. Who told you to? No wonder; walking! And the sun on your head, heat, fag, solitude, all the day long, and then, I suppose, you go to bed and try very hard—eh?"

Isbister stopped short and looked at the sufferer doubtfully.

"Look at these rocks!" cried the seated man with a sudden force of gesture. "Look at that sea that has shone and quivered there for ever! See the white spume rush into darkness under that great cliff. And this blue vault, with the blinding sun pouring from the dome of it. It is your world. You accept it, you rejoice in it. It warms and supports and delights you. And for me—"

He turned his head and showed a ghastly face, bloodshot pallid eyes and bloodless lips. He spoke almost in a whisper. "It is the garment of my misery. The whole world ... is the garment of my misery."

Isbister looked at all the wild beauty of the sunlit cliffs about them and back to that face of despair. For a moment he was silent.

He started, and made a gesture of impatient rejection. "You get a night's sleep," he said, "and you won't see much misery out here. Take my word for it."

He was quite sure now that this was a providential encounter. Only half an hour ago he had been feeling horribly bored. Here was employment the bare thought of which, was righteous self-applause. He took possession forthwith. The first need of this exhausted being was companionship. He flung himself down on the steeply sloping turf beside the motionless seated figure, and threw out a skirmishing line of gossip.

His hearer lapsed into apathy; he stared dismally seaward, and spoke only in answer to Isbister's direct questions—and not to all of those. But he made no objection to this benevolent intrusion upon his despair.

He seemed even grateful, and when presently Isbister, feeling that his unsupported talk was losing vigour, suggested that they should reascend the steep and return towards Boscastle, alleging the view into Blackapit, he submitted quietly. Halfway up he began talking to himself, and abruptly turned a ghastly face on his helper. "What can be happening?" he asked with a gaunt illustrative hand. "What can be happening? Spin, spin, spin, spin. It goes round and round, round and round for evermore."

He stood with his hand circling.

"It's all right, old chap," said Isbister with the air of an old friend. "Don't worry yourself. Trust to me."

The man dropped his hand and turned again. They went over the brow and to the headland beyond Penally, with the sleepless man gesticulating ever and again, and speaking fragmentary things concerning his whirling brain. At the headland they stood by the seat that looks into the dark mysteries of Blackapit, and then he sat down. Isbister had resumed his talk whenever the path had widened sufficiently for them to walk abreast.

He was enlarging upon the complex difficulty of making Boscastle Harbour in bad weather, when suddenly and quite irrelevantly his companion interrupted him again.

"My head is not like what it was," he said, gesticulating for want of expressive phrases. "It's not like what it was. There is a sort of oppression, a weight. No—not drowsiness, would God that it were! It is like a shadow, a deep shadow falling suddenly and swiftly across something busy. Spin, spin into the darkness. The tumult of thought, the confusion, the eddy and eddy. I can't express it. I can hardly keep my mind on it—steadily enough to tell you."

He stopped feebly.

"Don't trouble, old chap," said Isbister. "I think I can understand. At any rate, it don't matter very much just at present about telling me, you know."

The sleepless man thrust his knuckles into his eyes and rubbed them. Isbister talked while this rubbing continued, and then he had a fresh idea. "Come down to my room," he said, "and try a pipe. I can show you some sketches of this Blackapit. If you'd care?"

The other rose obediently and followed him down the steep.

Several times Isbister heard him stumble as they came down, and his movements were slow and hesitating. "Come in with me," said Isbister, "and try some cigarettes and the blessed gift of alcohol. If you take alcohol?"

The stranger hesitated at the garden gate. He seemed no longer aware of his actions. "I don't drink," he said slowly, coming up the garden path, and after a moment's interval repeated absently, "No—I don't drink. It goes round. Spin, it goes—spin—"

He stumbled at the doorstep and entered the room with the bearing of one who sees nothing.

Then he sat down heavily in the easy chair, seemed almost to fall into it. He leant forward with his brows on his hands and became motionless. Presently he made a faint sound in his throat.

Isbister moved about the room with the nervousness of an inexperienced host, making little remarks that scarcely required answering. He crossed the room to his portfolio, placed it on the table and noticed the mantel clock.

"I don't know if you'd care to have supper with me," he said with an unlighted cigarette in his hand—his mind troubled with ideas of a furtive administration of chloral. "Only cold mutton, you know, but passing sweet. Welsh. And a tart, I believe." He repeated this after momentary silence.

The seated man made no answer. Isbister stopped, match in hand, regarding him.

The stillness lengthened. The match went out, the cigarette was put down unlit. The man was certainly very still. Isbister took up the portfolio, opened it, put it down, hesitated, seemed about to speak. "Perhaps," he whispered doubtfully. Presently he glanced at the door and back to the figure. Then he stole on tiptoe out of the room, glancing at his companion after each elaborate pace.

He closed the door noiselessly. The house door was standing open, and he went out beyond the porch, and stood where the monkshood rose at the corner of the garden bed. From this point he could see the stranger through the open window, still and dim, sitting head on hand. He had not moved.

A number of children going along the road stopped and regarded the artist curiously. A boatman exchanged civilities with him. He felt that possibly his circumspect attitude and position looked peculiar and unaccountable. Smoking, perhaps, might seem more natural. He drew pipe and pouch from his pocket, filled the pipe slowly.

"I wonder," ... he said, with a scarcely perceptible loss of complacency. "At any rate one must give him a chance." He struck a match in the virile way, and proceeded to light his pipe.

He heard his landlady behind him, coming with his lamp lit from the kitchen. He turned, gesticulating with his pipe, and stopped her at the door of his sitting-room. He had some difficulty in explaining the situation in whispers, for she did not know he had a visitor. She retreated again with the lamp, still a little mystified to judge from her manner, and he resumed his hovering at the corner of the porch, flushed and less at his ease.

Long after he had smoked out his pipe, and when the bats were abroad, curiosity dominated his complex hesitations, and he stole back into his darkling sitting-room. He paused in the doorway. The stranger was still in the same attitude, dark against the window. Save for the singing of some sailors aboard one of the little slate-carrying ships in the harbour the evening was very still. Outside, the spikes of monkshood and delphinium stood erect and motionless against the shadow of the hillside. Something flashed into Isbister's mind; he started, and leaning over the table, listened. An unpleasant suspicion grew stronger; became conviction. Astonishment seized him and became—dread!

No sound of breathing came from the seated figure!

He crept slowly and noiselessly round the table, pausing twice to listen. At last he could lay his hand on the back of the armchair. He bent down until the two heads were ear to ear.

Then he bent still lower to look up at his visitor's face. He started violently and uttered an exclamation. The eyes were void spaces of white.

He looked again and saw that they were open and with the pupils rolled under the lids. He was afraid. He took the man by the shoulder and shook him. "Are you asleep?" he said, with his voice jumping, and again, "Are you asleep?"

A conviction took possession of his mind that this man was dead. He became active and noisy, strode across the room, blundering against the table as he did so, and rang the bell.

"Please bring a light at once," he said in the passage. "There is something wrong with my friend."

He returned to the motionless seated figure, grasped the shoulder, shook it, shouted. The room was flooded with yellow glare as his landlady entered with the light. His face was white as he turned blinking towards her. "I must fetch a doctor," he said. "It is either death or a fit. Is there a doctor in the village? Where is a doctor to be found?"

2

___

THE TRANCE

THE STATE OF CATALEPTIC RIGOUR INTO WHICH THIS MAN HAD FALLEN, lasted for an unprecedented length of time, and then he passed slowly to the flaccid state, to a lax attitude suggestive of profound repose. Then it was his eyes could be closed.

He was removed from the hotel to the Boscastle surgery, and from the surgery, after some weeks, to London. But he still resisted every attempt at reanimation. After a time, for reasons that will appear later, these attempts were discontinued. For a great space he lay in that strange condition, inert and still—neither dead nor living but, as it were, suspended, hanging midway between nothingness and existence. His was a darkness unbroken by a ray of thought or sensation, a dreamless inanition, a vast space of peace. The tumult of his mind had swelled and risen to an abrupt climax of silence. Where was the man? Where is any man when insensibility takes hold of him?

"It seems only yesterday," said Isbister. "I remember it all as though it happened yesterday—clearer, perhaps, than if it had happened yesterday."

It was the Isbister of the last §, but he was no longer a young man. The hair that had been brown and a trifle in excess of the fashionable length, was iron grey and clipped close, and the face that had been pink and white was buff and ruddy. He had a pointed beard shot with grey. He talked to an elderly man who wore a summer suit of drill (the summer of that year was unusually hot). This was Warming, a London solicitor and next of kin to

Graham, the man who had fallen into the trance. And the two men stood side by side in a room in a house in London regarding his recumbent figure.

It was a yellow figure lying lax upon a water-bed and clad in a flowing shirt, a figure with a shrunken face and a stubby beard, lean limbs and lank nails, and about it was a case of thin glass. This glass seemed to mark off the sleeper from the reality of life about him, he was a thing apart, a strange, isolated abnormality. The two men stood close to the glass, peering in.

"The thing gave me a shock," said Isbister. "I feel a queer sort of surprise even now when I think of his white eyes. They were white, you know, rolled up. Coming here again brings it all back to me."

"Have you never seen him since that time?" asked Warming.

"Often wanted to come," said Isbister; "but business nowadays is too serious a thing for much holiday keeping. I've been in America most of the time."

"If I remember rightly," said Warming, "you were an artist?"

"Was. And then I became a married man. I saw it was all up with black and white, very soon—at least for a mediocrity, and I jumped on to process. Those posters on the Cliffs at Dover are by my people."

"Good posters," admitted the solicitor, "though I was sorry to see them there."

"Last as long as the cliffs, if necessary," exclaimed Isbister with satisfaction. "The world changes. When he fell asleep, twenty years ago, I was down at Boscastle with a box of water-colours and a noble, old-fashioned ambition. I didn't expect that some day my pigments would glorify the whole blessed coast of England, from Land's End round again to the Lizard. Luck comes to a man very often when he's not looking."

Warming seemed to doubt the quality of the luck. "I just missed seeing you, if I recollect aright."

"You came back by the trap that took me to Camelford railway station. It was close on the Jubilee, Victoria's Jubilee, because I remember the seats and flags in Westminster, and the row with the cabman at Chelsea."

"The Diamond Jubilee, it was," said Warming; "the second one."

"Ah, yes! At the proper Jubilee—the Fifty Year affair—I was down at Wookey—a boy. I missed all that.... What a fuss we had with him! My landlady wouldn't take him in, wouldn't let him stay—he looked so queer when he was rigid. We had to carry him in a chair up to the hotel. And the Boscastle doctor—it wasn't the present chap, but the G.P. before him—

was at him until nearly two, with me and the landlord holding lights and so forth."

"Do you mean—he was stiff and hard?"

"Stiff!—wherever you bent him he stuck. You might have stood him on his head and he'd have stopped. I never saw such stiffness. Of course this"—he indicated the prostrate figure by a movement of his head—"is quite different. And the little doctor—what was his name?"

"Smithers?"

"Smithers it was—was quite wrong in trying to fetch him round too soon, according to all accounts. The things he did! Even now it makes me feel all—ugh! Mustard, snuff, pricking. And one of those beastly little things, not dynamos—"

"Coils."

"Yes. You could see his muscles throb and jump, and he twisted about. There were just two flaring yellow candles, and all the shadows were shivering, and the little doctor nervous and putting on side, and *him*—stark and squirming in the most unnatural ways. Well, it made me dream."

Pause.

"It's a strange state," said Warming.

"It's a sort of complete absence," said Isbister. "Here's the body, empty. Not dead a bit, and yet not alive. It's like a seat vacant and marked 'engaged.' No feeling, no digestion, no beating of the heart—not a flutter. *That* doesn't make me feel as if there was a man present. In a sense it's more dead than death, for these doctors tell me that even the hair has stopped growing. Now with the proper dead, the hair will go on growing—"

"I know," said Warming, with a flash of pain in his expression.

They peered through the glass again. Graham was indeed in a strange state, in the flaccid phase of a trance, but a trance unprecedented in medical history. Trances had lasted for as much as a year before—but at the end of that time it had ever been a waking or a death; sometimes first one and then the other. Isbister noted the marks the physicians had made in injecting nourishment, for that had been resorted to to postpone collapse; he pointed them out to Warming, who had been trying not to see them.

"And while he has been lying here," said Isbister, with the zest of a life freely spent, "I have changed my plans in life; married, raised a family, my eldest lad—I hadn't begun to think of sons then—is an American citizen, and looking forward to leaving Harvard. There's a touch of grey in my hair.

And this man, not a day older nor wiser (practically) than I was in my downy days. It's curious to think of."

Warming turned. "And I have grown old too. I played cricket with him when I was still only a boy. And he looks a young man still. Yellow perhaps. But that *is* a young man nevertheless."

"And there's been the War," said Isbister.

"From beginning to end."

"I've understood," said Isbister after a pause, "that he had some moderate property of his own?"

"That is so," said Warming. He coughed primly. "As it happens—I have charge of it."

"Ah!" Isbister thought, hesitated and spoke: "No doubt—his keep here is not expensive—no doubt it will have improved—accumulated?"

"It has. He will wake up very much better off—if he wakes—than when he slept."

"As a business man," said Isbister, "that thought has naturally been in my mind. I have, indeed, sometimes thought that, speaking commercially, of course, this sleep may be a very good thing for him. That he knows what he is about, so to speak, in being insensible so long. If he had lived straight on—"

"I doubt if he would have premeditated as much," said Warming. "He was not a far-sighted man. In fact—"

"Yes?"

"We differed on that point. I stood to him somewhat in the relation of a guardian. You have probably seen enough of affairs to recognize that occasionally a certain friction—. But even if that was the case, there is a doubt whether he will ever wake. This sleep exhausts slowly, but it exhausts. Apparently he is sliding slowly, very slowly and tediously, down a long slope, if you can understand me?"

"It will be a pity to lose his surprise. There's been a lot of change these twenty years. It's Rip Van Winkle come real."

"There has been a lot of change certainly," said Warming. "And, among other changes, I have changed. I am an old man."

Isbister hesitated, and then feigned a belated surprise. "I shouldn't have thought it."

"I was forty-three when his bankers—you remember you wired to his bankers—sent on to me."

"I got their address from the cheque book in his pocket," said Isbister.

"Well, the addition is not difficult," said Warming.

There was another pause, and then Isbister gave way to an unavoidable curiosity. "He may go on for years yet," he said, and had a moment of hesitation. "We have to consider that. His affairs, you know, may fall some day into the hands of—someone else, you know."

"That, if you will believe me, Mr. Isbister, is one of the problems most constantly before my mind. We happen to be—as a matter of fact, there are no very trustworthy connexions of ours. It is a grotesque and unprecedented position."

"Rather," said Isbister.

"It seems to me it's a case of some public body, some practically undying guardian. If he really is going on living—as the doctors, some of them, think. As a matter of fact, I have gone to one or two public men about it. But, so far, nothing has been done."

"It wouldn't be a bad idea to hand him over to some public body—the British Museum Trustees, or the Royal College of Physicians. Sounds a bit odd, of course, but the whole situation is odd."

"The difficulty is to induce them to take him."

"Red tape, I suppose?"

"Partly."

Pause. "It's a curious business, certainly," said Isbister. "And compound interest has a way of mounting up."

"It has," said Warming. "And now the gold supplies are running short there is a tendency towards ... appreciation."

"I've felt that," said Isbister with a grimace. "But it makes it better for *him*."

"*If* he awakes."

"If he awakes," echoed Isbister. "Do you notice the pinched-in look of his nose, and the way in which his eyelids sink?"

Warming looked and thought for a space. "I doubt if he will wake," he said at last.

"I never properly understood," said Isbister, "what it was brought this on. He told me something about overstudy. I've often been curious."

"He was a man of considerable gifts, but spasmodic, emotional. He had grave domestic troubles, divorced his wife, in fact, and it was as a relief from that, I think, that he took up politics of the rabid sort. He was a fanatical Radical—a Socialist—or typical Liberal, as they used to call themselves, of the advanced school. Energetic—flighty—undisciplined. Overwork upon a controversy did this for him. I remember the pamphlet he wrote—a curious production. Wild, whirling stuff. There were one or two prophecies. Some of them are already exploded, some of them are established facts. But for the most part to read such a thesis is to realise how full the world is of unanticipated things. He will have much to learn, much to unlearn, when he wakes. If ever a waking comes."

"I'd give anything to be there," said Isbister, "just to hear what he would say to it all."

"So would I," said Warming. "Aye! so would I," with an old man's sudden turn to self pity. "But I shall never see him wake."

He stood looking thoughtfully at the waxen figure. "He will never awake," he said at last. He sighed. "He will never awake again."

3

THE AWAKENING

But Warming was wrong in that. An awakening came.

What a wonderfully complex thing! this simple seeming unity—the self! Who can trace its reintegration as morning after morning we awaken, the flux and confluence of its countless factors interweaving, rebuilding, the dim first stirrings of the soul, the growth and synthesis of the unconscious to the subconscious, the subconscious to dawning consciousness, until at last we recognize ourselves again. And as it happens to most of us after the night's sleep, so it was with Graham at the end of his vast slumber. A dim cloud of sensation taking shape, a cloudy dreariness, and he found himself vaguely somewhere, recumbent, faint, but alive.

The pilgrimage towards a personal being seemed to traverse vast gulfs, to occupy epochs. Gigantic dreams that were terrible realities at the time, left vague perplexing memories, strange creatures, strange scenery, as if from another planet. There was a distinct impression, too, of a momentous conversation, of a name—he could not tell what name—that was subsequently to recur, of some queer long-forgotten sensation of vein and muscle, of a feeling of vast hopeless effort, the effort of a man near drowning in darkness. Then came a panorama of dazzling unstable confluent scenes....

Graham became aware that his eyes were open and regarding some unfamiliar thing.

It was something white, the edge of something, a frame of wood. He moved his head slightly, following the contour of this shape. It went up beyond the top of his eyes. He tried to think where he might be. Did it matter, seeing he was so wretched? The colour of his thoughts was a dark depression. He felt the featureless misery of one who wakes towards the hour of dawn. He had an uncertain sense of whispers and footsteps hastily receding.

The movement of his head involved a perception of extreme physical weakness. He supposed he was in bed in the hotel at the place in the valley —but he could not recall that white edge. He must have slept. He remembered now that he had wanted to sleep. He recalled the cliff and Waterfall again, and then recollected something about talking to a passer-by....

How long had he slept? What was that sound of pattering feet? And that rise and fall, like the murmur of breakers on pebbles? He put out a languid hand to reach his watch from the chair whereon it was his habit to place it, and touched some smooth hard surface like glass. This was so unexpected that it startled him extremely. Quite suddenly he rolled over, stared for a moment, and struggled into a sitting position. The effort was unexpectedly difficult, and it left him giddy and weak—and amazed.

He rubbed his eyes. The riddle of his surroundings was confusing but his mind was quite clear—evidently his sleep had benefited him. He was not in a bed at all as he understood the word, but lying naked on a very soft and yielding mattress, in a trough of dark glass. The mattress was partly transparent, a fact he observed with a sense of insecurity, and below it was a mirror reflecting him greyly. About his arm—and he saw with a shock that his skin was strangely dry and yellow—was bound a curious apparatus of rubber, bound so cunningly that it seemed to pass into his skin above and below. And this bed was placed in a case of greenish coloured glass (as it seemed to him), a bar in the white framework of which had first arrested his attention. In the corner of the case was a stand of glittering and delicately made apparatus, for the most part quite strange appliances, though a maximum and minimum thermometer was recognizable.

The slightly greenish tint of the glass-like substance which surrounded him on every hand obscured what lay behind, but he perceived it was a vast apartment of splendid appearance, and with a very large and simple white archway facing him. Close to the walls of the cage were articles of furniture, a table covered with a silvery cloth, silvery like the side of a fish, a couple of graceful chairs, and on the table a number of dishes with substances piled on them, a bottle and two glasses. He realized that he was intensely hungry.

He could see no one, and after a period of hesitation scrambled off the translucent mattress and tried to stand on the clean white floor of his little apartment. He had miscalculated his strength, however, and staggered and put his hand against the glass-like pane before him to steady himself. For a moment it resisted his hand, bending outward like a distended bladder, then it broke with a slight report and vanished—a pricked bubble. He reeled out into the general space of the hall, greatly astonished. He caught at the table to save himself, knocking one of the glasses to the floor—it rang but did not break—and sat down in one of the armchairs.

When he had a little recovered he filled the remaining glass from the bottle and drank—a colourless liquid it was, but not water, with a pleasing faint aroma and taste and a quality of immediate support and stimulus. He put down the vessel and looked about him.

The apartment lost none of its size and magnificence now that the greenish transparency that had intervened was removed. The archway he saw led to a flight of steps, going downward without the intermediation of a door, to a spacious transverse passage. This passage ran between polished pillars of some white-veined substance of deep ultramarine, and along it came the sound of human movements, and voices and a deep undeviating droning note. He sat, now fully awake, listening alertly, forgetting the viands in his attention.

Then with a shock he remembered that he was naked, and casting about him for covering, saw a long black robe thrown on one of the chairs beside him. This he wrapped about him and sat down again, trembling.

His mind was still a surging perplexity. Clearly he had slept, and had been removed in his sleep. But where? And who were those people, the distant crowd beyond the deep blue pillars? Boscastle? He poured out and partially drank another glass of the colourless fluid.

What was this place?—this place that to his senses seemed subtly quivering like a thing alive? He looked about him at the clean and beautiful form of the apartment, unstained by ornament, and saw that the roof was broken in one place by a circular shaft full of light, and, as he looked, a steady, sweeping shadow blotted it out and passed, and came again and passed. "Beat, beat," that sweeping shadow had a note of its own in the subdued tumult that filled the air.

He would have called out, but only a little sound came into his throat. Then he stood up, and, with the uncertain steps of a drunkard, made his way towards the archway. He staggered down the steps, tripped on the corner of the black cloak he had wrapped about himself, and saved himself by catching at one of the blue pillars.

The passage ran down a cool vista of blue and purple and ended remotely in a railed space like a balcony brightly lit and projecting into a space of haze, a space like the interior of some gigantic building. Beyond and remote were vast and vague architectural forms. The tumult of voices rose now loud and clear, and on the balcony and with their backs to him, gesticulating and apparently in animated conversation, were three figures, richly dressed in loose and easy garments of bright soft colourings. The noise of a great multitude of people poured up over the balcony, and once it seemed the top of a banner passed, and once some brightly coloured object, a pale blue cap or garment thrown up into the air perhaps, flashed athwart the space and fell. The shouts sounded like English, there was a reiteration of "Wake!" He heard some indistinct shrill cry, and abruptly these three men began laughing.

"Ha, ha, ha!" laughed one—a red-haired man in a short purple robe. "When the Sleeper wakes—*When!*"

He turned his eyes full of merriment along the passage. His face changed, the whole man changed, became rigid. The other two turned swiftly at his exclamation and stood motionless. Their faces assumed an expression of consternation, an expression that deepened into awe.

Suddenly Graham's knees bent beneath him, his arm against the pillar collapsed limply, he staggered forward and fell upon his face.

4

THE SOUND OF A TUMULT

GRAHAM'S LAST IMPRESSION BEFORE HE FAINTED WAS OF THE RINGING of bells. He learnt afterwards that he was insensible, hanging between life and death, for the better part of an hour. When he recovered his senses, he was back on his translucent couch, and there was a stirring warmth at heart and throat. The dark apparatus, he perceived, had been removed from his arm, which was bandaged. The white framework was still about him, but the greenish transparent substance that had filled it was altogether gone. A man in a deep violet robe, one of those who had been on the balcony, was looking keenly into his face.

Remote but insistent was a clamour of bells and confused sounds, that suggested to his mind the picture of a great number of people shouting together. Something seemed to fall across this tumult, a door suddenly closed.

Graham moved his head. "What does this all mean?" he said slowly. "Where am I?"

He saw the red-haired man who had been first to discover him. A voice seemed to be asking what he had said, and was abruptly stilled.

The man in violet answered in a soft voice, speaking English with a slightly foreign accent, or so at least it seemed to the Sleeper's ears. "You are quite safe. You were brought hither from where you fell asleep. It is quite safe. You have been here some time—sleeping. In a trance."

He said something further that Graham could not hear, and a little phial was handed across to him. Graham felt a cooling spray, a fragrant mist played over his forehead for a moment, and his sense of refreshment increased. He closed his eyes in satisfaction.

"Better?" asked the man in violet, as Graham's eyes reopened. He was a pleasant-faced man of thirty, perhaps, with a pointed flaxen beard, and a clasp of gold at the neck of his violet robe.

"Yes," said Graham.

"You have been asleep some time. In a cataleptic trance. You have heard? Catalepsy? It may seem strange to you at first, but I can assure you everything is well."

Graham did not answer, but these words served their reassuring purpose. His eyes went from face to face of the three people about him. They were regarding him strangely. He knew he ought to be somewhere in Cornwall, but he could not square these things with that impression.

A matter that had been in his mind during his last waking moments at Boscastle recurred, a thing resolved upon and somehow neglected. He cleared his throat.

"Have you wired my cousin?" he asked. "E. Warming, 27, Chancery Lane?"

They were all assiduous to hear. But he had to repeat it. "What an odd *blurr* in his accent!" whispered the red-haired man. "Wire, sir?" said the young man with the flaxen beard, evidently puzzled.

"He means send an electric telegram," volunteered the third, a pleasant-faced youth of nineteen or twenty. The flaxen-bearded man gave a cry of comprehension. "How stupid of me! You may be sure everything shall be done, sir," he said to Graham. "I am afraid it would be difficult to—*wire* to your cousin. He is not in London now. But don't trouble about arrangements yet; you have been asleep a very long time and the important thing is to get over that, sir." (Graham concluded the word was *sir*, but this man pronounced it "*Sire*.")

"Oh!" said Graham, and became quiet.

It was all very puzzling, but apparently these people in unfamiliar dress knew what they were about. Yet they were odd and the room was odd. It seemed he was in some newly established place. He had a sudden flash of suspicion! Surely this wasn't some hall of public exhibition! If it was he would give Warming a piece of his mind. But it scarcely had that character. And in a place of public exhibition he would not have discovered himself naked.

Then suddenly, quite abruptly, he realized what had happened. There was no perceptible interval of suspicion, no dawn to his knowledge. Abruptly he knew that his trance had lasted for a vast interval; as if by some processes of thought-reading he interpreted the awe in the faces that peered into his. He looked at them strangely, full of intense emotion. It seemed they read his eyes. He framed his lips to speak and could not. A queer impulse to hide his knowledge came into his mind almost at the moment of his discovery. He looked at his bare feet, regarding them silently. His impulse to speak passed. He was trembling exceedingly.

They gave him some pink fluid with a greenish fluorescence and a meaty taste, and the assurance of returning strength grew.

"That—that makes me feel better," he said hoarsely, and there were murmurs of respectful approval. He knew now quite clearly. He made to speak again, and again he could not.

He pressed his throat and tried a third time. "How long?" he asked in a level voice. "How long have I been asleep?"

"Some considerable time," said the flaxen-bearded man, glancing quickly at the others.

"How long?"

"A very long time."

"Yes—yes," said Graham, suddenly testy. "But I want—Is it—it is— some years? Many years? There was something—I forget what. I feel— confused. But you—" He sobbed. "You need not fence with me. How long—?"

He stopped, breathing irregularly. He squeezed his eyes with his knuckles and sat waiting for an answer.

They spoke in undertones.

"Five or six?" he asked faintly. "More?"

"Very much more than that."

"More!"

"More."

He looked at them and it seemed as though imps were twitching the muscles of his face. He looked his question.

"Many years," said the man with the red beard.

Graham struggled into a sitting position. He wiped a rheumy tear from his face with a lean hand. "Many years!" he repeated. He shut his eyes tight, opened them, and sat looking about him from one unfamiliar thing to another.

"How many years?" he asked.

"You must be prepared to be surprised."

"Well?"

"More than a gross of years."

He was irritated at the strange word. "More than a *what?*"

Two of them spoke together. Some quick remarks that were made about "decimal" he did not catch.

"How long did you say?" asked Graham. "How long? Don't look like that. Tell me."

Among the remarks in an undertone, his ear caught six words: "More than a couple of centuries."

"*What?*" he cried, turning on the youth who he thought had spoken. "Who says—? What was that? A couple of *centuries!*"

"Yes," said the man with the red beard. "Two hundred years."

Graham repeated the words. He had been prepared to hear of a vast repose, and yet these concrete centuries defeated him.

"Two hundred years," he said again, with the figure of a great gulf opening very slowly in his mind; and then, "Oh, but—!"

They said nothing.

"You—did you say—?"

"Two hundred years. Two centuries of years," said the man with the red beard.

There was a pause. Graham looked at their faces and saw that what he had heard was indeed true.

"But it can't be," he said querulously. "I am dreaming. Trances—trances don't last. That is not right—this is a joke you have played upon me! Tell me—some days ago, perhaps, I was walking along the coast of Cornwall—?"

His voice failed him.

The man with the flaxen beard hesitated. "I'm not very strong in history, sir," he said weakly, and glanced at the others.

"That was it, sir," said the youngster. "Boscastle, in the old Duchy of Cornwall—it's in the south-west country beyond the dairy meadows. There is a house there still. I have been there."

"Boscastle!" Graham turned his eyes to the youngster. "That was it— Boscastle. Little Boscastle. I fell asleep—somewhere there. I don't exactly remember. I don't exactly remember."

He pressed his brows and whispered, "More than *two hundred years!*"

He began to speak quickly with a twitching face, but his heart was cold within him. "But if it *is* two hundred years, every soul I know, every human being that ever I saw or spoke to before I went to sleep, must be dead."

They did not answer him.

"The Queen and the Royal Family, her Ministers, Church and State. High and low, rich and poor, one with another ... Is there England still?"

"That's a comfort! Is there London?"

"This *is* London, eh? And you are my assistant-custodian; assistant-custodian. And these—? Eh? Assistant-custodians too!"

He sat with a gaunt stare on his face. "But why am I here? No! Don't talk. Be quiet. Let me—"

He sat silent, rubbed his eyes, and, uncovering them, found another little glass of pinkish fluid held towards him. He took the dose. Directly after he had taken it he began to weep naturally and refreshingly.

Presently he looked at their faces, suddenly laughed through his tears, a little foolishly. "But—two—hun—dred—years!" he said. He grimaced hysterically and covered his face again.

After a space he grew calm. He sat up, his hands hanging over his knees in almost precisely the same attitude in which Isbister had found him on the cliff at Pentargen. His attention was attracted by a thick domineering voice, the footsteps of an advancing personage. "What are you doing? Why was I not warned? Surely you could tell? Someone will suffer for this. The man must be kept quiet. Are the doorways closed? All the doorways? He must be kept perfectly quiet. He must not be told. Has he been told anything?"

The man with the fair beard made some inaudible remark, and Graham looking over his shoulder saw approaching a short, fat, and thickset beardless man, with aquiline nose and heavy neck and chin. Very thick black and slightly sloping eyebrows that almost met over his nose and overhung deep grey eyes, gave his face an oddly formidable expression. He scowled momentarily at Graham and then his regard returned to the man with the flaxen beard. "These others," he said in a voice of extreme irritation. "You had better go."

"Go?" said the red-bearded man.

"Certainly—go now. But see the doorways are closed as you go."

The two men addressed turned obediently, after one reluctant glance at Graham, and instead of going through the archway as he expected, walked straight to the dead wall of the apartment opposite the archway. A long strip of this apparently solid wall rolled up with a snap, hung over the two retreating men and fell again, and immediately Graham was alone with the new-comer and the purple-robed man with the flaxen beard.

For a space the thickset man took not the slightest notice of Graham, but proceeded to interrogate the other—obviously his subordinate—upon the treatment of their charge. He spoke clearly, but in phrases only partially intelligible to Graham. The awakening seemed not only a matter of surprise but of consternation and annoyance to him. He was evidently profoundly excited.

"You must not confuse his mind by telling him things," he repeated again and again. "You must not confuse his mind."

His questions answered, he turned quickly and eyed the awakened sleeper with an ambiguous expression.

"Feel queer?" he asked.

"Very."

"The world, what you see of it, seems strange to you?"

"I suppose I have to live in it, strange as it seems."

"I suppose so, now."

"In the first place, hadn't I better have some clothes?"

"They—" said the thickset man and stopped, and the flaxen-bearded man met his eye and went away. "You will very speedily have clothes," said the thickset man.

"Is it true indeed, that I have been asleep two hundred—?" asked Graham.

"They have told you that, have they? Two hundred and three, as a matter of fact."

Graham accepted the indisputable now with raised eyebrows and depressed mouth. He sat silent for a moment, and then asked a question, "Is there a mill or dynamo near here?" He did not wait for an answer. "Things have changed tremendously, I suppose?" he said.

"What is that shouting?" he asked abruptly.

"Nothing," said the thickset man impatiently. "It's people. You'll understand better later—perhaps. As you say, things have changed." He spoke shortly, his brows were knit, and he glanced about him like a man trying to decide in an emergency. "We must get you clothes and so forth, at any rate. Better wait here until they can be procured. No one will come near you. You want shaving."

Graham rubbed his chin.

The man with the flaxen beard came back towards them, turned suddenly, listened for a moment, lifted his eyebrows at the older man, and hurried off through the archway towards the balcony. The tumult of shouting grew louder, and the thickset man turned and listened also. He cursed suddenly under his breath, and turned his eyes upon Graham with an unfriendly expression. It was a surge of many voices, rising and falling, shouting and screaming, and once came a sound like blows and sharp cries, and then a snapping like the crackling of dry sticks. Graham strained his ears to draw some single thread of sound from the woven tumult.

Then he perceived, repeated again and again, a certain formula. For a time he doubted his ears. But surely these were the words: "Show us the Sleeper! Show us the Sleeper!"

The thickset man rushed suddenly to the archway.

"Wild!" he cried. "How do they know? Do they know? Or is it guessing?"

There was perhaps an answer.

"I can't come," said the thickset man; "I have *him* to see to. But shout from the balcony."

There was an inaudible reply.

"Say he is not awake. Anything! I leave it to you."

He came hurrying back to Graham. "You must have clothes at once," he said. "You cannot stop here—and it will be impossible to—"

He rushed away, Graham shouting unanswered questions after him. In a moment he was back.

"I can't tell you what is happening. It is too complex to explain. In a moment you shall have your clothes made. Yes—in a moment. And then I can take you away from here. You will find out our troubles soon enough."

"But those voices. They were shouting—?"

"Something about the Sleeper—that's you. They have some twisted idea. I don't know what it is. I know nothing."

A shrill bell jetted acutely across the indistinct mingling of remote noises, and this brusque person sprang to a little group of appliances in the corner of the room. He listened for a moment, regarding a ball of crystal, nodded, and said a few indistinct words; then he walked to the wall through which the two men had vanished. It rolled up again like a curtain, and he stood waiting.

Graham lifted his arm and was astonished to find what strength the restoratives had given him. He thrust one leg over the side of the couch and then the other. His head no longer swam. He could scarcely credit his rapid recovery. He sat feeling his limbs.

The man with the flaxen beard re-entered from the archway, and as he did so the cage of a lift came sliding down in front of the thickset man, and a lean, grey-bearded man, carrying a roll, and wearing a tightly-fitting costume of dark green, appeared therein.

"This is the tailor," said the thickset man with an introductory gesture. "It will never do for you to wear that black. I cannot understand how it got here. But I shall. I shall. You will be as rapid as possible?" he said to the tailor.

The man in green bowed, and, advancing, seated himself by Graham on the bed. His manner was calm, but his eyes were full of curiosity. "You will find the fashions altered, Sire," he said. He glanced from under his brows at the thickset man.

He opened the roller with a quick movement, and a confusion of brilliant fabrics poured out over his knees. "You lived, Sire, in a period essentially cylindrical—the Victorian. With a tendency to the hemisphere in hats. Circular curves always. Now—" He flicked out a little appliance the size and appearance of a keyless watch, whirled the knob, and behold—a little figure in white appeared kinetoscope fashion on the dial, walking and turning. The tailor caught up a pattern of bluish white satin. "That is my conception of your immediate treatment," he said.

The thickset man came and stood by the shoulder of Graham.

"We have very little time," he said.

"Trust me," said the tailor. "My machine follows. What do you think of this?"

"What is that?" asked the man from the nineteenth century.

"In your days they showed you a fashion-plate," said the tailor, "but this is our modern development. See here." The little figure repeated its evolutions, but in a different costume. "Or this," and with a click another small figure in a more voluminous type of robe marched on to the dial. The tailor was very quick in his movements, and glanced twice towards the lift as he did these things.

It rumbled again, and a crop-haired anaemic lad with features of the Chinese type, clad in coarse pale blue canvas, appeared together with a complicated machine, which he pushed noiselessly on little castors into the room. Incontinently the little kinetoscope was dropped, Graham was invited to stand in front of the machine and the tailor muttered some instructions to the crop-haired lad, who answered in guttural tones and with words Graham did not recognize. The boy then went to conduct an incomprehensible monologue in the corner, and the tailor pulled out a number of slotted arms terminating in little discs, pulling them out until the discs were flat against the body of Graham, one at each shoulder blade, one at the elbows, one at the neck and so forth, so that at last there were, perhaps, two score of them upon his body and limbs. At the same time, some other person entered the room by the lift, behind Graham. The tailor set moving a mechanism that initiated a faint-sounding rhythmic movement of parts in the machine, and in another moment he was knocking up the levers and Graham was released. The tailor replaced his cloak of black, and the man with the flaxen beard proffered him a little glass of some refreshing fluid. Graham saw over the rim of the glass a pale-faced young man regarding him with a singular fixity.

The thickset man had been pacing the room fretfully, and now turned and went through the archway towards the balcony, from which the noise of a distant crowd still came in gusts and cadences. The crop-headed lad handed the tailor a roll of the bluish satin and the two began fixing this in the mechanism in a manner reminiscent of a roll of paper in a nineteenth century printing machine. Then they ran the entire thing on its easy, noiseless bearings across the room to a remote corner where a twisted cable looped rather gracefully from the wall. They made some connexion and the machine became energetic and swift.

"What is that doing?" asked Graham, pointing with the empty glass to the busy figures and trying to ignore the scrutiny of the new comer. "Is that—some sort of force—laid on?"

"Yes," said the man with the flaxen beard.

"Who is *that*?" He indicated the archway behind him.

The man in purple stroked his little beard, hesitated, and answered in an undertone, "He is Howard, your chief guardian. You see, Sire—it's a little difficult to explain. The Council appoints a guardian and assistants. This hall has under certain restrictions been public. In order that people might satisfy themselves. We have barred the doorways for the first time. But I think—if you don't mind, I will leave him to explain."

"Odd!" said Graham. "Guardian? Council?" Then turning his back on the new comer, he asked in an undertone, "Why is this man *glaring* at me? Is he a mesmerist?"

"Mesmerist! He is a capillotomist."

"Capillotomist!"

"Yes—one of the chief. His yearly fee is sixdoz lions."

It sounded sheer nonsense. Graham snatched at the last phrase with an unsteady mind. "Sixdoz lions?" he said.

"Didn't you have lions? I suppose not. You had the old pounds? They are our monetary units."

"But what was that you said—sixdoz?"

"Yes. Six dozen, Sire. Of course things, even these little things, have altered. You lived in the days of the decimal system, the Arab system—tens, and little hundreds and thousands. We have eleven numerals now. We have single figures for both ten and eleven, two figures for a dozen, and a dozen dozen makes a gross, a great hundred, you know, a dozen gross a dozand, and a dozand dozand a myriad. Very simple?"

"I suppose so," said Graham. "But about this cap—what was it?"

The man with the flaxen beard glanced over his shoulder.

"Here are your clothes!" he said. Graham turned round sharply and saw the tailor standing at his elbow smiling, and holding some palpably new garments over his arm. The crop-headed boy, by means of one ringer, was impelling the complicated machine towards the lift by which he had arrived. Graham stared at the completed suit. "You don't mean to say—!"

"Just made," said the tailor. He dropped the garments at the feet of Graham, walked to the bed, on which Graham had so recently been lying, flung out the translucent mattress, and turned up the looking-glass. As he did so a furious bell summoned the thickset man to the corner. The man with the flaxen beard rushed across to him and then hurried out by the archway.

The tailor was assisting Graham into a dark purple combination garment, stockings, vest, and pants in one, as the thickset man came back from the corner to meet the man with the flaxen beard returning from the balcony. They began speaking quickly in an undertone, their bearing had an unmistakable quality of anxiety. Over the purple under-garment came a complex garment of bluish white, and Graham was clothed in the fashion once more and saw himself, sallow-faced, unshaven and shaggy still, but at least naked no longer, and in some indefinable unprecedented way graceful.

"I must shave," he said regarding himself in the glass.

"In a moment," said Howard.

The persistent stare ceased. The young man closed his eyes, reopened them, and with a lean hand extended, advanced on Graham. Then he stopped, with his hand slowly gesticulating, and looked about him.

"A seat," said Howard impatiently, and in a moment the flaxen-bearded man had a chair behind Graham. "Sit down, please," said Howard.

Graham hesitated, and in the other hand of the wild-eyed man he saw the glint of steel.

"Don't you understand, Sire?" cried the flaxen-bearded man with hurried politeness. "He is going to cut your hair."

"Oh!" cried Graham enlightened. "But you called him—"

"A capillotomist—precisely! He is one of the finest artists in the world."

Graham sat down abruptly. The flaxen-bearded man disappeared. The capillotomist came forward, examined Graham's ears and surveyed him, felt the back of his head, and would have sat down again to regard him but for Howard's audible impatience. Forthwith with rapid movements and a succession of deftly handled implements he shaved Graham's chin, clipped his moustache, and cut and arranged his hair. All this he did without a word, with something of the rapt air of a poet inspired. And as soon as he had finished Graham was handed a pair of shoes.

Suddenly a loud voice shouted—it seemed from a piece of machinery in the corner—"At once—at once. The people know all over the city. Work is being stopped. Work is being stopped. Wait for nothing, but come."

This shout appeared to perturb Howard exceedingly. By his gestures it seemed to Graham that he hesitated between two directions. Abruptly he went towards the corner where the apparatus stood about the little crystal ball. As he did so the undertone of tumultuous shouting from the archway that had continued during all these occurrences rose to a mighty sound, roared as if it were sweeping past, and fell again as if receding swiftly. It drew Graham after it with an irresistible attraction. He glanced at the thickset man, and then obeyed his impulse. In two strides he was down the steps and in the passage, and in a score he was out upon the balcony upon which the three men had been standing.

5

THE MOVING WAYS

HE WENT TO THE RAILINGS OF THE BALCONY AND STARED UPWARD. AN exclamation of surprise at his appearance, and the movements of a number of people came from the great area below.

His first impression was of overwhelming architecture. The place into which he looked was an aisle of Titanic buildings, curving spaciously in either direction. Overhead mighty cantilevers sprang together across the huge width of the place, and a tracery of translucent material shut out the sky. Gigantic globes of cool white light shamed the pale sunbeams that filtered down through the girders and wires. Here and there a gossamer suspension bridge dotted with foot passengers flung across the chasm and the air was webbed with slender cables. A cliff of edifice hung above him, he perceived as he glanced upward, and the opposite façade was grey and dim and broken by great archings, circular perforations, balconies, buttresses, turret projections, myriads of vast windows, and an intricate scheme of architectural relief. Athwart these ran inscriptions horizontally and obliquely in an unfamiliar lettering. Here and there close to the roof cables of a peculiar stoutness were fastened, and drooped in a steep curve to circular openings on the opposite side of the space, and even as Graham noted these a remote and tiny figure of a man clad in pale blue arrested his attention. This little figure was far overhead across the space beside the higher fastening of one of these festoons, hanging forward from a little ledge of masonry and handling some well-nigh invisible strings dependent from the line. Then suddenly, with a swoop that sent Graham's heart into his mouth, this man had rushed down the curve and vanished through a round opening on the hither side of the way. Graham had been looking up as he came out upon the balcony, and the things he saw above and opposed to him had at first seized his attention to the exclusion of anything else. Then suddenly he discovered the roadway! It was not a roadway at all, as Graham understood such things, for in the nineteenth century the only roads and streets were beaten tracks of motionless earth, jostling rivulets of vehicles between narrow footways. But this roadway was three hundred feet across, and it moved; it moved, all save the middle, the lowest part. For a moment, the motion dazzled his mind. Then he understood. Under the balcony this extraordinary roadway ran swiftly to Graham's right, an endless flow rushing along as fast as a nineteenth century express train, an endless platform of narrow transverse overlapping slats with little interspaces that permitted it to follow the curvatures of the street. Upon it were seats, and here and there little kiosks, but they swept by too swiftly for him to see what might be therein. From this nearest and swiftest platform a series of others descended to the centre of the space. Each moved to the right, each perceptibly slower than the one above it, but the difference in pace was small enough to permit anyone to step from any platform to the one adjacent, and so walk uninterruptedly from the swiftest to the motionless middle way. Beyond this middle way was another series of endless platforms rushing with varying pace to Graham's left. And seated in crowds upon the two widest and swiftest platforms, or stepping from one to another down the steps, or swarming over the central space, was an innumerable and wonderfully diversified multitude of people.

"You must not stop here," shouted Howard suddenly at his side. "You must come away at once."

Graham made no answer. He heard without hearing. The platforms ran with a roar and the people were shouting. He perceived women and girls with flowing hair, beautifully robed, with bands crossing between the breasts. These first came out of the confusion. Then he perceived that the dominant note in that kaleidoscope of costume was the pale blue that the tailor's boy had worn. He became aware of cries of "The Sleeper. What has happened to the Sleeper?" and it seemed as though the rushing platforms before him were suddenly spattered with the pale buff of human faces, and then still more thickly. He saw pointing fingers. He perceived that the motionless central area of this huge arcade just opposite to the balcony was densely crowded with blue-clad people. Some sort of struggle had sprung into life. People seemed to be pushed up the running platforms on either side, and carried away against their will. They would spring off so soon as they were beyond the thick of the confusion, and run back towards the conflict.

"It is the Sleeper. Verily it is the Sleeper," shouted voices. "That is never the Sleeper," shouted others. More and more faces were turned to him. At the intervals along this central area Graham noted openings, pits, apparently the heads of staircases going down with people ascending out of them and descending into them. The struggle it seemed centred about the one of these nearest to him. People were running down the moving platforms to this, leaping dexterously from platform to platform. The clustering people on the higher platforms seemed to divide their interest between this point and the balcony. A number of sturdy little figures clad in a uniform of bright red, and working methodically together, were employed it seemed in preventing access to this descending staircase. About them a crowd was rapidly accumulating. Their brilliant colour contrasted vividly with the whitish-blue of their antagonists, for the struggle was indisputable.

He saw these things with Howard shouting in his ear and shaking his arm. And then suddenly Howard was gone and he stood alone.

He perceived that the cries of "The Sleeper!" grew in volume, and that the people on the nearer platform were standing up. The nearer platform he perceived was empty to the right of him, and far across the space the platform running in the opposite direction was coming crowded and passing away bare. With incredible swiftness a vast crowd had gathered in the central space before his eyes; a dense swaying mass of people, and the shouts grew from a fitful crying to a voluminous incessant clamour: "The Sleeper! The Sleeper!" and yells and cheers, a waving of garments and cries of "Stop the Ways!" They were also crying another name strange to Graham. It sounded like "Ostrog." The slower platforms were soon thick with active people, running against the movement so as to keep themselves opposite to him.

"Stop the Ways," they cried. Agile figures ran up from the centre to the swift road nearest to him, were borne rapidly past him, shouting strange, unintelligible things, and ran back obliquely to the central way. One thing he distinguished: "It is indeed the Sleeper. It is indeed the Sleeper," they testified.

For a space Graham stood motionless. Then he became vividly aware that all this concerned him. He was pleased at his wonderful popularity, he bowed, and, seeking a gesture of longer range, waved his arm. He was astonished at the violence of uproar that this provoked. The tumult about the descending stairway rose to furious violence. He became aware of crowded balconies, of men sliding along ropes, of men in trapeze-like seats hurling athwart the space. He heard voices behind him, a number of people descending the steps through the archway; he suddenly perceived that his guardian Howard was back again and gripping his arm painfully, and shouting inaudibly in his ear.

He turned, and Howard's face was white. "Come back," he heard. "They will stop the ways. The whole city will be in confusion."

He perceived a number of men hurrying along the passage of blue pillars behind Howard, the red-haired man, the man with the flaxen beard, a tall man in vivid vermilion, a crowd of others in red carrying staves, and all these people had anxious eager faces.

"Get him away," cried Howard.

"But why?" said Graham. "I don't see—"

"You must come away!" said the man in red in a resolute voice. His face and eyes were resolute, too. Graham's glances went from face to face, and he was suddenly aware of that most disagreeable flavour in life, compulsion. Someone gripped his arm....

He was being dragged away. It seemed as though the tumult suddenly became two, as if half the shouts that had come in from this wonderful roadway had sprung into the passages of the great building behind him. Marvelling and confused, feeling an impotent desire to resist, Graham was half led, half thrust, along the passage of blue pillars, and suddenly he found himself alone with Howard in a lift and moving swiftly upward.

⬤
6

THE HALL OF THE ATLAS

FROM THE MOMENT WHEN THE TAILOR HAD BOWED HIS FAREWELL TO the moment when Graham found himself in the lift, was altogether barely five minutes. As yet the haze of his vast interval of sleep hung about him, as yet the initial strangeness of his being alive at all in this remote age touched everything with wonder, with a sense of the irrational, with something of the quality of a realistic dream. He was still detached, an astonished spectator, still but half involved in life. What he had seen, and especially the last crowded tumult, framed in the setting of the balcony, had a spectacular turn, like a thing witnessed from the box of a theatre. "I don't understand," he said. "What was the trouble? My mind is in a whirl. Why were they shouting? What is the danger?"

"We have our troubles," said Howard. His eyes avoided Graham's enquiry. "This is a time of unrest. And, in fact, your appearance, your waking just now, has a sort of connexion—"

He spoke jerkily, like a man not quite sure of his breathing. He stopped abruptly.

"I don't understand," said Graham.

"It will be clearer later," said Howard.

He glanced uneasily upward, as though he found the progress of the lift slow.

"I shall understand better, no doubt, when I have seen my way about a little," said Graham puzzled. "It will be—it is bound to be perplexing. At present it is all so strange. Anything seems possible. Anything. In the details even. Your counting, I understand, is different."

The lift stopped, and they stepped out into a narrow but very long passage between high walls, along which ran an extraordinary number of tubes and big cables.

"What a huge place this is!" said Graham. "Is it all one building? What place is it?"

"This is one of the city ways for various public services. Light and so forth."

"Was it a social trouble—that—in the great roadway place? How are you governed? Have you still a police?"

"Several," said Howard.

"Several?"

"About fourteen."

"I don't understand."

"Very probably not. Our social order will probably seem very complex to you. To tell you the truth, I don't understand it myself very clearly. Nobody does. You will, perhaps—bye and bye. We have to go to the Council."

Graham's attention was divided between the urgent necessity of his inquiries and the people in the passages and halls they were traversing. For a moment his mind would be concentrated upon Howard and the halting answers he made, and then he would lose the thread in response to some vivid unexpected impression. Along the passages, in the halls, half the people seemed to be men in the red uniform. The pale blue canvas that had been so abundant in the aisle of moving ways did not appear. Invariably these men looked at him, and saluted him and Howard as they passed.

He had a clear vision of entering a long corridor, and there were a number of girls sitting on low seats, as though in a class. He saw no teacher, but only a novel apparatus from which he fancied a voice proceeded. The girls regarded him and his conductor, he thought, with curiosity and astonishment. But he was hurried on before he could form a clear idea of the gathering. He judged they knew Howard and not himself, and that they wondered who he was. This Howard, it seemed, was a person of importance. But then he was also merely Graham's guardian. That was odd.

There came a passage in twilight, and into this passage a footway hung so that he could see the feet and ankles of people going to and fro thereon, but no more of them. Then vague impressions of galleries and of casual astonished passers-by turning round to stare after the two of them with their red-clad guard.

The stimulus of the restoratives he had taken was only temporary. He was speedily fatigued by this excessive haste. He asked Howard to slacken his speed. Presently he was in a lift that had a window upon the great street space, but this was glazed and did not open, and they were too high for him to see the moving platforms below. But he saw people going to and fro along cables and along strange, frail-looking bridges.

Thence they passed across the street and at a vast height above it. They crossed by means of a narrow bridge closed in with glass, so clear that it made him giddy even to remember it. The floor of it also was of glass. From his memory of the cliffs between New Quay and Boscastle, so remote in time, and so recent in his experience, it seemed to him that they must be near four hundred feet above the moving ways. He stopped, looked down between his legs upon the swarming blue and red multitudes, minute and foreshortened, struggling and gesticulating still towards the little balcony far below, a little toy balcony, it seemed, where he had so recently been standing. A thin haze and the glare of the mighty globes of light obscured everything. A man seated in a little openwork cradle shot by from some point still higher than the little narrow bridge, rushing down a cable as swiftly almost as if he were falling. Graham stopped involuntarily to watch this strange passenger vanish below, and then his eyes went back to the tumultuous struggle.

Along one of the faster ways rushed a thick crowd of red spots. This broke up into individuals as it approached the balcony, and went pouring down the slower ways towards the dense struggling crowd on the central area. These men in red appeared to be armed with sticks or truncheons; they seemed to be striking and thrusting. A great shouting, cries of wrath, screaming, burst out and came up to Graham, faint and thin. "Go on," cried Howard, laying hands on him.

Another man rushed down a cable. Graham suddenly glanced up to see whence he came, and beheld through the glassy roof and the network of cables and girders, dim rhythmically passing forms like the vanes of windmills, and between them glimpses of a remote and pallid sky. Then Howard had thrust him forward across the bridge, and he was in a little narrow passage decorated with geometrical patterns.

"I want to see more of that," cried Graham, resisting.

"No, no," cried Howard, still gripping his arm. "This way. You must go this way." And the men in red following them seemed ready to enforce his orders.

Some negroes in a curious wasp-like uniform of black and yellow appeared down the passage, and one hastened to throw up a sliding shutter that had seemed a door to Graham, and led the way through it. Graham found himself in a gallery overhanging the end of a great chamber. The attendant in black and yellow crossed this, thrust up a second shutter and stood waiting.

This place had the appearance of an ante-room. He saw a number of people in the central space, and at the opposite end a large and imposing doorway at the top of a flight of steps, heavily curtained but giving a glimpse of some still larger hall beyond. He perceived white men in red and other negroes in black and yellow standing stiffly about those portals.

As they crossed the gallery he heard a whisper from below, "The Sleeper," and was aware of a turning of heads, a hum of observation. They entered another little passage in the wall of this antechamber, and then he found himself on an iron-railed gallery of metal that passed round the side of the great hall he had already seen through the curtains. He entered the place at the corner, so that he received the fullest impression of its huge proportions. The black in the wasp uniform stood aside like a well-trained servant, and closed the valve behind him.

Compared with any of the places Graham had seen thus far, this second hall appeared to be decorated with extreme richness. On a pedestal at the remoter end, and more brilliantly lit than any other object, was a gigantic white figure of Atlas, strong and strenuous, the globe upon his bowed shoulders. It was the first thing to strike his attention, it was so vast, so patiently and painfully real, so white and simple. Save for this figure and for a dais in the centre, the wide floor of the place was a shining vacancy. The dais was remote in the greatness of the area; it would have looked a mere slab of metal had it not been for the group of seven men who stood about a table on it, and gave an inkling of its proportions. They were all dressed in white robes, they seemed to have arisen that moment from their seats, and they were regarding Graham steadfastly. At the end of the table he perceived the glitter of some mechanical appliances.

Howard led him along the end gallery until they were opposite this mighty labouring figure. Then he stopped. The two men in red who had followed them into the gallery came and stood on either hand of Graham.

"You must remain here," murmured Howard, "for a few moments," and, without waiting for a reply, hurried away along the gallery.

"But, *why*—?" began Graham.

He moved as if to follow Howard, and found his path obstructed by one of the men in red. "You have to wait here, Sire," said the man in red.

"*Why?*"

"Orders, Sire."

"Whose orders?"

"Our orders, Sire."

Graham looked his exasperation.

"What place is this?" he said presently. "Who are those men?"

"They are the lords of the Council, Sire."

"What Council?"

"*The* Council."

"Oh!" said Graham, and after an equally ineffectual attempt at the other man, went to the railing and stared at the distant men in white, who stood watching him and whispering together.

The Council? He perceived there were now eight, though how the new-comer had arrived he had not observed. They made no gestures of greeting; they stood regarding him as in the nineteenth century a group of men might have stood in the street regarding a distant balloon that had suddenly floated into view. What council could it be that gathered there, that little body of men beneath the significant white Atlas, secluded from every eavesdropper in this impressive spaciousness? And why should he be brought to them, and be looked at strangely and spoken of inaudibly? Howard appeared beneath, walking quickly across the polished floor towards them. As he drew near he bowed and performed certain peculiar movements, apparently of a ceremonious nature. Then he ascended the steps of the dais, and stood by the apparatus at the end of the table.

Graham watched that visible inaudible conversation. Occasionally, one of the white-robed men would glance towards him. He strained his ears in vain. The gesticulation of two of the speakers became animated. He glanced from them to the passive faces of his attendants.... When he looked again Howard was extending his hands and moving his head like a man who protests. He was interrupted, it seemed, by one of the white-robed men rapping the table.

The conversation lasted an interminable time to Graham's sense. His eyes rose to the still giant at whose feet the Council sat. Thence they wandered to the walls of the hall. It was decorated in long painted panels of a quasi-Japanese type, many of them very beautiful. These panels were grouped in a great and elaborate framing of dark metal, which passed into the metallic caryatidae of the galleries, and the great structural lines of the interior. The facile grace of these panels enhanced the mighty white effort that laboured in the centre of the scheme. Graham's eyes came back to the Council, and Howard was descending the steps. As he drew nearer his features could be distinguished, and Graham saw that he was flushed and blowing out his cheeks. His countenance was still disturbed when presently he reappeared along the gallery.

"This way," he said concisely, and they went on in silence to a little door that opened at their approach. The two men in red stopped on either side of this door. Howard and Graham passed in, and Graham, glancing back, saw the white-robed Council still standing in a close group and looking at him. Then the door closed behind him with a heavy thud, and for the first time since his awakening he was in silence. The floor, even, was noiseless to his feet.

Howard opened another door, and they were in the first of two contiguous chambers furnished in white and green. "What Council was that?" began Graham. "What were they discussing? What have they to do with me?" Howard closed the door carefully, heaved a huge sigh, and said something in an undertone. He walked slantingways across the room and turned, blowing out his cheeks again. "Ugh!" he grunted, a man relieved.

Graham stood regarding him.

"You must understand," began Howard abruptly, avoiding Graham's eyes, "that our social order is very complex. A half explanation, a bare unqualified statement would give you false impressions. As a matter of fact —it is a case of compound interest partly—your small fortune, and the fortune of your cousin Warming which was left to you—and certain other beginnings—have become very considerable. And in other ways that will be hard for you to understand, you have become a person of significance— of very considerable significance—involved in the world's affairs."

He stopped.

"Yes?" said Graham.

"We have grave social troubles."

"Yes?"

"Things have come to such a pass that, in fact, it is advisable to seclude you here."

"Keep me prisoner!" exclaimed Graham.

"Well—to ask you to keep in seclusion."

Graham turned on him. "This is strange!" he said.

"No harm will be done you."

"No harm!"

"But you must be kept here—"

"While I learn my position, I presume."

"Precisely."

"Very well then. Begin. Why *harm*?"

"Not now."

"Why not?"

"It is too long a story, Sire."

"All the more reason I should begin at once. You say I am a person of importance. What was that shouting I heard? Why is a great multitude shouting and excited because my trance is over, and who are the men in white in that huge council chamber?"

"All in good time, Sire," said Howard. "But not crudely, not crudely. This is one of those flimsy times when no man has a settled mind. Your awakening—no one expected your awakening. The Council is consulting."

"What council?"

"The Council you saw."

Graham made a petulant movement. "This is not right," he said. "I should be told what is happening."

"You must wait. Really you must wait."

Graham sat down abruptly. "I suppose since I have waited so long to resume life," he said, "that I must wait a little longer."

"That is better," said Howard. "Yes, that is much better. And I must leave you alone. For a space. While I attend the discussion in the Council.... I am sorry."

He went towards the noiseless door, hesitated and vanished.

Graham walked to the door, tried it, found it securely fastened in some way he never came to understand, turned about, paced the room restlessly, made the circuit of the room, and sat down. He remained sitting for some time with folded arms and knitted brow, biting his finger nails and trying to piece together the kaleidoscopic impressions of this first hour of awakened life; the vast mechanical spaces, the endless series of chambers and passages, the great struggle that roared and splashed through these strange ways, the little group of remote unsympathetic men beneath the colossal Atlas, Howard's mysterious behaviour. There was an inkling of some vast inheritance already in his mind—a vast inheritance perhaps misapplied—of some unprecedented importance and opportunity. What had he to do? And this room's secluded silence was eloquent of imprisonment!

It came into Graham's mind with irresistible conviction that this series of magnificent impressions was a dream. He tried to shut his eyes and succeeded, but that time-honoured device led to no awakening.

Presently he began to touch and examine all the unfamiliar appointments of the two small rooms in which he found himself.

In a long oval panel of mirror he saw himself and stopped astonished. He was clad in a graceful costume of purple and bluish white, with a little grey-shot beard trimmed to a point, and his hair, its blackness streaked now with bands of grey, arranged over his forehead in an unfamiliar but pleasing manner. He seemed a man of five-and-forty perhaps. For a moment he did not perceive this was himself.

A flash of laughter came with the recognition. "To call on old Warming like this!" he exclaimed, "and make him take me out to lunch!"

Then he thought of meeting first one and then another of the few familiar acquaintances of his early manhood, and in the midst of his amusement realized that every soul with whom he might jest had died many score of years ago. The thought smote him abruptly and keenly; he stopped short, the expression of his face changed to a white consternation.

The tumultuous memory of the moving platforms and the huge façade of that wonderful street reasserted itself. The shouting multitudes came back clear and vivid, and those remote, inaudible, unfriendly councillors in white. He felt himself a little figure, very small and ineffectual, pitifully conspicuous. And all about him, the world was—*strange*.

7

IN THE SILENT ROOMS

PRESENTLY GRAHAM RESUMED HIS EXAMINATION OF HIS APARTMENTS. Curiosity kept him moving in spite of his fatigue. The inner room, he perceived, was high, and its ceiling dome-shaped, with an oblong aperture in the centre, opening into a funnel in which a wheel of broad vanes seemed to be rotating, apparently driving the air up the shaft. The faint humming note of its easy motion was the only clear sound in that quiet place. As these vanes sprang up one after the other, Graham could get transient glimpses of the sky. He was surprised to see a star.

This drew his attention to the fact that the bright lighting of these rooms was due to a multitude of very faint glow lamps set about the cornices. There were no windows. And he began to recall that along all the vast chambers and passages he had traversed with Howard he had observed no windows at all. Had there been windows? There were windows on the street indeed, but were they for light? Or was the whole city lit day and night for evermore, so that there was no night there?

And another thing dawned upon him. There was no fireplace in either room. Was the season summer, and were these merely summer apartments, or was the whole city uniformly heated or cooled? He became interested in these questions, began examining the smooth texture of the walls, the simply constructed bed, the ingenious arrangements by which the labour of bedroom service was practically abolished. And over everything was a curious absence of deliberate ornament, a bare grace of form and colour, that he found very pleasing to the eye. There were several very comfortable chairs, a light table on silent runners carrying several bottles of fluids and glasses, and two plates bearing a clear substance like jelly. Then he noticed there were no books, no newspapers, no writing materials. "The world has changed indeed," he said.

He observed one entire side of the outer room was set with rows of peculiar double cylinders inscribed with green lettering on white that harmonised with the decorative scheme of the room, and in the centre of this side projected a little apparatus about a yard square and having a white smooth face to the room. A chair faced this. He had a transitory idea that these cylinders might be books, or a modern substitute for books, but at first it did not seem so.

The lettering on the cylinders puzzled him. At first sight it seemed like Russian. Then he noticed a suggestion of mutilated English about certain of the words.

"Ɵi Man huwdbi Kiŋ" forced itself on him as "The Man who would be King."

"Phonetic spelling," he said. He remembered reading a story with that title, then he recalled the story vividly, one of the best stories in the world. But this thing before him was not a book as he understood it. He puzzled out the titles of two adjacent cylinders. "The Heart of Darkness" he had never heard of before nor "The Madonna of the Future"—no doubt if they were indeed stories, they were by post-Victorian authors.

He puzzled over this peculiar cylinder for some time and replaced it. Then he turned to the square apparatus and examined that. He opened a sort of lid and found one of the double cylinders within, and on the upper edge a little stud like the stud of an electric bell. He pressed this and a rapid clicking began and ceased. He became aware of voices and music, and noticed a play of colour on the smooth front face. He suddenly realized what this might be, and stepped back to regard it.

On the flat surface was now a little picture, very vividly coloured, and in this picture were figures that moved. Not only did they move, but they were conversing in clear small voices. It was exactly like reality viewed through an inverted opera glass and heard through a long tube. His interest was seized at once by the situation, which presented a man pacing up and down and vociferating angry things to a pretty but petulant woman. Both were in the picturesque costume that seemed so strange to Graham. "I have worked," said the man, "but what have you been doing?"

"Ah!" said Graham. He forgot everything else, and sat down in the chair. Within five minutes he heard himself, named, heard "when the Sleeper wakes," used jestingly as a proverb for remote postponement, and passed himself by, a thing remote and incredible. But in a little while he knew those two people like intimate friends.

At last the miniature drama came to an end, and the square face of the apparatus was blank again.

It was a strange world into which he had been permitted to see, unscrupulous, pleasure-seeking, energetic, subtle, a world too of dire economic struggle; there were allusions he did not understand, incidents that conveyed strange suggestions of altered moral ideals, flashes of dubious enlightenment. The blue canvas that bulked so largely in his first impression of the city ways appeared again and again as the costume of the common people. He had no doubt the story was contemporary, and its intense realism was undeniable. And the end had been a tragedy that oppressed him. He sat staring at the blankness.

He started and rubbed his eyes. He had been so absorbed in the latter-day substitute for a novel, that he awoke to the little green and white room with more than a touch of the surprise of his first awakening.

He stood up, and abruptly he was back in his own wonderland. The clearness of the kinetoscope drama passed, and the struggle in the vast place of streets, the ambiguous Council, the swift phases of his waking hour, came back. These people had spoken of the Council with suggestions of a vague universality of power. And they had spoken of the Sleeper; it had not really struck him vividly at the time that he was the Sleeper. He had to recall precisely what they had said....

He walked into the bedroom and peered up through the quick intervals of the revolving fan. As the fan swept round, a dim turmoil like the noise of machinery came in rhythmic eddies. All else was silence. Though the perpetual day still irradiated his apartments, he perceived the little intermittent strip of sky was now deep blue—black almost, with a dust of little stars ....

He resumed his examination of the rooms. He could find no way of opening the padded door, no bell nor other means of calling for attendance. His feeling of wonder was in abeyance; but he was curious, anxious for information. He wanted to know exactly how he stood to these new things. He tried to compose himself to wait until someone came to him. Presently he became restless and eager for information, for distraction, for fresh sensations.

He went back to the apparatus in the other room, and had soon puzzled out the method of replacing the cylinders by others. As he did so, it came into his mind that it must be these little appliances had fixed the language so that it was still clear and understandable after two hundred years. The haphazard cylinders he substituted displayed a musical fantasia. At first it was beautiful, and then it was sensuous. He presently recognised what appeared to him to be an altered version of the story of Tannhauser. The music was unfamiliar. But the rendering was realistic, and with a contemporary unfamiliarity. Tannhauser did not go to a Venusberg, but to a Pleasure City. What was a Pleasure City? A dream, surely, the fancy of a fantastic, voluptuous writer.

He became interested, curious. The story developed with a flavour of strangely twisted sentimentality. Suddenly he did not like it. He liked it less as it proceeded.

He had a revulsion of feeling. These were no pictures, no idealisations, but photographed realities. He wanted no more of the twenty-second century Venusberg. He forgot the part played by the model in nineteenth century art, and gave way to an archaic indignation. He rose, angry and half ashamed at himself for witnessing this thing even in solitude. He pulled forward the apparatus, and with some violence sought for a means of stopping its action. Something snapped. A violet spark stung and convulsed his arm and the thing was still. When he attempted the next day to replace these Tannhauser cylinders by another pair, he found the apparatus broken....

He struck out a path oblique to the room and paced to and fro, struggling with intolerable vast impressions. The things he had derived from the cylinders and the things he had seen, conflicted, confused him. It seemed to him the most amazing thing of all that in his thirty years of life he had never tried to shape a picture of these coming times. "We were making the future," he said, "and hardly any of us troubled to think what future we were making. And here it is!

"What have they got to, what has been done? How do I come into the midst of it all?" The vastness of street and house he was prepared for, the multitudes of people. But conflicts in the city ways! And the systematised sensuality of a class of rich men!

He thought of Bellamy, the hero of whose Socialistic Utopia had so oddly anticipated this actual experience. But here was no Utopia, no Socialistic state. He had already seen enough to realize that the ancient antithesis of luxury, waste and sensuality on the one hand and abject poverty on the other, still prevailed. He knew enough of the essential factors of life to understand that correlation. And not only were the buildings of the city gigantic and the crowds in the street gigantic, but the voices he had heard in the ways, the uneasiness of Howard, the very atmosphere spoke of gigantic discontent. What country was he in? Still England it seemed, and yet strangely "un-English." His mind glanced at the rest of the world, and saw only an enigmatical veil.

He prowled about his apartment, examining everything as a caged animal might do. He was very tired, with that feverish exhaustion that does not admit of rest. He listened for long spaces under the ventilator to catch some distant echo of the tumults he felt must be proceeding in the city.

He began to talk to himself. "Two hundred and three years!" he said to himself over and over again, laughing stupidly. "Then I am two hundred and thirty-three years old! The oldest inhabitant. Surely they haven't reversed the tendency of our time and gone back to the rule of the oldest. My claims are indisputable. Mumble, mumble. I remember the Bulgarian atrocities as though it was yesterday. 'Tis a great age! Ha ha!" He was surprised at first to hear himself laughing, and then laughed again deliberately and louder. Then he realized that he was behaving foolishly. "Steady," he said. "Steady!"

His pacing became more regular. "This new world," he said. "I don't understand it. *Why?* ... But it is all *why!*"

"I suppose they can fly and do all sorts of things. Let me try and remember just how it began."

He was surprised at first to find how vague the memories of his first thirty years had become. He remembered fragments, for the most part trivial moments, things of no great importance that he had observed. His boyhood seemed the most accessible at first, he recalled school books and certain lessons in mensuration. Then he revived the more salient features of his life, memories of the wife long since dead, her magic influence now gone beyond corruption, of his rivals and friends and betrayers, of the decision of this issue and that, and then of his last years of misery, of fluctuating resolves, and at last of his strenuous studies. In a little while he perceived he had it all again; dim perhaps, like metal long laid aside, but in no way defective or injured, capable of re-polishing. And the hue of it was a deepening misery. Was it worth re-polishing? By a miracle he had been lifted out of a life that had become intolerable....

He reverted to his present condition. He wrestled with the facts in vain. It became an inextricable tangle. He saw the sky through the ventilator pink with dawn. An old persuasion came out of the dark recesses of his memory. "I must sleep," he said. It appeared as a delightful relief from this mental distress and from the growing pain and heaviness of his limbs. He went to the strange little bed, lay down and was presently asleep....

He was destined to become very familiar indeed with these apartments before he left them, for he remained imprisoned for three days. During that time no one, except Howard, entered the rooms. The marvel of his fate mingled with and in some way minimised the marvel of his survival. He had awakened to mankind it seemed only to be snatched away into this unaccountable solitude. Howard came regularly with subtly sustaining and nutritive fluids, and light and pleasant foods, quite strange to Graham. He always closed the door carefully as he entered. On matters of detail he was increasingly obliging, but the bearing of Graham on the great issues that were evidently being contested so closely beyond the sound-proof walls that enclosed him, he would not elucidate. He evaded, as politely as possible, every question on the position of affairs in the outer world.

And in those three days Graham's incessant thoughts went far and wide. All that he had seen, all this elaborate contrivance to prevent him seeing, worked together in his mind. Almost every possible interpretation of his position he debated—even as it chanced, the right interpretation. Things that presently happened to him, came to him at last credible, by virtue of this seclusion. When at length the moment of his release arrived, it found him prepared....

Howard's bearing went far to deepen Graham's impression of his own strange importance; the door between its opening and closing seemed to admit with him a breath of momentous happening. His enquiries became more definite and searching. Howard retreated through protests and difficulties. The awakening was unforeseen, he repeated; it happened to have fallen in with the trend of a social convulsion. "To explain it I must tell you the history of a gross and a half of years," protested Howard.

"The thing is this," said Graham. "You are afraid of something I shall do. In some way I am arbitrator—I might be arbitrator."

"It is not that. But you have—I may tell you this much—the automatic increase of your property puts great possibilities of interference in your hands. And in certain other ways you have influence, with your eighteenth century notions."

"Nineteenth century," corrected Graham.

"With your old-world notions, anyhow, ignorant as you are of every feature of our State."

"Am I a fool?"

"Certainly not."

"Do I seem to be the sort of man who would act rashly?"

"You were never expected to act at all. No one counted on your awakening. No one dreamt you would ever awake. The Council had surrounded you with antiseptic conditions. As a matter of fact, we thought that you were dead—a mere arrest of decay. And—but it is too complex. We dare not suddenly—while you are still half awake."

"It won't do," said Graham. "Suppose it is as you say—why am I not being crammed night and day with facts and warnings and all the wisdom of the time to fit me for my responsibilities? Am I any wiser now than two days ago, if it is two days, when I awoke?"

Howard pulled his lip.

"I am beginning to feel—every hour I feel more clearly—a system of concealment of which you are the face. Is this Council, or committee, or whatever they are, cooking the accounts of my estate? Is that it?"

"That note of suspicion—" said Howard.

"Ugh!" said Graham. "Now, mark my words, it will be ill for those who have put me here. It will be ill. I am alive. Make no doubt of it, I am alive. Every day my pulse is stronger and my mind clearer and more vigorous. No more quiescence. I am a man come back to life. And I want to *live*—"

"*Live!*"

Howard's face lit with an idea. He came towards Graham and spoke in an easy confidential tone.

"The Council secludes you here for your good. You are restless. Naturally—an energetic man! You find it dull here. But we are anxious that everything you may desire—every desire—every sort of desire.... There may be something. Is there any sort of company?"

He paused meaningly.

"Yes," said Graham thoughtfully. "There is."

"Ah! *Now*! We have treated you neglectfully."

"The crowds in yonder streets of yours."

"That," said Howard, "I am afraid—But—"

Graham began pacing the room. Howard stood near the door watching him. The implication of Howard's suggestion was only half evident to Graham. Company? Suppose he were to accept the proposal, demand some sort of *company*? Would there be any possibilities of gathering from the conversation of this additional person some vague inkling of the struggle that had broken out so vividly at his waking moment? He meditated again, and the suggestion took colour. He turned on Howard abruptly.

"What do you mean by company?"

Howard raised his eyes and shrugged his shoulders. "Human beings," he said, with a curious smile on his heavy face. "Our social ideas," he said, "have a certain increased liberality, perhaps, in comparison with your times. If a man wishes to relieve such a tedium as this—by feminine society, for instance. We think it no scandal. We have cleared our minds of formulae. There is in our city a class, a necessary class, no longer despised—discreet—"

Graham stopped dead.

"It would pass the time," said Howard. "It is a thing I should perhaps have thought of before, but, as a matter of fact, so much is happening—"

He indicated the exterior world.

Graham hesitated. For a moment the figure of a possible woman dominated his mind with an intense attraction. Then he flashed into anger.

"*No!*" he shouted.

He began striding rapidly up and down the room. "Everything you say, everything you do, convinces me—of some great issue in which I am concerned. I do not want to pass the time, as you call it. Yes, I know. Desire and indulgence are life in a sense—and Death! Extinction! In my life before I slept I had worked out that pitiful question. I will not begin again. There is a city, a multitude—. And meanwhile I am here like a rabbit in a bag."

His rage surged high. He choked for a moment and began to wave his clenched fists. He gave way to an anger fit, he swore archaic curses. His gestures had the quality of physical threats.

"I do not know who your party may be. I am in the dark, and you keep me in the dark. But I know this, that I am secluded here for no good purpose. For no good purpose. I warn you, I warn you of the consequences. Once I come at my power—"

He realized that to threaten thus might be a danger to himself. He stopped. Howard stood regarding him with a curious expression.

"I take it this is a message to the Council," said Howard.

Graham had a momentary impulse to leap upon the man, fell or stun him. It must have shown upon his face; at any rate Howard's movement was quick. In a second the noiseless door had closed again, and the man from the nineteenth century was alone.

For a moment he stood rigid, with clenched hands half raised. Then he flung them down. "What a fool I have been!" he said, and gave way to his anger again, stamping about the room and shouting curses.... For a long time he kept himself in a sort of frenzy, raging at his position, at his own folly, at the knaves who had imprisoned him. He did this because he did not want to look calmly at his position. He clung to his anger—because he was afraid of fear.

Presently he found himself reasoning with himself. This imprisonment was unaccountable, but no doubt the legal forms—new legal forms—of the time permitted it. It must, of course, be legal. These people were two hundred years further on in the march of civilisation than the Victorian generation. It was not likely they would be less—humane. Yet they had cleared their minds of formulae! Was humanity a formula as well as chastity?

His imagination set to work to suggest things that might be done to him. The attempts of his reason to dispose of these suggestions, though for the most part logically valid, were quite unavailing. "Why should anything be done to me?"

"If the worst comes to the worst," he found himself saying at last, "I can give up what they want. But what do they want? And why don't they ask me for it instead of cooping me up?"

He returned to his former preoccupation with the Council's possible intentions. He began to reconsider the details of Howard's behaviour, sinister glances, inexplicable hesitations. Then, for a time, his mind circled about the idea of escaping from these rooms; but whither could he escape into this vast, crowded world? He would be worse off than a Saxon yeoman suddenly dropped into nineteenth century London. And besides, how could anyone escape from these rooms?

"How can it benefit anyone if harm should happen to me?"

He thought of the tumult, the great social trouble of which he was so unaccountably the axis. A text, irrelevant enough, and yet curiously insistent, came floating up out of the darkness of his memory. This also a Council had said:

"It is expedient for us that one man should die for the people."

8

THE ROOF SPACES

As the fans in the circular aperture of the inner room rotated and permitted glimpses of the night, dim sounds drifted in thereby. And Graham, standing underneath, was startled by the sound of a voice.

He peered up and saw in the intervals of the rotation, dark and dim, the face and shoulders of a man regarding him. Then a dark hand was extended, the swift vane struck it, swung round and beat on with a little brownish patch on the edge of its thin blade, and something began to fall therefrom upon the floor, dripping silently.

Graham looked down, and there were spots of blood at his feet. He looked up again in a strange excitement. The figure had gone.

He remained motionless—his every sense intent upon the flickering patch of darkness. He became aware of some faint, remote, dark specks floating lightly through the outer air. They came down towards him, fitfully, eddyingly, and passed aside out of the uprush from the fan. A gleam of light flickered, the specks flashed white, and then the darkness came again. Warmed and lit as he was, he perceived that it was snowing within a few feet of him.

Graham walked across the room and came back to the ventilator again. He saw the head of a man pass near. There was a sound of whispering. Then a smart blow on some metallic substance, effort, voices, and the vanes stopped. A gust of snowflakes whirled into the room, and vanished before they touched the floor. "Don't be afraid," said a voice.

Graham stood under the vane. "Who are you?" he whispered.

For a moment there was nothing but a swaying of the fan, and then the head of a man was thrust cautiously into the opening. His face appeared nearly inverted to Graham; his dark hair was wet with dissolving flakes of snow upon it. His arm went up into the darkness holding something unseen. He had a youthful face and bright eyes, and the veins of his forehead were swollen. He seemed to be exerting himself to maintain his position.

For several seconds neither he nor Graham spoke.

"You were the Sleeper?" said the stranger at last.

"Yes," said Graham. "What do you want with me?"

"I come from Ostrog, Sire."

"Ostrog?"

The man in the ventilator twisted his head round so that his profile was towards Graham. He appeared to be listening. Suddenly there was a hasty exclamation, and the intruder sprang back just in time to escape the sweep of the released fan. And when Graham peered up there was nothing visible but the slowly falling snow.

It was perhaps a quarter of an hour before anything returned to the ventilator. But at last came the same metallic interference again; the fans stopped and the face reappeared. Graham had remained all this time in the same place, alert and tremulously excited.

"Who are you? What do you want?" he said.

"We want to speak to you, Sire," said the intruder. "We want—I can't hold the thing. We have been trying to find a way to you—these three days."

"Is it rescue?" whispered Graham. "Escape?"

"Yes, Sire. If you will."

"You are my party—the party of the Sleeper?"

"Yes, Sire."

"What am I to do?" said Graham.

There was a struggle. The stranger's arm appeared, and his hand was bleeding. His knees came into view over the edge of the funnel. "Stand away from me," he said, and he dropped rather heavily on his hands and one shoulder at Graham's feet. The released ventilator whirled noisily. The stranger rolled over, sprang up nimbly and stood panting, hand to a bruised shoulder, and with his bright eyes on Graham.

"You are indeed the Sleeper," he said. "I saw you asleep. When it was the law that anyone might see you."

"I am the man who was in the trance," said Graham. "They have imprisoned me here. I have been here since I awoke—at least three days."

The intruder seemed about to speak, heard something, glanced swiftly at the door, and suddenly left Graham and ran towards it, shouting quick incoherent words. A bright wedge of steel flashed in his hand, and he began tap, tap, a quick succession of blows upon the hinges. "Mind!" cried a voice. "Oh!" The voice came from above.

Graham glanced up, saw the soles of two feet, ducked, was struck on the shoulder by one of them, and a heavy weight bore him to the earth. He fell on his knees and forward, and the weight went over his head. He knelt up and saw a second man from above seated before him.

"I did not see you, Sire," panted the man. He rose and assisted Graham to rise. "Are you hurt, Sire?" he panted. A succession of heavy blows on the ventilator began, something fell close to Graham's face, and a shivering edge of white metal danced, fell over, and lay flat upon the floor.

"What is this?" cried Graham, confused and looking at the ventilator. "Who are you? What are you going to do? Remember, I understand nothing."

"Stand back," said the stranger, and drew him from under the ventilator as another fragment of metal fell heavily.

"We want you to come, Sire," panted the newcomer, and Graham glancing at his face again, saw a new cut had changed from white to red on his forehead, and a couple of little trickles of blood starting therefrom. "Your people call for you."

"Come where? My people?"

"To the hall about the markets. Your life is in danger here. We have spies. We learned but just in time. The Council has decided—this very day —either to drug or kill you. And everything is ready. The people are drilled, the Wind-Vane police, the engineers, and half the way-gearers are with us. We have the halls crowded—shouting. The whole city shouts against the Council. We have arms." He wiped the blood with his hand. "Your life here is not worth—"

"But why arms?"

"The people have risen to protect you, Sire. What?"

He turned quickly as the man who had first come down made a hissing with his teeth. Graham saw the latter start back, gesticulate to them to conceal themselves, and move as if to hide behind the opening door.

As he did so Howard appeared, a little tray in one hand and his heavy face downcast. He started, looked up, the door slammed behind him, the tray tilted side-ways, and the steel wedge struck him behind the ear. He went down like a felled tree, and lay as he fell athwart the floor of the outer room. The man who had struck him bent hastily, studied his face for a moment, rose, and returned to his work at the door.

"Your poison!" said a voice in Graham's ear.

Then abruptly they were in darkness. The innumerable cornice lights had been extinguished. Graham saw the aperture of the ventilator with ghostly snow whirling above it and dark figures moving hastily. Three knelt on the vane. Some dim thing—a ladder—was being lowered through the opening, and a hand appeared holding a fitful yellow light.

He had a moment of hesitation. But the manner of these men, their swift alacrity, their words, marched so completely with his own fears of the Council, with his idea and hope of a rescue, that it lasted not a moment. And his people awaited him!

"I do not understand," he said. "I trust. Tell me what to do."

The man with the cut brow gripped Graham's arm. "Clamber up the ladder," he whispered. "Quick. They will have heard—"

Graham felt for the ladder with extended hands, put his foot on the lower rung, and, turning his head, saw over the shoulder of the nearest man, in the yellow flicker of the light, the first-comer astride over Howard and still working at the door. Graham turned to the ladder again, and was thrust by his conductor and helped up by those above, and then he was standing on something hard and cold and slippery outside the ventilating funnel.

He shivered. He was aware of a great difference in the temperature. Half a dozen men stood about him, and light flakes of snow touched hands and face and melted. For a moment it was dark, then for a flash a ghastly violet white, and then everything was dark again.

He saw he had come out upon the roof of the vast city structure which had replaced the miscellaneous houses, streets and open spaces of Victorian London. The place upon which he stood was level, with huge serpentine cables lying athwart it in every direction. The circular wheels of a number of windmills loomed indistinct and gigantic through the darkness and snowfall, and roared with a varying loudness as the fitful wind rose and fell. Some way off an intermittent white light smote up from below, touched the snow eddies with a transient glitter, and made an evanescent spectre in the night; and here and there, low down, some vaguely outlined wind-driven mechanism flickered with livid sparks.

All this he appreciated in a fragmentary manner as his rescuers stood about him. Someone threw a thick soft cloak of fur-like texture about him, and fastened it by buckled straps at waist and shoulders. Things were said briefly, decisively. Some one thrust him forward.

Before his mind was yet clear a dark shape gripped his arm. "This way," said this shape, urging him along, and pointed Graham across the flat roof in the direction of a dim semi-circular haze of light. Graham obeyed.

"Mind!" said a voice, as Graham stumbled against a cable. "Between them and not across them," said the voice. And, "We must hurry."

"Where are the people?" said Graham. "The people you said awaited me?"

The stranger did not answer. He left Graham's arm as the path grew narrower, and led the way with rapid strides. Graham followed blindly. In a minute he found himself running. "Are the others coming?" he panted, but received no reply. His companion glanced back and ran on. They came to a sort of pathway of open metal-work, transverse to the direction they had come, and they turned aside to follow this. Graham looked back, but the snowstorm had hidden the others.

"Come on!" said his guide. Running now, they drew near a little wind-mill spinning high in the air. "Stoop," said Graham's guide, and they avoided an endless band running roaring up to the shaft of the vane. "This way!" and they were ankle deep in a gutter full of drifted thawing snow, between two low walls of metal that presently rose waist high. "I will go first," said the guide. Graham drew his cloak about him and followed. Then suddenly came a narrow abyss across which the gutter leapt to the snowy darkness of the further side. Graham peeped over the side once and the gulf was black. For a moment he regretted his flight. He dared not look again, and his brain spun as he waded through the half liquid snow.

Then out of the gutter they clambered and hurried across a wide flat space damp with thawing snow, and for half its extent dimly translucent to lights that went to and fro underneath. He hesitated at this unstable looking substance, but his guide ran on unheeding, and so they came to and clambered up slippery steps to the rim of a great dome of glass. Round this they went. Far below a number of people seemed to be dancing, and music filtered through the dome.... Graham fancied he heard a shouting through the snowstorm, and his guide hurried him on with a new spurt of haste. They clambered panting to a space of huge windmills, one so vast that only the lower edge of its vanes came rushing into sight and rushed up again and was lost in the night and the snow. They hurried for a time through the colossal metallic tracery of its supports, and came at last above a place of moving platforms like the place into which Graham had looked from the balcony. They crawled across the sloping transparency that covered this street of platforms, crawling on hands and knees because of the slipperiness of the snowfall.

For the most part the glass was bedewed, and Graham saw only hazy suggestions of the forms below, but near the pitch of the transparent roof the glass was clear, and he found himself looking sheerly down upon it all. For a while, in spite of the urgency of his guide, he gave way to vertigo and lay spread-eagled on the glass, sick and paralyzed. Far below, mere stirring specks and dots, went the people of the unsleeping city in their perpetual daylight, and the moving platforms ran on their incessant journey. Messengers and men on unknown businesses shot along the drooping cables and the frail bridges were crowded with men. It was like peering into a gigantic glass hive, and it lay vertically below him with only a tough glass of unknown thickness to save him from a fall. The street showed warm and lit, and Graham was wet now to the skin with thawing snow, and his feet were numbed with cold. For a space he could not move. "Come on!" cried his guide, with terror in his voice. "Come on!"

Graham reached the pitch of the roof by an effort.

Over the ridge, following his guide's example, he turned about and slid backward down the opposite slope very swiftly, amid a little avalanche of snow. While he was sliding he thought of what would happen if some broken gap should come in his way. At the edge he stumbled to his feet ankle deep in slush, thanking heaven for an opaque footing again. His guide was already clambering up a metal screen to a level expanse.

Through the spare snowflakes above this loomed another line of vast windmills, and then suddenly the amorphous tumult of the rotating wheels was pierced with a deafening sound. It was a mechanical shrilling of extraordinary intensity that seemed to come simultaneously from every point of the compass.

"They have missed us already!" cried Graham's guide in an accent of terror, and suddenly, with a blinding flash, the night became day.

Above the driving snow, from the summits of the wind-wheels, appeared vast masts carrying globes of livid light. They receded in illimitable vistas in every direction. As far as his eye could penetrate the snowfall they glared.

"Get on this," cried Graham's conductor, and thrust him forward to a long grating of snowless metal that ran like a band between two slightly sloping expanses of snow. It felt warm to Graham's benumbed feet, and a faint eddy of steam rose from it.

"Come on!" shouted his guide ten yards off, and, without waiting, ran swiftly through the incandescent glare towards the iron supports of the next range of wind-wheels. Graham, recovering from his astonishment, followed as fast, convinced of his imminent capture....

In a score of seconds they were within a tracery of glare and black shadows shot with moving bars beneath the monstrous wheels. Graham's conductor ran on for some time, and suddenly darted sideways and vanished into a black shadow in the corner of the foot of a huge support. In another moment Graham was beside him.

They cowered panting and stared out.

The scene upon which Graham looked was very wild and strange. The snow had now almost ceased; only a belated flake passed now and again across the picture. But the broad stretch of level before them was a ghastly white, broken only by gigantic masses and moving shapes and lengthy strips of impenetrable darkness, vast ungainly Titans of shadow. All about them, huge metallic structures, iron girders, inhumanly vast as it seemed to him, interlaced, and the edges of wind-wheels, scarcely moving in the lull, passed in great shining curves steeper and steeper up into a luminous haze. Wherever the snow-spangled light struck down, beams and girders, and incessant bands running with a halting, indomitable reso-lution, passed upward and downward into the black. And with all that mighty activity, with an omnipresent sense of motive and design, this snow-clad desolation of mechanism seemed void of all human presence save themselves, seemed as trackless and deserted and unfrequented by men as some inaccessible Alpine snowfield.

"They will be chasing us," cried the leader. "We are scarcely halfway there yet. Cold as it is we must hide here for a space—at least until it snows more thickly again."

His teeth chattered in his head.

"Where are the markets?" asked Graham staring out. "Where are all the people?"

The other made no answer.

"*Look!*" whispered Graham, crouched close, and became very still.

The snow had suddenly become thick again, and sliding with the whirling eddies out of the black pit of the sky came something, vague and large and very swift. It came down in a steep curve and swept round, wide wings extended and a trail of white condensing steam behind it, rose with an easy swiftness and went gliding up the air, swept horizontally forward in a wide curve, and vanished again in the steaming specks of snow. And, through the ribs of its body, Graham saw two little men, very minute and active, searching the snowy areas about him, as it seemed to him, with field glasses. For a second they were clear, then hazy through a thick whirl of snow, then small and distant, and in a minute they were gone.

"*Now!*" cried his companion. "Come!"

He pulled Graham's sleeve, and incontinently the two were running headlong down the arcade of ironwork beneath the wind-wheels. Graham, running blindly, collided with his leader, who had turned back on him suddenly. He found himself within a dozen yards of a black chasm. It extended as far as he could see right and left. It seemed to cut off their progress in either direction.

"Do as I do," whispered his guide. He lay down and crawled to the edge, thrust his head over and twisted until one leg hung. He seemed to feel for something with his foot, found it, and went sliding over the edge into the gulf. His head reappeared. "It is a ledge," he whispered. "In the dark all the way along. Do as I did."

Graham hesitated, went down upon all fours, crawled to the edge, and peered into a velvety blackness. For a sickly moment he had courage neither to go on nor retreat, then he sat and hung his leg down, felt his guide's hands pulling at him, had a horrible sensation of sliding over the edge into the unfathomable, splashed, and felt himself in a slushy gutter, impenetrably dark.

"This way," whispered the voice, and he began crawling along the gutter through the trickling thaw, pressing himself against the wall. They continued along it for some minutes. He seemed to pass through a hundred stages of misery, to pass minute after minute through a hundred degrees of cold, damp, and exhaustion. In a little while he ceased to feel his hands and feet.

The gutter sloped downwards. He observed that they were now many feet below the edge of the buildings. Rows of spectral white shapes like the ghosts of blind-drawn windows rose above them. They came to the end of a cable fastened above one of these white windows, dimly visible and dropping into impenetrable shadows. Suddenly his hand came against his guide's. "*Still!*" whispered the latter very softly.

He looked up with a start and saw the huge wings of the flying machine gliding slowly and noiselessly overhead athwart the broad band of snow-flecked grey-blue sky. In a moment it was hidden again.

"Keep still; they were just turning."

For a while both were motionless, then Graham's companion stood up, and reaching towards the fastenings of the cable fumbled with some indistinct tackle.

"What is that?" asked Graham.

The only answer was a faint cry. The man crouched motionless. Graham peered and saw his face dimly. He was staring down the long ribbon of sky, and Graham, following his eyes, saw the flying machine small and faint and remote. Then he saw that the wings spread on either side, that it headed towards them, that every moment it grew larger. It was following the edge of the chasm towards them.

The man's movements became convulsive. He thrust two cross bars into Graham's hand. Graham could not see them, he ascertained their form by feeling. They were slung by thin cords to the cable. On the cord were hand grips of some soft elastic substance. "Put the cross between your legs," whispered the guide hysterically, "and grip the holdfasts. Grip tightly, grip!"

Graham did as he was told.

"Jump," said the voice. "In heaven's name, jump!"

For one momentous second Graham could not speak. He was glad afterwards that darkness hid his face. He said nothing. He began to tremble violently. He looked sideways at the swift shadow that swallowed up the sky as it rushed upon him.

"Jump! Jump—in God's name! Or they will have us," cried Graham's guide, and in the violence of his passion thrust him forward.

Graham tottered convulsively, gave a sobbing cry, a cry in spite of himself, and then, as the flying machine swept over them, fell forward into the pit of that darkness, seated on the cross wood and holding the ropes with the clutch of death. Something cracked, something rapped smartly against a wall. He heard the pulley of the cradle hum on its rope. He heard the aeronauts shout. He felt a pair of knees digging into his back.... He was sweeping headlong through the air, falling through the air. All his strength was in his hands. He would have screamed but he had no breath.

He shot into a blinding light that made him grip the tighter. He recognised the great passage with the running ways, the hanging lights and interlacing girders. They rushed upward and by him. He had a momentary impression of a great round mouth yawning to swallow him up.

He was in the dark again, falling, falling, gripping with aching hands, and behold! a clap of sound, a burst of light, and he was in a brightly lit hall with a roaring multitude of people beneath his feet. The people! His people! A proscenium, a stage rushed up towards him, and his cable swept down to a circular aperture to the right of this. He felt he was travelling slower, and suddenly very much slower. He distinguished shouts of "Saved! The Master. He is safe!" The stage rushed up towards him with rapidly diminishing swiftness. Then—

He heard the man clinging behind him shout as if suddenly terrified, and this shout was echoed by a shout from below. He felt that he was no longer gliding along the cable but falling with it. There was a tumult of yells, screams, and cries. He felt something soft against his extended hand, and the impact of a broken fall quivering through his arm....

He wanted to be still and the people were lifting him. He believed afterwards he was carried to the platform and given some drink, but he was never sure. He did not notice what became of his guide. When his mind was clear again he was on his feet; eager hands were assisting him to stand. He was in a big alcove, occupying the position that in his previous experience had been devoted to the lower boxes. If this was indeed a theatre.

A mighty tumult was in his ears, a thunderous roar, the shouting of a countless multitude. "It is the Sleeper! The Sleeper is with us!"

"The Sleeper is with us! The Master—the Owner! The Master is with us. He is safe."

Graham had a surging vision of a great hall crowded with people. He saw no individuals, he was conscious of a froth of pink faces, of waving arms and garments, he felt the occult influence of a vast crowd pouring over him, buoying him up. There were balconies, galleries, great archways giving remoter perspectives, and everywhere people, a vast arena of people, densely packed and cheering. Across the nearer space lay the collapsed cable like a huge snake. It had been cut by the men of the flying machine at its upper end, and had crumpled down into the hall. Men seemed to be hauling this out of the way. But the whole effect was vague, the very buildings throbbed and leapt with the roar of the voices.

He stood unsteadily and looked at those about him. Someone supported him by one arm. "Let me go into a little room," he said, weeping; "a little room," and could say no more. A man in black stepped forward, took his disengaged arm. He was aware of officious men opening a door before him. Someone guided him to a seat. He staggered. He sat down heavily and covered his face with his hands; he was trembling violently, his nervous control was at an end. He was relieved of his cloak, he could not remember how; his purple hose he saw were black with wet. People were running about him, things were happening, but for some time he gave no heed to them.

He had escaped. A myriad of cries told him that. He was safe. These were the people who were on his side. For a space he sobbed for breath, and then he sat still with his face covered. The air was full of the shouting of innumerable men.

9

THE PEOPLE MARCH

HE BECAME AWARE OF SOMEONE URGING A GLASS OF CLEAR FLUID UPON his attention, looked up and discovered this was a dark young man in a yellow garment. He took the dose forthwith, and in a moment he was glowing. A tall man in a black robe stood by his shoulder, and pointed to the half open door into the hall. This man was shouting close to his ear and yet what was said was indistinct because of the tremendous uproar from the great theatre. Behind the man was a girl in a silvery grey robe, whom Graham, even in this confusion, perceived to be beautiful. Her dark eyes, full of wonder and curiosity, were fixed on him, her lips trembled apart. A partially opened door gave a glimpse of the crowded hall, and admitted a vast uneven tumult, a hammering, clapping and shouting that died away and began again, and rose to a thunderous pitch, and so continued intermittently all the time that Graham remained in the little room. He watched the lips of the man in black and gathered that he was making some explanation.

He stared stupidly for some moments at these things and then stood up abruptly; he grasped the arm of this shouting person.

"Tell me!" he cried. "Who am I? Who am I?"

The others came nearer to hear his words. "Who am I?" His eyes searched their faces.

"They have told him nothing!" cried the girl.

"Tell me, tell me!" cried Graham.

"You are the Master of the Earth. You are owner of the world."

He did not believe he heard aright. He resisted the persuasion. He pretended not to understand, not to hear. He lifted his voice again. "I have been awake three days—a prisoner three days. I judge there is some struggle between a number of people in this city—it is London?"

"Yes," said the younger man.

"And those who meet in the great hall with the white Atlas? How does it concern me? In some way it has to do with me. *Why*, I don't know. Drugs? It seems to me that while I have slept the world has gone mad. I have gone mad...."

"Who are those Councillors under the Atlas? Why should they try to drug me?"

"To keep you insensible," said the man in yellow. "To prevent your interference."

"But *why*?"

"Because *you* are the Atlas, Sire," said the man in yellow. "The world is on your shoulders. They rule it in your name."

The sounds from the hall had died into a silence threaded by one monotonous voice. Now suddenly, trampling on these last words, came a deafening tumult, a roaring and thundering, cheer crowded on cheer, voices hoarse and shrill, beating, overlapping, and while it lasted the people in the little room could not hear each other shout.

Graham stood, his intelligence clinging helplessly to the thing he had just heard. "The Council," he repeated blankly, and then snatched at a name that had struck him. "But who is Ostrog?" he said.

"He is the organiser—the organiser of the revolt. Our Leader—in your name."

"In my name?—And you? Why is he not here?"

"He—has deputed us. I am his brother—his half-brother, Lincoln. He wants you to show yourself to these people and then come on to him. That is why he has sent. He is at the Wind-Vane offices directing. The people are marching."

"In your name," shouted the younger man. "They have ruled, crushed, tyrannised. At last even—"

"In my name! My name! Master?"

The younger man suddenly became audible in a pause of the outer thunder, indignant and vociferous, a high penetrating voice under his red aquiline nose and bushy moustache. "No one expected you to wake. No one expected you to wake. They were cunning. Damned tyrants! But they were taken by surprise. They did not know whether to drug you, hypnotise you, kill you."

Again the hall dominated everything.

"Ostrog is at the Wind-Vane offices ready—. Even now there is a rumour of fighting beginning."

The man who had called himself Lincoln came close to him. "Ostrog has it planned. Trust him. We have our organizations ready. We shall seize the flying stages—. Even now he may be doing that. Then—"

"This public theatre," bawled the man in yellow, "is only a contingent. We have five myriads of drilled men—"

"We have arms," cried Lincoln. "We have plans. A leader. Their police have gone from the streets and are massed in the—" (inaudible). "It is now or never. The Council is rocking—They cannot trust even their drilled men—"

"Hear the people calling to you!"

Graham's mind was like a night of moon and swift clouds, now dark and hopeless, now clear and ghastly. He was Master of the Earth, he was a man sodden with thawing snow. Of all his fluctuating impressions the dominant ones presented an antagonism; on the one hand was the White Council, powerful, disciplined, few, the White Council from which he had just escaped; and on the other, monstrous crowds, packed masses of indistinguishable people clamouring his name, hailing him Master. The other side had imprisoned him, debated his death. These shouting thousands beyond the little doorway had rescued him. But why these things should be so he could not understand.

The door opened, Lincoln's voice was swept away and drowned, and a rash of people followed on the heels of the tumult. These intruders came towards him and Lincoln gesticulating. The voices without explained their soundless lips. "Show us the Sleeper, show us the Sleeper!" was the burden of the uproar. Men were bawling for "Order! Silence!"

Graham glanced towards the open doorway, and saw a tall, oblong picture of the hall beyond, a waving, incessant confusion of crowded, shouting faces, men and women together, waving pale blue garments, extended hands. Many were standing, one man in rags of dark brown, a gaunt figure, stood on the seat and waved a black cloth. He met the wonder and expectation of the girl's eyes. What did these people expect from him? He was dimly aware that the tumult outside had changed its character, was in some way beating, marching. His own mind, too, changed. For a space he did not recognize the influence that was transforming him. But a moment that was near to panic passed. He tried to make audible inquiries of what was required of him.

Lincoln was shouting in his ear, but Graham was deafened to that. All the others save the woman gesticulated towards the hall. He perceived what had happened to the uproar. The whole mass of people was chanting together. It was not simply a song, the voices were gathered together and upborne by a torrent of instrumental music, music like the music of an organ, a woven texture of sounds, full of trumpets, full of flaunting banners, full of the march and pageantry of opening war. And the feet of the people were beating time—tramp, tramp.

He was urged towards the door. He obeyed mechanically. The strength of that chant took hold of him, stirred him, emboldened him. The hall opened to him, a vast welter of fluttering colour swaying to the music.

"Wave your arm to them," said Lincoln. "Wave your arm to them."

"This," said a voice on the other side, "he must have this." Arms were about his neck detaining him in the doorway, and a black subtly-folding mantle hung from his shoulders. He threw his arm free of this and followed Lincoln. He perceived the girl in grey close to him, her face lit, her gesture onward. For the instant she became to him, flushed and eager as she was, an embodiment of the song. He emerged in the alcove again. Incontinently the mounting waves of the song broke upon his appearing, and flashed up into a foam of shouting. Guided by Lincoln's hand he marched obliquely across the centre of the stage facing the people.

The hall was a vast and intricate space—galleries, balconies, broad spaces of amphitheatral steps, and great archways. Far away, high up, seemed the mouth of a huge passage full of struggling humanity. The whole multitude was swaying in congested masses. Individual figures sprang out of the tumult, impressed him momentarily, and lost definition again. Close to the platform swayed a beautiful fair woman, carried by three men, her hair across her face and brandishing a green staff. Next to this group an old careworn man in blue canvas maintained his place in the crush with difficulty, and behind shouted a hairless face, a great cavity of toothless mouth. A voice called that enigmatical word 'Ostrog.' All his impressions were vague save the massive emotion of that trampling song. The multitude were beating time with their feet—marking time, tramp,

tramp, tramp, tramp. The green weapons waved, flashed and slanted. Then he saw those nearest to him on a level space before the stage were marching in front of him, passing towards a great archway, shouting "To the Council!" Tramp, tramp, tramp, tramp. He raised his arm, and the roaring was redoubled. He remembered he had to shout "March!" His mouth shaped inaudible heroic words. He waved his arm again and pointed to the archway, shouting "Onward!" They were no longer marking time, they were marching; tramp, tramp, tramp, tramp. In that host were bearded men, old men, youths, fluttering robed bare-armed women, girls. Men and women of the new age! Rich robes, grey rags fluttered together in the whirl of their movement amidst the dominant blue. A monstrous black banner jerked its way to the right. He perceived a blue-clad negro, a shrivelled woman in yellow, then a group of tall fair-haired, white-faced, blue-clad men pushed theatrically past him. He noted two Chinamen. A tall, sallow, dark-haired, shining-eyed youth, white clad from top to toe, clambered up towards the platform shouting loyally, and sprang down again and receded, looking backward. Heads, shoulders, hands clutching weapons, all were swinging with those marching cadences.

Faces came out of the confusion to him as he stood there, eyes met his and passed and vanished. Men gesticulated to him, shouted inaudible personal things. Most of the faces were flushed, but many were ghastly white. And disease was there, and many a hand that waved to him was gaunt and lean. Men and women of the new age! Strange and incredible meeting! As the broad stream passed before him to the right, tributary gangways from the remote uplands of the hall thrust downward in an incessant replacement of people; tramp, tramp, tramp, tramp. The unison of the song was enriched and complicated by the massive echoes of arches and passages. Men and women mingled in the ranks; tramp, tramp, tramp, tramp. The whole world seemed marching. Tramp, tramp, tramp, tramp; his brain was tramping. The garments waved onward, the faces poured by more abundantly.

Tramp, tramp, tramp, tramp; at Lincoln's pressure he turned towards the archway, walking unconsciously in that rhythm, scarcely noticing his movement for the melody and stir of it. The multitude, the gesture and song, all moved in that direction, the flow of people smote downward until the upturned faces were below the level of his feet. He was aware of a path before him, of a suite about him, of guards and dignities, and Lincoln on his right hand. Attendants intervened, and ever and again blotted out the sight of the multitude to the left. Before him went the backs of the guards in black—three and three and three. He was marched along a little railed way, and crossed above the archway, with the torrent dipping to flow beneath, and shouting up to him. He did not know whither he went; he did not want to know. He glanced back across a flaming spaciousness of hall. Tramp, tramp, tramp, tramp.

10

THE BATTLE OF THE DARKNESS

HE WAS NO LONGER IN THE HALL. HE WAS MARCHING ALONG A GALLERY overhanging one of the great streets of the moving platforms that traversed the city. Before him and behind him tramped his guards. The whole concave of the moving ways below was a congested mass of people marching, tramping to the left, shouting, waving hands and arms, pouring along a huge vista, shouting as they came into view, shouting as they passed, shouting as they receded, until the globes of electric light receding in perspective dropped down it seemed and hid the swarming bare heads. Tramp, tramp, tramp, tramp.

The song roared up to Graham now, no longer upborne by music, but coarse and noisy, and the beating of the marching feet, tramp, tramp, tramp, tramp, interwove with a thunderous irregularity of footsteps from the undisciplined rabble that poured along the higher ways.

Abruptly he noted a contrast. The buildings on the opposite side of the way seemed deserted, the cables and bridges that laced across the aisle were empty and shadowy. It came into Graham's mind that these also should have swarmed with people.

He felt a curious emotion—throbbing—very fast! He stopped again. The guards before him marched on; those about him stopped as he did. He saw anxiety and fear in their faces. The throbbing had something to do with the lights. He too looked up.

At first it seemed to him a thing that affected the lights simply, an isolated phenomenon, having no bearing on the things below. Each huge globe of blinding whiteness was as it were clutched, compressed in a systole that was followed by a transitory diastole, and again a systole like a tightening grip, darkness, light, darkness, in rapid alternation.

Graham became aware that this strange behaviour of the lights had to do with the people below. The appearance of the houses and ways, the appearance of the packed masses changed, became a confusion of vivid lights and leaping shadows. He saw a multitude of shadows had sprung into aggressive existence, seemed rushing up, broadening, widening, growing with steady swiftness—to leap suddenly back and return reinforced. The song and the tramping had ceased. The unanimous march, he discovered, was arrested, there were eddies, a flow sideways, shouts of "The lights!" Voices were crying together one thing. "The lights!" cried these voices. "The lights!" He looked down. In this dancing death of the lights the area of the street had suddenly become a monstrous struggle. The huge white globes became purple-white, purple with a reddish glow, flickered, flickered faster and faster, fluttered between light and extinction, ceased to flicker and became mere fading specks of glowing red in a vast obscurity. In ten seconds the extinction was accomplished, and there was only this roaring darkness, a black monstrosity that had suddenly swallowed up those glittering myriads of men.

He felt invisible forms about him; his arms were gripped. Something rapped sharply against his shin. A voice bawled in his ear, "It is all right—all right."

Graham shook off the paralysis of his first astonishment. He struck his forehead against Lincoln's and bawled, "What is this darkness?"

"The Council has cut the currents that light the city. We must wait—stop. The people will go on. They will—"

His voice was drowned. Voices were shouting, "Save the Sleeper. Take care of the Sleeper." A guard stumbled against Graham and hurt his hand by an inadvertent blow of his weapon. A wild tumult tossed and whirled about him, growing, as it seemed, louder, denser, more furious each moment. Fragments of recognizable sounds drove towards him, were whirled away from him as his mind reached out to grasp them. Voices seemed to be shouting conflicting orders, other voices answered. There were suddenly a succession of piercing screams close beneath them.

A voice bawled in his ear, "The red police," and receded forthwith beyond his questions.

A crackling sound grew to distinctness, and therewith a leaping of faint flashes along the edge of the further ways. By their light Graham saw the heads and bodies of a number of men, armed with weapons like those of his guards, leap into an instant's dim visibility. The whole area began to crackle, to flash with little instantaneous streaks of light, and abruptly the darkness rolled back like a curtain.

A glare of light dazzled his eyes, a vast seething expanse of struggling men confused his mind. A shout, a burst of cheering, came across the ways. He looked up to see the source of the light. A man hung far overhead from the upper part of a cable, holding by a rope the blinding star that had driven the darkness back.

Graham's eyes fell to the ways again. A wedge of red a little way along the vista caught his eye. He saw it was a dense mass of red-clad men jammed on the higher further way, their backs against the pitiless cliff of building, and surrounded by a dense crowd of antagonists. They were fighting. Weapons flashed and rose and fell, heads vanished at the edge of the contest, and other heads replaced them, the little flashes from the green weapons became little jets of smoky grey while the light lasted.

Abruptly the flare was extinguished and the ways were an inky darkness once more, a tumultuous mystery.

He felt something thrusting against him. He was being pushed along the gallery. Some one was shouting—it might be at him. He was too confused to hear. He was thrust against the wall, and a number of people blundered past him. It seemed to him that his guards were struggling with one another.

Suddenly the cable-hung star-holder appeared again, and the whole scene was white and dazzling. The band of red-coats seemed broader and nearer; its apex was halfway down the ways towards the central aisle. And raising his eyes Graham saw that a number of these men had also appeared now in the darkened lower galleries of the opposite building, and were firing over the heads of their fellows below at the boiling confusion of people on the lower ways. The meaning of these things dawned upon him. The march of the people had come upon an ambush at the very outset. Thrown into confusion by the extinction of the lights they were now being attacked by the red police. Then he became aware that he was standing alone, that his guards and Lincoln were along the gallery in the direction along which he had come before the darkness fell. He saw they were gesticulating to him wildly, running back towards him. A great shouting came from across the ways. Then it seemed as though the whole face of the darkened building opposite was lined and speckled with red-clad men. And they were pointing over to him and shouting. "The Sleeper! Save the Sleeper!" shouted a multitude of throats.

Something struck the wall above his head. He looked up at the impact and saw a star-shaped splash of silvery metal. He saw Lincoln near him. Felt his arm gripped. Then, pat, pat; he had been missed twice.

For a moment he did not understand this. The street was hidden, everything was hidden, as he looked. The second flare had burned out.

Lincoln had gripped Graham by the arm, was lugging him along the gallery. "Before the next light!" he cried. His haste was contagious. Graham's instinct of self-preservation overcame the paralysis of his incredulous astonishment. He became for a time the blind creature of the fear of death. He ran, stumbling because of the uncertainty of the darkness, blundered into his guards as they turned to run with him. Haste was his one desire, to escape this perilous gallery upon which he was exposed. A third glare came close on its predecessors. With it came a great shouting across the ways, an answering tumult from the ways. The red-coats below, he saw, had now almost gained the central passage. Their countless faces turned towards him, and they shouted. The white façade opposite was densely stippled with red. All these wonderful things concerned him, turned upon him as a pivot. These were the guards of the Council attempting to recapture him.

Lucky it was for him that these shots were the first fired in anger for a hundred and fifty years. He heard bullets whacking over his head, felt a splash of molten metal sting his ear, and perceived without looking that the whole opposite façade, an unmasked ambuscade of red police, was crowded and bawling and firing at him.

Down went one of his guards before him, and Graham, unable to stop, leapt the writhing body.

In another second he had plunged, unhurt, into a black passage, and incontinently someone, coming, it may be, in a transverse direction, blundered violently into him. He was hurling down a staircase in absolute darkness. He reeled, and was struck again, and came against a wall with his hands. He was crushed by a weight of struggling bodies, whirled round, and thrust to the right. A vast pressure pinned him. He could not breathe, his ribs seemed cracking. He felt a momentary relaxation, and then the whole mass of people moving together, bore him back towards the great theatre from which he had so recently come. There were moments when his feet did not touch the ground. Then he was staggering and shoving. He heard shouts of "They are coming!" and a muffled cry close to him. His foot blundered against something soft, he heard a hoarse scream under foot. He heard shouts of "The Sleeper!" but he was too confused to speak. He heard the green weapons crackling. For a space he lost his individual will, became an atom in a panic, blind, unthinking, mechanical. He thrust and pressed back and writhed in the pressure, kicked presently against a step, and found himself ascending a slope. And abruptly the faces all about him leapt out of the black, visible, ghastly-white and astonished, terrified, perspiring, in a livid glare. One face, a young man's, was very near to him, not twenty inches away. At the time it was but a passing incident of no emotional value, but afterwards it came back to him in his dreams. For this young man, wedged upright in the crowd for a time, had been shot and was already dead.

A fourth white star must have been lit by the man on the cable. Its light came glaring in through vast windows and arches and showed Graham that he was now one of a dense mass of flying black figures pressed back across the lower area of the great theatre. This time the picture was livid and fragmentary, slashed and barred with black shadows. He saw that quite near to him the red guards were fighting their way through the people. He could not tell whether they saw him. He looked for Lincoln and his guards. He saw Lincoln near the stage of the theatre surrounded in a crowd of black-badged revolutionaries, lifted up and staring to and fro as if seeking him. Graham perceived that he himself was near the opposite edge of the crowd, that behind him, separated by a barrier, sloped the now vacant seats of the theatre. A sudden idea came to him, and he began fighting his way towards the barrier. As he reached it the glare came to an end.

In a moment he had thrown off the great cloak that not only impeded his movements but made him conspicuous, and had slipped it from his shoulders. He heard someone trip in its folds. In another he was scaling the barrier and had dropped into the blackness on the further side. Then feeling his way he came to the lower end of an ascending gangway. In the darkness the sound of firing ceased and the roar of feet and voices lulled. Then suddenly he came to an unexpected step and tripped and fell. As he did so pools and islands amidst the darkness about him leapt to vivid light again, the uproar surged louder and the glare of the fifth white star shone through the vast fenestrations of the theatre walls.

He rolled over among some seats, heard a shouting and the whirring rattle of weapons, struggled up and was knocked back again, perceived that a number of black-badged men were all about him firing at the reds below, leaping from seat to seat, crouching among the seats to reload. Instinctively he crouched amidst the seats, as stray shots ripped the pneumatic cushions and cut bright slashes on their soft metal frames. Instinctively he marked the direction of the gangways, the most plausible way of escape for him so soon as the veil of darkness fell again.

A young man in faded blue garments came vaulting over the seats. "Hallo!" he said, with his flying feet within six inches of the crouching Sleeper's face.

He stared without any sign of recognition, turned to fire, fired, and shouting, "To hell with the Council!" was about to fire again. Then it seemed to Graham that the half of this man's neck had vanished. A drop of moisture fell on Graham's cheek. The green weapon stopped half raised. For a moment the man stood still with his face suddenly expressionless, then he began to slant forward. His knees bent. Man and darkness fell together. At the sound of his fall Graham rose up and ran for his life until a step down to the gangway tripped him. He scrambled to his feet, turned up the gangway and ran on.

When the sixth star glared he was already close to the yawning throat of a passage. He ran on the swifter for the light, entered the passage and turned a corner into absolute night again. He was knocked sideways, rolled over, and recovered his feet. He found himself one of a crowd of invisible fugitives pressing in one direction. His one thought now was their thought also; to escape out of this fighting. He thrust and struck, staggered, ran, was wedged tightly, lost ground and then was clear again.

For some minutes he was running through the darkness along a winding passage, and then he crossed some wide and open space, passed down a long incline, and came at last down a flight of steps to a level place. Many people were shouting, "They are coming! The guards are coming. They are firing. Get out of the fighting. The guards are firing. It will be safe in Seventh Way. Along here to Seventh Way!" There were women and children in the crowd as well as men.

The crowd converged on an archway, passed through a short throat and emerged on a wider space again, lit dimly. The black figures about him spread out and ran up what seemed in the twilight to be a gigantic series of steps. He followed. The people dispersed to the right and left.... He perceived that he was no longer in a crowd. He stopped near the highest step. Before him, on that level, were groups of seats and a little kiosk. He went up to this and, stopping in the shadow of its eaves, looked about him panting.

Everything was vague and grey, but he recognised that these great steps were a series of platforms of the "ways," now motionless again. The platform slanted up on either side, and the tall buildings rose beyond, vast dim ghosts, their inscriptions and advertisements indistinctly seen, and up through the girders and cables was a faint interrupted ribbon of pallid sky. A number of people hurried by. From their shouts and voices, it seemed they were hurrying to join the fighting. Other less noisy figures flitted timidly among the shadows.

From very far away down the street he could hear the sound of a struggle. But it was evident to him that this was not the street into which the theatre opened. That former fight, it seemed, had suddenly dropped out of sound and hearing. And they were fighting for him!

For a space he was like a man who pauses in the reading of a vivid book, and suddenly doubts what he has been taking unquestionably. At that time he had little mind for details; the whole effect was a huge astonishment. Oddly enough, while the flight from the Council prison, the great crowd in the hall, and the attack of the red police upon the swarming people were clearly present in his mind, it cost him an effort to piece in his awakening and to revive the meditative interval of the Silent Rooms. At first his memory leapt these things and took him back to the cascade at Pentargen quivering in the wind, and all the sombre splendours of the sunlit Cornish coast. The contrast touched everything with unreality. And then the gap filled, and he began to comprehend his position.

It was no longer absolutely a riddle, as it had been in the Silent Rooms. At least he had the strange, bare outline now. He was in some way the owner of the world, and great political parties were fighting to possess him. On the one hand was the Council, with its red police, set resolutely, it seemed, on the usurpation of his property and perhaps his murder; on the other, the revolution that had liberated him, with this unseen "Ostrog" as its leader. And the whole of this gigantic city was convulsed by their struggle. Frantic development of his world! "I do not understand," he cried. "I do not understand!"

He had slipped out between the contending parties into this liberty of the twilight. What would happen next? What was happening? He figured the red-clad men as busily hunting him, driving the black-badged revolutionists before them.

At any rate chance had given him a breathing space. He could lurk unchallenged by the passers-by, and watch the course of things. His eye followed up the intricate dim immensity of the twilight buildings, and it came to him as a thing infinitely wonderful, that above there the sun was rising, and the world was lit and glowing with the old familiar light of day. In a little while he had recovered his breath. His clothing had already dried upon him from the snow.

He wandered for miles along these twilight ways, speaking to no one, accosted by no one—a dark figure among dark figures—the coveted man out of the past, the inestimable unintentional owner of the world. Wherever there were lights or dense crowds, or exceptional excitement, he was afraid of recognition, and watched and turned back or went up and down by the middle stairways, into some transverse system of ways at a lower or higher level. And though he came on no more fighting, the whole city stirred with battle. Once he had to run to avoid a marching multitude of men that swept the street. Every one abroad seemed involved. For the most part they were men, and they carried what he judged were weapons. It seemed as though the struggle was concentrated mainly in the quarter of the city from which he came. Ever and again a distant roaring, the remote suggestion of that conflict, reached his ears. Then his caution and his curiosity struggled together. But his caution prevailed, and he continued wandering away from the fighting—so far as he could judge. He went unmolested, unsuspected through the dark. After a time he ceased to hear even a remote echo of the battle, fewer and fewer people passed him, until at last the streets became deserted. The frontages of the buildings grew plain, and harsh; he seemed to have come to a district of vacant warehouses. Solitude crept upon him—his pace slackened.

He became aware of a growing fatigue. At times he would turn aside and sit down on one of the numerous benches of the upper ways. But a feverish restlessness, the knowledge of his vital implication in this struggle, would not let him rest in any place for long. Was the struggle on his behalf alone?

And then in a desolate place came the shock of an earthquake—a roaring and thundering—a mighty wind of cold air pouring through the city, the smash of glass, the slip and thud of falling masonry—a series of gigantic concussions. A mass of glass and ironwork fell from the remote roofs into the middle gallery, not a hundred yards away from him, and in the distance were shouts and running. He, too, was startled to an aimless activity, and ran first one way and then as aimlessly back.

A man came running towards him. His self-control returned. "What have they blown up?" asked the man breathlessly. "That was an explosion," and before Graham could speak he had hurried on.

The great buildings rose dimly, veiled by a perplexing twilight, albeit the rivulet of sky above was now bright with day. He noted many strange features, understanding none at the time; he even spelt out many of the inscriptions in phonetic lettering. But what profit is it to decipher a confusion of odd-looking letters resolving itself, after painful strain of eye and mind, into "Here is Eadhamite," or, "Labour Bureau—Little Side"? Grotesque thought, that all these cliff-like houses were his!

The perversity of his experience came to him vividly. In actual fact he had made such a leap in time as romancers have imagined again and again. And that fact realized, he had been prepared. His mind had, as it were, seated itself for a spectacle. And no spectacle unfolded itself, but a great vague danger, unsympathetic shadows and veils of darkness. Somewhere through the labyrinthine obscurity his death sought him. Would he, after all, be killed before he saw? It might be that even at the next corner his destruction ambushed. A great desire to see, a great longing to know, arose in him.

He became fearful of corners. It seemed to him that there was safety in concealment. Where could he hide to be inconspicuous when the lights returned? At last he sat down upon a seat in a recess on one of the higher ways, conceiving he was alone there.

He squeezed his knuckles into his weary eyes. Suppose when he looked again he found the dark trough of parallel ways and that intolerable altitude of edifice gone. Suppose he were to discover the whole story of these last few days, the awakening, the shouting multitudes, the darkness and the fighting, a phantasmagoria, a new and more vivid sort of dream. It must be a dream; it was so inconsecutive, so reasonless. Why were the people fighting for him? Why should this saner world regard him as Owner and Master?

So he thought, sitting blinded, and then he looked again, half hoping in spite of his ears to see some familiar aspect of the life of the nineteenth century, to see, perhaps, the little harbour of Boscastle about him, the cliffs of Pentargen, or the bedroom of his home. But fact takes no heed of human hopes. A squad of men with a black banner tramped athwart the nearer shadows, intent on conflict, and beyond rose that giddy wall of frontage, vast and dark, with the dim incomprehensible lettering showing faintly on its face.

"It is no dream," he said, "no dream." And he bowed his face upon his hands.

11

THE OLD MAN WHO KNEW EVERYTHING

HE WAS STARTLED BY A COUGH CLOSE AT HAND.

He turned sharply, and peering, saw a small, hunched up figure sitting a couple of yards off in the shadow of the enclosure.

"Have ye any news?" asked the high-pitched wheezy voice of a very old man.

Graham hesitated. "None," he said.

"I stay here till the lights come again," said the old man. "These blue scoundrels are everywhere—everywhere."

Graham's answer was inarticulate assent. He tried to see the old man but the darkness hid his face. He wanted very much to respond, to talk, but he did not know how to begin.

"Dark and damnable," said the old man suddenly. "Dark and damnable. Turned out of my room among all these dangers."

"That's hard," ventured Graham. "That's hard on you."

"Darkness. An old man lost in the darkness. And all the world gone mad. War and fighting. The police beaten and rogues abroad. Why don't they bring some negroes to protect us? ... No more dark passages for me. I fell over a dead man."

"You're safer with company," said the old man, "if it's company of the right sort," and peered frankly. He rose suddenly and came towards Graham.

Apparently the scrutiny was satisfactory. The old man sat down as if relieved to be no longer alone. "Eh!" he said, "but this is a terrible time! War and fighting, and the dead lying there—men, strong men, dying in the dark. Sons! I have three sons. God knows where they are to-night."

The voice ceased. Then repeated quavering: "God knows where they are to-night."

Graham stood revolving a question that should not betray his ignorance. Again the old man's voice ended the pause.

"This Ostrog will win," he said. "He will win. And what the world will be like under him no one can tell. My sons are under the wind vanes, all three. One of my daughters-in-law was his mistress for a while. His mistress! We're not common people. Though they've sent me to wander to-night and take my chance .... I knew what was going on. Before most people. But this darkness! And to fall over a dead body suddenly in the dark!"

His wheezy breathing could be heard.

"Ostrog!" said Graham.

"The greatest Boss the world has ever seen," said the voice.

Graham ransacked his mind. "The Council has few friends among the people," he hazarded.

"Few friends. And poor ones at that. They've had their time. Eh! They should have kept to the clever ones. But twice they held election. And Ostrog—. And now it has burst out and nothing can stay it, nothing can stay it. Twice they rejected Ostrog—Ostrog the Boss. I heard of his rages at the time—he was terrible. Heaven save them! For nothing on earth can now he has raised the Labour Companies upon them. No one else would have dared. All the blue canvas armed and marching! He will go through with it. He will go through."

He was silent for a little while. "This Sleeper," he said, and stopped.

"Yes," said Graham. "Well?"

The senile voice sank to a confidential whisper, the dim, pale face came close. "The real Sleeper—"

"Yes," said Graham.

"Died years ago."

"What?" said Graham, sharply.

"Years ago. Died. Years ago."

"You don't say so!" said Graham.

"I do. I do say so. He died. This Sleeper who's woke up—they changed in the night. A poor, drugged insensible creature. But I mustn't tell all I know. I mustn't tell all I know."

For a little while he muttered inaudibly. His secret was too much for him. "I don't know the ones that put him to sleep—that was before my time—but I know the man who injected the stimulants and woke him again. It was ten to one—wake or kill. Wake or kill. Ostrog's way."

Graham was so astonished at these things that he had to interrupt, to make the old man repeat his words, to re-question vaguely, before he was sure of the meaning and folly of what he heard. And his awakening had not been natural! Was that an old man's senile superstition, too, or had it any truth in it? Feeling in the dark corners of his memory, he presently came on something that might conceivably be an impression of some such stimulating effect. It dawned upon him that he had happened upon a lucky encounter, that at last he might learn something of the new age. The old man wheezed awhile and spat, and then the piping, reminiscent voice resumed:

"The first time they rejected him. I've followed it all."

"Rejected whom?" said Graham. "The Sleeper?"

"Sleeper? *No.* Ostrog. He was terrible—terrible! And he was promised then, promised certainly the next time. Fools they were—not to be more afraid of him. Now all the city's his millstone, and such as we dust ground upon it. Dust ground upon it. Until he set to work—the workers cut each other's throats, and murdered a Chinaman or a Labour policeman at times, and left the rest of us in peace. Dead bodies! Robbing! Darkness! Such a thing hasn't been this gross of years. Eh!—but 'tis ill on small folks when the great fall out! It's ill."

"Did you say—there had not been—what?—for a gross of years?"

"Eh?" said the old man.

The old man said something about clipping his words, and made him repeat this a third time. "Fighting and slaying, and weapons in hand, and fools bawling freedom and the like," said the old man. "Not in all my life has there been that. These are like the old days—for sure—when the Paris people broke out—three gross of years ago. That's what I mean hasn't been. But it's the world's way. It had to come back. I know. I know. This five years Ostrog has been working, and there has been trouble and trouble, and hunger and threats and high talk and arms. Blue canvas and murmurs. No one safe. Everything sliding and slipping. And now here we are! Revolt and fighting, and the Council come to its end."

"You are rather well-informed on these things," said Graham.

"I know what I hear. It isn't all Babble Machine with me."

"No," said Graham, wondering what Babble Machine might be. "And you are certain this Ostrog—you are certain Ostrog organised this rebellion and arranged for the waking of the Sleeper? Just to assert himself—because he was not elected to the Council?"

"Everyone knows that, I should think," said the old man. "Except—just fools. He meant to be master somehow. In the Council or not. Everyone who knows anything knows that. And here we are with dead bodies lying in the dark! Why, where have you been if you haven't heard all about the trouble between Ostrog and the Verneys? And what do you think the troubles are about? The Sleeper? Eh? You think the Sleeper's real and woke of his own accord—eh?"

"I'm a dull man, older than I look, and forgetful," said Graham. "Lots of things that have happened—especially of late years—. If I was the Sleeper, to tell you the truth, I couldn't know less about them."

"Eh!" said the voice. "Old, are you? You don't sound so very old! But it's not everyone keeps his memory to my time of life—truly. But these notorious things! But you're not so old as me—not nearly so old as me. Well! I ought not to judge other men by myself, perhaps. I'm young—for so old a man. Maybe you're old for so young."

"That's it," said Graham. "And I've a queer history. I know very little. And history! Practically I know no history. The Sleeper and Julius Caesar are all the same to me. It's interesting to hear you talk of these things."

"I know a few things," said the old man. "I know a thing or two. But—. Hark!"

The two men became silent, listening. There was a heavy thud, a concussion that made their seat shiver. The passers-by stopped, shouted to one another. The old man was full of questions; he shouted to a man who passed near. Graham, emboldened by his example, got up and accosted others. None knew what had happened.

He returned to the seat and found the old man muttering vague interrogations in an undertone. For a while they said nothing to one another.

The sense of this gigantic struggle, so near and yet so remote, oppressed Graham's imagination. Was this old man right, was the report of the people right, and were the revolutionaries winning? Or were they all in error, and were the red guards driving all before them? At any time the flood of warfare might pour into this silent quarter of the city and seize upon him again. It behoved him to learn all he could while there was time. He turned suddenly to the old man with a question and left it unsaid. But his motion moved the old man to speech again.

"Eh! but how things work together!" said the old man. "This Sleeper that all the fools put their trust in! I've the whole history of it—I was always a good one for histories. When I was a boy—I'm that old—I used to read printed books. You'd hardly think it. Likely you've seen none—they rot and dust so—and the Sanitary Company burns them to make ashlarite. But they were convenient in their dirty way. One learnt a lot. These new-fangled Babble Machines—they don't seem new-fangled to you, eh?—they're easy to hear, easy to forget. But I've traced all the Sleeper business from the first."

"You will scarcely believe it," said Graham slowly, "I'm so ignorant—I've been so preoccupied in my own little affairs, my circumstances have been so odd—I know nothing of this Sleeper's history. Who was he?"

"Eh!" said the old man. "I know, I know. He was a poor nobody, and set on a playful woman, poor soul! And he fell into a trance. There's the old things they had, those brown things—silver photographs—still showing him as he lay, a gross and a half years ago—a gross and a half of years."

"Set on a playful woman, poor soul," said Graham softly to himself, and then aloud, "Yes—well go on."

"You must know he had a cousin named Warming, a solitary man without children, who made a big fortune speculating in roads—the first Eadhamite roads. But surely you've heard? No? Why? He bought all the patent rights and made a big company. In those days there were grosses of grosses of separate businesses and business companies. Grosses of grosses! His roads killed the railroads—the old things—in two dozen years; he bought up and Eadhamited the tracks. And because he didn't want to break up his great property or let in shareholders, he left it all to the Sleeper, and put it under a Board of Trustees that he had picked and trained. He knew then the Sleeper wouldn't wake, that he would go on sleeping, sleeping till he died. He knew that quite well! And plump! a man in the United States, who had lost two sons in a boat accident, followed that up with another great bequest. His trustees found themselves with a dozen myriads of lions'-worth or more of property at the very beginning."

"What was his name?"

"Graham."

"No—I mean—that American's."

"Isbister."

"Isbister!" cried Graham. "Why, I don't even know the name."

"Of course not," said the old man. "Of course not. People don't learn much in the schools nowadays. But I know all about him. He was a rich American who went from England, and he left the Sleeper even more than

Warming. How he made it? That I don't know. Something about pictures by machinery. But he made it and left it, and so the Council had its start. It was just a council of trustees at first."

"And how did it grow?"

"Eh!—but you're not up to things. Money attracts money—and twelve brains are better than one. They played it cleverly. They worked politics with money, and kept on adding to the money by working currency and tariffs. They grew—they grew. And for years the twelve trustees hid the growing of the Sleeper's estate under double names and company titles and all that. The Council spread by title deed, mortgage, share, every political party, every newspaper they bought. If you listen to the old stories you will see the Council growing and growing. Billions and billions of lions at last—the Sleeper's estate. And all growing out of a whim—out of this Warming's will, and an accident to Isbister's sons.

"Men are strange," said the old man. "The strange thing to me is how the Council worked together so long. As many as twelve. But they worked in cliques from the first. And they've slipped back. In my young days speaking of the Council was like an ignorant man speaking of God. We didn't think they could do wrong. We didn't know of their women and all that! Or else I've got wiser.

"Men are strange," said the old man. "Here are you, young and ignorant, and me—sevendy years old, and I might reasonably before getting—explaining it all to you short and clear.

"Sevendy," he said, "sevendy, and I hear and see—hear better than I see. And reason clearly, and keep myself up to all the happenings of things. Sevendy!

"Life is strange. I was twaindy before Ostrog was a baby. I remember him long before he'd pushed his way to the head of the Wind-Vanes Control. I've seen many changes. Eh! I've worn the blue. And at last I've come to see this crush and darkness and tumult and dead men carried by in heaps on the ways. And all his doing! All his doing!"

His voice died away in scarcely articulate praises of Ostrog.

Graham thought. "Let me see," he said, "if I have it right."

He extended a hand and ticked off points upon his fingers. "The Sleeper has been asleep—"

"Changed," said the old man.

"Perhaps. And meanwhile the Sleeper's property grew in the hands of Twelve Trustees, until it swallowed up nearly all the great ownership of the world. The Twelve Trustees—by virtue of this property have become masters of the world. Because they are the paying power—just as the old English Parliament used to be—"

"Eh!" said the old man. "That's so—that's a good comparison. You're not so—"

"And now this Ostrog—has suddenly revolutionised the world by waking the Sleeper—whom no one but the superstitious, common people had ever dreamt would wake again—raising the Sleeper to claim his property from the Council, after all these years."

The old man endorsed this statement with a cough. "It's strange," he said, "to meet a man who learns these things for the first time to-night."

"Aye," said Graham, "it's strange."

"Have you been in a Pleasure City?" said the old man. "All my life I've longed—" He laughed. "Even now," he said, "I could enjoy a little fun. Enjoy seeing things, anyhow." He mumbled a sentence Graham did not understand.

"The Sleeper—when did he awake?" said Graham suddenly.

"Three days ago."

"Where is he?"

"Ostrog has him. He escaped from the Council not four hours ago. My dear sir, where were you at the time? He was in the hall of the markets—where the fighting has been. All the city was screaming about it. All the Babble Machines. Everywhere it was shouted. Even the fools who speak for the Council were admitting it. Everyone was rushing off to see him—everyone was getting arms. Were you drunk or asleep? And even then! But you're joking! Surely you're pretending. It was to stop the shouting of the Babble Machines and prevent the people gathering that they turned off the electricity—and put this damned darkness upon us. Do you mean to say—?"

"I had heard the Sleeper was rescued," said Graham. "But—to come back a minute. Are you sure Ostrog has him?"

"He won't let him go," said the old man.

"And the Sleeper. Are you sure he is not genuine? I have never heard—"

"So all the fools think. So they think. As if there wasn't a thousand things that were never heard. I know Ostrog too well for that. Did I tell you? In a way I'm a sort of relation of Ostrog's. A sort of relation. Through my daughter-in-law."

"I suppose—"

"Well?"

"I suppose there's no chance of this Sleeper asserting himself. I suppose he's certain to be a puppet—in Ostrog's hands or the Council's, as soon as the struggle is over."

"In Ostrog's hands—certainly. Why shouldn't he be a puppet? Look at his position. Everything done for him, every pleasure possible. Why should he want to assert himself?"

"What are these Pleasure Cities?" said Graham, abruptly.

The old man made him repeat the question. When at last he was assured of Graham's words, he nudged him violently. "That's *too* much," said he. "You're poking fun at an old man. I've been suspecting you know more than you pretend."

"Perhaps I do," said Graham. "But no! why should I go on acting? No, I do not know what a Pleasure City is."

The old man laughed in an intimate way.

"What is more, I do not know how to read your letters, I do not know what money you use, I do not know what foreign countries there are. I do not know where I am. I cannot count. I do not know where to get food, nor drink, nor shelter."

"Come, come," said the old man, "if you had a glass of drink now, would you put it in your ear or your eye?"

"I want you to tell me all these things."

"He, he! Well, gentlemen who dress in silk must have their fun." A withered hand caressed Graham's arm for a moment. "Silk. Well, well! But, all the same, I wish I was the man who was put up as the Sleeper. He'll have a fine time of it. All the pomp and pleasure. He's a queer looking face. When they used to let anyone go to see him, I've got tickets and been. The image of the real one, as the photographs show him, this substitute used to be. Yellow. But he'll get fed up. It's a queer world. Think of the luck of it. The luck of it. I expect he'll be sent to Capri. It's the best fun for a greener."

His cough overtook him again. Then he began mumbling enviously of pleasures and strange delights. "The luck of it, the luck of it! All my life I've been in London, hoping to get my chance."

"But you don't know that the Sleeper died," said Graham, suddenly.

The old man made him repeat his words.

"Men don't live beyond ten dozen. It's not in the order of things," said the old man. "I'm not a fool. Fools may believe it, but not me."

Graham became angry with the old man's assurance. "Whether you are a fool or not," he said, "it happens you are wrong about the Sleeper."

"Eh?"

"You are wrong about the Sleeper. I haven't told you before, but I will tell you now. You are wrong about the Sleeper."

"How do you know? I thought you didn't know anything—not even about Pleasure Cities."

Graham paused.

"You don't know," said the old man. "How are you to know? It's very few men—"

"I *am* the Sleeper."

He had to repeat it.

There was a brief pause. "There's a silly thing to say, sir, if you'll excuse me. It might get you into trouble in a time like this," said the old man.

Graham, slightly dashed, repeated his assertion.

"I was saying I was the Sleeper. That years and years ago I did, indeed, fall asleep, in a little stone-built village, in the days when there were hedgerows, and villages, and inns, and all the countryside cut up into little pieces, little fields. Have you never heard of those days? And it is I—I who speak to you—who awakened again these four days since."

"Four days since!—the Sleeper! But they've *got* the Sleeper. They have him and they won't let him go. Nonsense! You've been talking sensibly enough up to now. I can see it as though I was there. There will be Lincoln like a keeper just behind him; they won't let him go about alone. Trust them. You're a queer fellow. One of these fun pokers. I see now why you have been clipping your words so oddly, but—"

He stopped abruptly, and Graham could see his gesture.

"As if Ostrog would let the Sleeper run about alone! No, you're telling that to the wrong man altogether. Eh! as if I should believe. What's your game? And besides, we've been talking of the Sleeper."

Graham stood up. "Listen," he said. "I am the Sleeper."

"You're an odd man," said the old man, "to sit here in the dark, talking clipped, and telling a lie of that sort. But—"

Graham's exasperation fell to laughter. "It is preposterous," he cried. "Preposterous. The dream must end. It gets wilder and wilder. Here am I —in this damned twilight—I never knew a dream in twilight before—an anachronism by two hundred years and trying to persuade an old fool that I am myself, and meanwhile—Ugh!"

He moved in gusty irritation and went striding. In a moment the old man was pursuing him. "Eh! but don't go!" cried the old man. "I'm an old fool, I know. Don't go. Don't leave me in all this darkness."

Graham hesitated, stopped. Suddenly the folly of telling his secret flashed into his mind.

"I didn't mean to offend you—disbelieving you," said the old man coming near. "It's no manner of harm. Call yourself the Sleeper if it pleases you. 'Tis a foolish trick—"

Graham hesitated, turned abruptly and went on his way.

For a time he heard the old man's hobbling pursuit and his wheezy cries receding. But at last the darkness swallowed him, and Graham saw him no more.

12

OSTROG

GRAHAM COULD NOW TAKE A CLEARER VIEW OF HIS POSITION. FOR A long time yet he wandered, but after the talk of the old man his discovery of this Ostrog was clear in his mind as the final inevitable decision. One thing was evident, those who were at the headquarters of the revolt had succeeded very admirably in suppressing the fact of his disappearance. But every moment he expected to hear the report of his death or of his recapture by the Council.

Presently a man stopped before him. "Have you heard?" he said.

"No!" said Graham, starting.

"Near a dozand," said the man, "a dozand men!" and hurried on.

A number of men and a girl passed in the darkness, gesticulating and shouting: "Capitulated! Given up!" "A dozand of men." "Two dozand of men." "Ostrog, Hurrah! Ostrog, Hurrah!" These cries receded, became indistinct.

Other shouting men followed. For a time his attention was absorbed in the fragments of speech he heard. He had a doubt whether all were speaking English. Scraps floated to him, scraps like Pigeon English, like "nigger" dialect, blurred and mangled distortions. He dared accost no one with questions. The impression the people gave him jarred altogether with his preconceptions of the struggle and confirmed the old man's faith in Ostrog. It was only slowly he could bring himself to believe that all these people were rejoicing at the defeat of the Council, that the Council which had pursued him with such power and vigour was after all the weaker of the two sides in conflict. And if that was so, how did it affect him? Several times he hesitated on the verge of fundamental questions. Once he turned and walked for a long way after a little man of rotund inviting outline, but he was unable to master confidence to address him.

It was only slowly that it came to him that he might ask for the "Wind-Vane offices" whatever the "Wind-Vane offices" might be. His first enquiry simply resulted in a direction to go on towards Westminster. His second led to the discovery of a short cut in which he was speedily lost. He was told to leave the ways to which he had hitherto confined himself—knowing no other means of transit—and to plunge down one of the middle staircases into the blackness of a cross-way. Thereupon came some trivial adventures; chief of these an ambiguous encounter with a gruff-voiced invisible creature speaking in a strange dialect that seemed at first a strange tongue, a thick flow of speech with the drifting corpses of English words therein, the dialect of the latter-day vile. Then another voice drew near, a girl's voice singing, "tralala tralala." She spoke to Graham, her English touched with something of the same quality. She professed to have lost her sister, she blundered needlessly into him he thought, caught hold of him and laughed. But a word of vague remonstrance sent her into the unseen again.

The sounds about him increased. Stumbling people passed him, speaking excitedly. "They have surrendered!" "The Council! Surely not the Council!" "They are saying so in the Ways." The passage seemed wider. Suddenly the wall fell away. He was in a great space and people were stirring remotely. He inquired his way of an indistinct figure. "Strike straight across," said a woman's voice. He left his guiding wall, and in a moment had stumbled against a little table on which were utensils of glass. Graham's eyes, now attuned to darkness, made out a long vista with tables on either side. He went down this. At one or two of the tables he heard a clang of glass and a sound of eating. There were people then cool enough to dine, or daring enough to steal a meal in spite of social convulsion and darkness. Far off and high up he presently saw a pallid light of a semi-circular shape. As he approached this, a black edge came up and hid it. He stumbled at steps and found himself in a gallery. He heard a sobbing, and found two scared little girls crouched by a railing. These children became silent at the near sound of feet. He tried to console them, but they were very still until he left them. Then as he receded he could hear them sobbing again.

Presently he found himself at the foot of a staircase and near a wide opening. He saw a dim twilight above this and ascended out of the blackness into a street of moving ways again. Along this a disorderly swarm of people marched shouting. They were singing snatches of the song of the revolt, most of them out of tune. Here and there torches flared creating brief hysterical shadows. He asked his way and was twice puzzled by that same thick dialect. His third attempt won an answer he could understand. He was two miles from the Wind-Vane offices in Westminster, but the way was easy to follow.

When at last he did approach the district of the Wind-Vane Offices it seemed to him, from the cheering processions that came marching along the Ways, from the tumult of rejoicing, and finally from the restoration of the lighting of the city, that the overthrow of the Council must already be accomplished. And still no news of his absence came to his ears.

The re-illumination of the city came with startling abruptness. Suddenly he stood blinking, all about him men halted dazzled, and the world was incandescent. The light found him already upon the outskirts of the excited crowds that choked the ways near the Wind-Vane Offices, and the sense of visibility and exposure that came with it turned his colourless intention of joining Ostrog to a keen anxiety.

For a time he was jostled, obstructed, and endangered by men hoarse and weary with cheering his name, some of them bandaged and bloody in his cause. The frontage of the Wind-Vane Offices was illuminated by some moving picture, but what it was he could not see, because in spite of his strenuous attempts the density of the crowd prevented his approaching it. From the fragments of speech he caught, he judged it conveyed news of the fighting about the Council House. Ignorance and indecision made him slow and ineffective in his movements. For a time he could not conceive how he was to get within the unbroken façade of this place. He made his way slowly into the midst of this mass of people, until he realized that the descending staircase of the central way led to the interior of the buildings. This gave him a goal, but the crowding in the central path was so dense that it was long before he could reach it. And even then he encountered intricate obstruction, and had an hour of vivid argument first in this guard room and then in that before he could get a note taken to the one man of all men who was most eager to see him. His story was laughed to scorn at one place, and wiser for that, when at last he reached a second stairway he professed simply to have news of extraordinary importance for Ostrog. What it was he would not say. They sent his note reluctantly. For a long time he waited in a little room at the foot of the lift shaft, and thither at last came Lincoln, eager, apologetic, astonished. He stopped in the doorway scrutinizing Graham, then rushed forward effusively.

"Yes," he cried. "It is you. And you are not dead!"

Graham made a brief explanation.

"My brother is waiting," explained Lincoln. "He is alone in the Wind-Vane Offices. We feared you had been killed in the theatre. He doubted—and things are very urgent still in spite of what we are telling them *there*—or he would have come to you."

They ascended a lift, passed along a narrow passage, crossed a great hall, empty save for two hurrying messengers, and entered a comparatively little room, whose only furniture was a long settee and a large oval disc of cloudy, shifting grey, hung by cables from the wall. There Lincoln left Graham for a space, and he remained alone without understanding the smoky shapes that drove slowly across this disc.

His attention was arrested by a sound that began abruptly. It was cheering, the frantic cheering of a vast but very remote crowd, a roaring exultation. This ended as sharply as it had begun, like a sound heard between the opening and shutting of a door. In the outer room was a noise of hurrying steps and a melodious clinking as if a loose chain was running over the teeth of a wheel.

Then he heard the voice of a woman, the rustle of unseen garments. "It is Ostrog!" he heard her say. A little bell rang fitfully, and then everything was still again.

Presently came voices, footsteps and movement without. The footsteps of some one person detached itself from the other sounds, and drew near, firm, evenly measured steps. The curtain lifted slowly. A tall, white-haired man, clad in garments of cream-coloured silk, appeared, regarding Graham from under his raised arm.

For a moment the white form remained holding the curtain, then dropped it and stood before it. Graham's first impression was of a very broad forehead, very pale blue eyes deep sunken under white brows, an aquiline nose, and a heavily-lined resolute mouth. The folds of flesh over the eyes, the drooping of the corners of the mouth contradicted the upright bearing, and said the man was old. Graham rose to his feet instinctively, and for a moment the two men stood in silence, regarding each other.

"You are Ostrog?" said Graham.

"I am Ostrog."

"The Boss?"

"So I am called."

Graham felt the inconvenience of the silence. "I have to thank you chiefly, I understand, for my safety," he said presently.

"We were afraid you were killed," said Ostrog. "Or sent to sleep again —for ever. We have been doing everything to keep our secret—the secret of your disappearance. Where have you been? How did you get here?"

Graham told him briefly.

Ostrog listened in silence.

He smiled faintly. "Do you know what I was doing when they came to tell me you had come?"

"How can I guess?"

"Preparing your double."

"My double?"

"A man as like you as we could find. We were going to hypnotise him, to save him the difficulty of acting. It was imperative. The whole of this revolt depends on the idea that you are awake, alive, and with us. Even now a great multitude of people has gathered in the theatre clamouring to see you. They do not trust ... You know, of course—something of your position?"

"Very little," said Graham.

"It is like this." Ostrog walked a pace or two into the room and turned. "You are absolute owner," he said, "of the world. You are King of the Earth. Your powers are limited in many intricate ways, but you are the figure-head, the popular symbol of government. This White Council, the Council of Trustees as it is called—"

"I have heard the vague outline of these things."

"I wondered."

"I came upon a garrulous old man."

"I see.... Our masses—the word comes from your days—you know, of course, that we still have masses—regard you as our actual ruler. Just as a great number of people in your days regarded the Crown as the ruler. They are discontented—the masses all over the earth—with the rule of your Trustees. For the most part it is the old discontent, the old quarrel of the common man with his commonness—the misery of work and discipline and unfitness. But your Trustees have ruled ill. In certain matters, in the administration of the Labour Companies, for example, they have been unwise. They have given endless opportunities. Already we of the popular party were agitating for reforms—when your waking came. Came! If it had been contrived it could not have come more opportunely." He smiled. "The public mind, making no allowance for your years of quiescence, had already hit on the thought of waking you and appealing to you, and —Flash!"

He indicated the outbreak by a gesture, and Graham moved his head to show that he understood.

"The Council muddled—quarrelled. They always do. They could not decide what to do with you. You know how they imprisoned you?"

"I see. I see. And now—we win?"

"We win. Indeed we win. To-night, in five swift hours. Suddenly we struck everywhere. The Wind-Vane people, the Labour Company and its millions, burst the bonds. We got the pull of the aeroplanes."

"Yes," said Graham.

"That was, of course, essential. Or they could have got away. All the city rose, every third man almost was in it! All the blue, all the public services, save only just a few aeronauts and about half the red police. You were rescued, and their own police of the ways—not half of them could be massed at the Council House—have been broken up, disarmed or killed. All London is ours—now. Only the Council House remains.

"Half of those who remain to them of the red police were lost in that foolish attempt to recapture you. They lost their heads when they lost you. They flung all they had at the theatre. We cut them off from the Council House there. Truly to-night has been a night of victory. Everywhere your star has blazed. A day ago—the White Council ruled as it has ruled for a gross of years, for a century and a half of years, and then, with only a little whispering, a covert arming here and there, suddenly—So!"

"I am very ignorant," said Graham. "I suppose—I do not clearly understand the conditions of this fighting. If you could explain. Where is the Council? Where is the fight?"

Ostrog stepped across the room, something clicked, and suddenly, save for an oval glow, they were in darkness. For a moment Graham was puzzled.

Then he saw that the cloudy grey disc had taken depth and colour, had assumed the appearance of an oval window looking out upon a strange unfamiliar scene.

At the first glance he was unable to guess what this scene might be. It was a daylight scene, the daylight of a wintry day, grey and clear. Across the picture, and half-way as it seemed between him and the remoter view, a stout cable of twisted white wire stretched vertically. Then he perceived that the rows of great wind-wheels he saw, the wide intervals, the occasional gulfs of darkness, were akin to those through which he had fled from the Council House. He distinguished an orderly file of red figures marching across an open space between files of men in black, and realized before Ostrog spoke that he was looking down on the upper surface of latter-day London. The overnight snows had gone. He judged that this mirror was some modern replacement of the camera obscura, but that matter was not explained to him. He saw that though the file of red figures was trotting from left to right, yet they were passing out of the picture to the left. He wondered momentarily, and then saw that the picture was passing slowly, panorama fashion, across the oval.

"In a moment you will see the fighting," said Ostrog at his elbow. "Those fellows in red you notice are prisoners. This is the roof space of London—all the houses are practically continuous now. The streets and public squares are covered in. The gaps and chasms of your time have disappeared."

Something out of focus obliterated half the picture. Its form suggested a man. There was a gleam of metal, a flash, something that swept across the oval, as the eyelid of a bird sweeps across its eye, and the picture was clear again. And now Graham beheld men running down among the wind-wheels, pointing weapons from which jetted out little smoky flashes. They swarmed thicker and thicker to the right, gesticulating—it might be they were shouting, but of that the picture told nothing. They and the wind-wheels passed slowly and steadily across the field of the mirror.

"Now," said Ostrog, "comes the Council House," and slowly a black edge crept into view and gathered Graham's attention. Soon it was no longer an edge but a cavity, a huge blackened space amidst the clustering edifices, and from it thin spires of smoke rose into the pallid winter sky. Gaunt ruinous masses of the building, mighty truncated piers and girders, rose dismally out of this cavernous darkness. And over these vestiges of some splendid place, countless minute men were clambering, leaping, swarming.

"This is the Council House," said Ostrog. "Their last stronghold. And the fools wasted enough ammunition to hold out for a month in blowing up the buildings all about them—to stop our attack. You heard the smash? It shattered half the brittle glass in the city."

And while he spoke, Graham saw that beyond this area of ruins, overhanging it and rising to a great height, was a ragged mass of white building. This mass had been isolated by the ruthless destruction of its surroundings. Black gaps marked the passages the disaster had torn apart; big halls had been slashed open and the decoration of their interiors showed dismally in the wintry dawn, and down the jagged walls hung festoons of divided cables and twisted ends of lines and metallic rods. And amidst all the vast details moved little red specks, the red-clothed defenders of the Council. Every now and then faint flashes illuminated the bleak shadows. At the first sight it seemed to Graham that an attack upon this isolated white building was in progress, but then he perceived that the party of the revolt was not advancing, but sheltered amidst the colossal wreckage that encircled this last ragged stronghold of the red-garbed men, was keeping up a fitful firing.

And not ten hours ago he had stood beneath the ventilating fans in a little chamber within that remote building wondering what was happening in the world!

Looking more attentively as this war-like episode moved silently across the centre of the mirror, Graham saw that the white building was surrounded on every side by ruins, and Ostrog proceeded to describe in concise phrases how its defenders had sought by such destruction to isolate themselves from a storm. He spoke of the loss of men that huge downfall had entailed in an indifferent tone. He indicated an improvised mortuary among the wreckage, showed ambulances swarming like cheese-mites along a ruinous groove that had once been a street of moving ways. He was more interested in pointing out the parts of the Council House, the distribution of the besiegers. In a little while the civil contest that had convulsed London was no longer a mystery to Graham. It was no tumultuous revolt had occurred that night, no equal warfare, but a splendidly organised *coup d'état*. Ostrog's grasp of details was astonishing; he seemed to know the business of even the smallest knot of black and red specks that crawled amidst these places.

He stretched a huge black arm across the luminous picture, and showed the room whence Graham had escaped, and across the chasm of ruins the course of his flight. Graham recognised the gulf across which the gutter ran, and the wind-wheels where he had crouched from the flying machine. The rest of his path had succumbed to the explosion. He looked again at the Council House, and it was already half hidden, and on the right a hillside with a cluster of domes and pinnacles, hazy, dim and distant, was gliding into view.

"And the Council is really overthrown?" he said.

"Overthrown," said Ostrog.

"And I—. Is it indeed true that I—?"

"You are Master of the World."

"But that white flag—"

"That is the flag of the Council—the flag of the Rule of the World. It will fall. The fight is over. Their attack on the theatre was their last frantic struggle. They have only a thousand men or so, and some of these men will be disloyal. They have little ammunition. And we are reviving the ancient arts. We are casting guns."

"But—help. Is this city the world?"

"Practically this is all they have left to them of their empire. Abroad the cities have either revolted with us or wait the issue. Your awakening has perplexed them, paralyzed them."

"But haven't the Council flying machines? Why is there no fighting with them?"

"They had. But the greater part of the aeronauts were in the revolt with us. They wouldn't take the risk of fighting on our side, but they would not stir against us. We *had* to get a pull with the aeronauts. Quite half were with us, and the others knew it. Directly they knew you had got away, those looking for you dropped. We killed the man who shot at you— an hour ago. And we occupied the flying stages at the outset in every city we could, and so stopped and captured the greater aeroplanes, and as for the little flying machines that turned out—for some did—we kept up too straight and steady a fire for them to get near the Council House. If they dropped they couldn't rise again, because there's no clear space about there for them to get up. Several we have smashed, several others have dropped and surrendered, the rest have gone off to the Continent to find a friendly city if they can before their fuel runs out. Most of these men were only too glad to be taken prisoner and kept out of harm's way. Upsetting in a flying machine isn't a very attractive prospect. There's no chance for the Council that way. Its days are done."

He laughed and turned to the oval reflection again to show Graham what he meant by flying stages. Even the four nearer ones were remote and obscured by a thin morning haze. But Graham could perceive they were very vast structures, judged even by the standard of the things about them.

And then as these dim shapes passed to the left there came again the sight of the expanse across which the disarmed men in red had been marching. And then the black ruins, and then again the beleaguered white fastness of the Council. It appeared no longer a ghostly pile, but glowing amber in the sunlight, for a cloud shadow had passed. About it the pigmy struggle still hung in suspense, but now the red defenders were no longer firing.

So, in a dusky stillness, the man from the nineteenth century saw the closing scene of the great revolt, the forcible establishment of his rule. With a quality of startling discovery it came to him that this was his world, and not that other he had left behind; that this was no spectacle to culminate and cease; that in this world lay whatever life was still before him, lay all his duties and dangers and responsibilities. He turned with fresh questions. Ostrog began to answer them, and then broke off abruptly. "But these things I must explain more fully later. At present there are—duties. The people are coming by the moving ways towards this ward from every part of the city—the markets and theatres are densely crowded. You are just in time for them. They are clamouring to see you. And abroad they want to see you. Paris, New York, Chicago, Denver, Capri—thousands of cities are up and in a tumult, undecided, and clamouring to see you. They have clamoured that you should be awakened for years, and now it is done they will scarcely believe—"

"But surely—I can't go...."

Ostrog answered from the other side of the room, and the picture on the oval disc paled and vanished as the light jerked back again. "There are kineto-telephoto-graphs," he said. "As you bow to the people here—all over the world myriads of myriads of people, packed and still in darkened halls, will see you also. In black and white, of course—not like this. And you will hear their shouts reinforcing the shouting in the hall.

"And there is an optical contrivance we shall use," said Ostrog, "used by some of the posturers and women dancers. It may be novel to you. You stand in a very bright light, and they see not you but a magnified image of you thrown on a screen—so that even the farthest man in the remotest gallery can, if he chooses, count your eyelashes."

Graham clutched desperately at one of the questions in his mind. "What is the population of London?" he said.

"Eight and twaindy myriads."

"Eight and what?"

"More than thirty-three millions."

These figures went beyond Graham's imagination.

"You will be expected to say something," said Ostrog. "Not what you used to call a Speech, but what our people call a word—just one sentence, six or seven words. Something formal. If I might suggest—'I have awakened and my heart is with you.' That is the sort of thing they want."

"What was that?" asked Graham.

"'I am awakened and my heart is with you.' And bow—bow royally. But first we must get you black robes—for black is your colour. Do you mind? And then they will disperse to their homes."

Graham hesitated. "I am in your hands," he said.

Ostrog was clearly of that opinion. He thought for a moment, turned to the curtain and called brief directions to some unseen attendants. Almost immediately a black robe, the very fellow of the black robe Graham had worn in the theatre, was brought. And as he threw it about his shoulders there came from the room without the shrilling of a high-pitched bell. Ostrog turned in interrogation to the attendant, then suddenly seemed to change his mind, pulled the curtain aside and disappeared.

For a moment Graham stood with the deferential attendant listening to Ostrog's retreating steps. There was a sound of quick question and answer and of men running. The curtain was snatched back and Ostrog reappeared, his massive face glowing with excitement. He crossed the room in a stride, clicked the room into darkness, gripped Graham's arm and pointed to the mirror.

"Even as we turned away," he said.

Graham saw his index finger, black and colossal, above the mirrored Council House. For a moment he did not understand. And then he perceived that the flagstaff that had carried the white banner was bare.

"Do you mean—?" he began.

"The Council has surrendered. Its rule is at an end for evermore."

"Look!" and Ostrog pointed to a coil of black that crept in little jerks up the vacant flagstaff, unfolding as it rose.

The oval picture paled as Lincoln pulled the curtain aside and entered.

"They are clamorous," he said.

Ostrog kept his grip of Graham's arm.

"We have raised the people," he said. "We have given them arms. For to-day at least their wishes must be law."

Lincoln held the curtain open for Graham and Ostrog to pass through....

On his way to the markets Graham had a transitory glance of a long narrow white-walled room in which men in the universal blue canvas were carrying covered things like biers, and about which men in medical purple hurried to and fro. From this room came groans and wailing. He had an impression of an empty blood-stained couch, of men on other couches, bandaged and blood-stained. It was just a glimpse from a railed footway and then a buttress hid the place and they were going on towards the markets....

The roar of the multitude was near now: it leapt to thunder. And, arresting his attention, a fluttering of black banners, the waving of blue canvas and brown rags, and the swarming vastness of the theatre near the public markets came into view down a long passage. The picture opened out. He perceived they were entering the great theatre of his first appearance, the great theatre he had last seen as a chequer-work of glare and blackness in his flight from the red police. This time he entered it along a gallery at a level high above the stage. The place was now brilliantly lit again. His eyes sought the gangway up which he had fled, but he could not tell it from among its dozens of fellows; nor could he see anything of the smashed seats, deflated cushions, and such like traces of the fight because of the density of the people. Except the stage the whole place was closely packed. Looking down the effect was a vast area of stippled pink, each dot a still upturned face regarding him. At his appearance with Ostrog the cheering died away, the singing died away, a common interest stilled and unified the disorder. It seemed as though every individual of those myriads was watching him.

$$13$$

THE END OF THE OLD ORDER

So far as Graham was able to judge, it was near midday when the white banner of the Council fell. But some hours had to elapse before it was possible to effect the formal capitulation, and so after he had spoken his "Word" he retired to his new apartments in the Wind-Vane Offices. The continuous excitement of the last twelve hours had left him inordinately fatigued, even his curiosity was exhausted; for a space he sat inert and passive with open eyes, and for a space he slept. He was roused by two medical attendants, come prepared with stimulants to sustain him through the next occasion. After he had taken their drugs and bathed by their advice in cold water, he felt a rapid return of interest and energy, and was presently able and willing to accompany Ostrog through several miles (as it seemed) of passages, lifts, and slides to the closing scene of the White Council's rule.

The way ran deviously through a maze of buildings. They came at last to a passage that curved about, and showed broadening before him an oblong opening, clouds hot with sunset, and the ragged skyline of the ruinous Council House. A tumult of shouts came drifting up to him. In another moment they had come out high up on the brow of the cliff of torn buildings that overhung the wreckage. The vast area opened to Graham's eyes, none the less strange and wonderful for the remote view he had had of it in the oval mirror.

This rudely amphitheatral space seemed now the better part of a mile to its outer edge. It was gold lit on the left hand, catching the sunlight, and below and to the right clear and cold in the shadow. Above the shadowy grey Council House that stood in the midst of it, the great black banner of the surrender still hung in sluggish folds against the blazing sunset. Severed rooms, halls and passages gaped strangely, broken masses of metal projected dismally from the complex wreckage, vast masses of twisted cable dropped like tangled seaweed, and from its base came a tumult of innumerable voices, violent concussions, and the sound of trumpets. All about this great white pile was a ring of desolation; the smashed and blackened masses, the gaunt foundations and ruinous lumber of the fabric that had been destroyed by the Council's orders, skeletons of girders, Titanic masses of wall, forests of stout pillars. Amongst the sombre wreckage beneath, running water flashed and glistened, and far away across the space, out of the midst of a vague vast mass of buildings, there thrust the twisted end of a water-main, two hundred feet in the air, thunderously spouting a shining cascade. And everywhere great multitudes of people.

Wherever there was space and foothold, people swarmed, little people, small and minutely clear, except where the sunset touched them to indistinguishable gold. They clambered up the tottering walls, they clung in wreaths and groups about the high-standing pillars. They swarmed along the edges of the circle of ruins. The air was full of their shouting, and they were pressing and swaying towards the central space.

The upper storeys of the Council House seemed deserted, not a human being was visible. Only the drooping banner of the surrender hung heavily against the light. The dead were within the Council House, or hidden by the swarming people, or carried away. Graham could see only a few neglected bodies in gaps and corners of the ruins, and amidst the flowing water.

"Will you let them see you, Sire?" said Ostrog. "They are very anxious to see you."

Graham hesitated, and then walked forward to where the broken verge of wall dropped sheer. He stood looking down, a lonely, tall, black figure against the sky.

Very slowly the swarming ruins became aware of him. And as they did so little bands of black-uniformed men appeared remotely, thrusting through the crowds towards the Council House. He saw little black heads become pink, looking at him, saw by that means a wave of recognition sweep across the space. It occurred to him that he should accord them some recognition. He held up his arm, then pointed to the Council House and dropped his hand. The voices below became unanimous, gathered volume, came up to him as multitudinous wavelets of cheering.

The western sky was a pallid bluish green, and Jupiter shone high in the south, before the capitulation was accomplished. Above was a slow insensible change, the advance of night serene and beautiful; below was hurry, excitement, conflicting orders, pauses, spasmodic developments of organization, a vast ascending clamour and confusion. Before the Council came out, toiling perspiring men, directed by a conflict of shouts, carried forth hundreds of those who had perished in the hand-to-hand conflict within those long passages and chambers....

Guards in black lined the way that the Council would come, and as far as the eye could reach into the hazy blue twilight of the ruins, and swarming now at every possible point in the captured Council House and along the shattered cliff of its circumadjacent buildings, were innumerable people, and their voices, even when they were not cheering, were as the soughing of the sea upon a pebble beach. Ostrog had chosen a huge commanding pile of crushed and overthrown masonry, and on this a stage of timbers and metal girders was being hastily constructed. Its essential parts were complete, but humming and clangorous machinery still glared fitfully in the shadows beneath this temporary edifice.

The stage had a small higher portion on which Graham stood with Ostrog and Lincoln close beside him, a little in advance of a group of minor officers. A broader lower stage surrounded this quarter-deck, and on this were the black-uniformed guards of the revolt armed with the little green weapons whose very names Graham still did not know. Those standing about him perceived that his eyes wandered perpetually from the swarming people in the twilight ruins about him to the darkling mass of the White Council House, whence the Trustees would presently come, and to the gaunt cliffs of ruin that encircled him, and so back to the people. The voices of the crowd swelled to a deafening tumult.

He saw the Councillors first afar off in the glare of one of the temporary lights that marked their path, a little group of white figures in a black archway. In the Council House they had been in darkness. He watched them approaching, drawing nearer past first this blazing electric star and then that; the minatory roar of the crowd over whom their power had lasted for a hundred and fifty years marched along beside them. As they drew still nearer their faces came out weary, white, and anxious. He saw them blinking up through the glare about him and Ostrog. He contrasted their strange cold looks in the Hall of Atlas.... Presently he could recognize several of them; the man who had rapped the table at Howard, a burly man with a red beard, and one delicate-featured, short, dark man with a peculiarly long skull. He noted that two were whispering together and looking behind him at Ostrog. Next there came a tall, dark and handsome man, walking downcast. Abruptly he glanced up, his eyes touched Graham for a moment, and passed beyond him to Ostrog. The way that had been made for them was so contrived that they had to march past and curve about before they came to the sloping path of planks that ascended to the stage where their surrender was to be made.

"The Master, the Master! God and the Master," shouted the people. "To hell with the Council!" Graham looked at their multitudes, receding beyond counting into a shouting haze, and then at Ostrog beside him, white and steadfast and still. His eye went again to the little group of White Councillors. And then he looked up at the familiar quiet stars overhead. The marvellous element in his fate was suddenly vivid. Could that be his indeed, that little life in his memory two hundred years gone by— and this as well?

14

FROM THE CROW'S NEST

AND SO AFTER STRANGE DELAYS AND THROUGH AN AVENUE OF DOUBT and battle, this man from the nineteenth century came at last to his position at the head of that complex world.

At first when he rose from the long deep sleep that followed his rescue and the surrender of the Council, he did not recognize his surroundings. By an effort he gained a clue in his mind, and all that had happened came back to him, at first with a quality of insincerity like a story heard, like something read out of a book. And even before his memories were clear, the exultation of his escape, the wonder of his prominence were back in his mind. He was owner of the world; Master of the Earth. This new great age was in the completest sense his. He no longer hoped to discover his experiences a dream; he became anxious now to convince himself that they were real.

An obsequious valet assisted him to dress under the direction of a dignified chief attendant, a little man whose face proclaimed him Japanese, albeit he spoke English like an Englishman. From the latter he learnt something of the state of affairs. Already the revolution was an accepted fact; already business was being resumed throughout the city. Abroad the downfall of the Council had been received for the most part with delight. Nowhere was the Council popular, and the thousand cities of Western America, after two hundred years still jealous of New York, London, and the East, had risen almost unanimously two days before at the news of Graham's imprisonment. Paris was fighting within itself. The rest of the world hung in suspense.

While he was breaking his fast, the sound of a telephone bell jetted from a corner, and his chief attendant called his attention to the voice of Ostrog making polite enquiries. Graham interrupted his refreshment to reply. Very shortly Lincoln arrived, and Graham at once expressed a strong desire to talk to people and to be shown more of the new life that was opening before him. Lincoln informed him that in three hours' time a representative gathering of officials and their wives would be held in the state apartments of the Wind-Vane chief. Graham's desire to traverse the ways of the city was, however, at present impossible, because of the enormous excitement of the people. It was, however, quite possible for him to take a bird's-eye view of the city from the crow's nest of the Wind-Vane keeper. To this accordingly Graham was conducted by his attendant. Lincoln; with a graceful compliment to the attendant, apologized for not accompanying them, on account of the present pressure of administrative work.

Higher even than the most gigantic, wind-wheels hung this crow's nest, a clear thousand feet above the roofs, a little disc-shaped speck on a spear of metallic filigree, cable stayed. To its summit Graham was drawn in a little wire-hung cradle. Half-way down the frail-seeming stem was a light gallery about which hung a cluster of tubes—minute they looked from above—rotating slowly on the ring of its outer rail. These were the specula, *en rapport* with the Wind-Vane Keeper's mirrors, in one of which Ostrog had shown him the coming of his rule. His Japanese attendant ascended before him and they spent nearly an hour asking and answering questions.

It was a day full of the promise and quality of spring. The touch of the wind warmed. The sky was an intense blue and the vast expanse of London shone dazzling under the morning sun. The air was clear of smoke and haze, sweet as the air of a mountain glen.

Save for the irregular oval of ruins about the House of the Council and the black flag of the surrender that fluttered there, the mighty city seen from above showed few signs of the swift revolution that had, to his imagination, in one night and one day, changed the destinies of the world. A multitude of people still swarmed over these ruins, and the huge open-work stagings in the distance from which started in times of peace the service of aeroplanes to the various great cities of Europe and America, were also black with the victors. Across a narrow way of planking raised on trestles that crossed the ruins a crowd of workmen were busy restoring the connection between the cables and wires of the Council House and the rest of the city, preparatory to the transfer thither of Ostrog's headquarters from the Wind-Vane buildings.

For the rest the luminous expanse was undisturbed. So vast was its serenity in comparison with the areas of disturbance, that presently Graham, looking beyond them, could almost forget the thousands of men lying out of sight in the artificial glare within the quasi-subterranean labyrinth, dead or dying of the overnight wounds, forget the improvised wards with the hosts of surgeons, nurses, and bearers feverishly busy, forget, indeed, all the wonder, consternation and novelty under the electric lights. Down there in the hidden ways of the anthill he knew that the revolution triumphed, that black everywhere carried the day, black favours, black banners, black festoons across the streets. And out here, under the fresh sunlight, beyond the crater of the fight, as if nothing had happened to the earth, the forest of Wind-Vanes that had grown from one or two while the Council had ruled, roared peacefully upon their incessant duty.

Far away, spiked, jagged and indented by the wind vanes, the Surrey Hills rose blue and faint; to the north and nearer, the sharp contours of Highgate and Muswell Hill were similarly jagged. And all over the countryside, he knew, on every crest and hill, where once the hedges had interlaced, and cottages, churches, inns, and farm houses had nestled among their trees, wind-wheels similar to those he saw and bearing like them vast advertisements, gaunt and distinctive symbols of the new age, cast their whirling shadows and stored incessantly the energy that flowed away incessantly through all the arteries of the city. And underneath these wandered the countless flocks and herds of the British Food Trust, his property, with their lonely guards and keepers.

Not a familiar outline anywhere broke the cluster of gigantic shapes below. St. Paul's he knew survived, and many of the old buildings in Westminster, embedded out of sight, arched over and covered in among the giant growths of this great age. The Thames, too, made no fall and gleam of silver to break the wilderness of the city; the thirsty water mains drank up every drop of its waters before they reached the walls. Its bed and estuary, scoured and sunken, was now a canal of sea water, and a race of grimy bargemen brought the heavy materials of trade from the Pool thereby beneath the very feet of the workers. Faint and dim in the eastward between earth and sky hung the clustering masts of the colossal shipping in the Pool. For all the heavy traffic, for which there was no need of haste, came in gigantic sailing ships from the ends of the earth, and the heavy goods for which there was urgency in mechanical ships of a smaller swifter sort.

And to the south over the hills came vast aqueducts with sea water for the sewers, and in three separate directions ran pallid lines—the roads, stippled with moving grey specks. On the first occasion that offered he was determined to go out and see these roads. That would come after the flying ship he was presently to try. His attendant officer described them as a pair of gently curving surfaces a hundred yards wide, each one for the traffic going in one direction, and made of a substance called Eadhamite—an artificial substance, so far as he could gather, resembling toughened glass. Along this shot a strange traffic of narrow rubber-shod vehicles, great single wheels, two and four wheeled vehicles, sweeping along at velocities of from one to six miles a minute. Railroads had vanished; a few embankments remained as rust-crowned trenches here and there. Some few formed the cores of Eadhamite ways.

Among the first things to strike his attention had been the great fleets of advertisement balloons and kites that receded in irregular vistas northward and southward along the lines of the aeroplane journeys. No great aeroplanes were to be seen. Their passages had ceased, and only one little-seeming monoplane circled high in the blue distance above the Surrey Hills, an unimpressive soaring speck.

A thing Graham had already learnt, and which he found very hard to imagine, was that nearly all the towns in the country, and almost all the villages, had disappeared. Here and there only, he understood, some gigantic hotel-like edifice stood amid square miles of some single cultivation and preserved the name of a town—as Bournemouth, Wareham, or Swanage. Yet the officer had speedily convinced him how inevitable such a change had been. The old order had dotted the country with farmhouses, and every two or three miles was the ruling landlord's estate, and the place of the inn and cobbler, the grocer's shop and church—the village. Every eight miles or so was the country town, where lawyer, corn merchant, wool-stapler, saddler, veterinary surgeon, doctor, draper, milliner and so forth lived. Every eight miles—simply because that eight mile marketing journey, four there and back, was as much as was comfortable for the farmer. But directly the railways came into play, and after them the light railways, and all the swift new motor cars that had replaced waggons and horses, and so soon as the high roads began to be made of wood, and rubber, and Eadhamite, and all sorts of elastic durable substances—the necessity of having such frequent market towns disappeared. And the big towns grew. They drew the worker with the gravitational force of seemingly endless work, the employer with their suggestion of an infinite ocean of labour.

And as the standard of comfort rose, as the complexity of the mechanism of living increased, life in the country had become more and more costly, or narrow and impossible. The disappearance of vicar and squire, the extinction of the general practitioner by the city specialist; had robbed the village of its last touch of culture. After telephone, kinematograph and phonograph had replaced newspaper, book, schoolmaster, and letter, to live outside the range of the electric cables was to live an isolated savage. In the country were neither means of being clothed nor fed (according to the refined conceptions of the time), no efficient doctors for an emergency, no company and no pursuits.

Moreover, mechanical appliances in agriculture made one engineer the equivalent of thirty labourers. So, inverting the condition of the city clerk in the days when London was scarce inhabitable because of the coaly foulness of its air, the labourers now came to the city and its life and delights at night to leave it again in the morning. The city had swallowed up humanity; man had entered upon a new stage in his development. First had come the nomad, the hunter, then had followed the agriculturist of the agricultural state, whose towns and cities and ports were but the headquarters and markets of the countryside. And now, logical consequence of an epoch of invention, was this huge new aggregation of men.

Such things as these, simple statements of fact though they were to contemporary men, strained Graham's imagination to picture. And when he glanced "over beyond there" at the strange things that existed on the Continent, it failed him altogether.

He had a vision of city beyond city; cities on great plains, cities beside great rivers, vast cities along the sea margin, cities girdled by snowy mountains. Over a great part of the earth the English tongue was spoken; taken together with its Spanish American and Hindoo and Negro and "Pidgin" dialects, it was the everyday language of two-thirds of humanity. On the Continent, save as remote and curious survivals, three other languages alone held sway—German, which reached to Antioch and Genoa and jostled Spanish-English at Cadiz; a Gallicised Russian which met the Indian English in Persia and Kurdistan and the "Pidgin" English in Pekin; and French still clear and brilliant, the language of lucidity, which shared the Mediterranean with the Indian English and German and reached through a negro dialect to the Congo.

And everywhere now through the city-set earth, save in the administered "black belt" territories of the tropics, the same cosmopolitan social organization prevailed, and everywhere from Pole to Equator his property and his responsibilities extended. The whole world was civilised; the whole world dwelt in cities; the whole world was his property....

Out of the dim south-west, glittering and strange, voluptuous, and in some way terrible, shone those Pleasure Cities of which the kinemato-graph-phonograph and the old man in the street had spoken. Strange places reminiscent of the legendary Sybaris, cities of art and beauty, mercenary art and mercenary beauty, sterile wonderful cities of motion and music, whither repaired all who profited by the fierce, inglorious, economic struggle that went on in the glaring labyrinth below.

Fierce he knew it was. How fierce he could judge from the fact that these latter-day people referred back to the England of the nineteenth century as the figure of an idyllic easy-going life. He turned his eyes to the scene immediately before him again, trying to conceive the big factories of that intricate maze....

●15

PROMINENT PEOPLE

THE STATE APARTMENTS OF THE WIND-VANE KEEPER WOULD HAVE astonished Graham had he entered them fresh from his nineteenth century life, but already he was growing accustomed to the scale of the new time. He came out through one of the now familiar sliding panels upon a plateau of landing at the head of a flight of very broad and gentle steps, with men and women far more brilliantly dressed than any he had hitherto seen, ascending and descending. From this position he looked down a vista of subtle and varied ornament in lustreless white and mauve and purple, spanned by bridges that seemed wrought of porcelain and filigree, and terminating far off in a cloudy mystery of perforated screens.

Glancing upward, he saw tier above tier of ascending galleries with faces looking down upon him. The air was full of the babble of innumerable voices and of a music that descended from above, a gay and exhilarating music whose source he did not discover.

The central aisle was thick with people, but by no means uncomfortably crowded; altogether that assembly must have numbered many thousands. They were brilliantly, even fantastically dressed, the men as fancifully as the women, for the sobering influence of the Puritan conception of dignity upon masculine dress had long since passed away. The hair of the men, too, though it was rarely worn long, was commonly curled in a manner that suggested the barber, and baldness had vanished from the earth. Frizzy straight-cut masses that would have charmed Rossetti abounded, and one gentleman, who was pointed out to Graham under the mysterious title of an "amorist," wore his hair in two becoming plaits *à la* Marguerite. The pigtail was in evidence; it would seem that citizens of Chinese extraction were no longer ashamed of their race. There was little uniformity of fashion apparent in the forms of clothing worn. The more shapely men displayed their symmetry in trunk hose, and here were puffs and slashes, and there a cloak and there a robe. The fashions of the days of Leo the Tenth were perhaps the prevailing influence, but the aesthetic conceptions of the far east were also patent. Masculine embonpoint, which, in Victorian times, would have been subjected to the buttoned perils, the ruthless exaggeration of tight-legged tight-armed evening dress, now formed but the basis of a wealth of dignity and drooping folds. Graceful slenderness abounded also. To Graham, a typically stiff man from a typically stiff period, not only did these men seem altogether too graceful in person, but altogether too expressive in their vividly expressive faces. They gesticulated, they expressed surprise, interest, amusement, above all, they expressed the emotions excited in their minds by the ladies about them with astonishing frankness. Even at the first glance it was evident that women were in a great majority.

The ladies in the company of these gentlemen displayed in dress, bearing and manner alike, less emphasis and more intricacy. Some affected a classical simplicity of robing and subtlety of fold, after the fashion of the First French Empire, and flashed conquering arms and shoulders as Graham passed. Others had closely-fitting dresses without seam or belt at the waist, sometimes with long folds falling from the shoulders. The delightful confidences of evening dress had not been diminished by the passage of two centuries.

Everyone's movements seemed graceful. Graham remarked to Lincoln that he saw men as Raphael's cartoons walking, and Lincoln told him that the attainment of an appropriate set of gestures was part of every rich person's education. The Master's entry was greeted with a sort of tittering applause, but these people showed their distinguished manners by not crowding upon him nor annoying him by any persistent scrutiny, as he descended the steps towards the floor of the aisle.

He had already learnt from Lincoln that these were the leaders of existing London society; almost every person there that night was either a powerful official or the immediate connexion of a powerful official. Many had returned from the European Pleasure Cities expressly to welcome him. The aeronautic authorities, whose defection had played a part in the overthrow of the Council only second to Graham's, were very prominent, and so, too, was the Wind-Vane Control. Amongst others there were several of the more prominent officers of the Food Department; the controller of the European Piggeries had a particularly melancholy and interesting countenance and a daintily cynical manner. A bishop in full canonicals passed athwart Graham's vision, conversing with a gentleman dressed exactly like the traditional Chaucer, including even the laurel wreath.

"Who is that?" he asked almost involuntarily.

"The Bishop of London," said Lincoln.

"No—the other, I mean."

"Poet Laureate."

"You still—?"

"He doesn't make poetry, of course. He's a cousin of Wotton—one of the Councillors. But he's one of the Red Rose Royalists—a delightful club —and they keep up the tradition of these things."

"Asano told me there was a King."

"The King doesn't belong. They had to expel him. It's the Stuart blood, I suppose; but really—"

"Too much?"

"Far too much."

Graham did not quite follow all this, but it seemed part of the general inversion of the new age. He bowed condescendingly to his first introduction. It was evident that subtle distinctions of class prevailed even in this assembly, that only to a small proportion of the guests, to an inner group, did Lincoln consider it appropriate to introduce him. This first introduction was the Master Aeronaut, a man whose sun-tanned face contrasted oddly with the delicate complexions about him. Just at present his critical defection from the Council made him a very important person indeed.

His manner contrasted very favourably, according to Graham's ideas, with the general bearing. He offered a few commonplace remarks, assurances of loyalty and frank inquiries about the Master's health. His manner was breezy, his accent lacked the easy staccato of latter-day English. He made it admirably clear to Graham that he was a bluff "aerial dog"—he used that phrase—that there was no nonsense about him, that he was a thoroughly manly fellow and old-fashioned at that, that he didn't profess to know much, and that what he did not know was not worth knowing. He made a curt bow, ostentatiously free from obsequiousness, and passed.

"I am glad to see that type endures," said Graham.

"Phonographs and kinematographs," said Lincoln, a little spitefully. "He has studied from the life." Graham glanced at the burly form again. It was oddly reminiscent.

"As a matter of fact we bought him," said Lincoln. "Partly. And partly he was afraid of Ostrog. Everything rested with him."

He turned sharply to introduce the Surveyor-General of the Public Schools. This person was a willowy figure in a blue-grey academic gown, he beamed down upon Graham through pince-nez of a Victorian pattern, and illustrated his remarks by gestures of a beautifully manicured hand. Graham was immediately interested in this gentleman's functions, and asked him a number of singularly direct questions. The Surveyor-General seemed quietly amused at the Master's fundamental bluntness. He was a little vague as to the monopoly of education his Company possessed; it was done by contract with the syndicate that ran the numerous London Municipalities, but he waxed enthusiastic over educational progress since the Victorian times. "We have conquered Cram," he said, "completely conquered Cram—there is not an examination left in the world. Aren't you glad?"

"How do you get the work done?" asked Graham.

"We make it attractive—as attractive as possible. And if it does not attract then—we let it go. We cover an immense field."

He proceeded to details, and they had a lengthy conversation. Graham learnt that University Extension still existed in a modified form. "There is a certain type of girl, for example," said the Surveyor-General, dilating with a sense of his usefulness, "with a perfect passion for severe studies— when they are not too difficult you know. We cater for them by the thousand. At this moment," he said with a Napoleonic touch, "nearly five hundred phonographs are lecturing in different parts of London on the influence exercised by Plato and Swift on the love affairs of Shelley, Hazlitt, and Burns. And afterwards they write essays on the lectures, and the names in order of merit are put in conspicuous places. You see how your little germ has grown? The illiterate middle-class of your days has quite passed away."

"About the public elementary schools," said Graham. "Do you control them?"

The Surveyor-General did, "entirely." Now, Graham, in his later democratic days, had taken a keen interest in these and his questioning quickened. Certain casual phrases that had fallen from the old man with whom he had talked in the darkness recurred to him. The Surveyor-General, in effect, endorsed the old man's words. "We try and make the elementary schools very pleasant for the little children. They will have to work so soon. Just a few simple principles—obedience—industry."

"You teach them very little?"

"Why should we? It only leads to trouble and discontent. We amuse them. Even as it is—there are troubles—agitations. Where the labourers get the ideas, one cannot tell. They tell one another. There are socialistic dreams—anarchy even! Agitators *will* get to work among them. I take it— I have always taken it—that my foremost duty is to fight against popular discontent. Why should people be made unhappy?"

"I wonder," said Graham thoughtfully. "But there are a great many things I want to know."

Lincoln, who had stood watching Graham's face throughout the conversation, intervened. "There are others," he said in an undertone.

The Surveyor-General of schools gesticulated himself away. "Perhaps," said Lincoln, intercepting a casual glance, "you would like to know some of these ladies?"

The daughter of the Manager of the Piggeries was a particularly charming little person with red hair and animated blue eyes. Lincoln left him awhile to converse with her, and she displayed herself as quite an enthusiast for the "dear old days," as she called them, that had seen the beginning of his trance. As she talked she smiled, and her eyes smiled in a manner that demanded reciprocity.

"I have tried," she said, "countless times—to imagine those old romantic days. And to you—they are memories. How strange and crowded the world must seem to you! I have seen photographs and pictures of the past, the little isolated houses built of bricks made out of burnt mud and all black with soot from your fires, the railway bridges, the simple advertisements, the solemn savage Puritanical men in strange black coats and those tall hats of theirs, iron railway trains on iron bridges overhead, horses and cattle, and even dogs running half wild about the streets. And suddenly, you have come into this!"

"Into this," said Graham.

"Out of your life—out of all that was familiar."

"The old life was not a happy one," said Graham. "I do not regret that."

She looked at him quickly. There was a brief pause. She sighed encouragingly. "No?"

"No," said Graham. "It was a little life—and unmeaning. But this—We thought the world complex and crowded and civilised enough. Yet I see—although in this world I am barely four days old—looking back on my own time, that it was a queer, barbaric time—the mere beginning of this new order. The mere beginning of this new order. You will find it hard to understand how little I know."

"You may ask me what you like," she said, smiling at him.

"Then tell me who these people are. I'm still very much in the dark about them. It's puzzling. Are there any Generals?"

"Men in hats and feathers?"

"Of course not. No. I suppose they are the men who control the great public businesses. Who is that distinguished looking man?"

"That? He's a most important officer. That is Morden. He is managing director of the Antibilious Pill Department. I have heard that his workers sometimes turn out a myriad myriad pills a day in the twenty-four hours. Fancy a myriad myriad!"

"A myriad myriad. No wonder he looks proud," said Graham. "Pills! What a wonderful time it is! That man in purple?"

"He is not quite one of the inner circle, you know. But we like him. He is really clever and very amusing. He is one of the heads of the Medical Faculty of our London University. All medical men, you know, wear that purple. But, of course, people who are paid by fees for *doing* something—" She smiled away the social pretensions of all such people.

"Are any of your great artists or authors here?"

"No authors. They are mostly such queer people—and so preoccupied about themselves. And they quarrel so dreadfully! They will fight, some of them, for precedence on staircases! Dreadful, isn't it? But I think Wraysbury, the fashionable capillotomist, is here. From Capri."

"Capillotomist," said Graham. "Ah! I remember. An artist! Why not?"

"We have to cultivate him," she said apologetically. "Our heads are in his hands." She smiled.

Graham hesitated at the invited compliment, but his glance was expressive. "Have the arts grown with the rest of civilised things?" he said. "Who are your great painters?"

She looked at him doubtfully. Then laughed. "For a moment," she said, "I thought you meant—" She laughed again. "You mean, of course, those good men you used to think so much of because they could cover great spaces of canvas with oil-colours? Great oblongs. And people used to put the things in gilt frames and hang them up in rows in their square rooms. We haven't any. People grew tired of that sort of thing."

"But what did you think I meant?"

She put a finger significantly on a cheek whose glow was above suspicion, and smiled and looked very arch and pretty and inviting. "And here," and she indicated her eyelid.

Graham had an adventurous moment. Then a grotesque memory of a picture he had somewhere seen of Uncle Toby and the widow flashed across his mind. An archaic shame came upon him. He became acutely aware that he was visible to a great number of interested people. "I see," he remarked inadequately. He turned awkwardly away from her fascinating facility. He looked about him to meet a number of eyes that immediately occupied themselves with other things. Possibly he coloured a little. "Who is that talking with the lady in saffron?" he asked, avoiding her eyes.

The person in question he learnt was one of the great organisers of the American theatres just fresh from a gigantic production at Mexico. His face reminded Graham of a bust of Caligula. Another striking looking man was the Black Labour Master. The phrase at the time made no deep impression, but afterwards it recurred;—the Black Labour Master? The little lady in no degree embarrassed, pointed out to him a charming little woman as one of the subsidiary wives of the Anglican Bishop of London. She added encomiums on the episcopal courage—hitherto there had been a rule of clerical monogamy—"neither a natural nor an expedient condition of things. Why should the natural development of the affections be dwarfed and restricted because a man is a priest?"

"And, by the bye," she added, "are you an Anglican?" Graham was on the verge of hesitating inquiries about the status of a "subsidiary wife," apparently an euphemistic phrase, when Lincoln's return broke off this very suggestive and interesting conversation. They crossed the aisle to where a tall man in crimson, and two charming persons in Burmese costume (as it seemed to him) awaited him diffidently. From their civilities he passed to other presentations.

In a little while his multitudinous impressions began to organise themselves into a general effect. At first the glitter of the gathering had raised all the democrat in Graham; he had felt hostile and satirical. But it is not in human nature to resist an atmosphere of courteous regard. Soon the music, the light, the play of colours, the shining arms and shoulders about him, the touch of hands, the transient interest of smiling faces, the frothing sound of skilfully modulated voices, the atmosphere of compliment, interest and respect, had woven together into a fabric of indisputable pleasure. Graham for a time forgot his spacious resolutions. He gave way insensibly to the intoxication of the position that was conceded him, his manner became more convincingly regal, his feet walked assuredly, the black robe fell with a bolder fold and pride ennobled his voice. After all, this was a brilliant interesting world.

He looked up and saw passing across a bridge of porcelain and looking down upon him, a face that was almost immediately hidden, the face of the girl he had seen overnight in the little room beyond the theatre after his escape from the Council. And she was watching him.

For the moment he did not remember when he had seen her, and then came a vague memory of the stirring emotions of their first encounter. But the dancing web of melody about him kept the air of that great marching song from his memory.

The lady to whom he talked repeated her remark, and Graham recalled himself to the quasi-regal flirtation upon which he was engaged.

Yet, unaccountably, a vague restlessness, a feeling that grew to dissatisfaction, came into his mind. He was troubled as if by some half-forgotten duty, by the sense of things important slipping from him amidst this light and brilliance. The attraction that these ladies who crowded about him were beginning to exercise ceased. He no longer gave vague and clumsy responses to the subtly amorous advances that he was now assured were being made to him, and his eyes wandered for another sight of the girl of the first revolt.

Where, precisely, had he seen her?...

Graham was in one of the upper galleries in conversation with a bright-eyed lady on the subject of Eadhamite—the subject was his choice and not hers. He had interrupted her warm assurances of personal devotion with a matter-of-fact inquiry. He found her, as he had already found several other latter-day women that night, less well informed than charming. Suddenly, struggling against the eddying drift of nearer melody, the song of the Revolt, the great song he had heard in the Hall, hoarse and massive, came beating down to him.

Ah! Now he remembered!

He glanced up startled, and perceived above him an *oeil-de-boeuf* through which this song had come, and beyond, the upper courses of cable, the blue haze, and the pendant fabric of the lights of the public ways. He heard the song break into a tumult of voices and cease. He perceived quite clearly the drone and tumult of the moving platforms and a murmur of many people. He had a vague persuasion that he could not account for, a sort of instinctive feeling that outside in the ways a huge crowd must be watching this place in which their Master amused himself.

Though the song had stopped so abruptly, though the special music of this gathering reasserted itself, the *motif* of the marching song, once it had begun, lingered in his mind.

The bright-eyed lady was still struggling with the mysteries of Eadhamite when he perceived the girl he had seen in the theatre again. She was coming now along the gallery towards him; he saw her first before she saw him. She was dressed in a faintly luminous grey, her dark hair about her brows was like a cloud, and as he saw her the cold light from the circular opening into the ways fell upon her downcast face.

The lady in trouble about the Eadhamite saw the change in his expression, and grasped her opportunity to escape. "Would you care to know that girl, Sire?" she asked boldly. "She is Helen Wotton—a niece of Ostrog's. She knows a great many serious things. She is one of the most serious persons alive. I am sure you will like her."

In another moment Graham was talking to the girl, and the bright-eyed lady had fluttered away.

"I remember you quite well," said Graham. "You were in that little room. When all the people were singing and beating time with their feet. Before I walked across the Hall."

Her momentary embarrassment passed. She looked up at him, and her face was steady. "It was wonderful," she said, hesitated, and spoke with a sudden effort. "All those people would have died for you, Sire. Countless people did die for you that night."

Her face glowed. She glanced swiftly aside to see that no other heard her words.

Lincoln appeared some way off along the gallery, making his way through the press towards them. She saw him and turned to Graham strangely eager, with a swift change to confidence and intimacy. "Sire," she said quickly, "I cannot tell you now and here. But the common people are very unhappy; they are oppressed—they are misgoverned. Do not forget the people, who faced death—death that you might live."

"I know nothing—" began Graham.

"I cannot tell you now."

Lincoln's face appeared close to them. He bowed an apology to the girl.

"You find the new world amusing, Sire?" asked Lincoln, with smiling deference, and indicating the space and splendour of the gathering by one comprehensive gesture. "At any rate, you find it changed."

"Yes," said Graham, "changed. And yet, after all, not so greatly changed."

"Wait till you are in the air," said Lincoln. "The wind has fallen; even now an aeroplane awaits you."

The girl's attitude awaited dismissal.

Graham glanced at her face, was on the verge of a question, found a warning in her expression, bowed to her and turned to accompany Lincoln.

16

THE MONOPLANE

THE FLYING STAGES OF LONDON WERE COLLECTED TOGETHER IN AN irregular crescent on the southern side of the river. They formed three groups of two each and retained the names of ancient suburban hills or villages. They were named in order, Roehampton, Wimbledon Park, Streatham, Norwood, Blackheath, and Shooter's Hill. They were uniform structures rising high above the general roof surfaces. Each was about four thousand yards long and a thousand broad, and constructed of the compound of aluminium and iron that had replaced iron in architecture. Their higher tiers formed an openwork of girders through which lifts and staircases ascended. The upper surface was a uniform expanse, with portions—the starting carriers—that could be raised and were then able to run on very slightly inclined rails to the end of the fabric.

Graham went to the flying stages by the public ways. He was accompanied by Asano, his Japanese attendant. Lincoln was called away by Ostrog, who was busy with his administrative concerns. A strong guard of the Wind-Vane police awaited the Master outside the Wind-Vane Offices, and they cleared a space for him on the upper moving platform. His passage to the flying stages was unexpected, nevertheless a considerable crowd gathered and followed him to his destination. As he went along, he could hear the people shouting his name, and saw numberless men and women and children in blue come swarming up the staircases in the central path, gesticulating and shouting. He could not hear what they shouted. He was struck again by the evident existence of a vulgar dialect among the poor of the city. When at last he descended, his guards were immediately surrounded by a dense excited crowd. Afterwards it occurred to him that some had attempted to reach him with petitions. His guards cleared a passage for him with difficulty.

He found a monoplane in charge of an aeronaut awaiting him on the westward stage. Seen close this mechanism was no longer small. As it lay on its launching carrier upon the wide expanse of the flying stage, its aluminium body skeleton was as big as the hull of a twenty-ton yacht. Its lateral supporting sails braced and stayed with metal nerves almost like the nerves of a bee's wing, and made of some sort of glassy artificial membrane, cast their shadow over many hundreds of square yards. The chairs for the engineer and his passenger hung free to swing by a complex tackle, within the protecting ribs of the frame and well abaft the middle. The passenger's chair was protected by a wind-guard and guarded about with metallic rods carrying air cushions. It could, if desired, be completely closed in, but Graham was anxious for novel experiences, and desired that it should be left open. The aeronaut sat behind a glass that sheltered his face. The passenger could secure himself firmly in his seat, and this was almost unavoidable on landing, or he could move along by means of a little rail and rod to a locker at the stem of the machine, where his personal luggage, his wraps and restoratives were placed, and which also with the seats, served as a makeweight to the parts of the central engine that projected to the propeller at the stern.

The flying stage about him was empty save for Asano and their suite of attendants. Directed by the aeronaut he placed himself in his seat. Asano stepped through the bars of the hull, and stood below on the stage waving his hand. He seemed to slide along the stage to the right and vanish.

The engine was humming loudly, the propeller spinning, and for a second the stage and the buildings beyond were gliding swiftly and horizontally past Graham's eye; then these things seemed to tilt up abruptly. He gripped the little rods on either side of him instinctively. He felt himself moving upward, heard the air whistle over the top of the windscreen. The propeller screw moved round with powerful rhythmic impulses—one, two, three, pause; one, two, three—which the engineer controlled very delicately. The machine began a quivering vibration that continued throughout the flight, and the roof areas seemed running away to starboard very quickly and growing rapidly smaller. He looked from the face of the engineer through the ribs of the machine. Looking sideways, there was nothing very startling in what he saw—a rapid funicular railway might have given the same sensations. He recognised the Council House and the Highgate Ridge. And then he looked straight down between his feet.

Physical terror possessed him, a passionate sense of insecurity. He held tight. For a second or so he could not lift his eyes. Some hundred feet or more sheer below him was one of the big wind vanes of south-west London, and beyond it the southernmost flying stage crowded with little black dots. These things seemed to be falling away from him. For a second he had an impulse to pursue the earth. He set his teeth, he lifted his eyes by a muscular effort, and the moment of panic passed.

He remained for a space with his teeth set hard, his eyes staring into the sky. Throb, throb, throb—beat, went the engine; throb, throb, throb —beat. He gripped his bars tightly, glanced at the aeronaut, and saw a smile upon his sun-tanned face. He smiled in return—perhaps a little arti- ficially. "A little strange at first," he shouted before he recalled his dignity. But he dared not look down again for some time. He stared over the aero- naut's head to where a rim of vague blue horizon crept up the sky. For a little while he could not banish the thought of possible accidents from his mind. Throb, throb, throb—beat; suppose some trivial screw went wrong in that supporting engine! Suppose—! He made a grim effort to dismiss all such suppositions. After a while they did at least abandon the foreground of his thoughts. And up he went steadily, higher and higher into the clear air.

Once the mental shock of moving unsupported through the air was over, his sensations ceased to be unpleasant, became very speedily plea- surable. He had been warned of air sickness. But he found the pulsating movement of the monoplane as it drove up the faint south-west breeze was very little in excess of the pitching of a boat head on to broad rollers in a moderate gale, and he was constitutionally a good sailor. And the keenness of the more rarefied air into which they ascended produced a sense of lightness and exhilaration. He looked up and saw the blue sky above fretted with cirrus clouds. His eye came cautiously down through the ribs and bars to a shining flight of white birds that hung in the lower sky. For a space he watched these. Then going lower and less apprehensively, he saw the slender figure of the Wind-Vane Keeper's crow's nest shining golden in the sunlight and growing smaller every moment. As his eye fell with more confidence now, there came a blue line of hills, and then London, already to leeward, an intricate space of roofing. Its near edge came sharp and clear, and banished his last apprehensions in a shock of surprise. For the boundary of London was like a wall, like a cliff, a steep fall of three or four hundred feet, a frontage broken only by terraces here and there, a complex decorative façade.

That gradual passage of town into country through an extensive sponge of suburbs, which was so characteristic a feature of the great cities of the nineteenth century, existed no longer. Nothing remained of it here but a waste of ruins, variegated and dense with thickets of the heterogeneous growths that had once adorned the gardens of the belt, interspersed among levelled brown patches of sown ground, and verdant stretches of winter greens. The latter even spread among the vestiges of houses. But for the most part the reefs and skerries of ruins, the wreckage of suburban villas, stood among their streets and roads, queer islands amidst the levelled expanses of green and brown, abandoned indeed by the inhabitants years since, but too substantial, it seemed, to be cleared out of the way of the wholesale horticultural mechanisms of the time.

The vegetation of this waste undulated and frothed amidst the countless cells of crumbling house walls, and broke along the foot of the city wall in a surf of bramble and holly and ivy and teazle and tall grasses. Here and there gaudy pleasure palaces towered amidst the puny remains of Victorian times, and cable ways slanted to them from the city. That winter day they seemed deserted. Deserted, too, were the artificial gardens among the ruins. The city limits were indeed as sharply defined as in the ancient days when the gates were shut at nightfall and the robber foeman prowled to the very walls. A huge semi-circular throat poured out a vigorous traffic upon the Eadhamite Bath Road. So the first prospect of the world beyond the city flashed on Graham, and dwindled. And when at last he could look vertically downward again, he saw below him the vegetable fields of the Thames valley—innumerable minute oblongs of ruddy brown, intersected by shining threads, the sewage ditches.

His exhilaration increased rapidly, became a sort of intoxication. He found himself drawing deep breaths of air, laughing aloud, desiring to shout. After a time that desire became too strong for him, and he shouted. They curved about towards the south. They drove with a slight list to leeward, and with a slow alternation of movement, first a short, sharp ascent and then a long downward glide that was very swift and pleasing. During these downward glides the propeller was inactive altogether. These ascents gave Graham a glorious sense of successful effort; the descents through the rarefied air were beyond all experience. He wanted never to leave the upper air again.

For a time he was intent upon the landscape that ran swiftly northward beneath him. Its minute, clear detail pleased him exceedingly. He was impressed by the ruin of the houses that had once dotted the country, by the vast treeless expanse of country from which all farms and villages had gone, save for crumbling ruins. He had known the thing was so, but seeing it so was an altogether different matter. He tried to make out familiar places within the hollow basin of the world below, but at first he could distinguish no data now that the Thames valley was left behind. Soon, however, they were driving over a sharp chalk hill that he recognised as the Guildford Hog's Back, because of the familiar outline of the gorge at its eastward end, and because of the ruins of the town that rose steeply on either lip of this gorge. And from that he made out other points, Leith Hill, the sandy wastes of Aldershot, and so forth. Save where the broad Eadhamite Portsmouth Road, thickly dotted with rushing shapes, followed the course of the old railway, the gorge of the Wey was choked with thickets.

The whole expanse of the Downs escarpment, so far as the grey haze permitted him to see, was set with wind-wheels to which the largest of the city was but a younger brother. They stirred with a stately motion before the south-west wind. And here and there were patches dotted with the sheep of the British Food Trust, and here and there a mounted shepherd made a spot of black. Then rushing under the stern of the monoplane came the Wealden Heights, the line of Hindhead, Pitch Hill, and Leith Hill, with a second row of wind-wheels that seemed striving to rob the downland whirlers of their share of breeze. The purple heather was speckled with yellow gorse, and on the further side a drove of black oxen stampeded before a couple of mounted men. Swiftly these swept behind, and dwindled and lost colour, and became scarce moving specks that were swallowed up in haze.

And when these had vanished in the distance Graham heard a peewit wailing close at hand. He perceived he was now above the South Downs, and staring over his shoulder saw the battlements of Portsmouth Landing Stage towering over the ridge of Portsdown Hill. In another moment there came into sight a spread of shipping like floating cities, the little white cliffs of the Needles dwarfed and sunlit, and the grey and glittering waters of the narrow sea. They seemed to leap the Solent in a moment, and in a few seconds the Isle of Wight was running past, and then beneath him spread a wider and wider extent of sea, here purple with the shadow of a cloud, here grey, here a burnished mirror, and here a spread of cloudy greenish blue. The Isle of Wight grew smaller and smaller. In a few more minutes a strip of grey haze detached itself from other strips that were clouds, descended out of the sky and became a coast-line—sunlit and pleasant—the coast of northern France. It rose, it took colour, became definite and detailed, and the counterpart of the Downland of England was speeding by below.

In a little time, as it seemed, Paris came above the horizon, and hung there for a space, and sank out of sight again as the monoplane circled about to the north. But he perceived the Eiffel Tower still standing, and beside it a huge dome surmounted by a pin-point Colossus. And he perceived, too, though he did not understand it at the time, a slanting drift of smoke. The aeronaut said something about "trouble in the under-ways," that Graham did not heed. But he marked the minarets and towers and slender masses that streamed skyward above the city Wind-Vanes, and knew that in the matter of grace at least Paris still kept in front of her larger rival. And even as he looked a pale blue shape ascended very swiftly from the city like a dead leaf driving up before a gale. It curved round and soared towards them, growing rapidly larger and larger. The aeronaut was saying something. "What?" said Graham, loth to take his eyes from this. "London aeroplane, Sire," bawled the aeronaut, pointing.

They rose and curved about northward as it drew nearer. Nearer it came and nearer, larger and larger. The throb, throb, throb—beat, of the monoplane's flight, that had seemed so potent, and so swift, suddenly appeared slow by comparison with this tremendous rush. How great the monster seemed, how swift and steady! It passed quite closely beneath them, driving along silently, a vast spread of wire-netted translucent wings, a thing alive. Graham had a momentary glimpse of the rows and rows of wrapped-up passengers, slung in their little cradles behind wind-screens, of a white-clothed engineer crawling against the gale along a ladder way, of spouting engines beating together, of the whirling wind screw, and of a wide waste of wing. He exulted in the sight. And in an instant the thing had passed.

It rose slightly and their own little wings swayed in the rush of its flight. It fell and grew smaller. Scarcely had they moved, as it seemed, before it was again only a flat blue thing that dwindled in the sky. This was the aeroplane that went to and fro between London and Paris. In fair weather and in peaceful times it came and went four times a day.

They beat across the Channel, slowly as it seemed now to Graham's enlarged ideas, and Beachy Head rose greyly to the left of them.

"Land," called the aeronaut, his voice small against the whistling of the air over the wind-screen.

"Not yet," bawled Graham, laughing. "Not land yet. I want to learn more of this machine."

"I meant—" said the aeronaut.

"I want to learn more of this machine," repeated Graham.

"I'm coming to you," he said, and had flung himself free of his chair and taken a step along the guarded rail between them. He stopped for a moment, and his colour changed and his hands tightened. Another step and he was clinging close to the aeronaut. He felt a weight on his shoulder, the pressure of the air. His hat was a whirling speck behind. The wind came in gusts over his wind-screen and blew his hair in streamers past his cheek. The aeronaut made some hasty adjustments for the shifting of the centres of gravity and pressure.

"I want to have these things explained," said Graham. "What do you do when you move that engine forward?"

The aeronaut hesitated. Then he answered, "They are complex, Sire."

"I don't mind," shouted Graham. "I don't mind."

There was a moment's pause. "Aeronautics is the secret—the privilege—"

"I know. But I'm the Master, and I mean to know." He laughed, full of this novel realisation of power that was his gift from the upper air.

The monoplane curved about, and the keen fresh wind cut across Graham's face and his garment lugged at his body as the stem pointed round to the west. The two men looked into each other's eyes.

"Sire, there are rules—"

"Not where I am concerned," said Graham, "You seem to forget."

The aeronaut scrutinised his face "No," he said. "I do not forget, Sire. But in all the earth—no man who is not a sworn aeronaut—has ever a chance. They come as passengers—"

"I have heard something of the sort. But I'm not going to argue these points. Do you know why I have slept two hundred years? To fly!"

"Sire," said the aeronaut, "the rules—if I break the rules—"

Graham waved the penalties aside.

"Then if you will watch me—"

"No," said Graham, swaying and gripping tight as the machine lifted its nose again for an ascent. "That's not my game. I want to do it myself. Do it myself if I smash for it! No! I will. See I am going to clamber by this—to come and share your seat. Steady! I mean to fly of my own accord if I smash at the end of it. I will have something to pay for my sleep. Of all other things—. In my past it was my dream to fly. Now—keep your balance."

"A dozen spies are watching me, Sire!"

Graham's temper was at an end. Perhaps he chose it should be. He swore. He swung himself round the intervening mass of levers and the monoplane swayed.

"Am I Master of the earth?" he said. "Or is your Society? Now. Take your hands off those levers, and hold my wrists. Yes—so. And now, how do we turn her nose down to the glide?"

"Sire," said the aeronaut.

"What is it?"

"You will protect me?"

"Lord! Yes! If I have to burn London. Now!"

And with that promise Graham bought his first lesson in aerial navigation. "It's clearly to your advantage, this journey," he said with a loud laugh —for the air was like strong wine—"to teach me quickly and well. Do I pull this? Ah! So! Hullo!"

"Back, Sire! Back!"

"Back—right. One—two—three—good God! Ah! Up she goes! But this is living!"

And now the machine began to dance the strangest figures in the air. Now it would sweep round a spiral of scarcely a hundred yards diameter, now rush up into the air and swoop down again, steeply, swiftly, falling like a hawk, to recover in a rushing loop that swept it high again. In one of these descents it seemed driving straight at the drifting park of balloons in the southeast, and only curved about and cleared them by a sudden recovery of dexterity. The extraordinary swiftness and smoothness of the motion, the extraordinary effect of the rarefied air upon his constitution, threw Graham into a careless fury.

But at last a queer incident came to sober him, to send him flying down once more to the crowded life below with all its dark insoluble riddles. As he swooped, came a tap and something flying past, and a drop like a drop of rain. Then as he went on down he saw something like a white rag whirling down in his wake. "What was that?" he asked. "I did not see."

The aeronaut glanced, and then clutched at the lever to recover, for they were sweeping down. When the monoplane was rising again he drew a deep breath and replied, "That," and he indicated the white thing still fluttering down, "was a swan."

"I never saw it," said Graham.

The aeronaut made no answer, and Graham saw little drops upon his forehead.

They drove horizontally while Graham clambered back to the passenger's place out of the lash of the wind. And then came a swift rush down, with the wind-screw whirling to check their fall, and the flying stage growing broad and dark before them. The sun, sinking over the chalk hills in the west, fell with them, and left the sky a blaze of gold.

Soon men could be seen as little specks. He heard a noise coming up to meet him, a noise like the sound of waves upon a pebbly beach, and saw that the roofs about the flying stage were dense with his people rejoicing over his safe return. A black mass was crushed together under the stage, a darkness stippled with innumerable faces, and quivering with the minute oscillation of waved white handkerchiefs and waving hands.

17

THREE DAYS

L INCOLN AWAITED G RAHAM IN AN APARTMENT BENEATH THE FLYING stages. He seemed curious to learn all that had happened, pleased to hear of the extraordinary delight and interest which Graham took in flying. Graham was in a mood of enthusiasm. "I must learn to fly," he cried. "I must master that. I pity all poor souls who have died without this opportunity. The sweet swift air! It is the most wonderful experience in the world."

"You will find our new times full of wonderful experiences," said Lincoln. "I do not know what you will care to do now. We have music that may seem novel."

"For the present," said Graham, "flying holds me. Let me learn more of that. Your aeronaut was saying there is some trades union objection to one's learning."

"There is, I believe," said Lincoln. "But for you—! If you would like to occupy yourself with that, we can make you a sworn aeronaut to-morrow."

Graham expressed his wishes vividly and talked of his sensations for a while. "And as for affairs," he asked abruptly. "How are things going on?"

Lincoln waved affairs aside. "Ostrog will tell you that to-morrow," he said. "Everything is settling down. The Revolution accomplishes itself all over the world. Friction is inevitable here and there, of course; but your rule is assured. You may rest secure with things in Ostrog's hands."

"Would it be possible for me to be made a sworn aeronaut, as you call it, forthwith—before I sleep?" said Graham, pacing. "Then I could be at it the very first thing to-morrow again...."

"It would be possible," said Lincoln thoughtfully. "Quite possible. Indeed, it shall be done." He laughed. "I came prepared to suggest amusements, but you have found one for yourself. I will telephone to the aeronautical offices from here and we will return to your apartments in the Wind-Vane Control. By the time you have dined the aeronauts will be able to come. You don't think that after you have dined you might prefer—?" He paused.

"Yes," said Graham.

"We had prepared a show of dancers—they have been brought from the Capri theatre."

"I hate ballets," said Graham, shortly. "Always did. That other—That's not what I want to see. We had dancers in the old days. For the matter of that, they had them in ancient Egypt. But flying—"

"True," said Lincoln. "Though our dancers—"

"They can afford to wait," said Graham; "they can afford to wait. I know. I'm not a Latin. There's questions I want to ask some expert—about your machinery. I'm keen. I want no distractions."

"You have the world to choose from," said Lincoln; "whatever you want is yours."

Asano appeared, and under the escort of a strong guard they returned through the city streets to Graham's apartments. Far larger crowds had assembled to witness his return than his departure had gathered, and the shouts and cheering of these masses of people sometimes drowned Lincoln's answers to the endless questions Graham's aerial journey had suggested. At first Graham had acknowledged the cheering and cries of the crowd by bows and gestures, but Lincoln warned him that such a recognition would be considered incorrect behaviour. Graham, already a little wearied by rhythmic civilities, ignored his subjects for the remainder of his public progress.

Directly they arrived at his apartments and Asano departed in search of kinematographic renderings of machinery in motion, and Lincoln dispatched Graham's commands for models of machines and small machines to illustrate the various mechanical advances of the last two centuries. The little group of appliances for telegraphic communication attracted the Master so strongly that his delightfully prepared dinner, served by a number of charmingly dexterous girls, waited for a space. The habit of smoking had almost ceased from the face of the earth, but when he expressed a wish for that indulgence, enquiries were made and some excellent cigars were discovered in Florida, and sent to him by pneumatic dispatch while the dinner was still in progress. Afterwards came the aeronauts, and a feast of ingenious wonders in the hands of a latter-day engineer. For the time, at any rate, the neat dexterity of counting and numbering machines, building machines, spinning engines, patent doorways, explosive motors, grain and water elevators, slaughter-house machines and harvesting appliances, was more fascinating to Graham than any bayadere. "We were savages," was his refrain, "we were savages. We were in the stone age—compared with this.... And what else have you?"

There came also practical psychologists with some very interesting developments in the art of hypnotism. The names of Milne Bramwell, Fechner, Liebault, William James, Myers and Gurney, he found, bore a value now that would have astonished their contemporaries. Several practical applications of psychology were now in general use; it had largely superseded drugs, antiseptics and anaesthetics in medicine; was employed by almost all who had any need of mental concentration. A real enlargement of human faculty seemed to have been effected in this direction. The feats of "calculating boys," the wonders, as Graham had been wont to regard them, of mesmerisers, were now within the range of anyone who could afford the services of a skilled hypnotist. Long ago the old examination methods in education had been destroyed by these expedients. Instead of years of study, candidates had substituted a few weeks of trances, and during the trances expert coaches had simply to repeat all the points necessary for adequate answering, adding a suggestion of the post-hypnotic recollection of these points. In process mathematics particularly, this aid had been of singular service, and it was now invariably invoked by such players of chess and games of manual dexterity as were still to be found. In fact, all operations conducted under finite rules, of a quasi-mechanical sort that is, were now systematically relieved from the wanderings of imagination and emotion, and brought to an unexampled pitch of accuracy. Little children of the labouring classes, so soon as they were of sufficient age to be hypnotised, were thus converted into beautifully punctual and trustworthy machine minders, and released forthwith from the long, long thoughts of youth. Aeronautical pupils, who gave way to giddiness, could be relieved from their imaginary terrors. In every street were hypnotists ready to print permanent memories upon the mind. If anyone desired to remember a name, a series of numbers, a song or a speech, it could be done by this method, and conversely memories could be effaced, habits removed, and desires eradicated—a sort of psychic surgery was, in fact, in general use. Indignities, humbling experiences, were thus forgotten, widows would obliterate their previous husbands, angry lovers release themselves from their slavery. To graft desires, however, was still impossible, and the facts of thought transference were yet unsystematised. The psychologists illustrated their expositions with some astounding experiments in mnemonics made through the agency of a troupe of pale-faced children in blue.

Graham, like most of the people of his former time, distrusted the hypnotist, or he might then and there have eased his mind of many painful preoccupations. But in spite of Lincoln's assurances he held to the old theory that to be hypnotised was in some way the surrender of his personality, the abdication of his will. At the banquet of wonderful experiences that was beginning, he wanted very keenly to remain absolutely himself.

The next day, and another day, and yet another day passed in such interests as these. Each day Graham spent many hours in the glorious entertainment of flying. On the third, he soared across middle France, and within sight of the snow-clad Alps. These vigorous exercises gave him restful sleep; he recovered almost wholly from the spiritless anaemia of his first awakening. And whenever he was not in the air, and awake, Lincoln was assiduous in the cause of his amusement; all that was novel and curious in contemporary invention was brought to him, until at last his appetite for novelty was well-nigh glutted. One might fill a dozen inconsecutive volumes with the strange things they exhibited. Each afternoon he held his court for an hour or so. He found his interest in his contemporaries becoming personal and intimate. At first he had been alert chiefly for unfamiliarity and peculiarity; any foppishness in their dress, any discordance with his preconceptions of nobility in their status and manners had jarred upon him, and it was remarkable to him how soon that strangeness and the faint hostility that arose from it, disappeared; how soon he came to appreciate the true perspective of his position, and see the old Victorian days remote and quaint. He found himself particularly amused by the red-haired daughter of the Manager of the European Piggeries. On the second day after dinner he made the acquaintance of a latter-day dancing girl, and found her an astonishing artist. And after that, more hypnotic wonders. On the third day Lincoln was moved to suggest that the Master should repair to a Pleasure City, but this Graham declined, nor would he accept the services of the hypnotists in his aeronautical experiments. The link of locality held him to London; he found a delight in topographical identifications that he would have missed abroad. "Here—or a hundred feet below here," he could say, "I used to eat my midday cutlets during my London University days. Underneath here was Waterloo and the tiresome hunt for confusing trains. Often have I stood waiting down there, bag in hand, and stared up into the sky above the forest of signals, little thinking I should walk some day a hundred yards in the air. And now in that very sky that was once a grey smoke canopy, I circle in a monoplane."

During those three days Graham was so occupied with these distractions that the vast political movements in progress outside his quarters had but a small share of his attention. Those about him told him little. Daily came Ostrog, the Boss, his Grand Vizier, his mayor of the palace, to report in vague terms the steady establishment of his rule; "a little trouble" soon to be settled in this city, "a slight disturbance" in that. The song of the social revolt came to him no more; he never learned that it had been forbidden in the municipal limits; and all the great emotions of the crow's nest slumbered in his mind.

But on the second and third of the three days he found himself, in spite of his interest in the daughter of the Pig Manager, or it may be by reason of the thoughts her conversation suggested, remembering the girl Helen Wotton, who had spoken to him so oddly at the Wind-Vane Keeper's gathering. The impression, she had made was a deep one, albeit the incessant surprise of novel circumstances had kept him from brooding upon it for a space. But now her memory was coming to its own. He wondered what she had meant by those broken half-forgotten sentences; the picture of her eyes and the earnest passion of her face became more vivid as his mechanical interests faded. Her slender beauty came compellingly between him and certain immediate temptations of ignoble passion. But he did not see her again until three full days were past.

18

GRAHAM REMEMBERS

SHE CAME UPON HIM AT LAST IN A LITTLE GALLERY THAT RAN FROM the Wind-Vane Offices toward his state apartments. The gallery was long and narrow, with a series of recesses, each with an arched fenestration that looked upon a court of palms. He came upon her suddenly in one of these recesses. She was seated. She turned her head at the sound of his footsteps and started at the sight of him. Every touch of colour vanished from her face. She rose instantly, made a step toward him as if to address him, and hesitated. He stopped and stood still, expectant. Then he perceived that a nervous tumult silenced her, perceived, too, that she must have sought speech with him to be waiting for him in this place.

He felt a regal impulse to assist her. "I have wanted to see you," he said. "A few days ago you wanted to tell me something—you wanted to tell me of the people. What was it you had to tell me?"

She looked at him with troubled eyes.

"You said the people were unhappy?"

For a moment she was silent still.

"It must have seemed strange to you," she said abruptly.

"It did. And yet—"

"It was an impulse."

"Well?"

"That is all."

She looked at him with a face of hesitation. She spoke with an effort. "You forget," she said, drawing a deep breath.

"What?"

"The people—"

"Do you mean—?"

"You forget the people."

He looked interrogative.

"Yes. I know you are surprised. For you do not understand what you are. You do not know the things that are happening."

"Well?"

"You do not understand."

"Not clearly, perhaps. But—tell me."

She turned to him with sudden resolution. "It is so hard to explain. I have meant to, I have wanted to. And now—I cannot. I am not ready with words. But about you—there is something. It is wonder. Your sleep—your awakening. These things are miracles. To me at least—and to all the common people. You who lived and suffered and died, you who were a common citizen, wake again, live again, to find yourself Master almost of the earth."

"Master of the earth," he said. "So they tell me. But try and imagine how little I know of it."

"Cities—Trusts—the Labour Department—"

"Principalities, powers, dominions—the power and the glory. Yes, I have heard them shout. I know. I am Master. King, if you wish. With Ostrog, the Boss—"

He paused.

She turned upon him and surveyed his face with a curious scrutiny. "Well?"

He smiled. "To take the responsibility."

"That is what we have begun to fear." For a moment she said no more. "No," she said slowly. "*You* will take the responsibility. You will take the responsibility. The people look to you."

She spoke softly. "Listen! For at least half the years of your sleep—in every generation—multitudes of people, in every generation greater multitudes of people, have prayed that you might awake—*prayed.*"

Graham moved to speak and did not.

She hesitated, and a faint colour crept back to her cheek. "Do you know that you have been to myriads—King Arthur, Barbarossa—the King who would come in his own good time and put the world right for them?"

"I suppose the imagination of the people—"

"Have you not heard our proverb, 'When the Sleeper wakes'? While you lay insensible and motionless there—thousands came. Thousands. Every first of the month you lay in state with a white robe upon you and the people filed by you. When I was a little girl I saw you like that, with your face white and calm."

She turned her face from him and looked steadfastly at the painted wall before her. Her voice fell. "When I was a little girl I used to look at your face.... It seemed to me fixed and waiting, like the patience of God.

"That is what we thought of you," she said. "That is how you seemed to us."

She turned shining eyes to him, her voice was clear and strong. "In the city, in the earth, a myriad myriad men and women are waiting to see what you will do, full of strange incredible expectations."

"Yes?"

"Ostrog—no one—can take that responsibility."

Graham looked at her in surprise, at her face lit with emotion. She seemed at first to have spoken with an effort, and to have fired herself by speaking.

"Do you think," she said, "that you who have lived that little life so far away in the past, you who have fallen into and risen out of this miracle of sleep—do you think that the wonder and reverence and hope of half the world has gathered about you only that you may live another little life?... That you may shift the responsibility to any other man?"

"I know how great this kingship of mine is," he said haltingly. "I know how great it seems. But is it real? It is incredible—dreamlike. Is it real, or is it only a great delusion?"

"It is real," she said; "if you dare."

"After all, like all kingship, my kingship is belief. It is an illusion in the minds of men."

"If you dare!" she said.

"But—"

"Countless men," she said, "and while it is in their minds—they will obey."

"But I know nothing. That is what I had in mind. I know nothing. And these others—the Councillors, Ostrog. They are wiser, cooler, they know so much, every detail. And, indeed, what are these miseries of which you speak? What am I to know? Do you mean—"

He stopped blankly.

"I am still hardly more than a girl," she said. "But to me the world seems full of wretchedness. The world has altered since your day, altered very strangely. I have prayed that I might see you and tell you these things. The world has changed. As if a canker had seized it—and robbed life of—everything worth having."

She turned a flushed face upon him, moving suddenly. "Your days were the days of freedom. Yes—I have thought. I have been made to think, for my life—has not been happy. Men are no longer free—no greater, no better than the men of your time. That is not all. This city—is a prison. Every city now is a prison. Mammon grips the key in his hand. Myriads, countless myriads, toil from the cradle to the grave. Is that right? Is that to be—for ever? Yes, far worse than in your time. All about us, beneath us, sorrow and pain. All the shallow delight of such life as you find about you, is separated by just a little from a life of wretchedness beyond any telling. Yes, the poor know it—they know they suffer. These countless multitudes who faced death for you two nights since—! You owe your life to them."

"Yes," said Graham, slowly. "Yes. I owe my life to them."

"You come," she said, "from the days when this new tyranny of the cities was scarcely beginning. It is a tyranny—a tyranny. In your days the feudal war lords had gone, and the new lordship of wealth had still to come. Half the men in the world still lived out upon the free countryside. The cities had still to devour them. I have heard the stories out of the old books—there was nobility! Common men led lives of love and faithfulness then—they did a thousand things. And you—you come from that time."

"It was not—. But never mind. How is it now—?"

"Gain and the Pleasure Cities! Or slavery—unthanked, unhonoured, slavery."

"Slavery!" he said.

"Slavery."

"You don't mean to say that human beings are chattels."

"Worse. That is what I want you to know, what I want you to see. I know you do not know. They will keep things from you, they will take you presently to a Pleasure City. But you have noticed men and women and children in pale blue canvas, with thin yellow faces and dull eyes?"

"Everywhere."

"Speaking a horrible dialect, coarse and weak."

"I have heard it."

"They are the slaves—your slaves. They are the slaves of the Labour Department you own."

"The Labour Department! In some way—that is familiar. Ah! now I remember. I saw it when I was wandering about the city, after the lights returned, great fronts of buildings coloured pale blue. Do you really mean—?"

"Yes. How can I explain it to you? Of course the blue uniform struck you. Nearly a third of our people wear it—more assume it now every day. This Labour Department has grown imperceptibly."

"What *is* this Labour Department?" asked Graham.

"In the old times, how did you manage with starving people?"

"There was the workhouse—which the parishes maintained."

"Workhouse! Yes—there was something. In our history lessons. I remember now. The Labour Department ousted the workhouse. It grew—partly—out of something—you, perhaps, may remember it—an emotional religious organisation called the Salvation Army—that became a business company. In the first place it was almost a charity. To save people from workhouse rigours. There had been a great agitation against the workhouse. Now I come to think of it, it was one of the earliest properties your Trustees acquired. They bought the Salvation Army and reconstructed it as this. The idea in the first place was to organise the labour of starving homeless people."

"Yes."

"Nowadays there are no workhouses, no refuges and charities, nothing but that Department. Its offices are everywhere. That blue is its colour. And any man, woman or child who comes to be hungry and weary and with neither home nor friend nor resort, must go to the Department in the end—or seek some way of death. The Euthanasy is beyond their means—for the poor there is no easy death. And at any hour in the day or night there is food, shelter and a blue uniform for all comers—that is the first condition of the Department's incorporation—and in return for a day's shelter the Department extracts a day's work, and then returns the visitor's proper clothing and sends him or her out again."

"Yes?"

"Perhaps that does not seem so terrible to you. In your time men starved in your streets. That was bad. But they died—*men*. These people in blue—. The proverb runs: 'Blue canvas once and ever.' The Department trades in their labour, and it has taken care to assure itself of the supply. People come to it starving and helpless—they eat and sleep for a night and day, they work for a day, and at the end of the day they go out again. If they have worked well they have a penny or so—enough for a theatre or a cheap dancing place, or a kinematograph story, or a dinner or a bet. They wander about after that is spent. Begging is prevented by the police of the ways. Besides, no one gives. They come back again the next day or the day after—brought back by the same incapacity that brought them first. At last their proper clothing wears out, or their rags get so shabby that they are ashamed. Then they must work for months to get fresh. If they want fresh. A great number of children are born under the Department's care. The mother owes them a month thereafter—the children they cherish and educate until they are fourteen, and they pay two years' service. You may be sure these children are educated for the blue canvas. And so it is the Department works."

"And none are destitute in the city?"

"None. They are either in blue canvas or in prison. We have abolished destitution. It is engraved upon the Department's checks."

"If they will not work?"

"Most people will work at that pitch, and the Department has powers. There are stages of unpleasantness in the work—stoppage of food—and a man or woman who has refused to work once is known by a thumb-marking system in the Department's offices all over the world. Besides, who can leave the city poor? To go to Paris costs two Lions. And for insubordination there are the prisons—dark and miserable—out of sight below. There are prisons now for many things."

"And a third of the people wear this blue canvas?"

"More than a third. Toilers, living without pride or delight or hope, with the stories of Pleasure Cities ringing in their ears, mocking their shameful lives, their privations and hardships. Too poor even for the Euthanasy, the rich man's refuge from life. Dumb, crippled millions, countless millions, all the world about, ignorant of anything but limitations and unsatisfied desires. They are born, they are thwarted and they die. That is the state to which we have come."

For a space Graham sat downcast.

"But there has been a revolution," he said. "All these things will be changed. Ostrog—"

"That is our hope. That is the hope of the world. But Ostrog will not do it. He is a politician. To him it seems things must be like this. He does not mind. He takes it for granted. All the rich, all the influential, all who are happy, come at last to take these miseries for granted. They use the people in their politics, they live in ease by their degradation. But you— you who come from a happier age—it is to you the people look. To you."

He looked at her face. Her eyes were bright with unshed tears. He felt a rush of emotion. For a moment he forgot this city, he forgot the race, and all those vague remote voices, in the immediate humanity of her beauty.

"But what am I to do?" he said with his eyes upon her.

"Rule," she answered, bending towards him and speaking in a low tone. "Rule the world as it has never been ruled, for the good and happiness of men. For you might rule it—you could rule it.

"The people are stirring. All over the world the people are stirring. It wants but a word—but a word from you—to bring them all together. Even the middle sort of people are restless—unhappy.

"They are not telling you the things that are happening. The people will not go back to their drudgery—they refuse to be disarmed. Ostrog has awakened something greater than he dreamt of—he has awakened hopes."

His heart was beating fast. He tried to seem judicial, to weigh considerations.

"They only want their leader," she said.

"And then?"

"You could do what you would;—the world is yours."

He sat, no longer regarding her. Presently he spoke. "The old dreams, and the thing I have dreamt, liberty, happiness. Are they dreams? Could one man—*one man*—?" His voice sank and ceased.

"Not one man, but all men—give them only a leader to speak the desire of their hearts."

He shook his head, and for a time there was silence.

He looked up suddenly, and their eyes met. "I have not your faith," he said, "I have not your youth. I am here with power that mocks me. No— let me speak. I want to do—not right—I have not the strength for that— but something rather right than wrong. It will bring no millennium, but I am resolved now, that I will rule. What you have said has awakened me ... You are right. Ostrog must know his place. And I will learn—.... One thing I promise you. This Labour slavery shall end."

"And you will rule?"

"Yes. Provided—. There is one thing."

"Yes?"

"That you will help me."

"*I*—a girl!"

"Yes. Does it not occur to you I am absolutely alone?"

She started and for an instant her eyes had pity. "Need you ask whether I will help you?" she said.

There came a tense silence, and then the beating of a clock striking the hour. Graham rose.

"Even now," he said, "Ostrog will be waiting." He hesitated, facing her. "When I have asked him certain questions—. There is much I do not know. It may be, that I will go to see with my own eyes the things of which you have spoken. And when I return—?"

"I shall know of your going and coming. I will wait for you here again."

They regarded one another steadfastly, questioningly, and then he turned from her towards the Wind-Vane offices.

19

OSTROG'S POINT OF VIEW

Graham found Ostrog waiting to give a formal account of his day's stewardship. On previous occasions he had passed over this ceremony as speedily as possible, in order to resume his aerial experiences, but now he began to ask quick short questions. He was very anxious to take up his empire forthwith. Ostrog brought flattering reports of the development of affairs abroad. In Paris and Berlin, Graham perceived that he was saying, there had been trouble, not organised resistance indeed, but insubordinate proceedings. "After all these years," said Ostrog, when Graham pressed enquiries; "the Commune has lifted its head again. That is the real nature of the struggle, to be explicit." But order had been restored in these cities. Graham, the more deliberately judicial for the stirring emotions he felt, asked if there had been any fighting. "A little," said Ostrog. "In one quarter only. But the Senegalese division of our African agricultural police—the Consolidated African Companies have a very well-drilled police—was ready, and so were the aeroplanes. We expected a little trouble in the continental cities, and in America. But things are very quiet in America. They are satisfied with the overthrow of the Council. For the time."

"Why should you expect trouble?" asked Graham abruptly.

"There is a lot of discontent—social discontent."

"The Labour Department?"

"You are learning," said Ostrog with a touch of surprise. "Yes. It is chiefly the discontent with the Labour Department. It was that discontent supplied the motive force of this overthrow—that and your awakening."

"Yes?"

Ostrog smiled. He became explicit. "We had to stir up their discontent, we had to revive the old ideals of universal happiness—all men equal—all men happy—no luxury that everyone may not share—ideas that have slumbered for two hundred years. You know that? We had to revive these ideals, impossible as they are—in order to overthrow the Council. And now—"

"Well?"

"Our revolution is accomplished, and the Council is overthrown, and people whom we have stirred up—remain surging. There was scarcely enough fighting.... We made promises, of course. It is extraordinary how violently and rapidly this vague out-of-date humanitarianism has revived and spread. We who sowed the seed even, have been astonished. In Paris, as I say—we have had to call in a little external help."

"And here?"

"There is trouble. Multitudes will not go back to work. There is a general strike. Half the factories are empty and the people are swarming in the ways. They are talking of a Commune. Men in silk and satin have been insulted in the streets. The blue canvas is expecting all sorts of things from you.... Of course there is no need for you to trouble. We are setting the Babble Machines to work with counter suggestions in the cause of law and order. We must keep the grip tight; that is all."

Graham thought. He perceived a way of asserting himself. But he spoke with restraint.

"Even to the pitch of bringing a negro police," he said.

"They are useful," said Ostrog. "They are fine loyal brutes, with no wash of ideas in their heads—such as our rabble has. The Council should have had them as police of the ways, and things might have been different. Of course, there is nothing to fear except rioting and wreckage. You can manage your own wings now, and you can soar away to Capri if there is any smoke or fuss. We have the pull of all the great things; the aeronauts are privileged and rich, the closest trades union in the world, and so are the engineers of the wind vanes. We have the air, and the mastery of the air is the mastery of the earth. No one of any ability is organizing against us. They have no leaders—only the sectional leaders of the secret society we organised before your very opportune awakening. Mere busybodies and sentimentalists they are and bitterly jealous of each other. None of them is man enough for a central figure. The only trouble will be a disorganised upheaval. To be frank—that may happen. But it won't interrupt your aeronautics. The days when the People could make revolutions are past."

"I suppose they are," said Graham. "I suppose they are." He mused. "This world of yours has been full of surprises to me. In the old days we dreamt of a wonderful democratic life, of a time when all men would be equal and happy."

Ostrog looked at him steadfastly. "The day of democracy is past," he said. "Past for ever. That day began with the bowmen of Creçy, it ended when marching infantry, when common men in masses ceased to win the battles of the world, when costly cannon, great ironclads, and strategic railways became the means of power. To-day is the day of wealth. Wealth now is power as it never was power before—it commands earth and sea and sky. All power is for those who can handle wealth. On your behalf.... You must accept facts, and these are facts. The world for the Crowd! The Crowd as Ruler! Even in your days that creed had been tried and condemned. To-day it has only one believer—a multiplex, silly one—the man in the Crowd."

Graham did not answer immediately. He stood lost in sombre preoccupations.

"No," said Ostrog. "The day of the common man is past. On the open countryside one man is as good as another, or nearly as good. The earlier aristocracy had a precarious tenure of strength and audacity. They were tempered—tempered. There were insurrections, duels, riots. The first real aristocracy, the first permanent aristocracy, came in with castles and armour, and vanished before the musket and bow. But this is the second aristocracy. The real one. Those days of gunpowder and democracy were only an eddy in the stream. The common man now is a helpless unit. In these days we have this great machine of the city, and an organisation complex beyond his understanding."

"Yet," said Graham, "there is something that resists, something you are holding down—something that stirs and presses."

"You will see," said Ostrog, with a forced smile that would brush these difficult questions aside. "I have not roused the force to destroy myself —trust me."

"I wonder," said Graham.

Ostrog stared.

"*Must* the world go this way?" said Graham with his emotions at the speaking point. "Must it indeed go in this way? Have all our hopes been vain?"

"What do you mean?" said Ostrog. "Hopes?"

"I come from a democratic age. And I find an aristocratic tyranny!"

"Well,—but you are the chief tyrant."

Graham shook his head.

"Well," said Ostrog, "take the general question. It is the way that change has always travelled. Aristocracy, the prevalence of the best—the suffering and extinction of the unfit, and so to better things."

"But aristocracy! those people I met—"

"Oh! not *those!*" said Ostrog. "But for the most part they go to their death. Vice and pleasure! They have no children. That sort of stuff will die out. If the world keeps to one road, that is, if there is no turning back. An easy road to excess, convenient Euthanasia for the pleasure seekers singed in the flame, that is the way to improve the race!"

"Pleasant extinction," said Graham. "Yet—." He thought for an instant. "There is that other thing—the Crowd, the great mass of poor men. Will that die out? That will not die out. And it suffers, its suffering is a force that even you—"

Ostrog moved impatiently, and when he spoke, he spoke rather less evenly than before.

"Don't trouble about these things," he said. "Everything will be settled in a few days now. The Crowd is a huge foolish beast. What if it does not die out? Even if it does not die, it can still be tamed and driven. I have no sympathy with servile men. You heard those people shouting and singing two nights ago. They were *taught* that song. If you had taken any man there in cold blood and asked why he shouted, he could not have told you. They think they are shouting for you, that they are loyal and devoted to you. Just then they were ready to slaughter the Council. To-day—they are already murmuring against those who have overthrown the Council."

"No, no," said Graham. "They shouted because their lives were dreary, without joy or pride, and because in me—in me—they hoped."

"And what was their hope? What is their hope? What right have they to hope? They work ill and they want the reward of those who work well. The hope of mankind—what is it? That some day the Over-man may come, that some day the inferior, the weak and the bestial may be subdued or eliminated. Subdued if not eliminated. The world is no place for the bad, the stupid, the enervated. Their duty—it's a fine duty too!—is to die.

The death of the failure! That is the path by which the beast rose to manhood, by which man goes on to higher things."

Ostrog took a pace, seemed to think, and turned on Graham. "I can imagine how this great world-state of ours seems to a Victorian Englishman. You regret all the old forms of representative government—their spectres still haunt the world, the voting councils, and parliaments and all that eighteenth century tomfoolery. You feel moved against our Pleasure Cities. I might have thought of that,—had I not been busy. But you will learn better. The people are mad with envy—they would be in sympathy with you. Even in the streets now, they clamour to destroy the Pleasure Cities. But the Pleasure Cities are the excretory organs of the State, attractive places that year after year draw together all that is weak and vicious, all that is lascivious and lazy, all the easy roguery of the world, to a graceful destruction. They go there, they have their time, they die childless, all the pretty silly lascivious women die childless, and mankind is the better. If the people were sane they would not envy the rich their way of death. And you would emancipate the silly brainless workers that we have enslaved, and try to make their lives easy and pleasant again. Just as they have sunk to what they are fit for." He smiled a smile that irritated Graham oddly. "You will learn better. I know those ideas; in my boyhood I read your Shelley and dreamt of Liberty. There is no liberty, save wisdom and self-control. Liberty is within—not without. It is each man's own affair. Suppose—which is impossible—that these swarming yelping fools in blue get the upper hand of us, what then? They will only fall to other masters. So long as there are sheep Nature will insist on beasts of prey. It would mean but a few hundred years' delay. The coming of the aristocrat is fatal and assured. The end will be the Over-man—for all the mad protests of humanity. Let them revolt, let them win and kill me and my like. Others will arise—other masters. The end will be the same."

"I wonder," said Graham doggedly.

For a moment he stood downcast.

"But I must see these things for myself," he said, suddenly assuming a tone of confident mastery. "Only by seeing can I understand. I must learn. That is what I want to tell you, Ostrog. I do not want to be King in a Pleasure City; that is not my pleasure. I have spent enough time with aeronautics—and those other things. I must learn how people live now, how the common life has developed. Then I shall understand these things better. I must learn how common people live—the labour people more especially—how they work, marry, bear children, die—"

"You get that from our realistic novelists," suggested Ostrog, suddenly preoccupied.

"I want reality," said Graham.

"There are difficulties," said Ostrog, and thought. "On the whole—"

"I did not expect—"

"I had thought—. And yet perhaps—. You say you want to go through the ways of the city and see the common people."

Suddenly he came to some conclusion. "You would need to go disguised," he said. "The city is intensely excited, and the discovery of your presence among them might create a fearful tumult. Still this wish of yours to go into this city—this idea of yours—. Yes, now I think the thing over, it seems to me not altogether—. It can be contrived. If you would really find an interest in that! You are, of course, Master. You can go soon if you like. A disguise Asano will be able to manage. He would go with you. After all it is not a bad idea of yours."

"You will not want to consult me in any matter?" asked Graham suddenly, struck by an odd suspicion.

"Oh, dear no! No! I think you may trust affairs to me for a time, at any rate," said Ostrog, smiling. "Even if we differ—"

Graham glanced at him sharply.

"There is no fighting likely to happen soon?" he asked abruptly.

"Certainly not."

"I have been thinking about these negroes. I don't believe the people intend any hostility to me, and, after all, I am the Master. I do not want any negroes brought to London. It is an archaic prejudice perhaps, but I have peculiar feelings about Europeans and the subject races. Even about Paris—"

Ostrog stood watching him from under his drooping brows. "I am not bringing negroes to London," he said slowly. "But if—"

"You are not to bring armed negroes to London, whatever happens," said Graham. "In that matter I am quite decided."

Ostrog resolved not to speak, and bowed deferentially.

20

IN THE CITY WAYS

AND THAT NIGHT, UNKNOWN AND UNSUSPECTED, GRAHAM, DRESSED IN the costume of an inferior Wind-Vane official keeping holiday, and accompanied by Asano in Labour Department canvas, surveyed the city through which he had wandered when it was veiled in darkness. But now he saw it lit and waking, a whirlpool of life. In spite of the surging and swaying of the forces of revolution, in spite of the unusual discontent, the mutterings of the greater struggle of which the first revolt was but the prelude, the myriad streams of commerce still flowed wide and strong. He knew now something of the dimensions and quality of the new age, but he was not prepared for the infinite surprise of the detailed view, for the torrent of colour and vivid impressions that poured past him.

This was his first real contact with the people of these latter days. He realized that all that had gone before, saving his glimpses of the public theatres and markets, had had its element of seclusion, had been a movement within the comparatively narrow political quarter, that all his previous experiences had revolved immediately about the question of his own position. But here was the city at the busiest hours of night, the people to a large extent returned to their own immediate interests, the resumption of the real informal life, the common habits of the new time.

They emerged at first into a street whose opposite ways were crowded with the blue canvas liveries. This swarm Graham saw was a portion of a procession—it was odd to see a procession parading the city *seated*. They carried banners of coarse black stuff with red letters. "No disarmament," said the banners, for the most part in crudely daubed letters and with variant spelling, and "Why should we disarm?" "No disarming." "No disarming." Banner after banner went by, a stream of banners flowing past, and at last at the end, the song of the revolt and a noisy band of strange instruments. "They all ought to be at work," said Asano. "They have had no food these two days, or they have stolen it."

Presently Asano made a detour to avoid the congested crowd that gaped upon the occasional passage of dead bodies from hospital to a mortuary, the gleanings after death's harvest of the first revolt.

That night few people were sleeping, everyone was abroad. A vast excitement, perpetual crowds perpetually changing, surrounded Graham; his mind was confused and darkened by an incessant tumult, by the cries and enigmatical fragments of the social struggle that was as yet only beginning. Everywhere festoons and banners of black and strange decorations, intensified the quality of his popularity. Everywhere he caught snatches of that crude thick dialect that served the illiterate class, the class, that is, beyond the reach of phonograph culture, in their commonplace intercourse. Everywhere this trouble of disarmament was in the air, with a quality of immediate stress of which he had no inkling during his seclusion in the Wind-Vane quarter. He perceived that as soon as he returned he must discuss this with Ostrog, this and the greater issues of which it was the expression, in a far more conclusive way than he had so far done. Perpetually that night, even in the earlier hours of their wanderings about the city, the spirit of unrest and revolt swamped his attention, to the exclusion of countless strange things he might otherwise have observed.

This preoccupation made his impressions fragmentary. Yet amidst so much that was strange and vivid, no subject, however personal and insistent, could exert undivided sway. There were spaces when the revolutionary movement passed clean out of his mind, was drawn aside like a curtain from before some startling new aspect of the time. Helen had swayed his mind to this intense earnestness of enquiry, but there came times when she, even, receded beyond his conscious thoughts. At one moment, for example, he found they were traversing the religious quarter, for the easy transit about the city afforded by the moving ways rendered sporadic churches and chapels no longer necessary—and his attention was vividly arrested by the façade of one of the Christian sects.

They were travelling seated on one of the swift upper ways, the place leapt upon them at a bend and advanced rapidly towards them. It was covered with inscriptions from top to base, in vivid white and blue, save where a vast and glaring kinematograph transparency presented a realistic New Testament scene, and where a vast festoon of black to show that the popular religion followed the popular politics, hung across the lettering. Graham had already become familiar with the phonotype writing and these inscriptions arrested him, being to his sense for the most part almost incredible blasphemy. Among the less offensive were "Salvation on the First Floor and turn to the Right." "Put your Money on your Maker." "The Sharpest Conversion in London, Expert Operators! Look Slippy!" "What Christ would say to the Sleeper;—Join the Up-to-date Saints!" "Be a Christian—without hindrance to your present Occupation." "All the Brightest Bishops on the Bench to-night and Prices as Usual." "Brisk Blessings for Busy Business Men."

"But this is appalling!" said Graham, as that deafening scream of mercantile piety towered above them.

"What is appalling?" asked his little officer, apparently seeking vainly for anything unusual in this shrieking enamel.

"*This*! Surely the essence of religion is reverence."

"Oh *that*!" Asano looked at Graham. "Does it shock you?" he said in the tone of one who makes a discovery. "I suppose it would, of course. I had forgotten. Nowadays the competition for attention is so keen, and people simply haven't the leisure to attend to their souls, you know, as they used to do." He smiled. "In the old days you had quiet Sabbaths and the countryside. Though somewhere I've read of Sunday afternoons that—"

"But, *that*," said Graham, glancing back at the receding blue and white. "That is surely not the only—"

"There are hundreds of different ways. But, of course, if a sect doesn't *tell* it doesn't pay. Worship has moved with the times. There are high class sects with quieter ways—costly incense and personal attentions and all that. These people are extremely popular and prosperous. They pay several dozen lions for those apartments to the Council—to you, I should say."

Graham still felt a difficulty with the coinage, and this mention of a dozen lions brought him abruptly to that matter. In a moment the screaming temples and their swarming touts were forgotten in this new interest. A turn of a phrase suggested, and an answer confirmed the idea that gold and silver were both demonetised, that stamped gold which had begun its reign amidst the merchants of Phoenicia was at last dethroned.

The change had been graduated but swift, brought about by an extension of the system of cheques that had even in his previous life already practically superseded gold in all the larger business transactions. The common traffic of the city, the common currency indeed of all the world, was conducted by means of the little brown, green and pink council cheques for small amounts, printed with a blank payee. Asano had several with him, and at the first opportunity he supplied the gaps in his set. They were printed not on tearable paper, but on a semi-transparent fabric of silken flexibility, interwoven with silk. Across them all sprawled a facsimile of Graham's signature, his first encounter with the curves and turns of that familiar autograph for two hundred and three years.

Some intermediary experiences made no impression sufficiently vivid to prevent the matter of the disarmament claiming his thoughts again; a blurred picture of a Theosophist temple that promised MIRACLES in enormous letters of unsteady fire was least submerged perhaps, but then came the view of the dining hall in Northumberland Avenue. That interested him very greatly.

By the energy and thought of Asano he was able to view this place from a little screened gallery reserved for the attendants of the tables. The building was pervaded by a distant muffled hooting, piping and bawling, of which he did not at first understand the import, but which recalled a certain mysterious leathery voice he had heard after the resumption of the lights on the night of his solitary wandering.

He had grown accustomed to vastness and great numbers of people, nevertheless this spectacle held him for a long time. It was as he watched the table service more immediately beneath, and interspersed with many questions and answers concerning details, that the realisation of the full significance of the feast of several thousand people came to him.

It was his constant surprise to find that points that one might have expected to strike vividly at the very outset never occurred to him until some trivial detail suddenly shaped as a riddle and pointed to the obvious thing he had overlooked. He discovered only now that this continuity of the city, this exclusion of weather, these vast halls and ways, involved the disappearance of the household; that the typical Victorian "Home," the little brick cell containing kitchen and scullery, living rooms and bedrooms, had, save for the ruins that diversified the countryside, vanished as surely as the wattle hut. But now he saw what had indeed been manifest from the first, that London, regarded as a living place, was no longer an aggregation of houses but a prodigious hotel, an hotel with a thousand classes of accommodation, thousands of dining halls, chapels, theatres, markets and places of assembly, a synthesis of enterprises, of which he chiefly was the owner. People had their sleeping rooms, with, it might be, antechambers, rooms that were always sanitary at least whatever the degree of comfort and privacy, and for the rest they lived much as many people had lived in the new-made giant hotels of the Victorian days, eating, reading, thinking, playing, conversing, all in places of public resort, going to their work in the industrial quarters of the city or doing business in their offices in the trading section.

He perceived at once how necessarily this state of affairs had developed from the Victorian city. The fundamental reason for the modern city had ever been the economy of co-operation. The chief thing to prevent the merging of the separate households in his own generation was simply the still imperfect civilisation of the people, the strong barbaric pride, passions, and prejudices, the jealousies, rivalries, and violence of the middle and lower classes, which had necessitated the entire separation of contiguous households. But the change, the taming of the people, had been in rapid progress even then. In his brief thirty years of previous life he had seen an enormous extension of the habit of consuming meals from home, the casually patronised horse-box coffee-house had given place to the open and crowded Aerated Bread Shop for instance, women's clubs had had their beginning, and an immense development of reading-rooms, lounges and libraries had witnessed to the growth of social confidence. These promises had by this time attained to their complete fulfilment. The locked and barred household had passed away.

These people below him belonged, he learnt, to the lower middle-class, the class just above the blue labourers, a class so accustomed in the Victorian period to feed with every precaution of privacy that its members, when occasion confronted them with a public meal, would usually hide their embarrassment under horseplay or a markedly militant demeanour. But these gaily, if lightly dressed people below, albeit vivacious, hurried and uncommunicative, were dexterously mannered and certainly quite at their ease with regard to one another.

He noted a slight significant thing; the table, as far as he could see, was and remained delightfully neat, there was nothing to parallel the confusion, the broadcast crumbs, the splashes of viand and condiment, the overturned drink and displaced ornaments, which would have marked the stormy progress of the Victorian meal. The table furniture was very different. There were no ornaments, no flowers, and the table was without a cloth, being made, he learnt, of a solid substance having the texture and appearance of damask. He discerned that this damask substance was patterned with gracefully designed trade advertisements.

In a sort of recess before each diner was a complex apparatus of porcelain and metal. There was one plate of white porcelain, and by means of taps for hot and cold volatile fluids the diner washed this himself between the courses; he also washed his elegant white metal knife and fork and spoon as occasion required.

Soup and the chemical wine that was the common drink were delivered by similar taps, and the remaining covers travelled automatically in tastefully arranged dishes down the table along silver rails. The diner stopped these and helped himself at his discretion. They appeared at a little door at one end of the table, and vanished at the other. That turn of democratic sentiment in decay, that ugly pride of menial souls, which renders equals loth to wait on one another, was very strong he found among these people. He was so preoccupied with these details that it was only as he was leaving the place that he remarked the huge advertisement dioramas that marched majestically along the upper walls and proclaimed the most remarkable commodities.

Beyond this place they came into a crowded hall, and he discovered the cause of the noise that had perplexed him. They paused at a turnstile at which a payment was made.

Graham's attention was immediately arrested by a violent, loud hoot, followed by a vast leathery voice. "The Master is sleeping peacefully," it vociferated. "He is in excellent health. He is going to devote the rest of his life to aeronautics. He says women are more beautiful than ever. Galloop! Wow! Our wonderful civilisation astonishes him beyond measure. Beyond all measure. Galloop. He puts great trust in Boss Ostrog, absolute confidence in Boss Ostrog. Ostrog is to be his chief minister; is authorised to remove or reinstate public officers—all patronage will be in his hands. All patronage in the hands of Boss Ostrog! The Councillors have been sent back to their own prison above the Council House."

Graham stopped at the first sentence, and, looking up, beheld a foolish trumpet face from which this was brayed. This was the General Intelligence Machine. For a space it seemed to be gathering breath, and a regular throbbing from its cylindrical body was audible. Then it trumpeted "Galloop, Galloop," and broke out again.

"Paris is now pacified. All resistance is over. Galloop! The black police hold every position of importance in the city. They fought with great bravery, singing songs written in praise of their ancestors by the poet Kipling. Once or twice they got out of hand, and tortured and mutilated wounded and captured insurgents, men and women. Moral—don't go rebelling. Haha! Galloop, Galloop! They are lively fellows. Lively brave fellows. Let this be a lesson to the disorderly banderlog of this city. Yah! Banderlog! Filth of the earth! Galloop, Galloop!"

The voice ceased. There was a confused murmur of disapproval among the crowd. "Damned niggers." A man began to harangue near them. "Is this the Master's doing, brothers? Is this the Master's doing?"

"Black police!" said Graham. "What is that? You don't mean—"

Asano touched his arm and gave him a warning look, and forthwith another of these mechanisms screamed deafeningly and gave tongue in a shrill voice. "Yahaha, Yahah, Yap! Hear a live paper yelp! Live paper. Yaha! Shocking outrage in Paris. Yahahah! The Parisians exasperated by the black police to the pitch of assassination. Dreadful reprisals. Savage times come again. Blood! Blood! Yaha!" The nearer Babble Machine hooted stupendously, "Galloop, Galloop," drowned the end of the sentence, and proceeded in a rather flatter note than before with novel comments on the horrors of disorder. "Law and order must be maintained," said the nearer Babble Machine.

"But," began Graham.

"Don't ask questions here," said Asano, "or you will be involved in an argument."

"Then let us go on," said Graham, "for I want to know more of this."

As he and his companion pushed their way through the excited crowd that swarmed beneath these voices, towards the exit, Graham conceived more clearly the proportion and features of this room. Altogether, great and small, there must have been nearly a thousand of these erections, piping, hooting, bawling and gabbling in that great space, each with its crowd of excited listeners, the majority of them men dressed in blue canvas. There were all sizes of machines, from the little gossiping mechanisms that chuckled out mechanical sarcasm in odd corners, through a number of grades to such fifty-foot giants as that which had first hooted over Graham.

This place was unusually crowded, because of the intense public interest in the course of affairs in Paris. Evidently the struggle had been much more savage than Ostrog had represented it. All the mechanisms were discoursing upon that topic, and the repetition of the people made the huge hive buzz with such phrases as "Lynched policemen," "Women burnt alive," "Fuzzy Wuzzy." "But does the Master allow such things?" asked a man near him. "Is *this* the beginning of the Master's rule?"

Is *this* the beginning of the Master's rule? For a long time after he had left the place, the hooting, whistling and braying of the machines pursued him; "Galloop, Galloop," "Yahahah, Yaha, Yap! Yaha!" Is *this* the beginning of the Master's rule?

Directly as they were out upon the ways he began to question Asano closely on the nature of the Parisian struggle. "This disarmament! What was their trouble? What does it all mean?" Asano seemed chiefly anxious to reassure him that it was "all right."

"But these outrages!"

"You cannot have an omelette," said Asano, "without breaking eggs. It is only the rough people. Only in one part of the city. All the rest is all right. The Parisian labourers are the wildest in the world, except ours."

"What! the Londoners?"

"No, the Japanese. They have to be kept in order."

"But burning women alive!"

"A Commune!" said Asano. "They would rob you of your property. They would do away with property and give the world over to mob rule. You are Master, the world is yours. But there will be no Commune here. There is no need for black police here.

"And every consideration has been shown. It is their own negroes—French speaking negroes. Senegal regiments, and Niger and Timbuctoo."

"Regiments?" said Graham, "I thought there was only one—"

"No," said Asano, and glanced at him. "There is more than one."

Graham felt unpleasantly helpless.

"I did not think," he began and stopped abruptly. He went off at a tangent to ask for information about these Babble Machines. For the most part, the crowd present had been shabbily or even raggedly dressed, and Graham learnt that so far as the more prosperous classes were concerned, in all the more comfortable private apartments of the city were fixed Babble Machines that would speak directly when a lever was pulled. The tenant of the apartment could connect this with the cables of any of the great News Syndicates that he preferred. When he learnt this presently, he demanded the reason of their absence from his own suite of apartments. Asano was embarrassed. "I never thought," he said. "Ostrog must have had them removed."

Graham stared. "How was I to know?" he exclaimed.

"Perhaps he thought they would annoy you," said Asano.

"They must be replaced directly when I return," said Graham after an interval.

He found a difficulty in understanding that this news room and the dining hall were not great central places, that such establishments were repeated almost beyond counting all over the city. But ever and again during the night's expedition his ears would pick out from the tumult of the ways the peculiar hooting of the organ of Boss Ostrog, "Galloop, Galloop!" or the shrill "Yahaha, Yaha Yap!—Hear a live paper yelp!" of its chief rival.

Repeated, too, everywhere, were such *crêches* as the one he now entered. It was reached by a lift, and by a glass bridge that flung across the dining hall and traversed the ways at a slight upward angle. To enter the first section of the place necessitated the use of his solvent signature under Asano's direction. They were immediately attended to by a man in a violet robe and gold clasp, the insignia of practising medical men. He perceived from this man's manner that his identity was known, and proceeded to ask questions on the strange arrangements of the place without reserve.

On either side of the passage, which was silent and padded, as if to deaden the footfall, were narrow little doors, their size and arrangement suggestive of the cells of a Victorian prison. But the upper portion of each door was of the same greenish transparent stuff that had enclosed him at his awakening, and within, dimly seen, lay, in every case, a very young baby in a little nest of wadding. Elaborate apparatus watched the atmosphere and rang a bell far away in the central office at the slightest departure from the optimum of temperature and moisture. A system of such *crêches* had almost entirely replaced the hazardous adventures of the old-world nursing. The attendant presently called Graham's attention to the wet nurses, a vista of mechanical figures, with arms, shoulders, and breasts of astonishingly realistic modelling, articulation, and texture, but mere brass tripods below, and having in the place of features a flat disc bearing advertisements likely to be of interest to mothers.

Of all the strange things that Graham came upon that night, none jarred more upon his habits of thought than this place. The spectacle of the little pink creatures, their feeble limbs swaying uncertainly in vague first movements, left alone, without embrace or endearment, was wholly repugnant to him. The attendant doctor was of a different opinion. His statistical evidence showed beyond dispute that in the Victorian times the most dangerous passage of life was the arms of the mother, that there human mortality had ever been most terrible. On the other hand this *crêche* company, the International Crêche Syndicate, lost not one-half per cent, of the million babies or so that formed its peculiar care. But Graham's prejudice was too strong even for those figures.

Along one of the many passages of the place they presently came upon a young couple in the usual blue canvas peering through the transparency and laughing hysterically at the bald head of their first-born. Graham's face must have showed his estimate of them, for their merriment ceased and they looked abashed. But this little incident accentuated his sudden realisation of the gulf between his habits of thought and the ways of the new age. He passed on to the crawling rooms and the Kindergarten, perplexed and distressed. He found the endless long playrooms were empty! the latter-day children at least still spent their nights in sleep. As they went through these, the little officer pointed out the nature of the toys, developments of those devised by that inspired sentimentalist Froebel. There were nurses here, but much was done by machines that sang and danced and dandled.

Graham was still not clear upon many points. "But so many orphans," he said perplexed, reverting to a first misconception, and learnt again that they were not orphans.

So soon as they had left the *crêche* he began to speak of the horror the babies in their incubating cases had caused him. "Is motherhood gone?" he said. "Was it a cant? Surely it was an instinct. This seems so unnatural—abominable almost."

"Along here we shall come to the dancing place," said Asano by way of reply. "It is sure to be crowded. In spite of all the political unrest it will be crowded. The women take no great interest in politics—except a few here and there. You will see the mothers—most young women in London are mothers. In that class it is considered a creditable thing to have one child —a proof of animation. Few middle-class people have more than one. With the Labour Department it is different. As for motherhood! They still take an immense pride in the children. They come here to look at them quite often."

"Then do you mean that the population of the World—?"

"Is falling? Yes. Except among the people under the Labour Department. In spite of scientific discipline they are reckless—"

The air was suddenly dancing with music, and down a way they approached obliquely, set with gorgeous pillars as it seemed of clear amethyst, flowed a concourse of gay people and a tumult of merry cries and laughter. He saw curled heads, wreathed brows, and a happy intricate flutter of gamboge pass triumphant across the picture.

"You will see," said Asano with a faint smile. "The world has changed. In a moment you will see the mothers of the new age. Come this way. We shall see those yonder again very soon."

They ascended a certain height in a swift lift, and changed to a slower one. As they went on the music grew upon them, until it was near and full and splendid, and, moving with its glorious intricacies they could distinguish the beat of innumerable dancing feet. They made a payment at a turnstile, and emerged upon the wide gallery that overlooked the dancing place, and upon the full enchantment of sound and sight.

"Here," said Asano, "are the fathers and mothers of the little ones you saw."

The hall was not so richly decorated as that of the Atlas, but saving that, it was, for its size, the most splendid Graham had seen. The beautiful white-limbed figures that supported the galleries reminded him once more of the restored magnificence of sculpture; they seemed to writhe in engaging attitudes, their faces laughed. The source of the music that filled the place was hidden, and the whole vast shining floor was thick with dancing couples. "Look at them," said the little officer, "see how much they show of motherhood."

The gallery they stood upon ran along the upper edge of a huge screen that cut the dancing hall on one side from a sort of outer hall that showed through broad arches the incessant onward rush of the city ways. In this outer hall was a great crowd of less brilliantly dressed people, as numerous almost as those who danced within, the great majority wearing the blue uniform of the Labour Department that was now so familiar to Graham. Too poor to pass the turnstiles to the festival, they were yet unable to keep away from the sound of its seductions. Some of them even had cleared spaces, and were dancing also, fluttering their rags in the air. Some shouted as they danced, jests and odd allusions Graham did not understand. Once someone began whistling the refrain of the revolutionary song, but it seemed as though that beginning was promptly suppressed. The corner was dark and Graham could not see. He turned to the hall again. Above the caryatids were marble busts of men whom that age esteemed great moral emancipators and pioneers; for the most part their names were strange to Graham, though he recognised Grant Allen, Le Gallienne, Nietzsche, Shelley and Goodwin. Great black festoons and eloquent sentiments reinforced the huge inscription that partially defaced the upper end of the dancing place, and asserted that "The Festival of the Awakening" was in progress.

"Myriads are taking holiday or staying from work because of that, quite apart from the labourers who refuse to go back," said Asano. "These people are always ready for holidays."

Graham walked to the parapet and stood leaning over, looking down at the dancers. Save for two or three remote whispering couples, who had stolen apart, he and his guide had the gallery to themselves. A warm breath of scent and vitality came up to him. Both men and women below were lightly clad, bare-armed, open-necked, as the universal warmth of the city permitted. The hair of the men was often a mass of effeminate curls, their chins were always shaven, and many of them had flushed or coloured cheeks. Many of the women were very pretty, and all were dressed with elaborate coquetry. As they swept by beneath, he saw ecstatic faces with eyes half closed in pleasure.

"What sort of people are these?" he asked abruptly.

"Workers—prosperous workers. What you would have called the middle-class. Independent tradesmen with little separate businesses have vanished long ago, but there are store servers, managers, engineers of a hundred sorts. To-night is a holiday of course, and every dancing place in the city will be crowded, and every place of worship."

"But—the women?"

"The same. There's a thousand forms of work for women now. But you had the beginning of the independent working-woman in your days. Most women are independent now. Most of these are married more or less— there are a number of methods of contract—and that gives them more money, and enables them to enjoy themselves."

"I see," said Graham, looking at the flushed faces, the flash and swirl of movement, and still thinking of that nightmare of pink helpless limbs. "And these are—mothers."

"Most of them."

"The more I see of these things the more complex I find your problems. This, for instance, is a surprise. That news from Paris was a surprise."

In a little while he spoke again:

"These are mothers. Presently, I suppose, I shall get into the modern way of seeing things. I have old habits of mind clinging about me—habits based, I suppose, on needs that are over and done with. Of course, in our time, a woman was supposed not only to bear children, but to cherish them, to devote herself to them, to educate them—all the essentials of moral and mental education a child owed its mother. Or went without. Quite a number, I admit, went without. Nowadays, clearly, there is no more need for such care than if they were butterflies. I see that! Only there was an ideal—that figure of a grave, patient woman, silently and serenely mistress of a home, mother and maker of men—to love her was a sort of worship—"

He stopped and repeated, "A sort of worship."

"Ideals change," said the little man, "as needs change."

Graham awoke from an instant reverie and Asano repeated his words. Graham's mind returned to the thing at hand.

"Of course I see the perfect reasonableness of this. Restraint, soberness, the matured thought, the unselfish act, they are necessities of the barbarous state, the life of dangers. Dourness is man's tribute to unconquered nature. But man has conquered nature now for all practical purposes—his political affairs are managed by Bosses with a black police—and life is joyous."

He looked at the dancers again. "Joyous," he said.

"There are weary moments," said the little officer, reflectively.

"They all look young. Down there I should be visibly the oldest man. And in my own time I should have passed as middle-aged."

"They are young. There are few old people in this class in the work cities."

"How is that?"

"Old people's lives are not so pleasant as they used to be, unless they are rich to hire lovers and helpers. And we have an institution called Euthanasy."

"Ah! that Euthanasy!" said Graham. "The easy death?"

"The easy death. It is the last pleasure. The Euthanasy Company does it well. People will pay the sum—it is a costly thing—long beforehand, go off to some pleasure city and return impoverished and weary, very weary."

"There is a lot left for me to understand," said Graham after a pause. "Yet I see the logic of it all. Our array of angry virtues and sour restraints was the consequence of danger and insecurity. The Stoic, the Puritan, even in my time, were vanishing types. In the old days man was armed against Pain, now he is eager for Pleasure. There lies the difference. Civilisation has driven pain and danger so far off—for well-to-do people. And only well-to-do people matter now. I have been asleep two hundred years."

For a minute they leant on the balustrading, following the intricate evolution of the dance. Indeed the scene was very beautiful.

"Before God," said Graham, suddenly, "I would rather be a wounded sentinel freezing in the snow than one of these painted fools!"

"In the snow," said Asano, "one might think differently."

"I am uncivilised," said Graham, not heeding him. "That is the trouble. I am primitive—Palaeolithic. *Their* fountain of rage and fear and anger is sealed and closed, the habits of a lifetime make them cheerful and easy and delightful. You must bear with my nineteenth century shocks and disgusts. These people, you say, are skilled workers and so forth. And while these dance, men are fighting—men are dying in Paris to keep the world—that they may dance."

Asano smiled faintly. "For that matter, men are dying in London," he said.

There was a moment's silence.

"Where do these sleep?" asked Graham.

"Above and below—an intricate warren."

"And where do they work? This is—the domestic life."

"You will see little work to-night. Half the workers are out or under arms. Half these people are keeping holiday. But we will go to the work places if you wish it."

For a time Graham watched the dancers, then suddenly turned away. "I want to see the workers. I have seen enough of these," he said.

Asano led the way along the gallery across the dancing hall. Presently they came to a transverse passage that brought a breath of fresher, colder air.

Asano glanced at this passage as they went past, stopped, went back to it, and turned to Graham with a smile. "Here, Sire," he said, "is something —will be familiar to you at least—and yet—. But I will not tell you. Come!"

He led the way along a closed passage that presently became cold. The reverberation of their feet told that this passage was a bridge. They came into a circular gallery that was glazed in from the outer weather, and so reached a circular chamber which seemed familiar, though Graham could not recall distinctly when he had entered it before. In this was a ladder— the first ladder he had seen since his awakening—up which they went, and came into a high, dark, cold place in which was another almost vertical ladder. This they ascended, Graham still perplexed.

But at the top he understood, and recognised the metallic bars to which he clung. He was in the cage under the ball of St. Paul's. The dome rose but a little way above the general contour of the city, into the still twilight, and sloped away, shining greasily under a few distant lights, into a circumambient ditch of darkness.

Out between the bars he looked upon the wind-clear northern sky and saw the starry constellations all unchanged. Capella hung in the west, Vega was rising, and the seven glittering points of the Great Bear swept overhead in their stately circle about the Pole.

He saw these stars in a clear gap of sky. To the east and south the great circular shapes of complaining wind-wheels blotted out the heavens, so that the glare about the Council House was hidden. To the southwest hung Orion, showing like a pallid ghost through a tracery of ironwork and interlacing shapes above a dazzling coruscation of lights. A bellowing and siren screaming that came from the flying stages warned the world that one of the aeroplanes was ready to start. He remained for a space gazing towards the glaring stage. Then his eyes went back to the northward constellations.

For a long time he was silent. "This," he said at last, smiling in the shadow, "seems the strangest thing of all. To stand in the dome of St. Paul's and look once more upon these familiar, silent stars!"

Thence Graham was taken by Asano along devious ways to the great gambling and business quarters where the bulk of the fortunes in the city were lost and made. It impressed him as a well-nigh interminable series of very high halls, surrounded by tiers upon tiers of galleries into which opened thousands of offices, and traversed by a complicated multitude of bridges, footways, aerial motor rails, and trapeze and cable leaps. And here more than anywhere the note of vehement vitality, of uncontrollable, hasty activity, rose high. Everywhere was violent advertisement, until his brain swam at the tumult of light and colour. And Babble Machines of a peculiarly rancid tone were abundant and filled the air with strenuous squealing and an idiotic slang. "Skin your eyes and slide," "Gewhoop, Bonanza," "Gollipers come and hark!"

The place seemed to him to be dense with people either profoundly agitated or swelling with obscure cunning, yet he learnt that the place was comparatively empty, that the great political convulsion of the last few days had reduced transactions to an unprecedented minimum. In one huge place were long avenues of roulette tables, each with an excited, undignified crowd about it; in another a yelping Babel of white-faced women and red-necked leathery-lunged men bought and sold the shares of an absolutely fictitious business undertaking which, every five minutes, paid a dividend of ten per cent, and cancelled a certain proportion of its shares by means of a lottery wheel.

These business activities were prosecuted with an energy that readily passed into violence, and Graham approaching a dense crowd found at its centre a couple of prominent merchants in violent controversy with teeth and nails on some delicate point of business etiquette. Something still remained in life to be fought for. Further he had a shock at a vehement announcement in phonetic letters of scarlet flame, each twice the height of a man, that "WE ASSURE THE PROPRAIET'R. WE ASSURE THE PROPRAIET'R."

"Who's the proprietor?" he asked.

"You."

"But what do they assure me?" he asked. "What do they assure me?"

"Didn't you have assurance?"

Graham thought. "Insurance?"

"Yes—Insurance. I remember that was the older word. They are insuring your life. Dozands of people are taking out policies, myriads of lions are being put on you. And further on other people are buying annuities. They do that on everybody who is at all prominent. Look there!"

A crowd of people surged and roared, and Graham saw a vast black screen suddenly illuminated in still larger letters of burning purple. "Anuetes on the Propraiet'r—x 5 pr. G." The people began to boo and shout at this, a number of hard-breathing, wild-eyed men came running past, clawing with hooked fingers at the air. There was a furious crush about a little doorway.

Asano did a brief, inaccurate calculation. "Seventeen per cent, per annum is their annuity on you. They would not pay so much per cent, if they could see you now, Sire. But they do not know. Your own annuities used to be a very safe investment, but now you are sheer gambling, of course. This is probably a desperate bid. I doubt if people will get their money."

The crowd of would-be annuitants grew so thick about them that for some time they could move neither forward nor backward. Graham noticed what appeared to him to be a high proportion of women among the speculators, and was reminded again of the economic independence of their sex. They seemed remarkably well able to take care of themselves in the crowd, using their elbows with particular skill, as he learnt to his cost. One curly-headed person caught in the pressure for a space, looked steadfastly at him several times, almost as if she recognised him, and then, edging deliberately towards him, touched his hand with her arm in a scarcely accidental manner, and made it plain by a look as ancient as Chaldea that he had found favour in her eyes. And then a lank, grey-bearded man, perspiring copiously in a noble passion of self-help, blind to all earthly things save that glaring bait, thrust between them in a cataclysmal rush towards that alluring "X 5 pr. G."

"I want to get out of this," said Graham to Asano. "This is not what I came to see. Show me the workers. I want to see the people in blue. These parasitic lunatics—"

He found himself wedged into a straggling mass of people.

21

THE UNDER SIDE

FROM THE BUSINESS QUARTER THEY PRESENTLY PASSED BY THE RUNNING ways into a remote quarter of the city, where the bulk of the manufactures was done. On their way the platforms crossed the Thames twice, and passed in a broad viaduct across one of the great roads that entered the city from the North. In both cases his impression was swift and in both very vivid. The river was a broad wrinkled glitter of black sea water, over-arched by buildings, and vanishing either way into a blackness starred with receding lights. A string of black barges passed seaward, manned by blue-clad men. The road was a long and very broad and high tunnel, along which big-wheeled machines drove noiselessly and swiftly. Here, too, the distinctive blue of the Labour Department was in abundance. The smoothness of the double tracks, the largeness and the lightness of the big pneumatic wheels in proportion to the vehicular body, struck Graham most vividly. One lank and very high carriage with longitudinal metallic rods hung with the dripping carcasses of many hundred sheep arrested his attention unduly. Abruptly the edge of the archway cut and blotted out the picture.

Presently they left the way and descended by a lift and traversed a passage that sloped downward, and so came to a descending lift again. The appearance of things changed. Even the pretence of architectural orna-ment disappeared, the lights diminished in number and size, the architec-ture became more and more massive in proportion to the spaces as the factory quarters were reached. And in the dusty biscuit-making place of the potters, among the felspar mills, in the furnace rooms of the metal workers, among the incandescent lakes of crude Eadhamite, the blue canvas clothing was on man, woman and child.

Many of these great and dusty galleries were silent avenues of machinery, endless raked out ashen furnaces testified to the revolutionary dislocation, but wherever there was work it was being done by slow-moving workers in blue canvas. The only people not in blue canvas were the overlookers of the work-places and the orange-clad Labour Police. And fresh from the flushed faces of the dancing halls, the voluntary vigours of the business quarter, Graham could note the pinched faces, the feeble muscles, and weary eyes of many of the latter-day workers. Such as he saw at work were noticeably inferior in physique to the few gaily dressed managers and forewomen who were directing their labours. The burly labourers of the old Victorian times had followed that dray horse and all such living force producers, to extinction; the place of his costly muscles was taken by some dexterous machine. The latter-day labourer, male as well as female, was essentially a machine-minder and feeder, a servant and attendant, or an artist under direction.

The women, in comparison with those Graham remembered, were as a class distinctly plain and flat-chested. Two hundred years of emancipation from the moral restraints of Puritanical religion, two hundred years of city life, had done their work in eliminating the strain of feminine beauty and vigour from the blue canvas myriads. To be brilliant physically or mentally, to be in any way attractive or exceptional, had been and was still a certain way of emancipation to the drudge, a line of escape to the Pleasure City and its splendours and delights, and at last to the Euthanasy and peace. To be steadfast against such inducements was scarcely to be expected of meanly nourished souls. In the young cities of Graham's former life, the newly aggregated labouring mass had been a diverse multitude, still stirred by the tradition of personal honour and a high morality; now it was differentiating into an instinct class, with a moral and physical difference of its own—even with a dialect of its own.

They penetrated downward, ever downward, towards the working places. Presently they passed underneath one of the streets of the moving ways, and saw its platforms running on their rails far overhead, and chinks of white lights between the transverse slits. The factories that were not working were sparsely lighted; to Graham they and their shrouded aisles of giant machines seemed plunged in gloom, and even where work was going on the illumination was far less brilliant than upon the public ways.

Beyond the blazing lakes of Eadhamite he came to the warren of the jewellers, and, with some difficulty and by using his signature, obtained admission to these galleries. They were high and dark, and rather cold. In the first a few men were making ornaments of gold filigree, each man at a little bench by himself, and with a little shaded light. The long vista of light patches, with the nimble fingers brightly lit and moving among the gleaming yellow coils, and the intent face like the face of a ghost, in each shadow, had the oddest effect.

The work was beautifully executed, but without any strength of modelling or drawing, for the most part intricate grotesques or the ringing of the changes on a geometrical *motif*. These workers wore a peculiar white uniform without pockets or sleeves. They assumed this on coming to work, but at night they were stripped and examined before they left the premises of the Department. In spite of every precaution, the Labour policeman told them in a depressed tone, the Department was not infrequently robbed.

Beyond was a gallery of women busied in cutting and setting slabs of artificial ruby, and next these were men and women working together upon the slabs of copper net that formed the basis of *cloisonné* tiles. Many of these workers had lips and nostrils a livid white, due to a disease caused by a peculiar purple enamel that chanced to be much in fashion. Asano apologized to Graham for this offensive sight, but excused himself on the score of the convenience of this route. "This is what I wanted to see," said Graham; "this is what I wanted to see," trying to avoid a start at a particularly striking disfigurement.

"She might have done better with herself than that," said Asano.

Graham made some indignant comments.

"But, Sire, we simply could not stand that stuff without the purple," said Asano. "In your days people could stand such crudities, they were nearer the barbaric by two hundred years."

They continued along one of the lower galleries of this *cloisonné* factory, and came to a little bridge that spanned a vault. Looking over the parapet, Graham saw that beneath was a wharf under yet more tremendous archings than any he had seen. Three barges, smothered in floury dust, were being unloaded of their cargoes of powdered felspar by a multitude of coughing men, each guiding a little truck; the dust filled the place with a choking mist, and turned the electric glare yellow. The vague shadows of these workers gesticulated about their feet, and rushed to and fro against a long stretch of white-washed wall. Every now and then one would stop to cough.

A shadowy, huge mass of masonry rising out of the inky water, brought to Graham's mind the thought of the multitude of ways and galleries and lifts that rose floor above floor overhead between him and the sky. The men worked in silence under the supervision of two of the Labour Police; their feet made a hollow thunder on the planks along which they went to and fro. And as he looked at this scene, some hidden voice in the darkness began to sing.

"Stop that!" shouted one of the policemen, but the order was disobeyed, and first one and then all the white-stained men who were working there had taken up the beating refrain, singing it defiantly—the Song of the Revolt. The feet upon the planks thundered now to the rhythm of the song, tramp, tramp, tramp. The policeman who had shouted glanced at his fellow, and Graham saw him shrug his shoulders. He made no further effort to stop the singing.

And so they went through these factories and places of toil, seeing many painful and grim things. That walk left on Graham's mind a maze of memories, fluctuating pictures of swathed halls, and crowded vaults seen through clouds of dust, of intricate machines, the racing threads of looms, the heavy beat of stamping machinery, the roar and rattle of belt and armature, of ill-lit subterranean aisles of sleeping places, illimitable vistas of pin-point lights. Here was the smell of tanning, and here the reek of a brewery, and here unprecedented reeks. Everywhere were pillars and cross archings of such a massiveness as Graham had never before seen, thick Titans of greasy, shining brickwork crushed beneath the vast weight of that complex city world, even as these anaemic millions were crushed by its complexity. And everywhere were pale features, lean limbs, disfigurement and degradation.

Once and again, and again a third time, Graham heard the song of the revolt during his long, unpleasant research in these places, and once he saw a confused struggle down a passage, and learnt that a number of these serfs had seized their bread before their work was done. Graham was ascending towards the ways again when he saw a number of blue-clad children running down a transverse passage, and presently perceived the reason of their panic in a company of the Labour Police armed with clubs, trotting towards some unknown disturbance. And then came a remote disorder. But for the most part this remnant that worked, worked hopelessly. All the spirit that was left in fallen humanity was above in the streets that night, calling for the Master, and valiantly and noisily keeping its arms.

They emerged from these wanderings and stood blinking in the bright light of the middle passage of the platforms again. They became aware of the remote hooting and yelping of the machines of one of the General Intelligence Offices, and suddenly came men running, and along the platforms and about the ways everywhere was a shouting and crying. Then a woman with a face of mute white terror, and another who gasped and shrieked as she ran.

"What has happened now?" said Graham, puzzled, for he could not understand their thick speech. Then he heard it in English and perceived that the thing that everyone was shouting, that men yelled to one another, that women took up screaming, that was passing like the first breeze of a thunderstorm, chill and sudden through the city, was this: "Ostrog has ordered the Black Police to London. The Black Police are coming from South Africa.... The Black Police. The Black Police."

Asano's face was white and astonished; he hesitated, looked at Graham's face, and told him the thing he already knew. "But how can they know?" asked Asano.

Graham heard someone shouting. "Stop all work. Stop all work," and a swarthy hunchback, ridiculously gay in green and gold, came leaping down the platforms toward him, bawling again and again in good English, "This is Ostrog's doing, Ostrog the Knave! The Master is betrayed." His voice was hoarse and a thin foam dropped from his ugly shouting mouth. He yelled an unspeakable horror that the Black Police had done in Paris, and so passed shrieking, "Ostrog the Knave!"

For a moment Graham stood still, for it had come upon him again that these things were a dream. He looked up at the great cliff of buildings on either side, vanishing into blue haze at last above the lights, and down to the roaring tiers of platforms, and the shouting, running people who were gesticulating past. "The Master is betrayed!" they cried. "The Master is betrayed!"

Suddenly the situation shaped itself in his mind real and urgent. His heart began to beat fast and strong.

"It has come," he said. "I might have known. The hour has come."

He thought swiftly. "What am I to do?"

"Go back to the Council House," said Asano.

"Why should I not appeal—? The people are here."

"You will lose time. They will doubt if it is you. But they will mass about the Council House. There you will find their leaders. Your strength is there—with them."

"Suppose this is only a rumour?"

"It sounds true," said Asano.

"Let us have the facts," said Graham.

Asano shrugged his shoulders. "We had better get towards the Council House," he cried. "That is where they will swarm. Even now the ruins may be impassable."

Graham regarded him doubtfully and followed him.

They went up the stepped platforms to the swiftest one, and there Asano accosted a labourer. The answers to his questions were in the thick, vulgar speech.

"What did he say?" asked Graham.

"He knows little, but he told me that the Black Police would have arrived here before the people knew—had not someone in the Wind-Vane Offices learnt. He said a girl."

"A girl? Not—?"

"He said a girl—he did not know who she was. Who came out from the Council House crying aloud, and told the men at work among the ruins."

And then another thing was shouted, something that turned an aimless tumult into determinate movements, it came like a wind along the street. "To your Wards, to your Wards. Every man get arms. Every man to his Ward!"

22

THE STRUGGLE IN THE COUNCIL-HOUSE

As Asano and Graham hurried along to the ruins about the Council House, they saw everywhere the excitement of the people rising. "To your wards! To your wards!" Everywhere men and women in blue were hurrying from unknown subterranean employments, up the staircases of the middle path; at one place Graham saw an arsenal of the revolutionary committee besieged by a crowd of shouting men, at another a couple of men in the hated yellow uniform of the Labour Police, pursued by a gathering crowd, fled precipitately along the swift way that went in the opposite direction.

The cries of "To your wards!" became at last a continuous shouting as they drew near the Government quarter. Many of the shouts were unintelligible. "Ostrog has betrayed us," one man bawled in a hoarse voice, again and again, dinning that refrain into Graham's ear until it haunted him. This person stayed close beside Graham and Asano on the swift way, shouting to the people who swarmed on the lower platforms as he rushed past them. His cry about Ostrog alternated with some incomprehensible orders. Presently he went leaping down and disappeared.

Graham's mind was filled with the din. His plans were vague and unformed. He had one picture of some commanding position from which he could address the multitudes, another of meeting Ostrog face to face. He was full of rage, of tense muscular excitement, his hands gripped, his lips were pressed together.

The way to the Council House across the ruins was impassable, but Asano met that difficulty and took Graham into the premises of the central post-office. The post-office was nominally at work, but the blue-clothed porters moved sluggishly or had stopped to stare through the arches of their galleries at the shouting men who were going by outside. "Every man to his ward! Every man to his ward!" Here, by Asano's advice, Graham revealed his identity.

They crossed to the Council House by a cable cradle. Already in the brief interval since the capitulation of the Councillors a great change had been wrought in the appearance of the ruins. The spurting cascades of the ruptured sea-water mains had been captured and tamed, and huge temporary pipes ran overhead along a flimsy looking fabric of girders. The sky was laced with restored cables and wires that served the Council House, and a mass of new fabric with cranes and other building machines going to and fro upon it projected to the left of the white pile.

The moving ways that ran across this area had been restored, albeit for once running under the open sky. These were the ways that Graham had seen from the little balcony in the hour of his awakening, not nine days since, and the hall of his Trance had been on the further side, where now shapeless piles of smashed and shattered masonry were heaped together.

It was already high day and the sun was shining brightly. Out of their tall caverns of blue electric light came the swift ways crowded with multitudes of people, who poured off them and gathered ever denser over the wreckage and confusion of the ruins. The air was full of their shouting, and they were pressing and swaying towards the central building. For the most part that shouting mass consisted of shapeless swarms, but here and there Graham could see that a rude discipline struggled to establish itself. And every voice clamoured for order in the chaos. "To your wards! Every man to his ward!"

The cable carried them into a hall which Graham recognised as the antechamber to the Hall of the Atlas, about the gallery of which he had walked days ago with Howard to show himself to the Vanished Council, an hour from his awakening. Now the place was empty except for two cable attendants. These men seemed hugely astonished to recognize the Sleeper in the man who swung down from the cross seat.

"Where is Ostrog?" he demanded. "I must see Ostrog forthwith. He has disobeyed me. I have come back to take things out of his hands." Without waiting for Asano, he went straight across the place, ascended the steps at the further end, and, pulling the curtain aside, found himself facing the perpetually labouring Titan.

The hall was empty. Its appearance had changed very greatly since his first sight of it. It had suffered serious injury in the violent struggle of the first outbreak. On the right-hand side of the great figure the upper half of the wall had been torn away for nearly two hundred feet of its length, and a sheet of the same glassy film that had enclosed Graham at his awakening had been drawn across the gap. This deadened, but did not altogether exclude the roar of the people outside. "Wards! Wards! Wards!" they seemed to be saying. Through it there were visible the beams and supports of metal scaffoldings that rose and fell according to the requirements of a great crowd of workmen. An idle building machine, with lank arms of red painted metal stretched gauntly across this green tinted picture. On it were still a number of workmen staring at the crowd below. For a moment he stood regarding these things, and Asano overtook him.

"Ostrog," said Asano, "will be in the small offices beyond there." The little man looked livid now and his eyes searched Graham's face.

They had scarcely advanced ten paces from the curtain before a little panel to the left of the Atlas rolled up, and Ostrog, accompanied by Lincoln and followed by two black and yellow clad negroes, appeared crossing the remote corner of the hall, towards a second panel that was raised and open. "Ostrog," shouted Graham, and at the sound of his voice the little party turned astonished.

Ostrog said something to Lincoln and advanced alone.

Graham was the first to speak. His voice was loud and dictatorial. "What is this I hear?" he asked. "Are you bringing negroes here—to keep the people down?"

"It is none too soon," said Ostrog. "They have been getting out of hand more and more, since the revolt. I under-estimated—"

"Do you mean that these infernal negroes are on the way?"

"On the way. As it is, you have seen the people—outside?"

"No wonder! But—after what was said. You have taken too much on yourself, Ostrog."

Ostrog said nothing, but drew nearer.

"These negroes must not come to London," said Graham. "I am Master and they shall not come."

Ostrog glanced at Lincoln, who at once came towards them with his two attendants close behind him. "Why not?" asked Ostrog.

"White men must be mastered by white men. Besides—"

"The negroes are only an instrument."

"But that is not the question. I am the Master. I mean to be the Master. And I tell you these negroes shall not come."

"The people—"

"I believe in the people."

"Because you are an anachronism. You are a man out of the Past—an accident. You are Owner perhaps of the world. Nominally—legally. But you are not Master. You do not know enough to be Master."

He glanced at Lincoln again. "I know now what you think—I can guess something of what you mean to do. Even now it is not too late to warn you. You dream of human equality—of some sort of socialistic order—you have all those worn-out dreams of the nineteenth century fresh and vivid in your mind, and you would rule this age that you do not understand."

"Listen!" said Graham. "You can hear it—a sound like the sea. Not voices—but a voice. Do *you* altogether understand?"

"We taught them that," said Ostrog.

"Perhaps. Can you teach them to forget it? But enough of this! These negroes must not come."

There was a pause and Ostrog looked him in the eyes.

"They will," he said.

"I forbid it," said Graham.

"They have started."

"I will not have it."

"No," said Ostrog. "Sorry as I am to follow the method of the Council —. For your own good—you must not side with—Disorder. And now that you are here—. It was kind of you to come here."

Lincoln laid his hand on Graham's shoulder. Abruptly Graham realized the enormity of his blunder in coming to the Council House. He turned towards the curtains that separated the hall from the antechamber. The clutching hand of Asano intervened. In another moment Lincoln had grasped Graham's cloak.

He turned and struck at Lincoln's face, and incontinently a negro had him by collar and arm. He wrenched himself away, his sleeve tore noisily, and he stumbled back, to be tripped by the other attendant. Then he struck the ground heavily and he was staring at the distant ceiling of the hall.

He shouted, rolled over, struggling fiercely, clutched an attendant's leg and threw him headlong, and struggled to his feet.

Lincoln appeared before him, went down heavily again with a blow under the point of the jaw and lay still. Graham made two strides, stumbled. And then Ostrog's arm was round his neck, he was pulled over backward, fell heavily, and his arms were pinned to the ground. After a few violent efforts he ceased to struggle and lay staring at Ostrog's heaving throat.

"You—are—a prisoner," panted Ostrog, exulting. "You—were rather a fool—to come back."

Graham turned his head about and perceived through the irregular green window in the walls of the hall the men who had been working the building cranes gesticulating excitedly to the people below them. They had seen!

Ostrog followed his eyes and started. He shouted something to Lincoln, but Lincoln did not move. A bullet smashed among the mouldings above the Atlas. The two sheets of transparent matter that had been stretched across this gap were rent, the edges of the torn aperture darkened, curved, ran rapidly towards the framework, and in a moment the Council chamber stood open to the air. A chilly gust blew in by the gap, bringing with it a war of voices from the ruinous spaces without, an elvish babblement, "Save the Master!" "What are they doing to the Master?" "The Master is betrayed!"

And then he realized that Ostrog's attention was distracted, that Ostrog's grip had relaxed, and, wrenching his arms free, he struggled to his knees. In another moment he had thrust Ostrog back, and he was on one foot, his hand gripping Ostrog's throat, and Ostrog's hands clutching the silk about his neck.

But now men were coming towards them from the dais—men whose intentions he misunderstood. He had a glimpse of someone running in the distance towards the curtains of the antechamber, and then Ostrog had slipped from him and these newcomers were upon him. To his infinite astonishment, they seized him. They obeyed the shouts of Ostrog.

He was lugged a dozen yards before he realized that they were not friends—that they were dragging him towards the open panel. When he saw this he pulled back, he tried to fling himself down, he shouted for help with all his strength. And this time there were answering cries.

The grip upon his neck relaxed, and behold! in the lower corner of the rent upon the wall, first one and then a number of little black figures appeared shouting and waving arms. They came leaping down from the gap into the light gallery that had led to the Silent Rooms. They ran along it, so near were they that Graham could see the weapons in their hands.

Then Ostrog was shouting in his ear to the men who held him, and once more he was struggling with all his strength against their endeavours to thrust him towards the opening that yawned to receive him. "They can't come down," panted Ostrog. "They daren't fire. It's all right. We'll save him from them yet."

For long minutes as it seemed to Graham that inglorious struggle continued. His clothes were rent in a dozen places, he was covered in dust, one hand had been trodden upon. He could hear the shouts of his supporters, and once he heard shots. He could feel his strength giving way, feel his efforts wild and aimless. But no help came, and surely, irresistibly, that black, yawning opening came nearer.

The pressure upon him relaxed and he struggled up. He saw Ostrog's grey head receding and perceived that he was no longer held. He turned about and came full into a man in black. One of the green weapons cracked close to him, a drift of pungent smoke came into his face, and a steel blade flashed. The huge chamber span about him.

He saw a man in pale blue stabbing one of the black and yellow attendants not three yards from his face. Then hands were upon him again.

He was being pulled in two directions now. It seemed as though people were shouting to him. He wanted to understand and could not. Someone was clutching about his thighs, he was being hoisted in spite of his vigorous efforts. He understood suddenly, he ceased to struggle. He was lifted up on men's shoulders and carried away from that devouring panel. Ten thousand throats were cheering.

He saw men in blue and black hurrying after the retreating Ostrogites and firing. Lifted up, he saw now across the whole expanse of the hall beneath the Atlas image, saw that he was being carried towards the raised platform in the centre of the place. The far end of the hall was already full of people running towards him. They were looking at him and cheering.

He became aware that a bodyguard surrounded him. Active men about him shouted vague orders. He saw close at hand the black moustached man in yellow who had been among those who had greeted him in the public theatre, shouting directions. The hall was already densely packed with swaying people, the little metal gallery sagged with a shouting load, the curtains at the end had been torn away, and the antechamber was revealed densely crowded. He could scarcely make the man near him hear for the tumult about them. "Where has Ostrog gone?" he asked.

The man he questioned pointed over the heads towards the lower panels about the hall on the side opposite the gap. They stood open, and armed men, blue clad with black sashes, were running through them and vanishing into the chambers and passages beyond. It seemed to Graham that a sound of firing drifted through the riot. He was carried in a staggering curve across the great hall towards an opening beneath the gap.

He perceived men working with a sort of rude discipline to keep the crowd off him, to make a space clear about him. He passed out of the hall, and saw a crude, new wall rising blankly before him topped by blue sky. He was swung down to his feet; someone gripped his arm and guided him. He found the man in yellow close at hand. They were taking him up a narrow stairway of brick, and close at hand rose the great red painted masses, the cranes and levers and the still engines of the big building machine.

He was at the top of the steps. He was hurried across a narrow railed footway, and suddenly with a vast shouting the amphitheatre of ruins opened again before him. "The Master is with us! The Master! The Master!" The shout swept athwart the lake of faces like a wave, broke against the distant cliff of ruins, and came back in a welter of cries. "The Master is on our side!"

Graham perceived that he was no longer encompassed by people, that he was standing upon a little temporary platform of white metal, part of a flimsy seeming scaffolding that laced about the great mass of the Council House. Over all the huge expanse of the ruins swayed and eddied the shouting people; and here and there the black banners of the revolutionary societies ducked and swayed and formed rare nuclei of organization in the chaos. Up the steep stairs of wall and scaffolding by which his rescuers had reached the opening in the Atlas Chamber clung a solid crowd, and little energetic black figures clinging to pillars and projections were strenuous to induce these congested, masses to stir. Behind him, at a higher point on the scaffolding, a number of men struggled upwards with the flapping folds of a huge black standard. Through the yawning gap in the walls below him he could look down upon the packed attentive multitudes in the Hall of the Atlas. The distant flying stages to the south came out bright and vivid, brought nearer as it seemed by an unusual translucency of the air. A solitary monoplane beat up from the central stage as if to meet the coming aeroplanes.

"What has become of Ostrog?" asked Graham, and even as he spoke he saw that all eyes were turned from him towards the crest of the Council House building. He looked also in this direction of universal attention. For a moment he saw nothing but the jagged corner of a wall, hard and clear against the sky. Then in the shadow he perceived the interior of a room and recognised with a start the green and white decorations of his former prison. And coming quickly across this opened room and up to the very verge of the cliff of the ruins came a little white clad figure followed by two other smaller seeming figures in black and yellow. He heard the man beside him exclaim "Ostrog," and turned to ask a question. But he never did, because of the startled exclamation of another of those who were with him and a lank finger suddenly pointing. He looked, and behold! the monoplane that had been rising from the flying stage when last he had looked in that direction, was driving towards them. The swift steady flight was still novel enough to hold his attention.

Nearer it came, growing rapidly larger and larger, until it had swept over the further edge of the ruins and into view of the dense multitudes below. It drooped across the space and rose and passed overhead, rising to clear the mass of the Council House, a filmy translucent shape with the solitary aeronaut peering down through its ribs. It vanished beyond the skyline of the ruins.

Graham transferred his attention to Ostrog. He was signalling with his hands, and his attendants were busy breaking down the wall beside him. In another moment the monoplane came into view again, a little thing far away, coming round in a wide curve and going slower.

Then suddenly the man in yellow shouted: "What are they doing? What are the people doing? Why is Ostrog left there? Why is he not captured? They will lift him—the monoplane will lift him! Ah!"

The exclamation was echoed by a shout from the ruins. The rattling sound of the green weapons drifted across the intervening gulf to Graham, and, looking down, he saw a number of black and yellow uniforms running along one of the galleries that lay open to the air below the promontory upon which Ostrog stood. They fired as they ran at men unseen, and then emerged a number of pale blue figures in pursuit. These minute fighting figures had the oddest effect; they seemed as they ran like little model soldiers in a toy. This queer appearance of a house cut open gave that struggle amidst furniture and passages a quality of unreality. It was perhaps two hundred yards away from him, and very nearly fifty above the heads in the ruins below. The black and yellow men ran into an open archway, and turned and fired a volley. One of the blue pursuers striding forward close to the edge, flung up his arms, staggered sideways, seemed to Graham's sense to hang over the edge for several seconds, and fell headlong down. Graham saw him strike a projecting corner, fly out, head over heels, head over heels, and vanish behind the red arm of the building machine.

And then a shadow came between Graham and the sun. He looked up and the sky was clear, but he knew the little monoplane had passed. Ostrog had vanished. The man in yellow thrust before him, zealous and perspiring, pointing and blatant.

"They are grounding!" cried the man in yellow. "They are grounding. Tell the people to fire at him. Tell them to fire at him!"

Graham could not understand. He heard loud voices repeating these enigmatical orders.

Suddenly he saw the prow of the monoplane come gliding over the edge of the ruins and stop with a jerk. In a moment Graham understood that the thing had grounded in order that Ostrog might escape by it. He saw a blue haze climbing out of the gulf, perceived that the people below him were now firing up at the projecting stem.

A man beside him cheered hoarsely, and he saw that the blue rebels had gained the archway that had been contested by the men in black and yellow a moment before, and were running in a continual stream along the open passage.

And suddenly the monoplane slipped over the edge of the Council House and fell like a diving swallow. It dropped, tilting at an angle of forty-five degrees, so steeply that it seemed to Graham, it seemed perhaps to most of those below, that it could not possibly rise again.

It fell so closely past him that he could see Ostrog clutching the guides of the seat, with his grey hair streaming; see the white-faced aeronaut wrenching over the lever that turned the machine upward. He heard the apprehensive vague cry of innumerable men below.

Graham clutched the railing before him and gasped. The second seemed an age. The lower vane of the monoplane passed within an ace of touching the people, who yelled and screamed and trampled one another below.

And then it rose.

For a moment it looked as if it could not possibly clear the opposite cliff, and then that it could not possibly clear the wind-wheel that rotated beyond.

And behold! it was clear and soaring, still heeling sideways, upward, upward into the wind-swept sky.

The suspense of the moment gave place to a fury of exasperation as the swarming people realized that Ostrog had escaped them. With belated activity they renewed their fire, until the rattling wove into a roar, until the whole area became dim and blue and the air pungent with the thin smoke of their weapons.

Too late! The flying machine dwindled smaller and smaller, and curved about and swept gracefully downward to the flying stage from which it had so lately risen. Ostrog had escaped.

For a while a confused babblement arose from the ruins, and then the universal attention came back to Graham, perched high among the scaffolding. He saw the faces of the people turned towards him, heard their shouts at his rescue. From the throat of the ways came the song of the revolt spreading like a breeze across that swaying sea of men.

The little group of men about him shouted congratulations on his escape. The man in yellow was close to him, with a set face and shining eyes. And the song was rising, louder and louder; tramp, tramp, tramp, tramp.

Slowly the realisation came of the full meaning of these things to him, the perception of the swift change in his position. Ostrog, who had stood beside him whenever he had faced that shouting multitude before, was beyond there—the antagonist. There was no one to rule for him any longer. Even the people about him, the leaders and organisers of the multitude, looked to see what he would do, looked to him to act, awaited his orders. He was king indeed. His puppet reign was at an end.

He was very intent to do the thing that was expected of him. His nerves and muscles were quivering, his mind was perhaps a little confused, but he felt neither fear nor anger. His hand that had been trodden upon throbbed and was hot. He was a little nervous about his bearing. He knew he was not afraid, but he was anxious not to seem afraid. In his former life he had often been more excited in playing games of skill. He was desirous of immediate action, he knew he must not think too much in detail of the huge complexity of the struggle about him lest he should be paralyzed by the sense of its intricacy. Over there those square blue shapes, the flying stages, meant Ostrog; against Ostrog, who was so clear and definite and decisive, he who was so vague and undecided, was fighting for the whole future of the world.

23

GRAHAM SPEAKS HIS WORD

For a time the Master of the Earth was not even master of his own mind. Even his will seemed a will not his own, his own acts surprised him and were but a part of the confusion of strange experiences that poured across his being. These things were definite, the negroes were coming, Helen Wotton had warned the people of their coming, and he was Master of the Earth. Each of these facts seemed struggling for complete possession of his thoughts. They protruded from a background of swarming halls, elevated passages, rooms jammed with ward leaders in council, kinematograph and telephone rooms, and windows looking out on a seething sea of marching men. The men in yellow, and men whom he fancied were called Ward Leaders, were either propelling him forward or following him obediently; it was hard to tell. Perhaps they were doing a little of both. Perhaps some power unseen and unsuspected propelled them all. He was aware that he was going to make a proclamation to the People of the Earth, aware of certain grandiose phrases floating in his mind as the thing he meant to say. Many little things happened, and then he found himself with the man in yellow entering a little room where this proclamation of his was to be made.

This room was grotesquely latter-day in its appointments. In the centre was a bright oval lit by shaded electric lights from above. The rest was in shadow, and the double finely fitting doors through which he came from the swarming Hall of the Atlas made the place very still. The dead thud of these as they closed behind him, the sudden cessation of the tumult in which he had been living for hours, the quivering circle of light, the whispers and quick noiseless movements of vaguely visible attendants in the shadows, had a strange effect upon Graham. The huge ears of a phonographic mechanism gaped in a battery for his words, the black eyes of great photographic cameras awaited his beginning, beyond metal rods and coils glittered dimly, and something whirled about with a droning hum. He walked into the centre of the light, and his shadow drew together black and sharp to a little blot at his feet.

The vague shape of the thing he meant to say was already in his mind. But this silence, this isolation, the withdrawal from that contagious crowd, this audience of gaping, glaring machines, had not been in his anticipation. All his supports seemed withdrawn together; he seemed to have dropped into this suddenly, suddenly to have discovered himself. In a moment he was changed. He found that he now feared to be inadequate, he feared to be theatrical, he feared the quality of his voice, the quality of his wit; astonished, he turned to the man in yellow with a propitiatory gesture. "For a moment," he said, "I must wait. I did not think it would be like this. I must think of the thing I have to say."

While he was still hesitating there came an agitated messenger with news that the foremost aeroplanes were passing over Madrid.

"What news of the flying stages?" he asked.

"The people of the south-west wards are ready."

"Ready!"

He turned impatiently to the blank circles of the lenses again.

"I suppose it must be a sort of speech. Would to God I knew certainly the thing that should be said! Aeroplanes at Madrid! They must have started before the main fleet.

"Oh! what can it matter whether I speak well or ill?" he said, and felt the light grow brighter.

He had framed some vague sentence of democratic sentiment when suddenly doubts overwhelmed him. His belief in his heroic quality and calling he found had altogether lost its assured conviction. The picture of a little strutting futility in a windy waste of incomprehensible destinies replaced it. Abruptly it was perfectly clear to him that this revolt against Ostrog was premature, foredoomed to failure, the impulse of passionate inadequacy against inevitable things. He thought of that swift flight of aeroplanes like the swoop of Fate towards him. He was astonished that he could have seen things in any other light. In that final emergency he debated, thrust debate resolutely aside, determined at all costs to go through with the thing he had undertaken. And he could find no word to begin. Even as he stood, awkward, hesitating, with an indiscreet apology for his inability trembling on his lips, came the noise of many people crying out, the running to and fro of feet. "Wait," cried someone, and a door opened. Graham turned, and the watching lights waned.

Through the open doorway he saw a slight girlish figure approaching. His heart leapt. It was Helen Wotton. The man in yellow came out of the nearer shadows into the circle of light.

"This is the girl who told us what Ostrog had done," he said.

She came in very quietly, and stood still, as if she did not want to interrupt Graham's eloquence.... But his doubts and questionings fled before her presence. He remembered the things that he had meant to say. He faced the cameras again and the light about him grew brighter. He turned back to her.

"You have helped me," he said lamely—"helped me very much.... This is very difficult."

He paused. He addressed himself to the unseen multitudes who stared upon him through those grotesque black eyes. At first he spoke slowly.

"Men and women of the new age," he said; "you have arisen to do battle for the race!... There is no easy victory before us."

He stopped to gather words. He wished passionately for the gift of moving speech.

"This night is a beginning," he said. "This battle that is coming, this battle that rushes upon us to-night, is only a beginning. All your lives, it may be, you must fight. Take no thought though I am beaten, though I am utterly overthrown. I think I may be overthrown."

He found the thing in his mind too vague for words. He paused momentarily, and broke into vague exhortations, and then a rush of speech came upon him. Much that he said was but the humanitarian commonplace of a vanished age, but the conviction of his voice touched it to vitality. He stated the case of the old days to the people of the new age, to the girl at his side.

"I come out of the past to you," he said, "with the memory of an age that hoped. My age was an age of dreams—of beginnings, an age of noble hopes; throughout the world we had made an end of slavery; throughout the world we had spread the desire and anticipation that wars might cease, that all men and women might live nobly, in freedom and peace.... So we hoped in the days that are past. And what of those hopes? How is it with man after two hundred years?

"Great cities, vast powers, a collective greatness beyond our dreams. For that we did not work, and that has come. But how is it with the little lives that make up this greater life? How is it with the common lives? As it has ever been—sorrow and labour, lives cramped and unfulfilled, lives tempted by power, tempted by wealth, and gone to waste and folly. The old faiths have faded and changed, the new faith—. Is there a new faith?

"Charity and mercy," he floundered; "beauty and the love of beautiful things—effort and devotion! Give yourselves as I would give myself—as Christ gave Himself upon the Cross. It does not matter if you understand. It does not matter if you seem to fail. You *know*—in the core of your hearts you *know*. There is no promise, there is no security—nothing to go upon but Faith. There is no faith but faith—faith which is courage...."

Things that he had long wished to believe, he found that he believed. He spoke gustily, in broken incomplete sentences, but with all his heart and strength, of this new faith within him. He spoke of the greatness of self-abnegation, of his belief in an immortal life of Humanity in which we live and move and have our being. His voice rose and fell, and the recording appliances hummed as he spoke, dim attendants watched him out of the shadow....

His sense of that silent spectator beside him sustained his sincerity. For a few glorious moments he was carried away; he felt no doubt of his heroic quality, no doubt of his heroic words, he had it all straight and plain. His eloquence limped no longer. And at last he made an end to speaking. "Here and now," he cried, "I make my will. All that is mine in the world I give to the people of the world. All that is mine in the world I give to the people of the world. To all of you. I give it to you, and myself I give to you. And as God wills to-night, I will live for you, or I will die."

He ended. He found the light of his present exaltation reflected in the face of the girl. Their eyes met; her eyes were swimming with tears of enthusiasm.

"I knew," she whispered. "Oh! Father of the World—*Sire*! I knew you would say these things...."

"I have said what I could," he answered lamely and grasped and clung to her outstretched hands.

The man in yellow was beside them. Neither had noted his coming. He was saying that the south-west wards were marching. "I never expected it so soon," he cried. "They have done wonders. You must send them a word to help them on their way."

24

WHILE THE AEROPLANES WERE COMING

GRAHAM STARED AT HIM ABSENT-MINDEDLY. THEN WITH A START HE returned to his previous preoccupation about the flying stages.

"Yes," he said. "That is good, that is good." He weighed a message. "Tell them;—well done South West."

He turned his eyes to Helen Wotton again. His face expressed his struggle between conflicting ideas. "We must capture the flying stages," he explained. "Unless we can do that they will land negroes. At all costs we must prevent that."

He felt even as he spoke that this was not what had been in his mind before the interruption. He saw a touch of surprise in her eyes. She seemed about to speak and a shrill bell drowned her voice.

It occurred to Graham that she expected him to lead these marching people, that that was the thing he had to do. He made the offer abruptly. He addressed the man in yellow, but he spoke to her. He saw her face respond. "Here I am doing nothing," he said.

"It is impossible," protested the man in yellow. "It is a fight in a warren. Your place is here."

He explained elaborately. He motioned towards the room where Graham must wait, he insisted no other course was possible. "We must know where you are," he said. "At any moment a crisis may arise needing your presence and decision."

A picture had drifted through his mind of such a vast dramatic struggle as the masses in the ruins had suggested. But here was no spectacular battle-field such as he imagined. Instead was seclusion—and suspense. It was only as the afternoon wore on that he pieced together a truer picture of the fight that was raging, inaudibly and invisibly, within four miles of him, beneath the Roehampton stage. A strange and unprecedented contest it was, a battle that was a hundred thousand little battles, a battle in a sponge of ways and channels, fought out of sight of sky or sun under the electric glare, fought out in a vast confusion by multitudes untrained in arms, led chiefly by acclamation, multitudes dulled by mindless labour and enervated by the tradition of two hundred years of servile security against multitudes demoralised by lives of venial privilege and sensual indulgence. They had no artillery, no differentiation into this force or that; the only weapon on either side was the little green metal carbine, whose secret manufacture and sudden distribution in enormous quantities had been one of Ostrog's culminating moves against the Council. Few had had any experience with this weapon, many had never discharged one, many who carried it came unprovided with ammunition; never was wilder firing in the history of warfare. It was a battle of amateurs, a hideous experimental warfare, armed rioters fighting armed rioters, armed rioters swept forward by the words and fury of a song, by the tramping sympathy of their numbers, pouring in countless myriads towards the smaller ways, the disabled lifts, the galleries slippery with blood, the halls and passages choked with smoke, beneath the flying stages, to learn there when retreat was hopeless the ancient mysteries of warfare. And overhead save for a few sharpshooters upon the roof spaces and for a few bands and threads of vapour that multiplied and darkened towards the evening, the day was a clear serenity. Ostrog it seems had no bombs at command and in all the earlier phases of the battle the flying machines played no part. Not the smallest cloud was there to break the empty brilliance of the sky. It seemed as though it held itself vacant until the aeroplanes should come.

Ever and again there was news of these, drawing nearer, from this Spanish town and then that, and presently from France. But of the new guns that Ostrog had made and which were known to be in the city came no news in spite of Graham's urgency, nor any report of successes from the dense felt of fighting strands about the flying stages. Section after section of the Labour-Societies reported itself assembled, reported itself marching, and vanished from knowledge into the labyrinth of that warfare. What was happening there? Even the busy ward leaders did not know. In spite of the opening and closing of doors, the hasty messengers, the ringing of bells and the perpetual clitter-clack of recording implements, Graham felt isolated, strangely inactive, inoperative.

His isolation seemed at times the strangest, the most unexpected of all the things that had happened since his awakening. It had something of the quality of that inactivity that comes in dreams. A tumult, the stupendous realisation of a world struggle between Ostrog and himself, and then this confined quiet little room with its mouthpieces and bells and broken mirror!

Now the door would be closed and Graham and Helen were alone together; they seemed sharply marked off then from all the unprecedented world storm that rushed together without, vividly aware of one another, only concerned with one another. Then the door would open again, messengers would enter, or a sharp bell would stab their quiet privacy, and it was like a window in a brightly lit house flung open suddenly to a hurricane. The dark hurry and tumult, the stress and vehemence of the battle rushed in and overwhelmed them. They were no longer persons but mere spectators, mere impressions of a tremendous convulsion. They became unreal even to themselves, miniatures of personality, indescribably small, and the two antagonistic realities, the only realities in being were first the city, that throbbed and roared yonder in a belated frenzy of defence and secondly the aeroplanes hurling inexorably towards them over the round shoulder of the world.

There came a sudden stir outside, a running to and fro, and cries. The girl stood up, speechless, incredulous.

Metallic voices were shouting "Victory!" Yes it was "Victory!"

Bursting through the curtains appeared the man in yellow, startled and dishevelled with excitement, "Victory," he cried, "victory! The people are winning. Ostrog's people have collapsed."

She rose. "Victory?"

"What do you mean?" asked Graham. "Tell me! *What?*"

"We have driven them out of the under galleries at Norwood, Streatham is afire and burning wildly, and Roehampton is ours. *Ours!*—and we have taken the monoplane that lay thereon."

A shrill bell rang. An agitated grey-headed man appeared from the room of the Ward Leaders. "It is all over," he cried.

"What matters it now that we have Roehampton? The aeroplanes have been sighted at Boulogne!"

"The Channel!" said the man in yellow. He calculated swiftly. "Half an hour."

"They still have three of the flying stages," said the old man.

"Those guns?" cried Graham.

"We cannot mount them—in half an hour."

"Do you mean they are found?"

"Too late," said the old man.

"If we could stop them another hour!" cried the man in yellow.

"Nothing can stop them now," said the old man. "They have near a hundred aeroplanes in the first fleet."

"Another hour?" asked Graham.

"To be so near!" said the Ward Leader. "Now that we have found those guns. To be so near—. If once we could get them out upon the roof spaces."

"How long would that take?" asked Graham suddenly.

"An hour—certainly."

"Too late," cried the Ward Leader, "too late."

"*Is* it too late?" said Graham. "Even now—. An hour!"

He had suddenly perceived a possibility. He tried to speak calmly, but his face was white. "There is are chance. You said there was a monoplane—?"

"On the Roehampton stage, Sire."

"Smashed?"

"No. It is lying crossways to the carrier. It might be got upon the guides—easily. But there is no aeronaut—."

Graham glanced at the two men and then at Helen. He spoke after a long pause. "*We* have no aeronauts?"

"None."

He turned suddenly to Helen. His decision was made. "I must do it."

"Do what?"

"Go to this flying stage—to this machine."

"What do you mean?"

"I am an aeronaut. After all—. Those days for which you reproached me were not altogether wasted."

He turned to the old man in yellow. "Tell them to put it upon the guides."

The man in yellow hesitated.

"What do you mean to do?" cried Helen.

"This monoplane—it is a chance—."

"You don't mean—?"

"To fight—yes. To fight in the air. I have thought before—. A big aeroplane is a clumsy thing. A resolute man—!"

"But—never since flying began—" cried the man in yellow.

"There has been no need. But now the time has come. Tell them now —send them my message—to put it upon the guides. I see now something to do. I see now why I am here!"

The old man dumbly interrogated the man in yellow nodded, and hurried out.

Helen made a step towards Graham. Her face was white. "But, Sire!— How can one fight? You will be killed."

"Perhaps. Yet, not to do it—or to let some one else attempt it—."

"You will be killed," she repeated.

"I've said my word. Do you not see? It may save—London!"

He stopped, he could speak no more, he swept the alternative aside by a gesture, and they stood looking at one another.

They were both clear that he must go. There was no step back from these towering heroisms.

Her eyes brimmed with tears. She came towards him with a curious movement of her hands, as though she felt her way and could not see; she seized his hand and kissed it.

"To wake," she cried, "for this!"

He held her clumsily for a moment, and kissed the hair of her bowed head, and then thrust her away, and turned towards the man in yellow.

He could not speak. The gesture of his arm said "Onward."

25

THE COMING OF THE AEROPLANES

Two men in pale blue were lying in the irregular line that stretched along the edge of the captured Roehampton stage from end to end, grasping their carbines and peering into the shadows of the stage called Wimbledon Park. Now and then they spoke to one another. They spoke the mutilated English of their class and period. The fire of the Ostrogites had dwindled and ceased, and few of the enemy had been seen for some time. But the echoes of the fight that was going on now far below in the lower galleries of that stage, came every now and then between the staccato of shots from the popular side. One of these men was describing to the other how he had seen a man down below there dodge behind a girder, and had aimed at a guess and hit him cleanly as he dodged too far. "He's down there still," said the marksman. "See that little patch. Yes. Between those bars."

A few yards behind them lay a dead stranger, face upward to the sky, with the blue canvas of his jacket smouldering in a circle about the neat bullet hole on his chest. Close beside him a wounded man, with a leg swathed about, sat with an expressionless face and watched the progress of that burning. Behind them, athwart the carrier lay the captured monoplane.

"I can't see him *now*," said the second man in a tone of provocation.

The marksman became foul-mouthed and high-voiced in his earnest endeavour to make things plain. And suddenly, interrupting him, came a noisy shouting from the substage.

"What's going on now?" he said, and raised himself on one arm to survey the stairheads in the central groove of the stage. A number of blue figures were coming up these, and swarming across the stage.

"We don't want all these fools," said his friend. "They only crowd up and spoil shots. What are they after?"

"Ssh!—they're shouting something."

The two men listened. The new-comers had crowded densely about the machine. Three Ward Leaders, conspicuous by their black mantles and badges, clambered into the body and appeared above it. The rank and file flung themselves upon the vans, gripping hold of the edges, until the entire outline of the thing was manned, in some places three deep. One of the marksmen knelt up. "They're putting it on the carrier—that's what they're after."

He rose to his feet, his friend rose also. "What's the good?" said his friend. "We've got no aeronauts."

"That's what they're doing anyhow." He looked at his rifle, looked at the struggling crowd, and suddenly turned to the wounded man. "Mind these, mate," he said, handing his carbine and cartridge belt; and in a moment he was running towards the monoplane. For a quarter of an hour he was lugging, thrusting, shouting and heeding shouts, and then the thing was done, and he stood with a multitude of others cheering their own achievement. By this time he knew, what indeed everyone in the city knew, that the Master, raw learner though he was, intended to fly this machine himself, was coming even now to take control of it, would let no other man attempt it.

"He who takes the greatest danger, he who bears the heaviest burden, that man is King," so the Master was reported to have spoken. And even as this man cheered, and while the beads of sweat still chased one another from the disorder of his hair, he heard the thunder of a greater tumult, and in fitful snatches the beat and impulse of the revolutionary song. He saw through a gap in the people that a thick stream of heads still poured up the stairway. "The Master is coming," shouted voices, "the Master is coming," and the crowd about him grew denser and denser. He began to thrust himself towards the central groove. "The Master is coming!" "The Sleeper, the Master!" "God and the Master!" roared the voices.

And suddenly quite close to him were the black uniforms of the revolutionary guard, and for the first and last time in his life he saw Graham, saw him quite nearly. A tall, dark man in a flowing black robe he was, with a white, resolute face and eyes fixed steadfastly before him; a man who for all the little things about him had neither ears nor eyes nor thoughts....

For all his days that man remembered the passing of Graham's bloodless face. In a moment it had gone and he was fighting in the swaying crowd. A lad weeping with terror thrust against him, pressing towards the stairways, yelling "Clear for the start, you fools!" The bell that cleared the flying stage became a loud unmelodious clanging.

With that clanging in his ears Graham drew near the monoplane, marched into the shadow of its tilting wing. He became aware that a number of people about him were offering to accompany him, and waved their offers aside. He wanted to think how one started the engine. The bell clanged faster and faster, and the feet of the retreating people roared faster and louder. The man in yellow was assisting him to mount through the ribs of the body. He clambered into the aeronaut's place, fixing himself very carefully and deliberately. What was it? The man in yellow was pointing to two small flying machines driving upward in the southern sky. No doubt they were looking for the coming aeroplanes. That—presently —the thing to do now was to start. Things were being shouted at him, questions, warnings. They bothered him. He wanted to think about the machine, to recall every item of his previous experience. He waved the people from him, saw the man in yellow dropping off through the ribs, saw the crowd cleft down the line of the girders by his gesture.

For a moment he was motionless, staring at the levers, the wheel by which the engine shifted, and all the delicate appliances of which he knew so little. His eye caught a spirit level with the bubble towards him, and he remembered something, spent a dozen seconds in swinging the engine forward until the bubble floated in the centre of the tube. He noted that the people were not shouting, knew they watched his deliberation. A bullet smashed on the bar above his head. Who fired? Was the line clear of people? He stood up to see and sat down again.

In another second the propeller was spinning and he was rushing down the guides. He gripped the wheel and swung the engine back to lift the stem. Then it was the people shouted. In a moment he was throbbing with the quiver of the engine, and the shouts dwindled swiftly behind, rushed down to silence. The wind whistled over the edges of the screen, and the world sank away from him very swiftly.

Throb, throb, throb—throb, throb, throb; up he drove. He fancied himself free of all excitement, felt cool and deliberate. He lifted the stem still more, opened one valve on his left wing and swept round and up. He looked down with a steady head, and up. One of the Ostrogite monoplanes was driving across his course, so that he drove obliquely towards it and would pass below it at a steep angle. Its little aeronauts were peering down at him. What did they mean to do? His mind became active. One, he saw held a weapon pointing, seemed prepared to fire. What did they think he meant to do? In a moment he understood their tactics, and his resolution was taken. His momentary lethargy was past. He opened two more valves to his left, swung round, end on to this hostile machine, closed his valves, and shot straight at it, stem and wind-screen shielding him from the shot. They tilted a little as if to clear him. He flung up his stem.

Throb, throb, throb—pause—throb, throb—he set his teeth, his face into an involuntary grimace, and crash! He struck it! He struck upward beneath the nearer wing.

Very slowly the wing of his antagonist seemed to broaden as the impetus of his blow turned it up. He saw the full breadth of it and then it slid downward out of his sight.

He felt his stem going down, his hands tightened on the levers, whirled and rammed the engine back. He felt the jerk of a clearance, the nose of the machine jerked upward steeply, and for a moment he seemed to be lying on his back. The machine was reeling and staggering, it seemed to be dancing on its screw. He made a huge effort, hung for a moment on the levers, and slowly the engine came forward again. He was driving upward but no longer so steeply. He gasped for a moment and flung himself at the levers again. The wind whistled about him. One further effort and he was almost level. He could breathe. He turned his head for the first time to see what had become of his antagonists. Turned back to the levers for a moment and looked again. For a moment he could have believed they were annihilated. And then he saw between the two stages to the east was a chasm, and down this something, a slender edge, fell swiftly and vanished, as a sixpence falls down a crack.

At first he did not understand, and then a wild joy possessed him. He shouted at the top of his voice, an inarticulate shout, and drove higher and higher up the sky. Throb, throb, throb, pause, throb, throb, throb. "Where was the other?" he thought. "They too—." As he looked round the empty heavens he had a momentary fear that this second machine had risen above him, and then he saw it alighting on the Norwood stage. They had meant shooting. To risk being rammed headlong two thousand feet in the air was beyond their latter-day courage....

For a little while he circled, then swooped in a steep descent towards the westward stage. Throb throb throb, throb throb throb. The twilight was creeping on apace, the smoke from the Streatham stage that had been so dense and dark, was now a pillar of fire, and all the laced curves of the moving ways and the translucent roofs and domes and the chasms between the buildings were glowing softly now, lit by the tempered radiance of the electric light that the glare of the day overpowered. The three efficient stages that the Ostrogites held—for Wimbledon Park was useless because of the fire from Roehampton, and Streatham was a furnace—were glowing with guide lights for the coming aeroplanes. As he swept over the Roehampton stage he saw the dark masses of the people thereon. He heard a clap of frantic cheering, heard a bullet from the Wimbledon Park stage tweet through the air, and went beating up above the Surrey wastes. He felt a breath of wind from the southwest, and lifted his westward wing as he had learnt to do, and so drove upward heeling into the rare swift upper air. Whirr, whirr, whirr.

Up he drove and up, to that pulsating rhythm, until the country beneath was blue and indistinct, and London spread like a little map traced in light, like the mere model of a city near the brim of the horizon. The south-west was a sky of sapphire over the shadowy rim of the world, and ever as he drove upward the multitude of stars increased.

And behold! In the southward, low down and glittering swiftly nearer, were two little patches of nebulous light. And then two more, and then a glow of swiftly driving shapes. Presently he could count them. There were four-and-twenty. The first fleet of aeroplanes had come! Beyond appeared a yet greater glow.

He swept round in a half circle, staring at this advancing fleet. It flew in a wedge-like shape, a triangular flight of gigantic phosphorescent shapes sweeping nearer through the lower air. He made a swift calculation of their pace, and spun the little wheel that brought the engine forward. He touched a lever and the throbbing effort of the engine ceased. He began to fall, fell swifter and swifter. He aimed at the apex of the wedge. He dropped like a stone through the whistling air. It seemed scarce a second from that soaring moment before he struck the foremost aeroplane.

No man of all that black multitude saw the coming of his fate, no man among them dreamt of the hawk that struck downward upon him out of the sky. Those who were not limp in the agonies of air sickness, were craning their black necks and staring to see the filmy city that was rising out of the haze, the rich and splendid city to which "Massa Boss" had brought their obedient muscles. Bright teeth gleamed and the glossy faces shone. They had heard of Paris. They knew they were to have lordly times among the poor white trash.

Suddenly Graham hit them.

He had aimed at the body of the aeroplane, but at the very last instant a better idea had flashed into his mind. He twisted about and struck near the edge of the starboard wing with all his accumulated weight. He was jerked back as he struck. His prow went gliding across its smooth expanse towards the rim. He felt the forward rush of the huge fabric sweeping him and his monoplane along with it, and for a moment that seemed an age he could not tell what was happening. He heard a thousand throats yelling, and perceived that his machine was balanced on the edge of the gigantic float, and driving down, down; glanced over his shoulder and saw the back-bone of the aeroplane and the opposite float swaying up. He had a vision through the ribs of sliding chairs, staring faces, and hands clutching at the tilting guide bars. The fenestrations in the further float flashed open as the aeronaut tried to right her. Beyond, he saw a second aeroplane leaping steeply to escape the whirl of its heeling fellow. The broad area of swaying wings seemed to jerk upward. He felt he had dropped clear, that the monstrous fabric, clean overturned, hung like a sloping wall above him.

He did not clearly understand that he had struck the side float of the aeroplane and slipped off, but he perceived that he was flying free on the down glide and rapidly nearing earth. What had he done? His heart throbbed like a noisy engine in his throat and for a perilous instant he could not move his levers because of the paralysis of his hands. He wrenched the levers to throw his engine back, fought for two seconds against the weight of it, felt himself righting, driving horizontally, set the engine beating again.

He looked upward and saw two aeroplanes glide shouting far overhead, looked back, and saw the main body of the fleet opening out and rushing upward and outward; saw the one he had struck fall edgewise on and strike like a gigantic knife-blade along the wind-wheels below it.

He put down his stern and looked again. He drove up heedless of his direction as he watched. He saw the Wind-Vanes give, saw the huge fabric strike the earth, saw its downward vanes crumple with the weight of its descent, and then the whole mass turned over and smashed, upside down, upon the sloping wheels. Then from the heaving wreckage a thin tongue of white fire licked up towards the zenith. He was aware of a huge mass flying through the air towards him, and turned upwards just in time to escape the charge—if it was a charge—of a second aeroplane. It whirled by below, sucked him down a fathom, and nearly turned him over in the gust of its close passage.

He became aware of three others rushing towards him, aware of the urgent necessity of beating above them. Aeroplanes were all about him, circling wildly to avoid him, as it seemed. They drove past him, above, below, eastward and westward. Far away to the westward was the sound of a collision, and two falling flares. Far away to the southward a second squadron was coming. Steadily he beat upward. Presently all the aeroplanes were below him, but for a moment he doubted the height he had of them, and did not swoop again. And then he came down upon a second victim and all its load of soldiers saw him coming. The big machine heeled and swayed as the fear-maddened men scrambled to the stern for their weapons. A score of bullets sung through the air, and there flashed a star in the thick glass wind-screen that protected him. The aeroplane slowed and dropped to foil his stroke, and dropped too low. Just in time he saw the wind-wheels of Bromley hill rushing up towards him, and spun about and up as the aeroplane he had chased crashed among them. All its voices wove into a felt of yelling. The great fabric seemed to be standing on end for a second among the heeling and splintering vans, and then it flew to pieces. Huge splinters came flying through the air, its engines burst like shells. A hot rush of flame shot overhead into the darkling sky.

"*Two!*" he cried, with a bomb from overhead bursting as it fell, and forthwith he was beating up again. A glorious exhilaration possessed him now, a giant activity. His troubles about humanity, about his inadequacy, were gone for ever. He was a man in battle rejoicing in his power. Aeroplanes seemed radiating from him in every direction, intent only upon avoiding him, the yelling of their packed passengers came in short gusts as they swept by. He chose his third quarry, struck hastily and did but turn it on edge. It escaped him, to smash against the tall cliff of London wall. Flying from that impact he skimmed the darkling ground so nearly he could see a frightened rabbit bolting up a slope. He jerked up steeply, and found himself driving over south London with the air about him vacant. To the right of him a wild riot of signal rockets from the Ostrogites banged tumultuously in the sky. To the south the wreckage of half a dozen air ships flamed, and east and west and north they fled before him. They drove away to the east and north, and went about in the south, for they could not pause in the air. In their present confusion any attempt at evolution would have meant disastrous collisions.

He passed two hundred feet or so above the Roehampton stage. It was black with people and noisy with their frantic shouting. But why was the Wimbledon Park stage black and cheering, too? The smoke and flame of Streatham now hid the three further stages. He curved about and rose to see them and the northern quarters. First came the square masses of Shooter's Hill into sight, from behind the smoke, lit and orderly with the aeroplane that had landed and its disembarking negroes. Then came Blackheath, and then under the corner of the reek the Norwood stage. On Blackheath no aeroplane had landed. Norwood was covered by a swarm of little figures running to and fro in a passionate confusion. Why? Abruptly he understood. The stubborn defence of the flying stages was over, the people were pouring into the under-ways of these last strongholds of Ostrog's usurpation. And then, from far away on the northern border of the city, full of glorious import to him, came a sound, a signal, a note of triumph, the leaden thud of a gun. His lips fell apart, his face was disturbed with emotion.

He drew an immense breath. "They win," he shouted to the empty air; "the people win!" The sound of a second gun came like an answer. And then he saw the monoplane on Blackheath was running down its guides to launch. It lifted clean and rose. It shot up into the air, driving straight southward and away from him.

In an instant it came to him what this meant. It must needs be Ostrog in flight. He shouted and dropped towards it. He had the momentum of his elevation and fell slanting down the air and very swiftly. It rose steeply at his approach. He allowed for its velocity and drove straight upon it.

It suddenly became a mere flat edge, and behold! he was past it, and driving headlong down with all the force of his futile blow.

He was furiously angry. He reeled the engine back along its shaft and went circling up. He saw Ostrog's machine beating up a spiral before him. He rose straight towards it, won above it by virtue of the impetus of his swoop and by the advantage and weight of a man. He dropped headlong— dropped and missed again! As he rushed past he saw the face of Ostrog's aeronaut confident and cool and in Ostrog's attitude a wincing resolution. Ostrog was looking steadfastly away from him—to the south. He realized with a gleam of wrath how bungling his flight must be. Below he saw the Croydon hills. He jerked upward and once more he gained on his enemy.

He glanced over his shoulder and his attention was arrested. The eastward stage, the one on Shooter's Hill, appeared to lift; a flash changing to a tall grey shape, a cowled figure of smoke and dust, jerked into the air. For a moment this cowled figure stood motionless, dropping huge masses of metal from its shoulders, and then it began to uncoil a dense head of smoke. The people had blown it up, aeroplane and all! As suddenly a second flash and grey shape sprang up from the Norwood stage. And even as he stared at this came a dead report; and the air wave of the first explosion struck him. He was flung up and sideways.

For a moment his monoplane fell nearly edgewise with her nose down, and seemed to hesitate whether to overset altogether. He stood on his wind-shield, wrenching the wheel that swayed up over his head. And then the shock of the second explosion took his machine sideways.

He found himself clinging to one of the ribs of his machine, and the air was blowing past him and *upward*. He seemed to be hanging quite still in the air, with the wind blowing up past him. It occurred to him that he was falling. Then he was sure that he was falling. He could not look down.

He found himself recapitulating with incredible swiftness all that had happened since his awakening, the days of doubt, the days of Empire, and at last the tumultuous discovery of Ostrog's calculated treachery.

The vision had a quality of utter unreality. Who was he? Why was he holding so tightly with his hands? Why could he not let go? In such a fall as this countless dreams have ended. But in a moment he would wake....

His thoughts ran swifter and swifter. He wondered if he should see Helen again. It seemed so unreasonable that he should not see her again. It *must* be a dream! Yet surely he would meet her. She at least was real. She was real. He would wake and meet her.

Although he could not look at it, he was suddenly aware that the earth was very near.

Came a shock and a great crackling and popping of bars and stays.

MEN LIKE GODS

BOOK THE FIRST

The Irruption of the Earthlings

1

Mr. Barnstaple Takes A Holiday

~

MR. BARNSTAPLE FOUND HIMSELF IN URGENT NEED OF A HOLIDAY, AND he had no one to go with and nowhere to go. He was overworked. And he was tired of home.

He was a man of strong natural affections; he loved his family extremely so that he knew it by heart, and when he was in these jaded moods it bored him acutely. His three sons, who were all growing up, seemed to get leggier and larger every day; they sat down in the chairs he was just going to sit down in; they played him off his own pianola; they filled the house with hoarse, vast laughter at jokes that one couldn't demand to be told; they cut in on the elderly harmless flirtations that had hitherto been one of his chief consolations in this vale; they beat him at tennis; they fought playfully on the landings, and fell downstairs by twos and threes with an enormous racket. Their hats were everywhere. They were late for breakfast. They went to bed every night in a storm of uproar: "Haw, Haw, Haw—*bump*!" and their mother seemed to like it. They all cost money, with a cheerful disregard of the fact that everything had gone up except Mr. Barnstaple's earning power. And when he said a few plain truths about Mr. Lloyd George at meal-times, or made the slightest attempt to raise the tone of the table-talk above the level of the silliest persiflage, their attention wandered ostentatiously ...

At any rate it *seemed* ostentatiously.

He wanted badly to get away from his family to some place where he could think of its various members with quiet pride and affection, and otherwise not be disturbed by them....

And also he wanted to get away for a time from Mr. Peeve. The very streets were becoming a torment to him, he wanted never to see a newspaper or a newspaper placard again. He was obsessed by apprehensions of some sort of financial and economic smash that would make the Great War seem a mere incidental catastrophe. This was because he was subeditor and general factotum of the *Liberal*, that well-known organ of the more depressing aspects of advanced thought, and the unvarying pessimism of Mr. Peeve, his chief, was infecting him more and more. Formerly it had been possible to put up a sort of resistance to Mr. Peeve by joking furtively about his gloom with the other members of the staff, but now there were no other members of the staff: they had all been retrenched by Mr. Peeve in a mood of financial despondency. Practically, now, nobody wrote regularly for the *Liberal* except Mr. Barnstaple and Mr. Peeve.

So Mr. Peeve had it all his own way with Mr. Barnstaple. He would sit hunched up in the editorial chair, with his hands deep in his trouser pockets, taking a gloomy view of everything, sometimes for two hours together. Mr. Barnstaple's natural tendency was towards a modest hopefulness and a belief in progress, but Mr. Peeve held very strongly that a belief in progress was at least six years out of date, and that the brightest hope that remained to liberalism was for a good Day of Judgment soon. And having finished the copy of what the staff, when there was a staff, used to call his weekly indigest, Mr. Peeve would depart and leave Mr. Barnstaple to get the rest of the paper together for the next week.

Even in ordinary times Mr. Peeve would have been hard enough to live with; but the times were not ordinary, they were full of disagreeable occurrences that made his melancholy anticipations all too plausible. The great coal lock-out had been going on for a month and seemed to foreshadow the commercial ruin of England; every morning brought intelligence of fresh outrages from Ireland, unforgivable and unforgettable outrages; a prolonged drought threatened the harvests of the world; the League of Nations, of which Mr. Barnstaple had hoped enormous things in the great days of President Wilson, was a melancholy and self-satisfied futility; everywhere there was conflict, everywhere unreason; seven-eighths of the world seemed to be sinking down towards chronic disorder and social dissolution. Even without Mr. Peeve it would have been difficult enough to have made headway against the facts.

Mr. Barnstaple was, indeed, ceasing to secrete hope, and for such types as he, hope is the essential solvent without which there is no digesting life. His hope had always been in liberalism and generous liberal effort, but he was beginning to think that liberalism would never do anything more for ever than sit hunched up with its hands in its pockets grumbling and peeving at the activities of baser but more energetic men. Whose scrambling activities would inevitably wreck the world.

Night and day now, Mr. Barnstaple was worrying about the world at large. By night even more than by day, for sleep was leaving him. And he was haunted by a dreadful craving to bring out a number of the *Liberal* of his very own —to alter it all after Mr. Peeve had gone away, to cut out all the dyspeptic stuff, the miserable, empty girding at this wrong and that, the gloating on cruel and unhappy things, the exaggeration of the simple, natural, human misdeeds of Mr. Lloyd George, the appeals to Lord Grey, Lord Robert Cecil, Lord Lansdowne, the Pope, Queen Anne, or the Emperor Frederick Barbarossa (it varied from week to week), to arise and give voice and form to the young aspirations of a world reborn, and, instead, to fill the number with —Utopia! to say to the amazed readers of the *Liberal*: Here are things that have to be done! Here are the things we are going to do! What a blow it would be for Mr. Peeve at his Sunday breakfast! For once, too astonished to secrete abnormally, he might even digest that meal!

But this was the most foolish of dreaming. There were the three young Barnstaples at home and their need for a decent start in life to consider. And beautiful as the thing was as a dream, Mr. Barnstaple had a very unpleasant conviction that he was not really clever enough to pull such a thing off. He would make a mess of it somehow....

One might jump from the frying-pan into the fire. The *Liberal* was a dreary, discouraging, ungenerous paper, but anyhow it was not a base and wicked paper.

Still, if there was to be no such disastrous outbreak it was imperative that Mr. Barnstaple should rest from Mr. Peeve for a time. Once or twice already he had contradicted him. A row might occur anywhen. And the first step towards resting from Mr. Peeve was evidently to see a doctor. So Mr. Barnstaple went to a doctor.

"My nerves are getting out of control," said Mr. Barnstaple. "I feel horribly neurasthenic."

"You are suffering from neurasthenia," said the doctor.

"I dread my daily work."

"You want a holiday."

"You think I need a change?"

"As complete a change as you can manage."

"Can you recommend any place where I could go?"

"Where do you want to go?"

"Nowhere definite. I thought you could recommend—"

"Let some place attract you—and go there. Do nothing to force your inclinations at the present time."

Mr. Barnstaple paid the doctor the sum of one guinea, and armed with these instructions prepared to break the news of his illness and his necessary absence to Mr. Peeve whenever the occasion seemed ripe for doing so.

FOR A TIME THIS PROSPECTIVE HOLIDAY WAS MERELY A FRESH ADDITION to Mr. Barnstaple's already excessive burthen of worries. To decide to get away was to find oneself face to face at once with three apparently insurmountable problems: How to get away? Whither? And since Mr. Barnstaple was one of those people who tire very quickly of their own company: With whom? A sharp gleam of furtive scheming crept into the candid misery that had recently become Mr. Barnstaple's habitual expression. But then, no one took much notice of Mr. Barnstaple's expressions.

One thing was very clear in his mind. Not a word of this holiday must be breathed at home. If once Mrs. Barnstaple got wind of it, he knew exactly what would happen. She would, with an air of competent devotion, take charge of the entire business. "You must have a *good* holiday," she would say. She would select some rather distant and expensive resort in Cornwall or Scotland or Brittany, she would buy a lot of outfits, she would have afterthoughts to swell the luggage with inconvenient parcels at the last moment, and she would bring the boys. Probably she would arrange for one or two groups of acquaintances to come to the same place to "liven things up." If they did they were certain to bring the worst sides of their natures with them and to develop into the most indefatigable of bores. There would be no conversation. There would be much unreal laughter. There would be endless games.... *No!*

But how is a man to go away for a holiday without his wife getting wind of it? Somehow a bag must be packed and smuggled out of the house....

The most hopeful thing about Mr. Barnstaple's position from Mr. Barnstaple's point of view was that he owned a small automobile of his very own. It was natural that this car should play a large part in his secret plannings. It seemed to offer the easiest means of getting away; it converted the possible answer to Whither? from a fixed and definite place into what mathematicians call, I believe, a locus; and there was something so companionable about the little beast that it did to a slight but quite perceptible extent answer the question, With whom? It was a two-seater. It was known in the family as the Foot Bath, Colman's Mustard, and the Yellow Peril. As these names suggest, it was a low, open car of a clear yellow colour. Mr. Barnstaple used it to come up to the office from Sydenham because it did thirty-three miles to the gallon and was ever so much cheaper than a season ticket. It stood up in the court under the office window during the day. At Sydenham it lived in a shed of which Mr. Barnstaple carried the only key. So far he had managed to prevent the boys from either driving it or taking it to pieces. At times Mrs. Barnstaple made him drive her about Sydenham for her shopping, but she did not really like the little car because it exposed her to the elements too much and made her dusty and dishevelled. Both by reason of all that it made possible and by reason of all that it debarred; the little car was clearly indicated as the medium for the needed holiday. And Mr. Barnstaple really liked driving it. He drove very badly, but he drove very carefully; and though it sometimes stopped and refused to proceed, it did not do, or at any rate it had not so far done as most other things did in Mr. Barnstaple's life, which was to go due east when he turned the steering wheel west. So that it gave him an agreeable sense of mastery.

In the end Mr. Barnstaple made his decisions with great rapidity. Opportunity suddenly opened in front of him. Thursday was his day at the printer's, and he came home on Thursday evening feeling horribly jaded. The weather kept obstinately hot and dry. It made it none the less distressing that this drought presaged famine and misery for half the world. And London was in full season, smart and grinning: if anything, it was a sillier year than 1913, the great tango year, which, in the light of subsequent events, Mr. Barnstaple had hitherto regarded as the silliest year in the world's history.

The *Star* had the usual batch of bad news along the margin of the sporting and fashionable intelligence that got the displayed space. Fighting was going on between the Russians and Poles, and also in Ireland, Asia Minor, the India frontier, and Eastern Siberia. There had been three new horrible murders. The miners were still out, and a big engineering strike was threatened. There had been only standing room in the down train and it had started twenty minutes late.

He found a note from his wife explaining that her cousins at Wimbledon had telegraphed that there was an unexpected chance of seeing the tennis there with Mademoiselle Lenglen and all the rest of the champions, and that she had gone over with the boys and would not be back until late. It would do their game no end of good, she said, to see some really first-class tennis. Also it was the servants' social that night. Would he mind being left alone in the house for once? The servants would put him out some cold supper before they went.

Mr. Barnstaple read this note with resignation. While he ate his supper he ran his eye over a pamphlet a Chinese friend had sent him to show how the Japanese were deliberately breaking up what was left of the civilisation and education of China.

It was only as he was sitting and smoking a pipe in his little back garden after supper that he realized all that being left alone in the house meant for him.

Then suddenly he became very active. He rang up Mr. Peeve, told him of the doctor's verdict, explained that the affairs of the *Liberal* were just then in a particularly leavable state, and got his holiday. Then he went to his bedroom and packed up a hasty selection of things to take with him in an old Gladstone bag that was not likely to be immediately missed, and put this in the dickey of his car. After which he spent some time upon a letter which he addressed to his wife and put away very carefully in his breast pocket.

Then he locked up the car-shed and composed himself in a deck-chair in the garden with his pipe and a nice thoughtful book on the Bankruptcy of Europe, so as to look and feel as innocent as possible before his family came home.

When his wife returned he told her casually that he believed he was suffering from neurasthenia, and that he had arranged to run up to London on the morrow and consult a doctor in the matter.

Mrs. Barnstaple wanted to choose him a doctor, but he got out of that by saying that he had to consider Peeve in the matter and that Peeve was very strongly set on the man he had already in fact consulted. And when

Mrs. Barnstaple said that she believed they *all* wanted a good holiday, he just grunted in a non-committal manner.

In this way Mr. Barnstaple was able to get right away from his house with all the necessary luggage for some weeks' holiday, without arousing any insurmountable opposition. He started next morning Londonward. The traffic on the way was gay and plentiful, but by no means troublesome, and the Yellow Peril was running so sweetly that she might almost have been named the Golden Hope. In Camberwell he turned into the Camberwell New Road and made his way to the post-office at the top of Vauxhall Bridge Road. There he drew up. He was scared but elated by what he was doing. He went into the post-office and sent his wife a telegram. "Dr. Pagan," he wrote, "says solitude and rest urgently needed so am going off Lake District recuperate have got bag and things expecting this letter follows."

Then he came outside and fumbled in his pocket and produced and posted the letter he had written so carefully overnight. It was deliberately scrawled to suggest neurasthenia at an acute phase. Dr. Pagan, it explained, had ordered an immediate holiday and suggested that Mr. Barnstaple should "wander north." It would be better to cut off all letters for a few days, or even a week or so. He would not trouble to write unless something went wrong. No news would be good news. Rest assured all would be well. As soon as he had a certain address for letters he would wire it, but only very urgent things were to be sent on.

After this he resumed his seat in his car with such a sense of freedom as he had never felt since his first holidays from his first school. He made for the Great North Road, but at the traffic jam at Hyde Park Corner he allowed the policeman to turn him down towards Knightsbridge, and afterwards at the corner where the Bath Road forks away from the Oxford Road an obstructive van put him into the former. But it did not matter very much. Any way led to Elsewhere and he could work northward later.

THE DAY WAS ONE OF THOSE DAYS OF GAY SUNSHINE THAT WERE characteristic of the great drought of 1921. It was not in the least sultry. Indeed there was a freshness about it that blended with Mr. Barnstaple's mood to convince him that there were quite agreeable adventures before him. Hope had already returned to him. He knew he was on the way out of things, though as yet he had not the slightest suspicion how completely out of things the way was going to take him. It would be quite a little adventure presently to stop at an inn and get some lunch, and if he felt lonely as he went on he would give somebody a lift and talk. It would be quite easy to give people lifts because so long as his back was generally towards Sydenham. and the *Liberal* office, it did not matter at all now in which direction he went.

A little way out of Slough he was passed by an enormous grey touring car. It made him start and swerve. It came up alongside him without a sound, and though according to his only very slightly inaccurate speedometer, he was doing a good twenty-seven miles an hour, it had passed him in a moment. Its occupants, he noted, were three gentlemen and a lady. They were all sitting up and looking backward as though they were interested in something that was following them. They went by too quickly for him to note more than that the lady was radiantly lovely in an immediate and indisputable way, and that the gentleman nearest to him had a peculiarly elfin yet elderly face.

Before he could recover from the *éclat* of this passage a car with the voice of a prehistoric saurian warned him that he was again being overtaken. This was how Mr. Barnstaple liked being passed. By negotiation. He slowed down, abandoned any claim to the crown of the road and made encouraging gestures with his hand. A large, smooth, swift Limousine availed itself of his permission to use the thirty odd feet or so of road to the right of him. It was carrying a fair load of luggage, but except for a young gentleman with an eye-glass who was sitting beside the driver, he saw nothing of its passengers. It swept round a corner ahead in the wake of the touring car.

Now even a mechanical foot bath does not like being passed in this lordly fashion on a bright morning on the open road. Mr. Barnstaple's accelerator went down and he came round that corner a good ten miles per hour faster than his usual cautious practice. He found the road quite clear ahead of him.

Indeed he found the road much too clear ahead of him. It stretched straight in front of him for perhaps a third of a mile. On the left were a low, well-trimmed hedge, scattered trees, level fields, some small cottages lying back, remote poplars, and a distant view of Windsor Castle. On the right were level fields, a small inn, and a background of low, wooded hills. A conspicuous feature in this tranquil landscape was the board advertisement of a riverside hotel at Maidenhead. Before him was a sort of heat flicker in the air and two or three little dust whirls spinning along the road. And there was not a sign of the grey touring car and not a sign of the Limousine.

It took Mr. Barnstaple the better part of two seconds to realize the full astonishment of this fact. Neither to right nor left was there any possible side road down which either car could have vanished. And if they had already got round the further bend, then they must be travelling at the rate of two or three hundred miles per hour!

It was Mr. Barnstaple's excellent custom whenever he was in doubt to slow down. He slowed down now. He went on at a pace of perhaps fifteen miles an hour, staring open-mouthed about the empty landscape for some clue to this mysterious disappearance. Curiously enough he had no feeling that he himself was in any sort of danger.

Then his car seemed to strike something and skidded. It skidded round so violently that for a moment or so Mr. Barnstaple lost his head. He could not remember what ought to be done when a car skids. He recalled something vaguely about steering in the direction in which the car is skidding, but he could not make out in the excitement of the moment in what direction the car was skidding.

Afterwards he remembered that at this point he heard a sound. It was exactly the same sound, coming as the climax of an accumulating pressure, sharp like the snapping of a lute string, which one hears at the end—or beginning—of insensibility under anaesthetics.

He had seemed to twist round towards the hedge on the right, but now he found the road ahead of him again. He touched his accelerator and then slowed down and stopped. He stopped in the profoundest aston-ishment.

This was an entirely different road from the one he had been upon half a minute before. The hedges had changed, the trees had altered, Windsor Castle had vanished, and—a small compensation—the big Limousine was in sight again. It was standing by the roadside about two hundred yards away,

2

The Wonderful Road

～

FOR A TIME MR. BARNSTAPLE'S ATTENTION WAS VERY UNEQUALLY divided between the Limousine, whose passengers were now descending, and the scenery about him. This latter was indeed so strange and beautiful that it was only as people who must be sharing his admiration and amazement and who therefore might conceivably help to elucidate and relieve his growing and quite overwhelming perplexity, that the little group ahead presently arose to any importance in his consciousness.

The road itself instead of being the packed together pebbles and dirt smeared with tar with a surface of grit, dust, and animal excrement, of a normal English high road, was apparently made of glass, clear in places as still water and in places milky or opalescent, shot with streaks of soft colour or glittering richly with clouds of embedded golden flakes. It was perhaps twelve or fifteen yards wide. On either side was a band of greensward, of a finer grass than Mr. Barnstaple had ever seen before—and he was an expert and observant mower of lawns—and beyond this a wide border of flowers. Where Mr. Barnstaple sat agape in his car and perhaps for thirty yards in either direction this border was a mass of some unfamiliar blossom of forget-me-not blue. Then the colour was broken by an increasing number of tall, pure white spikes that finally ousted the blue altogether from the bed. On the opposite side of the way these same spikes were mingled with masses of plants bearing seed-pods equally strange to Mr. Barnstaple, which varied through a series of blues and mauves and purples to an intense crimson. Beyond this gloriously coloured foam of flowers spread flat meadows on which creamy cattle were grazing. Three close at hand, a little startled perhaps by Mr. Barnstaple's sudden apparition, chewed the cud and regarded him with benevolently speculative eyes. They had long horns and dewlaps like the cattle of South Europe and India. From these benign creatures Mr. Barnstaple's eyes went to a long line of flame-shaped trees, to a colonnade of white and gold, and to a background of snow-clad mountains. A few tall, white clouds were sailing across a sky of dazzling blue. The air impressed Mr. Barnstaple as being astonishingly clear and sweet.

Except for the cows and the little group of people standing by the Limousine Mr. Barnstaple could see no other living creature. The motorists were standing still and staring about them. A sound of querulous voices came to him.

A sharp crepitation at his back turned Mr. Barnstaple's attention round. By the side of the road in the direction from which conceivably he had come were the ruins of what appeared to be a very recently demolished stone house. Beside it were two large apple trees freshly twisted and riven, as if by some explosion, and out of the centre of it came a column of smoke and this sound of things catching fire. And the contorted lines of these shattered apple trees helped Mr. Barnstaple to realize that some of the flowers by the wayside near at hand were also bent down to one side as if by the passage of a recent violent gust of wind. Yet he had heard no explosion nor felt any wind.

He stared for a time and then turned as if for an explanation to the Limousine. Three of these people were now coming along the road towards him, led by a tall, slender, grey-headed gentleman in a felt hat and a long motoring dust-coat. He had a small upturned face with a little nose that scarce sufficed for the springs of his gilt glasses. Mr. Barnstaple restarted his engine and drove slowly to meet them.

As soon as he judged himself within hearing distance he stopped and put his head over the side of the Yellow Peril with a question. At the same moment the tall, grey-headed gentleman asked practically the same question: "Can you tell me at all, sir, where we *are*?"

"Five minutes ago," said Mr. Barnstaple, "I should have said we were on the Maidenhead Road. Near Slough."

"Exactly!" said the tall gentleman in earnest, argumentative tones. "Exactly! And I maintain that there is not the slightest reason for supposing that we are not still on the Maidenhead Road."

The challenge of the dialectician rang in his voice.

"It doesn't *look* like the Maidenhead Road," said Mr. Barnstaple.

"Agreed! But are we to judge by appearances or are we to judge by the direct continuity of our experience? The Maidenhead Road led to this, was in continuity with this, and therefore I hold that this is the Maidenhead Road."

"Those mountains?" considered Mr. Barnstaple.

"Windsor Castle ought to be there," said the tall gentleman brightly as if he gave a point in a gambit.

"*Was* there five minutes ago," said Mr. Barnstaple.

"Then obviously those mountains are some sort of a camouflage," said the tall gentleman triumphantly, "and the whole of this business is, as they say nowadays, a put-up thing."

"It seems to be remarkably well put up," said Mr. Barnstaple.

Came a pause during which Mr. Barnstaple surveyed the tall gentleman's companions. The tall gentleman he knew perfectly well. He had seen him a score of times at public meetings and public dinners. He was Mr. Cecil Burleigh, the great Conservative leader. He was not only distinguished as a politician; he was eminent as a private gentleman, a philosopher and a man of universal intelligence. Behind him stood a short, thickset, middle-aged young man, unknown to Mr. Barnstaple, the natural hostility of whose appearance was greatly enhanced by an eye-glass. The third member of the little group was also a familiar form, but for a time Mr. Barnstaple could not place him. He had a clean-shaven, round, plump face and a well-nourished person and his costume suggested either a High Church clergyman or a prosperous Roman Catholic priest.

The young man with the eye-glass now spoke in a kind of impotent falsetto. "I came down to Taplow Court by road not a month ago and there was certainly nothing of this sort on the way then."

"I admit there are difficulties," said Mr. Burleigh with gusto. "I admit there are considerable difficulties. Still, I venture to think my main proposition holds."

"*You* don't think this is the Maidenhead Road?" said the gentleman with the eye-glass flatly to Mr. Barnstaple.

"It seems too perfect for a put-up thing," said Mr. Barnstaple with a mild obstinacy.

"But, my dear Sir!" protested Mr. Burleigh, "this road is *notorious* for nursery seedsmen and sometimes they arrange the most astonishing displays. As an advertisement."

"Then why don't we go straight on to Taplow Court now?" asked the gentleman with the eye-glass.

"Because," said Mr. Burleigh, with the touch of asperity natural when one has to insist on a fact already clearly known, and obstinately overlooked, "Rupert insists that we are in some other world. And won't go on. That is why. He has always had too much imagination. He thinks that things that don't exist *can* exist. And now he imagines himself in some sort of scientific romance and out of our world altogether. In another dimension. I sometimes think it would have been better for all of us if Rupert had taken to writing romances—instead of living them. If you, as his secretary, think that you will be able to get him on to Taplow in time for lunch with the Windsor people—"

Mr. Burleigh indicated by a gesture ideas for which he found words inadequate.

Mr. Barnstaple had already noted a slow-moving, intent, sandy-complexioned figure in a grey top hat with a black band that the caricaturists had made familiar, exploring the flowery tangle beside the Limousine. This then must be no less well-known person than Rupert Catskill, the Secretary of State for War.

For once Mr. Barnstaple found himself in entire agreement with this all too adventurous politician. This *was* another world. Mr. Barnstaple got out of his car and addressed himself to Mr. Burleigh. "I think we may get a lot of light upon just where we are, Sir, if we explore this building which is burning here close at hand. I thought just now that I saw a figure lying on the slope close behind it. If we could catch one of the hoaxers—"

He left his sentence unfinished because he did not believe for a moment that they were being hoaxed. Mr. Burleigh had fallen very much in his opinion in the last five minutes.

All four men turned their faces to the smoking ruin.

"It's a very extraordinary thing that there isn't a soul in sight," remarked the eye-glass gentleman searching the horizon.

"Well, I see no harm whatever in finding out what is burning," said Mr. Burleigh and led the way, upholding an intelligent, anticipatory face, towards the wrecked house between the broken trees.

But before he had gone a dozen paces the attention of the little group was recalled to the Limousine by a loud scream of terror from the lady who had remained seated therein.

$\sim$

"REALLY THIS IS TOO MUCH!" CRIED MR. BURLEIGH WITH A NOTE OF genuine exasperation. "There must surely be police regulations to prevent this kind of thing."

"It's out of some travelling menagerie," said the gentleman with the eye-glass. "What ought we to do?"

"It looks tame," said Mr. Barnstaple, but without any impulse to put his theory to the test.

"It might easily frighten people very seriously," said Mr. Burleigh. And lifting up a bland voice he shouted: "Don't be alarmed, Stella! It's probably quite tame and harmless. Don't *irritate* it with that sunshade. It might fly at you. Stel-*la*!"

"It" was a big and beautifully marked leopard which had come very softly out of the flowers and sat down like a great cat in the middle of the glass road at the side of the big car. It was blinking and moving its head from side to side rhythmically, with an expression of puzzled interest, as the lady, in accordance with the best traditions of such cases, opened and shut her parasol at it as rapidly as she could. The chauffeur had taken cover behind the car. Mr. Rupert Catskill stood staring, knee-deep in flowers, apparently only made aware of the creature's existence by the same scream that had attracted the attention of Mr. Burleigh and his companions.

Mr. Catskill was the first to act, and his act showed his mettle. It was at once discreet and bold. "Stop flopping that sunshade, Lady Stella," he said. "Let me—I will—catch its eye."

He made a detour round the car so as to come face to face with the animal. Then for a moment he stood, as it were displaying himself, a resolute little figure in a grey frock coat and a black-banded top hat. He held out a cautious hand, not too suddenly for fear of startling the creature. "*Poossy!*" he said.

The leopard, relieved by the cessation of Lady Stella's sunshade, regarded him with interest and curiosity. He drew closer. The leopard extended its muzzle and sniffed.

"If it will only let me stroke it," said Mr. Catskill, and came within arm's length.

The beast sniffed the extended hand with an expression of incredulity. Then with a suddenness that sent Mr. Catskill back several paces, it sneezed. It sneezed again much more violently, regarded Mr. Catskill reproachfully for a moment and then leapt lightly over the flower-bed and made off in the direction of the white and golden colonnade. The grazing cattle in the field, Mr. Barnstaple noted, watched its passage without the slightest sign of dismay.

Mr. Catskill remained in a slightly expanded state in the middle of the road. "No animal," he remarked, "can stand up to the steadfast gaze of the human eye. Not one. It is a riddle for your materialist.... Shall we join Mr. Cecil, Lady Stella? He seems to have found something to look at down there. The man in the little yellow car may know where he is. Hm?"

He assisted the lady to get out of the car and the two came on after Mr. Barnstaple's party, which was now again approaching the burning house. The chauffeur, evidently not wishing to be left alone with the Limousine in this world of incredible possibilities, followed as closely as respect permitted.

3

The Beautiful People

THE FIRE IN THE LITTLE HOUSE DID NOT SEEM TO BE MAKING HEADWAY. The smoke that came from it was much less now than when Mr. Barnstaple had first observed it. As they came close they found a quantity of twisted bits of bright metal and fragments of broken glass among the shattered masonry. The suggestion of exploded scientific apparatus was very strong. Then almost simultaneously the entire party became aware of a body lying on the grassy slope behind the ruins. It was the body of a man in the prime of life, naked except for a couple of bracelets and a necklace and girdle, and blood was oozing from his mouth and nostrils. With a kind of awe Mr. Barnstaple knelt down beside this prostrate figure and felt its still heart. He had never seen so beautiful a face and body before.

"*Dead,*" he whispered.

"Look!" cried the shrill voice of the man with the eye-glass. "Another!"

He was pointing to something that was hidden from Mr. Barnstaple by a piece of wall. Mr. Barnstaple had to get up and climb over a heap of rubble before he could see this second find. It was a slender girl, clothed as little as the man. She had evidently been flung with enormous violence against the wall and killed instantaneously. Her face was quite undistorted although her skull had been crushed in from behind; her perfect mouth and green-grey eyes were a little open and her expression was that of one who is still thinking out some difficult but interesting problem. She did not seem in the least dead but merely disregardful. One hand still grasped a copper implement with a handle of glass. The other lay limp and prone.

For some seconds nobody spoke. It was as if they all feared to interrupt the current of her thoughts.

Then Mr. Barnstaple heard the voice of the priestly gentleman speaking very softly behind him. "What a *perfect* form!" he said.

"I admit I was wrong," said Mr. Burleigh with deliberation. "I have been wrong.... These are no earthly people. Manifestly. And ergo, we are not on earth. I cannot imagine what has happened nor where we are. In the face of sufficient evidence I have never hesitated to retract an opinion. This world we are in is not our world. It is something—"

He paused. "It is something very wonderful indeed."

"And the Windsor party," said Mr. Catskill without any apparent regret, "must have its lunch without us."

"But then," said the clerical gentleman, "what world *are* we in, and how did we get here?"

"Ah! *there*," said Mr. Burleigh blandly, "you go altogether beyond my poor powers of guessing. We are here in some world that is singularly like our world and singularly unlike it. It must be in some way related to our world or we could not be here. But how it can be related, is, I confess, a hopeless mystery to me. Maybe we are in some other dimension of space than those we wot of. But my poor head whirls at the thought of these dimensions. I am—I am *mazed-mazed*."

"Einstein," injected the gentleman with the eye-glass compactly and with evident self-satisfaction.

"Exactly!" said Mr. Burleigh. "Einstein might make it clear to us. Or dear old Haldane might undertake to explain it and fog us up with that adipose Hegelianism of his. But I am neither Haldane nor Einstein. Here we are in some world which is, for all practical purposes, including the purposes of our week-end engagements, Nowhere. Or if you prefer the Greek of it, we are in Utopia. And as I do not see that there is any manifest way out of it again, I suppose the thing we have to do as rational creatures is to make the best of it. And watch our opportunities.

"It is certainly a very lovely world. The loveliness is even greater than the wonder. And there are human beings here—with minds. I judge from all this material lying about, it is a world in which experimental chemistry is pursued—pursued indeed to the bitter end—under almost idyllic conditions. Chemistry—and nakedness. I feel bound to confess that whether we are to regard these two people who have apparently just blown themselves up here as Greek gods or as naked savages, seems to me to be altogether a question of individual taste. I admit a bias for the Greek god—and goddess."

"Except that it is a little difficult to think of two dead immortals," squeaked the gentleman of the eye-glass in the tone of one who scores a point.

Mr. Burleigh was about to reply, and to judge from his ruffled expression his reply would have been of a disciplinary nature. But instead he exclaimed sharply and turned round to face two newcomers. The whole party had become aware of them at the same moment. Two stark Apollos stood over the ruin and were regarding our Earthlings with an astonishment at least as great as that they created.

One spoke, and Mr. Barnstaple was astonished beyond measure to find understandable words reverberating in his mind.

"Red Gods!" cried the Utopian. "What things are you? And how did you get into the world?"

(English! It would have been far less astounding if they had spoken Greek. But that they should speak any known language was a matter for incredulous amazement.)

$$\sim$$

Mr. Cecil Burleigh was the least disconcerted of the party. "Now," he said, "we may hope to learn something definite—face to face with rational and articulate creatures."

He cleared his throat, grasped the lapels of his long dust-coat with two long nervous hands and assumed the duties of spokesman. "We are quite unable, gentlemen, to account for our presence here," he said. "We are as puzzled as you are. We have discovered ourselves suddenly in your world instead of our own."

"You come from another world?"

"Exactly. A quite different world. In which we have all our natural and proper places. We were travelling in that world of ours in—Ah!—certain vehicles, when suddenly we discovered ourselves here. Intruders, I admit, but, I can assure you, innocent and unpremeditated intruders."

"You do not know how it is that Arden and Greenlake have failed in their experiment and how it is that they are dead?"

"If Arden and Greenlake are the names of these two beautiful young people here, we know nothing about them except that we found them lying as you see them when we came from the road hither to find out or, in fact, to inquire—"

He cleared his throat and left his sentence with a floating end.

The Utopian, if we may for convenience call him that, who had first spoken, looked now at his companion and seemed to question him mutely. Then he turned to the Earthlings again. He spoke and again those clear tones rang, not —so it seemed to Mr. Barnstaple—in his ears but within his head.

"It will be well if you and your friends do not trample this wreckage. It will be well if you all return to the road. Come with me. My brother here will put an end to this burning and do what needs to be done to our brother and sister. And afterwards this place will be examined by those who understand the work that was going on here."

"We must throw ourselves entirely upon your hospitality," said Mr. Burleigh. "We are entirely at your disposal. This encounter, let me repeat, was not of our seeking."

"Though we should certainly have sought it if we had known of its possibility," said Mr. Catskill, addressing the world at large and glancing at Mr. Barnstaple as if for confirmation. "We find this world of yours—*most* attractive."

"At the first encounter," the gentleman with the eye-glass endorsed, "a *most* attractive world."

As they returned through the thick-growing flowers to the road, in the wake of the Utopian and Mr. Burleigh, Mr. Barnstaple found Lady Stella rustling up beside him. Her words, in this setting of pure wonder, filled him with amazement at their serene and invincible ordinariness. "Haven't we met before somewhere—at lunch or something—Mr.—Mr.—?"

Was all this no more than a show? He stared at her blankly for a moment before supplying her with:

"Barnstaple."

"Mr. Barnstaple?"

His mind came into line with hers.

"I've never had that pleasure, Lady Stella. Though, of course, I know you—I know you very well from your photographs in the weekly illus-trated papers."

"Did you hear what it was that Mr. Cecil was saying just now? About this being Utopia?"

"He said we might *call* it Utopia."

"So like Mr. Cecil. But is it Utopia?—*really* Utopia?

"I've always longed so to be in Utopia," the lady went on without waiting for Mr. Barnstaple's reply to her question. "What splendid young men these two Utopians appear to be! They must, I am sure, belong to its aristocracy—in spite of their—informal—costume. Or even because of it."....

Mr. Barnstaple had a happy thought. "I have also recognised Mr. Burleigh and Mr. Rupert Catskill, Lady Stella, but I should be so glad if you would tell me who the young gentleman with the eye-glass is, and the clerical gentleman. They are close behind us."

Lady Stella imparted her information in a charmingly confidential undertone. "The eye-glass," she murmured, "is—I am going to spell it — F.R.E.D.D.Y. M.U.S.H. Taste. Good taste. He is awfully clever at finding out young poets and all that sort of literary thing. And he's Rupert's secretary. If there is a literary Academy, they say, he's certain to be in it. He's dreadfully critical and sarcastic. We were going to Taplow for a perfectly intellectual week-end, quite like the old times. So soon as the Windsor people had gone again, that is.... Mr. Gosse was coming and Max Beerbohm—and everyone like that. But nowadays something always happens. Always.... The unexpected—almost excessively.... The clerical collar"—she glanced back to judge whether she was within earshot of the gentleman under discussion—"is Father Amerton, who is so dreadfully outspoken about the sins of society and all *that* sort of thing. It's odd, but out of the pulpit he's inclined to be shy and quiet and a little awkward with the forks and spoons. Paradoxical, isn't it?"

"Of *course!*" cried Mr. Barnstaple. "I remember him now. I knew his face but I couldn't place it. Thank you so much, Lady Stella."

THERE WAS SOMETHING VERY REASSURING TO MR. BARNSTAPLE IN THE company of these famous and conspicuous people and particularly in the company of Lady Stella. She was indeed heartening: she brought so much of the dear old world with her, and she was so manifestly prepared to subjugate this new world to its standards at the earliest possible opportunity. She fended off much of the wonder and beauty that had threatened to submerge Mr. Barnstaple altogether. Meeting her and her company was in itself for a man in his position a minor but considerable adventure that helped to bridge the gulf of astonishment between the humdrum of his normal experiences and this all too bracing Utopian air. It solidified, it—if one may use the word in such a connexion—it *degraded* the luminous splendour about him towards complete credibility that it should also be seen and commented on by her and by Mr. Burleigh, and viewed through the appraising monocle of Mr. Freddy Mush. It brought it within range of the things that get into the newspapers. Mr. Barnstaple alone in Utopia might have been so completely overawed as to have been mentally overthrown. This easy-mannered brown-skinned divinity who was now exchanging questions with Mr. Burleigh was made mentally accessible by that great man's intervention.

Yet it was with something very like a catching of the breath that Mr. Barnstaple's attention reverted from the Limousine people to this noble-seeming world into which he and they had fallen. What sort of beings really were these men and women of a world where ill-bred weeds, it seemed, had ceased to thrust and fight amidst the flowers, and where leopards void of feline malice looked out with friendly eyes upon the passer-by?

It was astounding that the first two inhabitants they had found in this world of subjugated nature should be lying dead, victims, it would seem, of some hazardous experiment. It was still more astonishing that this other pair who called themselves the brothers of the dead man and woman should betray so little grief or dismay at the tragedy. There had been no emotional scene at all, Mr. Barnstaple realized, no consternation or weeping. They were evidently much more puzzled and interested than either horrified or distressed.

The Utopian who had remained in the ruin, had carried out the body of the girl to lay it beside her companion's, and he had now, Mr. Barnstaple saw, returned to a close scrutiny of the wreckage of the experiment.

But now more of these people were coming upon the scene. They had aeroplanes in this world, for two small ones, noiseless and swift in their flight as swallows, had landed in the fields near by. A man had come up along the road on a machine like a small two-wheeled two-seater with its wheels in series, bicycle fashion; lighter and neater it was than any earthly automobile and mysteriously able to stand up on its two wheels while standing still. A burst of laughter from down the road called Mr. Barnstaple's attention to a group of these Utopians who had apparently found something exquisitely ridiculous in the engine of the Limousine. Most of these people were as scantily clothed and as beautifully built as the two dead experimentalists, but one or two were wearing big hats of straw, and one who seemed to be an older woman of thirty or more wore a robe of white bordered by an intense red line. She was speaking now to Mr. Burleigh.

Although she was a score of yards away, her speech presented itself in Mr. Barnstaple's mind with great distinctness.

"We do not even know as yet what connexion your coming into our world may have with the explosion that has just happened here or whether, indeed, it has any connexion. We want to inquire into both these things. It will be reasonable, we think, to take you and all the possessions you have brought with you to a convenient place for a conference not very far from here. We are arranging for machines to take you thither. There perhaps you will eat. I do not know when you are accustomed to eat?"

"Refreshment," said Mr. Burleigh, rather catching at the idea. "Some refreshment would certainly be acceptable before very long. In fact, had we not fallen so sharply out of our own world into yours, by this time we should have been lunching—lunching in the best of company."

Wonder and lunch, thought Mr. Barnstaple. Man is a creature who must eat by necessity whether he wonders or no. Mr. Barnstaple perceived indeed that he was already hungry and that the air he was breathing was a keen and appetizing air.

The Utopian seemed struck by a novel idea. "Do you eat several times a day? What sort of things do you eat?"

"Oh! Surely! They're *not* vegetarians!" cried Mr. Mush sharply in a protesting parenthesis, dropping his eye-glass from its socket.

They were all hungry. It showed upon their faces.

"We are all accustomed to eat several times a day," said Mr. Burleigh. "Perhaps it would be well if I were to give you a brief résumé of our dietary. There may be differences. We begin, as a rule, with a simple cup of tea and the thinnest slice of bread-and-butter brought to the bedside. Then comes breakfast.".... He proceeded to a masterly summary of his gastronomic day, giving clearly and attractively the particulars of an English breakfast, eggs to be boiled four and a half minutes, neither more nor less, lunch with any light wine, tea rather a social rally than a serious meal, dinner, in some detail, the occasional resort to supper. It was one of those clear statements which that would have rejoiced the House of Commons, light, even gay, and yet with a trace of earnestness. The Utopian woman regarded him with deepening interest as he proceeded. "Do you all eat in this fashion?" she asked.

Mr. Burleigh ran his eye over his party. "I cannot answer for Mr.—Mr. —?"

"Barnstaple.... Yes, I eat in much the same fashion."

For some reason the Utopian woman smiled at him. She had very pretty brown eyes, and though he liked her to smile he wished that she had not smiled in the way she did.

"And you sleep?" she asked.

"From six to ten hours, according to circumstances," said Mr. Burleigh.

"And you make love?"

The question perplexed and to a certain extent shocked our Earthlings. What exactly did she mean? For some moments no one framed a reply. Mr. Barnstaple's mind was filled with a hurrying rush of strange possibilities.

Then Mr. Burleigh, with his fine intelligence and the quick evasiveness of a modern leader of men, stepped into the breach. "Not habitually, I can assure you," he said. "Not habitually."

The woman with the red-bordered robe seemed to think this over for a swift moment. Then she smiled faintly.

"We must take you somewhere where we can talk of all these things," she said. "Manifestly you come from some strange other world. Our men of knowledge must get together with you and exchange ideas."

At half-past ten that morning Mr. Barnstaple had been motoring along the main road through Slough, and now at half-past one he was soaring through wonderland with his own world half forgotten. "Marvellous," he repeated. "Marvellous. I knew that I should have a good holiday. But *this, this*—!"

He was extraordinarily happy with the bright unclouded happiness of a perfect dream. Never before had he enjoyed the delights of an explorer in new lands, never before had he hoped to experience these delights. Only a few weeks before he had written an article for the *Liberal* lamenting the "End of the Age of Exploration," an article so thoroughly and aimlessly depressing that it had pleased Mr. Peeve extremely. He recalled that exploit now with but the faintest twinge of remorse.

The Earthling party had been distributed among four small aeroplanes, and as Mr. Barnstaple and his companion, Father Amerton, rose in the air, he looked back to see the automobiles and luggage being lifted with astonishing ease into two lightly built lorries. Each lorry put out a pair of glittering arms and lifted up its automobile as a nurse might lift up a baby.

By contemporary earthly standards of safety Mr. Barnstaple's aviator flew very low. There were times when he passed between trees rather than over them, and this, even if at first it was a little alarming, permitted a fairly close inspection of the landscape. For the earlier part of the journey it was garden pasture with grazing creamy cattle and patches of brilliantly coloured vegetation of a nature unknown to Mr. Barnstaple. Amidst this cultivation narrow tracks, which may have been foot or cycle tracks, threaded their way. Here and there ran a road bordered with flowers and shaded by fruit trees.

There were few houses and no towns or villages at all. The houses varied very greatly in size, from little isolated buildings which Mr. Barnstaple thought might be elegant summer-houses or little temples, to clusters of roofs and turrets which reminded him of country chateaux or suggested extensive farming or dairying establishments. Here and there people were working in the fields or going to and fro on foot or on machines, but the effect of the whole was of an extremely underpopulated land.

It became evident that they were going to cross the range of snowy mountains that had so suddenly blotted the distant view of Windsor Castle from the landscape.

As they approached these mountains, broad stretches of golden corn-land replaced the green of the pastures and then the cultivation became more diversified. He noted unmistakable vineyards on sunny slopes, and the number of workers visible and the habitations multiplied. The little squadron of aeroplanes flew up a broad valley towards a pass so that Mr. Barnstaple was able to scrutinize the mountain scenery. Came chestnut woods and at last pines. There were Cyclopean turbines athwart the mountain torrents and long, low, many-windowed buildings that might serve some industrial purpose. A skilfully graded road with exceedingly bold, light and beautiful viaducts mounted towards the pass. There were more people, he thought, in the highland country than in the levels below, though still far fewer than he would have seen upon any comparable countryside on earth.

Ten minutes of craggy desolation with the snow-fields of a great glacier on one side intervened before he descended into the upland valley on the Conference Place where presently he alighted. This was a sort of lap in the mountain, terraced by masonry so boldly designed that it seemed a part of the geological substance of the mountain itself. It faced towards a wide artificial lake retained by a stupendous dam from the lower reaches of the valley. At intervals along this dam there were great stone pillars dimly suggestive of seated figures. He glimpsed a wide plain beyond, which reminded him of the valley of the Po, and then as he descended the straight line of the dam came up to hide this further vision.

Upon these terraces, and particularly upon the lower ones, were groups and clusters of flowerlike buildings, and he distinguished paths and steps and pools of water as if the whole place were a garden.

The aeroplanes made an easy landing on a turfy expanse. Close at hand was a graceful chalet that ran out from the shores of the lake over the water, and afforded mooring to a flotilla of gaily coloured boats....

It was Father Amerton who had drawn Mr. Barnstaple's attention to the absence of villages. He now remarked that there was no church in sight and that nowhere had they seen any spires or belfries. But Mr. Barnstaple thought that some of the smaller buildings might be temples or shrines. "Religion may take different forms here," he said.

"And how few babies or little children are visible!" Father Amerton remarked. "Nowhere have I seen a mother with her child."

"On the other side of the mountains there was a place like the playing field of a big school. There were children there and one or two older people dressed in white."

"I saw that. But I was thinking of babes. Compare this with what one would see in Italy."

"The most beautiful and desirable young women," added the reverend gentleman; "*most* desirable—and not a sign of maternity!"

Their aviator, a sun-tanned blond with very blue eyes, helped them out of his machine, and they stood watching the descent of the other members of their party. Mr. Barnstaple was astonished to note how rapidly he was becoming familiarized with the colour and harmony of this new world; the strangest things in the whole spectacle now were the figures and clothing of his associates. Mr. Rupert Catskill in his celebrated grey top hat, Mr. Mush with his preposterous eye-glass, the peculiar long slenderness of Mr. Burleigh, and the square leather-clad lines of Mr. Burleigh's chauffeur, struck him as being far more incredible than the graceful Utopian forms about him.

The aviator's interest and amusement enhanced Mr. Barnstaple's perception of his companions' oddity. And then came a wave of profound doubt.

"I suppose this is *really* real," he said to Father Amerton.

"Really real! What else can it be?"

"I suppose we are not dreaming all this."

"Are your dreams and my dreams likely to coincide?"

"Yes; but there are quite impossible things—absolutely impossible things."

"As, for instance?"

"Well, how is it that these people are speaking to us in English—modern English?"

"I never thought of that. It is rather incredible. They don't talk in English to one another."

Mr. Barnstaple stared in round-eyed amazement at Father Amerton, struck for the first time by a still more incredible fact. "They don't talk in *anything* to one another," he said. "And we haven't noticed it until this moment!"

4

The Shadow of Einstein Falls Across the Story but Passes Lightly By

EXCEPT FOR THAT ONE PERPLEXING FACT THAT ALL THESE UTOPIANS had apparently a complete command of idiomatic English, Mr. Barnstaple found his vision of this new world developing with a congruity that no dream in his experience had ever possessed. It was so coherent, so orderly, that less and less was it like a strange world at all and more and more like an arrival in some foreign but very highly civilised country.

Under the direction of the brown-eyed woman in the scarlet-edged robe, the Earthlings were established in their quarters near the Conference Place in the most hospitable and comfortable fashion conceivable. Five or six youths and girls made it their business to initiate the strangers in the little details of Utopian domesticity. The separate buildings in which they were lodged had each an agreeable little dressing-room, and the bed, which had sheets of the finest linen and a very light puffy coverlet, stood in an open loggia—too open Lady Stella thought, but then as she said, "One feels so safe here." The luggage appeared and the valises were identified as if they were in some hospitable earthly mansion.

But Lady Stella had to turn two rather too friendly youths out of her apartment before she could open her dressing-bag and administer refreshment to her complexion.

A few minutes later some excitement was caused by an outbreak of wild laughter and the sounds of an amiable but hysterical struggle that came from Lady Stella's retreat. The girl who had remained with her had displayed a quite feminine interest in her equipment and had come upon a particularly charming and diaphanous sleeping suit. For some obscure reason this secret daintiness amused the young Utopian extremely, and it was with some difficulty that Lady Stella restrained her from putting the garment on and dancing out in it for a public display. "Then *you* put it on," the girl insisted.

"But you don't understand," cried Lady Stella. "It's almost—*sacred*! It's for nobody to see—*ever*."

"But *why?*" the Utopian asked, puzzled beyond measure.

Lady Stella found an answer impossible.

The light meal that followed was by terrestrial standards an entirely satisfactory one. The anxiety of Mr. Freddy Mush was completely allayed: there were cold chicken and ham and a very pleasant meat pate. There were also rather coarse-grained but most palatable bread, pure butter, an exquisite salad, fruit, cheese of the Gruyere type, and a light white wine which won from Mr. Burleigh the tribute that "Moselle never did anything better."

"You find our food very like your own?" asked the woman in the red-trimmed robe.

"Eckquithit quality," said Mr. Mush with his mouth rather full.

"Food has changed very little in the last three thousand years. People had found out all the best things to eat long before the Last Age of Confusion."

"It's too real to be real," Mr. Barnstaple repeated to himself. "Too real to be real."

He looked at his companions, elated, interested and eating with appreciation.

If it wasn't for the absurdity of these Utopians speaking English with a clearness that tapped like a hammer inside his head Mr. Barnstaple would have had no doubt whatever of its reality.

No servants waited at the clothless stone table; the woman in the white and scarlet robe and the two aviators shared the meal and the guests attended to each other's requirements. Mr. Burleigh's chauffeur was for modestly shrinking to another table until the great statesman reassured him with: "Sit down there, Perk. Next to Mr. Mush." Other Utopians with friendly but keenly observant eyes upon the Earthlings came into the great pillared veranda in which the meal had been set, and smiled and stood about or sat down. There were no introductions and few social formalities.

"All this is most reassuring," said Mr. Burleigh. "Most reassuring. I'm bound to say these beat the Chatsworth peaches. Is that cream, my dear Rupert, in the little brown jar in front of you?... I guessed as much. If you are sure you can spare it, Rupert.... Thank you."

SEVERAL OF THE UTOPIANS MADE THEMSELVES KNOWN BY NAME TO THE Earthlings. All their voices sounded singularly alike to Mr. Barnstaple and the words were as clear as print. The brown-eyed woman's name was Lychnis. A man with a beard who might perhaps, Mr. Barnstaple thought, have been as old as forty, was either Urthred or Adam or Edom, the name for all its sharpness of enunciation had been very difficult to catch. It was as if large print *hesitated*. Urthred conveyed that he was an ethnologist and historian and that he desired to learn all that he possibly could about the ways of our world. He impressed Mr. Barnstaple as having the easy carriage of some earthly financier or great newspaper proprietor rather than the diffidence natural in our own every-day world to a merely learned man. Another of their hosts, Serpentine, was also, Mr. Barnstaple learnt with surprise, for his bearing too was almost masterful, a scientific man. He called himself something that Mr. Barnstaple could not catch. First it sounded like "atomic mechanician," and then oddly enough it sounded like "molecular chemist." And then Mr. Barnstaple heard Mr. Burleigh say to Mr. Mush, "He said 'physio-chemist,' didn't he?"

"*I* thought he just called himself a materialist," said Mr. Mush.

"I thought he said he weighed things," said Lady Stella.

"Their intonation is peculiar," said Mr. Burleigh. "Sometimes they are almost too loud for comfort and then there is a kind of gap in the sounds."...

When the meal was at an end the whole party removed to another little building that was evidently planned for classes and discussions. It had a semi-circular apse round which ran a series of white tablets which evidently functioned at times as a lecturer's blackboard, since there were black and coloured pencils and cloths for erasure lying on a marble ledge at a convenient height below the tablets. The lecturer could walk from point to point of this semicircle as he talked. Lychnis, Urthred, Serpentine and the Earthlings seated themselves on a semi-circular bench below this lecturer's track, and there was accommodation for about eighty or a hundred people upon the seats before them. All these were occupied, and beyond stood a number of graceful groups against a background of rhododendron-like bushes, between which Mr. Barnstaple caught glimpses of grassy vistas leading down to the shining waters of the lake.

They were going to talk over this extraordinary irruption into their world. Could anything be more reasonable than to talk it over? Could anything be more fantastically impossible?

"Odd that there are no swallows," said Mr. Mush suddenly in Mr. Barnstaple's ear. "I wonder why there are no swallows."

Mr. Barnstaple's attention went to the empty sky. "No gnats nor flies perhaps," he suggested. It was odd that he had not missed the swallows before.

"Sssh!" said Lady Stella. "He's beginning."

THIS INCREDIBLE CONFERENCE BEGAN. IT WAS OPENED BY THE MAN named Serpentine, and he stood before his audience and seemed to make a speech. His lips moved, his hands assisted his statements; his expression followed his utterance. And yet Mr. Barnstaple had the most subtle and indefensible doubt whether indeed Serpentine was speaking. There was something odd about the whole thing. Sometimes the thing said sounded with a peculiar resonance in his head; sometimes it was indistinct and elusive like an object seen through troubled waters; sometimes though Serpentine still moved his fine hands and looked towards his hearers, there were gaps of absolute silence—as if for brief intervals Mr. Barnstaple had gone deaf.... Yet it was a discourse; it held together and it held Mr. Barnstaple's attention.

Serpentine had the manner of one who is taking great pains to be as simple as possible with a rather intricate question. He spoke, as it were, in propositions with a pause between each. "It had long been known," he began, "that the possible number of dimensions, like the possible number of anything else that could be enumerated, was unlimited!"

Yes, Mr. Barnstaple had got that, but it proved too much for Mr. Freddy Mush.

"Oh, Lord!" he said. "Dimensions!" and dropped his eye-glass and became despondently inattentive.

"For most practical purposes," Serpentine continued, "the particular universe, the particular system of events, in which we found ourselves and of which we formed part, could be regarded as occurring in a space of three rectilinear dimensions and as undergoing translation, which translation was in fact duration, through a fourth dimension, *time*. Such a system of events was necessarily a gravitational system."

"Er!" said Mr. Burleigh sharply. "Excuse me! I don't see that."

So he, at any rate, was following it too.

"Any universe that endures must necessarily gravitate," Serpentine repeated, as if he were asserting some self-evident fact.

"For the life of me I can't see that," said Mr. Burleigh after a moment's reflection.

Serpentine considered him for a moment. "It *is* so," he said, and went on with his discourse. Our minds, he continued, had been evolved in the form of this practical conception of things, they accepted it as true, and it was only by great efforts of sustained analysis that we were able to realize that this universe in which we lived not only extended but was, as it were, slightly bent and contorted, into a number of other long unsuspected spatial dimensions. It extended beyond its three chief spatial dimensions into these others just as a thin sheet of paper, which is practically two-dimensional, extended not only by virtue of its thickness but also of its crinkles and curvature into a third dimension.

"Am I going deaf?" asked Lady Stella in a stage whisper. "I can't catch a word of all this."

"Nor I," said Father Amerton.

Mr. Burleigh made a pacifying gesture towards these unfortunates without taking his eyes off Serpentine's face. Mr. Barnstaple knitted his brows, clasped his knees, knotted his fingers, held on desperately.

He *must* be hearing—of course he was hearing!

Serpentine proceeded to explain that just as it would be possible for any number of practically two-dimensional universes to lie side by side, like sheets of paper, in a three-dimensional space, so in the many-dimensional space about which the ill-equipped human mind is still slowly and painfully acquiring knowledge, it is possible for an innumerable quantity of practically three-dimensional universes to lie, as it were, side by side and to undergo a roughly parallel movement through time. The speculative work of Lonestone and Cephalus had long since given the soundest basis for the belief that there actually were a very great number of such space-and-time universes, parallel to one another and resembling each other, nearly but not exactly, much as the leaves of a book might resemble one another. All of them would have duration, all of them would be gravitating systems—

(Mr. Burleigh shook his head to show that still he didn't see it.)

—And those lying closest together would most nearly resemble each other. How closely they now had an opportunity of learning. For the daring attempts of those two great geniuses, Arden and Greenlake, to use the—(*inaudible*)—thrust of the atom to rotate a portion of the Utopian material universe in that dimension, the F dimension, into which it had long been known to extend for perhaps the length of a man's arm, to rotate this fragment of Utopian matter, much as a gate is swung on its hinges, had manifestly been altogether successful. The gate had swung back again bringing with it a breath of close air, a storm of dust and, to the immense amazement of Utopia, three sets of visitors from an unknown world.

"*Three?*" whispered Mr. Barnstaple doubtfully. "Did he say *three?*"

[Serpentine disregarded him.]

"Our brother and sister have been killed by some unexpected release of force, but their experiment has opened a way that now need never be closed again, out of the present spatial limitations of Utopia into a whole vast folio of hitherto unimagined worlds. Close at hand to us, even as Lonestone guessed ages ago, nearer to us, as he put it, than the blood in our hearts—"

("Nearer to us than breathing and closer than hands and feet," Father Amerton misquoted, waking up suddenly. "But what is he talking about? I don't catch it.")

"—we discover another planet, much the same size as ours to judge by the scale of its inhabitants, circulating, we may certainly assume, round a sun like that in our skies, a planet bearing life and being slowly subjugated, even as our own is being subjugated, by intelligent life which has evidently evolved under almost exactly parallel conditions to those of our own evolution. This sister universe to ours is, so far as we may judge by appearances, a little retarded in time in relation to our own. Our visitors wear something very like the clothing and display physical characteristics resembling those of our ancestors during the Last Age of Confusion....

"We are not yet justified in supposing that their history has been strictly parallel to ours. No two particles of matter are alike; no two vibrations. In all the dimensions of being, in all the universes of God, there has never been and there can never be an exact repetition. That we have come to realize is the one impossible thing. Nevertheless, this world you call Earth is manifestly very near and like to this universe of ours....

"We are eager to learn from you Earthlings, to check our history, which is still very imperfectly known, by your experiences, to show you what we know, to make out what may be possible and desirable in intercourse and help between the people of your planet and ours. We, here, are the merest beginners in knowledge; we have learnt as yet scarcely anything more than the immensity of the things that we have yet to learn and do. In a million kindred things our two worlds may perhaps teach each other and help each other....

"Possibly there are streaks of heredity in your planet that have failed to develop or that have died out in ours. Possibly there are elements or minerals in one world that are rare or wanting in the other.... The structure of your atoms (?)... our worlds may intermarry (?)...to their common invigoration...."

He passed into the inaudible just when Mr. Barnstaple was most moved and most eager to follow what he was saying. Yet a deaf man would have judged he was still speaking.

Mr. Barnstaple met the eye of Mr. Rupert Catskill, as distressed and puzzled as his own. Father Amerton's face was buried in his hands. Lady Stella and Mr. Mush were whispering softly together; they had long since given up any pretence of listening.

"Such," said Serpentine, abruptly becoming audible again, "is our first rough interpretation of your apparition in our world and of the possibilities of our interaction. I have put our ideas before you as plainly as I can. I would suggest that now one of you tell us simply and plainly what *you* conceive to be the truth about your world in relation to ours."

5

The Governance and History of Utopia

⁓

CAME A PAUSE. THE EARTHLINGS LOOKED AT ONE ANOTHER AND THEIR gaze seemed to converge upon Mr. Cecil Burleigh. That statesman feigned to be unaware of the general expectation. "Rupert," he said. "Won't *you?*"

"I reserve my comments," said Mr. Catskill. "Father Amerton, you are accustomed to treat of other worlds."

"Not in your presence, Mr. Cecil. No."

"But what am I to tell them?"

"What you think of it," said Mr. Barnstaple.

"Exactly," said Mr. Catskill. "Tell them what you think of it."

No one else appeared to be worthy of consideration. Mr. Burleigh rose slowly and walked thoughtfully to the centre of the semicircle. He grasped his coat lapels and remained for some moments with face downcast as if considering what he was about to say. "Mr. Serpentine," he began at last, raising a candid countenance and regarding the blue sky above the distant lake through his glasses. "Ladies and Gentlemen—"

He was going to make a speech!—as though he was at a Primrose League garden party—or Geneva. It was preposterous and yet, what else was there to be done?

"I must confess, Sir, that although I am by no means a novice at public speaking, I find myself on this occasion somewhat at a loss. Your

242

admirable discourse, Sir, simple, direct, lucid, compact, and rising at times to passages of unaffected eloquence, has set me a pattern that I would fain follow—and before which, in all modesty, I quail. You ask me to tell you as plainly and clearly as possible the outline facts as we conceive them about this kindred world out of which with so little premeditation we have come to you. So far as my poor powers of understanding or discussing such recondite matters go, I do not think I can better or indeed supplement in any way your marvellous exposition of the mathematical aspects of the case. What you have told us embodies the latest, finest thoughts of terrestrial science and goes, indeed, far beyond our current ideas. On certain matters, in, for example, the relationship of time and gravitation, I feel bound to admit that I do not go with you, but that is rather a failure to understand your position than any positive dissent. Upon the broader aspects of the case there need be no difficulties between us. We accept your main proposition unreservedly; namely, that we conceive ourselves to be living in a parallel universe to yours, on a planet the very brother of your own, indeed quite amazingly like yours, having regard to all the possible contrasts we might have found here. We are attracted by and strongly disposed to accept your view that our system is, in all probability, a little less seasoned and mellowed by the touch of time than yours, short perhaps by some hundreds or some thousands of years of your experiences. Assuming this, it is inevitable, Sir, that a certain humility should mingle in our attitude towards you. As your juniors it becomes us not to instruct but to learn. It is for us to ask: What have you done? To what have you reached? rather than to display to you with an artless arrogance all that still remains for us to learn and do...."

"No!" said Mr. Barnstaple to himself but half audibly. "This is a dream.... If it were anyone else...."

He rubbed his knuckles into his eyes and opened them again, and there he was still, sitting next to Mr. Mush in the midst of these Olympian divinities. And Mr. Burleigh, that polished sceptic, who never believed, who was never astonished, was leaning forward on his toes and speaking, speaking, with the assurance of a man who has made ten thousand speeches. He could not have been more sure of himself and his audience in the Guildhall in London. And they were understanding him! Which was absurd!

There was nothing to do but to fall in with this stupendous absurdity —and sit and listen. Sometimes Mr. Barnstaple's mind wandered altogether from what Mr. Burleigh was saying. Then it returned and hung desperately to his discourse. In his halting, parliamentary way, his hands trifling with his glasses or clinging to the lapels of his coat, Mr. Burleigh was giving Utopia a brief account of the world of men, seeking to be elementary and lucid and reasonable, telling them of states and empires, of wars and the Great War, of economic organization and disorganization, of revolutions and Bolshevism, of the terrible Russian famine that was beginning, of the difficulties of finding honest statesmen and officials, and of the unhelpfulness of newspapers, of all the dark and troubled spectacle of human life. Serpentine had used the term "the Last Age of Confusion," and Mr. Burleigh had seized upon the phrase and was making much of it....

It was a great oratorical impromptu. It must have gone on for an hour, and the Utopians listened with keen, attentive faces, now and then nodding their acceptance and recognition of this statement or that. "Very like," would come tapping into Mr. Barnstaple's brain. "With us also—in the Age of Confusion."

At last Mr. Burleigh, with the steady deliberation of an old parliamentary hand, drew to his end. Compliments.

He bowed. He had done. Mr. Mush startled everyone by a vigorous hand-clapping in which no one else joined.

The tension in Mr. Barnstaple's mind had become intolerable. He leapt to his feet.

HE STOOD MAKING THOSE WEAK PROPITIATORY GESTURES THAT COME SO naturally to the inexperienced speaker. "Ladies and Gentlemen," he said. "Utopians, Mr. Burleigh! I crave your pardon for a moment. There is a little matter. Urgent."

For a brief interval he was speechless.

Then he found attention and encouragement in the eye of Urthred.

"Something I don't understand. Something incredible—I mean, incompatible. The little rift. Turns everything into a fantastic phantasmagoria."

The intelligence in Urthred's eye was very encouraging. Mr. Barnstaple abandoned any attempt to address the company as a whole, and spoke directly to Urthred.

"You live in Utopia, hundreds of thousands of years in advance of us. How is it that you are able to talk contemporary English—to use exactly the same language that we do? I ask you, how is that? It is incredible. It jars. It makes a dream of you. And yet you are not a dream? It makes me feel—almost—insane."

Urthred smiled pleasantly. "We *don't* speak English," he said.

Mr. Barnstaple felt the ground slipping from under his feet. "But I *hear* you speaking English," he said.

"Nevertheless we do not speak it," said Urthred.

He smiled still more broadly. "We don't—for ordinary purposes—speak anything."

Mr. Barnstaple, with his brain resigning its functions, maintained his pose of deferential attention.

"Ages ago," Urthred continued, "we certainly used to speak languages. We made sounds and we heard sounds. People used to think, and then chose and arranged words and uttered them. The hearer heard, noted, and retranslated the sounds into ideas. Then, in some manner which we still do not understand perfectly, people began to *get* the idea before it was clothed in words and uttered in sounds. They began to hear in their minds, as soon as the speaker had arranged his ideas and before he put them into word symbols even in his own mind. They knew what he was going to say before he said it. This direct transmission presently became common; it was found out that with a little effort most people could get over to each other in this fashion to some extent, and the new mode of communication was developed systematically.

"That is what we do now habitually in this world. We think directly *to* each other. We determine to convey the thought and it is conveyed at once—provided the distance is not too great. We use sounds in this world now only for poetry and pleasure and in moments of emotion or to shout at a distance, or with animals, not for the transmission of ideas from human mind to kindred human mind any more. When I think to you, the thought, *so far as it finds corresponding ideas and suitable words in your mind*, is reflected in your mind. My thought clothes itself in words in your mind, which words you seem to hear—and naturally enough in your own language and your own habitual phrases. Very probably the members of your party are hearing what I am saying to you, each with his own individual difference of vocabulary and phrasing."

Mr. Barnstaple had been punctuating this discourse with sharp, intelligent nods, coming now and then to the verge of interruption. Now he broke out with: "And that is why occasionally—as for instance when Mr. Serpentine made his wonderful explanation just now—when you soar into ideas of which we haven't even a shadow in our minds, we just hear nothing at all."

"Are there such gaps?" asked Urthred.

"Many, I fear—for all of us," said Mr. Burleigh.

"It's like being deaf in spots," said Lady Stella. "Large spots."

Father Amerton nodded agreement.

"And that is why we cannot be clear whether you are called Urthred or Adam, and why I have found myself confusing Arden and Greentrees and Forest in my mind."

"I hope that now you are mentally more at your ease?" said Urthred.

"Oh, quite," said Mr. Barnstaple. "Quite. And all things considered, it is really very convenient for us that there should be this method of transmission. For otherwise I do not see how we could have avoided weeks of linguistic bother, first principles of our respective grammars, logic, significs, and so forth, boring stuff for the most part, before we could have got to anything like our present understanding."

"A very good point indeed," said Mr. Burleigh, turning round to Mr. Barnstaple in a very friendly way. "A very good point indeed. I should never have noted it if you had not called my attention to it. It is quite extraordinary; I had not noted anything of this—this difference. I was occupied, I am bound to confess, by my own thoughts. I supposed they were speaking English. Took it for granted."

IT SEEMED TO MR. BARNSTAPLE THAT THIS WONDERFUL EXPERIENCE WAS now so complete that there remained nothing more to wonder at except its absolute credibility. He sat in this beautiful little building looking out upon dreamland flowers and the sunlit lake amidst this strange mingling of week-end English costumes and this more than Olympian nudity that had already ceased to startle him, he listened and occasionally participated in the long informal conversation that now ensued. It was a discussion that brought to light the most amazing and fundamental differences of moral and social outlook. Yet everything had now assumed a reality that made it altogether natural to suppose that he would presently go home to write about it in the *Liberal* and tell his wife, as much as might seem advisable at the time, about the manners and costumes of this hitherto undiscovered world. He had not even a sense of intervening distances. Sydenham might have been just round the corner.

Presently two pretty young girls made tea at an equipage among the rhododendra and brought it round to people. Tea! It was what we should call China tea, very delicate, and served in little cups without handles, Chinese fashion, but it was real and very refreshing tea.

The earlier curiosities of the Earthlings turned upon methods of government. This was perhaps natural in the presence of two such statesmen as Mr. Burleigh and Mr. Catskill.

"What form of government do you have?" asked Mr. Burleigh. "Is it a monarchy or an autocracy or a pure democracy? Do you separate the executive and the legislative? And is there one central government for all your planet, or are there several governing centres?"

It was conveyed to Mr. Burleigh and his companions with some difficulty that there was no central government in Utopia at all.

"But surely," said Mr. Burleigh, "there is someone or something, some council or bureau or what not, somewhere, with which the final decision rests in cases of collective action for the common welfare? Some ultimate seat and organ of sovereignty, it seems to me, there *must* be.".....

No, the Utopians declared, there was no such concentration of authority in their world. In the past there had been, but it had long since diffused back into the general body of the community. Decisions in regard to any particular matter were made by the people who knew most about that matter.

"But suppose it is a decision that has to be generally observed? A rule affecting the public health, for example? Who would enforce it?"

"It would not need to be enforced. Why should it?"

"But suppose someone refused to obey your regulation?"

"We should inquire why he or she did not conform. There might be some exceptional reason."

"But failing that?"

"We should make an inquiry into his mental and moral health."

"The mind doctor takes the place of the policeman," said Mr. Burleigh.

"I should prefer the policeman," said Mr. Rupert Catskill.

"You *would*, Rupert," said Mr. Burleigh as who should say: "*Got* you that time."

"Then do you mean to say," he continued, addressing the Utopians with an expression of great intelligence, "that your affairs are all managed by special bodies or organizations—one scarcely knows what to call them —without any co-ordination of their activities?"

"The activities of our world," said Urthred, "are all co-ordinated to secure the general freedom. We have a number of intelligences directed to the general psychology of the race and to the interaction of one collective function upon another."

"Well, isn't that group of intelligences a governing class?" said Mr. Burleigh.

"Not in the sense that they exercise any arbitrary will," said Urthred. "They deal with general relations, that is all. But they rank no higher, they have no more precedence on that account than a philosopher has over a scientific specialist."

"This is a republic indeed!" said Mr. Burleigh. "But how it works and how it came about I cannot imagine. Your state is probably a highly socialistic one?"

"You live still in a world in which nearly everything except the air, the high roads, the high seas and the wilderness is privately owned?"

"We do," said Mr. Catskill. "Owned—and competed for."

"We have been through that stage. We found at last that private property in all but very personal things was an intolerable nuisance to mankind. We got rid of it. An artist or a scientific man has complete control of all the material he needs, we all own our tools and appliances and have rooms and places of our own, but there is no property for trade or speculation. All this militant property, this property of manoeuvre, has been quite got rid of. But how we got rid of it is a long story. It was not done in a few years. The exaggeration of private property was an entirely natural and necessary stage in the development of human nature. It led at last to monstrous results, but it was only through these monstrous and catastrophic results that men learnt the need and nature of the limitations of private property."

Mr. Burleigh had assumed an attitude which was obviously habitual to him. He sat very low in his chair with his long legs crossed in front of him and the thumb and fingers of one hand placed with meticulous exactness against those of the other.

"I must confess," he said, "that I am most interested in the peculiar form of Anarchism which seems to prevail here. Unless I misunderstand you completely every man attends to his own business as the servant of the state. I take it you have—you must correct me if I am wrong—a great number of people concerned in the production and distribution and preparation of food; they inquire, I assume, into the needs of the world, they satisfy them and they are a law unto themselves in their way of doing it. They conduct researches, they make experiments. Nobody compels, obliges, restrains or prevents them. ("People talk to them about it," said Urthred with a faint smile.) And again others produce and manufacture and study metals for all mankind and are also a law unto themselves. Others again see to the habitability of your world, plan and arrange these delightful habitations, say who shall use them and how they shall be used. Others pursue pure science. Others experiment with sensory and imaginative possibilities and are artists. Others again teach."

"They are very important," said Lychnis.

"And they all do it in harmony—and due proportion. Without either a central legislature or executive. I will admit that all this seems admirable—but impossible. Nothing of the sort has ever been even suggested yet in the world from which we come."

"Something of the sort was suggested long ago by the Guild Socialists," said Mr. Barnstaple.

"Dear me!" said Mr. Burleigh. "I know very little about the Guild Socialists. Who were they? Tell me."

Mr. Barnstaple tacitly declined that task. "The idea is quite familiar to our younger people," he said. "Laski calls it the pluralistic state, as distinguished from the monistic state in which sovereignty is concentrated. Even the Chinese have it. A Pekin professor, Mr. S. C. Chang, has written a pamphlet on what he calls 'Professionalism.' I read it only a few weeks ago. He sent it to the office of the *Liberal.* He points out how undesirable it is and how unnecessary for China to pass through a phase of democratic politics on the western model. He wants China to go right straight on to a collateral independence of functional classes, mandarins, industrials, agricultural workers and so forth, much as we seem to find it here. Though that of course involves an educational revolution. Decidedly the germ of what you call Anarchism here is also in the air we come from."

"Dear me!" said Mr. Burleigh, looking more intelligent and appreciative than ever. "And is that so? I had *no* idea—!"

THE CONVERSATION CONTINUED DESULTORY IN FORM AND YET THE exchange of ideas was rapid and effective. Quite soon, as it seemed to Mr. Barnstaple, an outline of the history of Utopia from the Last Age of Confusion onward shaped itself in his mind.

The more he learnt of that Last Age of Confusion the more it seemed to resemble the present time on earth. In those days the

Utopians had worn abundant clothing and lived in towns quite after the earthly fashion. A fortunate conspiracy of accidents rather than any set design had opened for them some centuries of opportunity and expansion. Climatic phases and political chances had smiled upon the race after a long period of recurrent shortage, pestilence and destructive warfare. For the first time the Utopians had been able to explore the whole planet on which they lived, and these explorations had brought great virgin areas under the axe, the spade and the plough. There had been an enormous increase in real wealth and in leisure and liberty. Many thousands of people were lifted out of the normal squalor of human life to positions in which they could, if they chose, think and act with unprecedented freedom. A few, a sufficient few, did. A vigorous development of scientific inquiry began and, trailing after it a multitude of ingenious inventions, produced a great enlargement of practical human power.

There had been previous outbreaks of the scientific intelligence in Utopia, but none before had ever occurred in such favourable circumstances or lasted long enough to come to abundant practical fruition. Now in a couple of brief centuries the Utopians, who had hitherto crawled about their planet like sluggish ants or travelled parasitically on larger and swifter animals, found themselves able to fly rapidly or speak instantaneously to any other point on the planet. They found themselves, too, in possession of mechanical power on a scale beyond all previous experience, and not simply of mechanical power; physiological and then psychological science followed in the wake of physics and chemistry, and extraordinary possibilities of control over his own body and over his social life dawned upon the Utopian. But these things came, when at last they did come, so rapidly and confusingly that it was only a small minority of people who realized the possibilities, as distinguished from the concrete achievements, of this tremendous expansion of knowledge. The rest took the novel inventions as they came, haphazard, with as little adjustment as possible of their thoughts and ways of living to the new necessities these novelties implied.

The first response of the general population of Utopia to the prospect of power, leisure and freedom thus opened out to it was proliferation. It behaved just as senselessly and mechanically as any other animal or vegetable species would have done. It bred until it had completely swamped the ampler opportunity that had opened before it. It spent the great gifts of science as rapidly as it got them in a mere insensate multiplication of the common life. At one time in the Last Age of Confusion the population of Utopia had mounted to over two thousand million....

"But what is it now?" asked Mr. Burleigh.

About two hundred and fifty million, the Utopians told him. That had been the maximum population that could live a fully developed life upon the surface of Utopia. But now with increasing resources the population was being increased.

A gasp of horror came from Father Amerton. He had been dreading this realisation for some time. It struck at his moral foundations. "And you dare to *regulate* increase! You control it! Your women consent to bear children as they are needed—or refrain!"

"Of course," said Urthred. "Why not?"

"I feared as much," said Father Amerton, and leaning forward he covered his face with his hands, murmuring, "I felt this in the atmosphere! The human stud farm! Refusing to create souls! The *wickedness* of it! Oh, my God!"

Mr. Burleigh regarded the emotion of the reverend gentleman through his glasses with a slightly shocked expression. He detested catchwords. But Father Amerton stood for very valuable conservative elements in the community. Mr. Burleigh turned to the Utopian again. "That is extremely interesting," he said. "Even at present our earth contrives to carry a population of at least five times that amount."

"But twenty millions or *so* will starve this winter, you told us a little while ago—in a place called Russia. And only a very small proportion of the rest are leading what even you would call full and spacious lives?"

"Nevertheless the contrast is very striking," said Mr. Burleigh.

"It is terrible!" said Father Amerton.

The overcrowding of the planet in the Last Age of Confusion was, these Utopians insisted, the fundamental evil out of which all the others that afflicted the race arose. An overwhelming flood of newcomers poured into the world and swamped every effort the intelligent minority could make to educate a sufficient proportion of them to meet the demands of the new and still rapidly changing conditions of life. And the intelligent minority was not itself in any position to control the racial destiny. These great masses of population that had been blundered into existence, swayed by damaged and decaying traditions and amenable to the crudest suggestions, were the natural prey and support of every adventurer with a mind blatant enough and a conception of success coarse enough to appeal to them. The economic system, clumsily and convulsively reconstructed to meet the new conditions of mechanical production and distribution, became more and more a cruel and impudent exploitation of the multitudinous congestion of the common man by the predatory and acquisitive few. That all too commonly common man was hustled through misery and subjection from his cradle to his grave; he was cajoled and lied to, he was bought, sold and dominated by an impudent minority, bolder and no doubt more energetic, but in all other respects no more intelligent than himself. It was difficult, Urthred said, for a Utopian nowadays to convey the monstrous stupidity, wastefulness and vulgarity to which these rich and powerful men of the Last Age of Confusion attained.

("We will not trouble you," said Mr. Burleigh. "Unhappily—we know.... We know. Only too well do we know.")

Upon this festering, excessive mass of population disasters descended at last like wasps upon a heap of rotting fruit. It was its natural, inevitable destiny. A war that affected nearly the whole planet dislocated its flimsy financial system and most of its economic machinery beyond any possibility of repair. Civil wars and clumsily conceived attempts at social revolution continued the disorganization. A series of years of bad weather accentuated the general shortage. The exploiting adventurers, too stupid to realize what had happened, continued to cheat and hoodwink the commonalty and burke any rally of honest men, as wasps will continue to eat even after their bodies have been cut away. The effort to make passed out of Utopian life, triumphantly superseded by the effort to get. Production dwindled down towards the vanishing point. Accumulated wealth vanished. An overwhelming system of debt, a swarm of creditors, morally incapable of helpful renunciation, crushed out all fresh initiative.

The long diastole in Utopian affairs that had begun with the great discoveries, passed into a phase of rapid systole. What plenty and pleasure was still possible in the world was filched all the more greedily by the adventurers of finance and speculative business. Organised science had long since been commercialized, and was "applied" now chiefly to a hunt for profitable patents and the forestalling of necessary supplies. The neglected lamp of pure science waned, flickered and seemed likely to go out again altogether, leaving Utopia in the beginning of a new series of Dark Ages like those before the age of discovery began....

"It is really *very* like a gloomy diagnosis of our own outlook," said Mr. Burleigh. "Extraordinarily like. How Dean Inge would have enjoyed all this!"

"To an infidel of his stamp, no doubt, it would seem most enjoyable," said Father Amerton a little incoherently.

These comments annoyed Mr. Barnstaple, who was urgent to hear more.

"And then," he said to Urthred, "what happened?"

WHAT HAPPENED, MR. BARNSTAPLE GATHERED, WAS A DELIBERATE change in Utopian thought. A growing number of people were coming to understand that amidst the powerful and easily released forces that science and organization had brought within reach of man, the old conception of social life in the state, as a limited and legalized struggle of men and women to get the better of one another, was becoming too dangerous to endure, just as the increased dreadfulness of modern weapons was making the separate sovereignty of nations too dangerous to endure. There had to be new ideas and new conventions of human association if history was not to end in disaster and collapse.

All societies were based on the limitation by laws and taboos and treaties of the primordial fierce combativeness of the ancestral man-ape; that ancient spirit of self-assertion had now to undergo new restrictions commensurate with the new powers and dangers of the race. The idea of competition to possess, as the ruling idea of intercourse, was, like some ill-controlled furnace, threatening to consume the machine it had formerly driven. The idea of creative service had to replace it. To that idea the human mind and will had to be turned if social life was to be saved. Propositions that had seemed, in former ages, to be inspired and exalted idealism began now to be recognised not simply as sober psychological truth but as practical and urgently necessary truth. In explaining this Urthred expressed himself in a manner that recalled to Mr. Barnstaple's mind certain very familiar phrases; he seemed to be saying that whosoever would save his life should lose it, and that whosoever would give his life should thereby gain the whole world.

Father Amerton's thoughts, it seemed, were also responding in the same manner. For he suddenly interrupted with: "But what you are saying is a quotation!"

Urthred admitted that he had a quotation in mind, a passage from the teachings of a man of great poetic power who had lived long ago in the days of spoken words.

He would have proceeded, but Father Amerton was too excited to let him do so. "But who was this teacher?" he asked. "Where did he live? How was he born? How did he die?"

A picture was flashed upon Mr. Barnstaple's consciousness of a solitary-looking pale-faced figure, beaten and bleeding, surrounded by armoured guards, in the midst of a thrusting, jostling, sun-bit crowd which filled a narrow, high-walled street. Behind, some huge ugly implement was borne along, dipping and swaying with the swaying of the multitude....

"Did he die upon the Cross in *this* world also?" cried Father Amerton. "Did he die upon the Cross?"

This prophet in Utopia they learnt had died very painfully, but not upon the Cross. He had been tortured in some way, but neither the Utopians nor these particular Earthlings had sufficient knowledge of the technicalities of torture to get any idea over about that, and then apparently he had been fastened upon a slowly turning wheel and exposed until he died. It was the abominable punishment of a cruel and conquering race, and it had been inflicted upon him because his doctrine of universal service had alarmed the rich and dominant who did not serve. Mr. Barnstaple had a momentary vision of a twisted figure upon that wheel of torture in the blazing sun. And, marvellous triumph over death! out of a world that could do such a deed had come this great peace and universal beauty about him!

But Father Amerton was pressing his questions. "But did you not realize who he was? Did not this world suspect?"

A great many people thought that this man was a God. But he had been accustomed to call himself merely a son of God or a son of Man.

Father Amerton stuck to his point. "But you worship him now?"

"We follow his teaching because it was wonderful and true," said Urthred.

"But worship?"

"No."

"But does nobody worship? There *were* those who worshipped him?"

There were those who worshipped him. There were those who quailed before the stern magnificence of his teaching and yet who had a tormenting sense that he was right in some profound way. So they played a trick upon their own uneasy consciences by treating him as a magical god instead of as a light to their souls. They interwove with his execution ancient traditions of sacrificial kings. Instead of receiving him frankly and clearly and making him a part of their understandings and wills they pretended to eat him mystically and make him a part of their bodies. They turned his wheel into a miraculous symbol, and they confused it with the equator and the sun and the ecliptic and indeed with anything else that was round. In cases of ill-luck, ill-health or bad weather it was believed to be very helpful for the believer to describe a circle in the air with the forefinger.

And since this teacher's memory was very dear to the ignorant multitude because of his gentleness and charity, it was seized upon by cunning and aggressive types who constituted themselves champions and exponents of the wheel, who grew rich and powerful in its name, led people into great wars for its sake and used it as a cover and justification for envy, hatred, tyranny and dark desires. Until at last men said that had that ancient prophet come again to Utopia, his own triumphant wheel would have crushed and destroyed him afresh....

Father Amerton seemed inattentive to this communication. He was seeing it from another angle. "But surely," he said, "there is a remnant of believers still! Despised perhaps—but a remnant?"

There was no remnant. The whole world followed that Teacher of Teachers, but no one worshipped him. On some old treasured buildings the wheel was still to be seen carved, often with the most fantastic decorative elaborations. And in museums and collections there were multitudes of pictures, images, charms and the like.

"I don't understand this," said Father Amerton. "It is too terrible. I am at a loss. I do not understand."

A FAIR AND RATHER SLENDER MAN WITH A DELICATELY BEAUTIFUL FACE whose name, Mr. Barnstaple was to learn later, was Lion, presently took over from Urthred the burthen of explaining and answering the questions of the Earthlings.

He was one of the educational co-ordinators in Utopia. He made it clear that the change over in Utopian affairs had been no sudden revolution. No new system of laws and customs, no new method of economic co-operation based on the idea of universal service to the common good, had sprung abruptly into being complete and finished. Throughout a long period, before and during the Last Age of Confusion, the foundations of the new state were laid by a growing multitude of inquirers and workers, having no set plan or preconceived method, but brought into unconscious co-operation by a common impulse to service and a common lucidity and veracity of mind. It was only towards the climax of the Last Age of Confusion in Utopia that psychological science began to develop with any vigour, comparable to the vigour of the development of geographical and physical science during the preceding centuries. And the social and economic disorder which was checking experimental science and crippling the organised work of the universities was stimulating inquiry into the processes of human association and making it desperate and fearless.

The impression given Mr. Barnstaple was not of one of those violent changes which our world has learnt to call revolutions, but of an increase of light, a dawn of new ideas, in which the things of the old order went on for a time with diminishing vigour until people began as a matter of common sense to do the new things in the place of the old.

The beginnings of the new order were in discussions, books and psychological laboratories; the soil in which it grew was found in schools and colleges. The old order gave small rewards to the schoolmaster, but its dominant types were too busy with the struggle for wealth and power to take much heed of teaching: it was left to any man or woman who would give thought and labour without much hope of tangible rewards, to shape the world anew in the minds of the young. And they did so shape it. In a world ruled ostensibly by adventurer politicians, in a world where men came to power through floundering business enterprises and financial cunning, it was presently being taught and understood that extensive private property was socially a nuisance, and that the state could not do its work properly nor education produce its proper results, side by side with a class of irresponsible rich people. For, by their very nature, they assailed, they corrupted, they undermined every state undertaking; their flaunting existences distorted and disguised all the values of life. They had to go, for the good of the race.

"Didn't they fight?" asked Mr. Catskill pugnaciously.

They had fought irregularly but fiercely. The fight to delay or arrest the coming of the universal scientific state, the educational state, in Utopia, had gone on as a conscious struggle for nearly five centuries. The fight against it was the fight of greedy, passionate, prejudiced and self-seeking men against the crystallization into concrete realities of this new idea of association for service. It was fought wherever ideas were spread; it was fought with dismissals and threats and boycotts and storms of violence, with lies and false accusations, with prosecutions and imprisonments, with lynching-rope, tar and feathers, paraffin, bludgeon and rifle, bomb and gun.

But the service of the new idea that had been launched into the world never failed; it seized upon the men and women it needed with compelling power. Before the scientific state was established in Utopia more than a million martyrs had been killed for it, and those who had suffered lesser wrongs were beyond all reckoning. Point after point was won in education, in social laws, in economic method. No date could be fixed for the change. A time came when Utopia perceived that it was day and that a new order of things had replaced the old....

"So it must be," said Mr. Barnstaple, as though Utopia were not already present about him. "So it must be."

A question was being answered. Every Utopian child is taught to the full measure of its possibilities and directed to the work that is indicated by its desires and capacity. It is born well. It is born of perfectly healthy parents; its mother has chosen to bear it after due thought and preparation. It grows up under perfectly healthy conditions; its natural impulses to play and learn are gratified by the subtlest educational methods; hands, eyes and limbs are given every opportunity of training and growth; it learns to draw, write, express itself, use a great variety of symbols to assist and extend its thought. Kindness and civility become ingrained habits, for all about it are kind and civil. And in particular the growth of its imagination is watched and encouraged. It learns the wonderful history of its world and its race, how man has struggled and still struggles out of his earlier animal narrowness and egotism towards an empire over being that is still but faintly apprehended through dense veils of ignorance. All its desires are made fine; it learns from poetry, from example and the love of those about it to lose its solicitude for itself in love; its sexual passions are turned against its selfishness, its curiosity flowers into scientific passion, its combativeness is set to fight disorder, its inherent pride and ambition are directed towards an honourable share in the common achievement. It goes to the work that attracts it and chooses what it will do.

If the individual is indolent there is no great loss, there is plenty for all in Utopia, but then it will find no lovers, nor will it ever bear children, because no one in Utopia loves those who have neither energy nor distinction. There is much pride of the mate in Utopian love. And there is no idle rich "society" in Utopia, nor games and shows for the mere looker-on. There is nothing for the mere looker-on. It is a pleasant world indeed for holidays, but not for those who would continuously do nothing.

For centuries now Utopian science has been able to discriminate among births, and nearly every Utopian alive would have ranked as an energetic creative spirit in former days. There are few dull and no really defective people in Utopia; the idle strains, the people of lethargic dispositions or weak imaginations, have mostly died out; the melancholic type has taken its dismissal and gone; spiteful and malignant characters are disappearing. The vast majority of Utopians are active, sanguine, inventive, receptive and good-tempered.

"And you have not even a parliament?" asked Mr. Burleigh, still incredulous.

Utopia has no parliament, no politics, no private wealth, no business competition, no police nor prisons, no lunatics, no defectives nor cripples, and it has none of these things because it has schools and teachers who are all that schools and teachers can be. Politics, trade and competition are the methods of adjustment of a crude society. Such methods of adjustment have been laid aside in Utopia for more than a thousand years. There is no rule nor government needed by adult Utopians because all the rule and government they need they have had in childhood and youth.

Said Lion: *"Our education is our government."*

6

Some Earthly Criticisms

⸱⸱⸱

AT TIMES DURING THAT MEMORABLE AFTERNOON AND EVENING IT
seemed to Mr. Barnstaple that he was involved in nothing more remarkable than an extraordinary dialogue about government and history, a
dialogue that had in some inexplicable way become spectacular; it was as if
all this was happening only in his mind; and then the absolute reality of his
adventure would return to him with overwhelming power and his intellectual interest fade to inattention in the astounding strangeness of his position. In these latter phases he would find his gaze wandering from face to
face of the Utopians who surrounded him, resting for a time on some
exquisite detail of the architecture of the building and then coming back
to these divinely graceful forms.

Then incredulously he would revert to his fellow Earthlings.

Not one of these Utopian faces but was as candid, earnest and beautiful as the angelic faces of an Italian painting. One woman was strangely
like Michelangelo's *Delphic Sibyl*. They sat in easy attitudes, men and
women together, for the most part concentrated on the discussion, but
every now and then Mr. Barnstaple would meet the direct scrutiny of a
pair of friendly eyes or find some Utopian face intent upon the costume of
Lady Stella or the eye-glass of Mr. Mush.

Mr. Barnstaple's first impression of the Utopians had been that they were all young people; now he perceived that many of these faces had a quality of vigorous maturity. None showed any of the distinctive marks of age as this world notes them, but both Urthred and Lion had lines of experience about eyes and lips and brow.

The effect of these people upon Mr. Barnstaple mingled stupefaction with familiarity in the strangest way. He had a feeling that he had always known that such a race could exist and that this knowledge had supplied the implicit standard of a thousand judgments upon human affairs, and at the same time he was astonished to the pitch of incredulity to find himself in the same world with them. They were at once normal and wonderful in comparison with himself and his companions who were, on their part, at the same time queer and perfectly matter-of-fact.

And together with a strong desire to become friendly and intimate with these fine and gracious persons, to give himself to them and to associate them with himself by service and reciprocal acts, there was an awe and fear of them that made him shrink from contact with them and quiver at their touch. He desired their personal recognition of himself as a fellow and companion so greatly that his sense of his own ungraciousness and unworthiness overwhelmed him. He wanted to bow down before them. Beneath all the light and loveliness of things about him lurked the intolerable premonition of his ultimate rejection from this new world.

So great was the impression made by the Utopians upon Mr. Barnstaple, so entirely did he yield himself up to his joyful acceptance of their grace and physical splendour, that for a time he had no attention left over to note how different from his own were the reactions of several of his Earthling companions. The aloofness of the Utopians from the queerness, grotesqueness and cruelty of normal earthly life made him ready for the most uncritical approval of their institutions and ways of life.

It was the behaviour of Father Amerton which first awakened him to the fact that it was possible to disapprove of these wonderful people very highly and to display a very considerable hostility to them. At first Father Amerton had kept a round-faced, round-eyed wonder above his round collar; he had shown a disposition to give the lead to anyone who chose to take it, and he had said not a word until the naked beauty of dead Green-lake had surprised him into an expression of unclerical appreciation. But during the journey to the lakeside and the meal and the opening arrangements of the conference there was a reaction, and this first naive and deferential astonishment gave place to an attitude of resistance and hostility. It was as if this new world which had begun by being a spectacle had taken on the quality of a proposition which he felt he had either to accept or confute. Perhaps it was that the habit of mind of a public censor was too strong for him and that he could not feel normal again until he began to condemn. Perhaps he was really shocked and distressed by the virtual nudity of these lovely bodies about him. But he began presently to make queer grunts and coughs, to mutter to himself, and to betray an increasing incapacity to keep still.

He broke out first into an interruption when the question of population was raised. For a little while his intelligence prevailed over this emotional stir when the prophet of the wheel was discussed, but then his gathering preoccupations resumed their sway.

"I must speak out," Mr. Barnstaple heard him mutter. "I must speak out."

"Now suddenly he began to ask questions. There are some things I want to have clear," he said. "I want to know what moral state this so-called Utopia is in. Excuse me!"

He got up. He stood with wavering hands, unable for a moment to begin. Then he went to the end of the row of seats and placed himself so that his hands could rest on the back of a seat. He passed his fingers through his hair and he seemed to be inhaling deeply. An unwonted animation came into his face, which reddened and began to shine. A horrible suspicion crossed the mind of Mr. Barnstaple that so it was he must stand when he began those weekly sermons of his, those fearless denunciations of almost everything, in the church of St. Barnabas in the West. The suspicion deepened to a still more horrible certainty.

"Friends, Brothers of this new world—I have certain things to say to you that I cannot delay saying. I want to ask you some soul-searching questions. I want to deal plainly with you about some plain and simple but very fundamental matters. I want to put things to you frankly and as man to man, not being mealy-mouthed about urgent if delicate things. Let me come without parley to what I have to say. I want to ask you if, in this so-called state of Utopia, you still have and respect and honour the most sacred thing in social life. Do you still respect the marriage bond?"

He paused, and in the pause the Utopian reply came through to Mr. Barnstaple: "In Utopia there are no bonds."

But Father Amerton was not asking questions with any desire for answers; he was asking questions pulpit-fashion.

"I want to know," he was booming out, "if that holy union revealed to our first parents in the Garden of Eden holds good here, if that sanctified life-long association of one man and one woman, in good fortune and ill fortune, excluding every other sort of intimacy, is the rule of your lives. I want to know—"

"But he *doesn't* want to know," came a Utopian intervention.

"—if that shielded and guarded dual purity—"

Mr. Burleigh raised a long white hand. "Father Amerton," he protested, "*please.*"

The hand of Mr. Burleigh was a potent hand that might still wave towards preferment. Few things under heaven could stop Father Amerton when he was once launched upon one of his soul storms, but the hand of Mr. Burleigh was among such things.

"—has followed another still more precious gift and been cast aside here and utterly rejected of men? What is it, Mr. Burleigh?"

"I wish you would not press this matter further just at present, Father Amerton. Until we have learnt a little more. Institutions are, manifestly, very different here. Even the institution of marriage may be different."

The preacher's face lowered. "Mr. Burleigh," he said, "I *must*. If my suspicions are right, I want to strip this world forthwith of its hectic pretence to a sort of health and virtue."

"Not much stripping required," said Mr. Burleigh's chauffeur, in a very audible aside.

A certain testiness became evident in Mr. Burleigh's voice.

"Then ask questions," he said. "Ask questions. Don't orate, please. They don't want us to orate."

"I've asked my question," said Father Amerton sulkily with a rhetorical glare at Urthred, and remained standing.

The answer came clear and explicit. In Utopia there was no compulsion for men and women to go about in indissoluble pairs. For most Utopians that would be inconvenient. Very often men and women, whose work brought them closely together, were lovers and kept very much together, as Arden and Greenlake had done. But they were not obliged to do that.

There had not always been this freedom. In the old crowded days of conflict, and especially among the agricultural workers and employed people of Utopia, men and women who had been lovers were bound together under severe penalties for life. They lived together in a small home which the woman kept in order for the man, she was his servant and bore him as many children as possible, while he got food for them. The children were desired because they were soon helpful on the land or as wage-earners. But the necessities that had subjugated women to that sort of pairing had passed away.

People paired indeed with their chosen mates, but they did so by an inner necessity and not by any outward compulsion.

Father Amerton had listened with ill-concealed impatience. Now he jumped with: "Then I was right, and you have abolished the family?" His finger pointed at Urthred made it almost a personal accusation.

No. Utopia had not abolished the family. It had enlarged and glorified the family until it embraced the whole world. Long ago that prophet of the wheel, whom Father Amerton seemed to respect, had preached that very enlargement of the ancient narrowness of home. They had told him while he preached that his mother and his brethren stood without and claimed his attention. But he would not go to them. He had turned to the crowd that listened to his words: "Behold my mother and my brethren!"

Father Amerton slapped the seat-back in front of him loudly and startlingly. "A quibble," he cried, "a quibble! Satan too can quote the scriptures."

It was clear to Mr. Barnstaple that Father Amerton was not in complete control of himself. He was frightened by what he was doing and yet impelled to do it. He was too excited to think clearly or control his voice properly, so that he shouted and boomed in the wildest way. He was "letting himself go" and trusting to the habits of the pulpit of St. Barnabas to bring him through.

"I perceive now how you stand. Only too well do I perceive how you stand. From the outset I guessed how things were with you. I waited—I waited to be perfectly sure, before I bore my testimony. But it speaks for itself —the shamelessness of your costume, the licentious freedom of your manners! Young men and women, smiling, joining hands, near to caressing, when averted eyes, averted eyes, are the least tribute you could pay to modesty! And this vile talk—of lovers loving—without bonds or blessings, without rules or restraint. What does it mean? Whither does it lead? Do not imagine because I am a priest, a man pure and virginal in spite of great temptations, do not imagine that I do not understand! Have I no vision of the secret places of the heart? Do not the wounded sinners, the broken potsherds, creep to me with their pitiful confessions? And I will tell you plainly whither you go and how you stand? This so-called freedom of yours is nothing but licence. Your so-called Utopia, I see plainly, is nothing but a hell of unbridled indulgence! Unbridled indulgence!"

Mr. Burleigh held up a protesting hand, but Father Amerton's eloquence soared over the obstruction.

He beat upon the back of the seat before him. "I will bear my witness," he shouted. "I will bear my witness. I will make no bones about it. I refuse to mince matters I tell you. You are all living—in promiscuity! That is the word for it. In animal promiscuity! In *bestial* promiscuity!"

Mr. Burleigh had sprung to his feet. He was holding up his two hands and motioning the London Boanerges to sit down. "No, no!" he cried. "You must *stop*, Mr. Amerton. Really, you must stop. You are being insulting. You do not understand. Sit *down*, please. I insist."

"*Sit down and hold your peace*," said a very clear voice. "Or you will be taken away."

Something made Father Amerton aware of a still figure at his elbow. He met the eyes of a lithe young man who was scrutinizing his build as a portrait painter might scrutinize a new sitter. There was no threat in his bearing, he stood quite still, and yet his appearance threw an extraordinary quality of evanescence about Father Amerton. The great preacher's voice died in his throat.

Mr. Burleigh's bland voice was lifted to avert a conflict. "Mr. Serpentine, Sir, I appeal to you and apologize. He is not fully responsible. We others regret the interruption—the incident. I pray you, please do not take him away, whatever taking away may mean. I will answer personally for his good behaviour.... *Do* sit down, Mr. Amerton, *please*; *now*; or I shall wash my hands of the whole business."

Father Amerton hesitated.

"My time will come," he said and looked the young man in the eyes for a moment and then went back to his seat.

Urthred spoke quietly and clearly. "You Earthlings are difficult guests to entertain. This is not all.... Manifestly this man's mind is very unclean. His sexual imagination is evidently inflamed and diseased. He is angry and anxious to insult and wound. And his noises are terrific. To-morrow he must be examined and dealt with."

"How?" said Father Amerton, his round face suddenly grey. "How do you mean—*dealt* with?"

"*Please* do not talk," said Mr. Burleigh. "*Please* do not talk any more. You have done quite enough mischief...."

For the time the incident seemed at an end, but it had left a queer little twinge of fear in Mr. Barnstaple's heart. These Utopians were very gentle-mannered and gracious people indeed, but just for a moment the hand of power had seemed to hover over the Earthling party. Sunlight and beauty were all about the visitors, nevertheless they were strangers and quite helpless strangers in an unknown world. The Utopian faces were kindly and their eyes curious and in a manner friendly, but much more observant than friendly. It was as if they looked across some impassable gulf of difference.

And then Mr. Barnstaple in the midst of his distress met the brown eyes of Lychnis, and they were kindlier than the eyes of the other Utopians. She, at least, understood the fear that had come to him, he felt, and she was willing to reassure him and be his friend. Mr. Barnstaple looked at her, feeling for the moment much as a stray dog might do who approaches a doubtfully amiable group and gets a friendly glance and a greeting.

ANOTHER MIND THAT WAS ALSO IN ACTIVE RESISTANCE TO UTOPIA WAS that of Mr. Freddy Mush. He had no quarrel indeed with the religion or morals or social organization of Utopia. He had long since learnt that no gentleman of serious aesthetic pretensions betrays any interest whatever in such matters. His perceptions were by hypothesis too fine for them. But presently he made it clear that there had been something very ancient and beautiful called the "Balance of Nature" which the scientific methods of Utopia had destroyed. What this Balance of Nature of his was, and how it worked on Earth, neither the Utopians nor Mr. Barnstaple were able to understand very clearly. Under cross-examination Mr. Mush grew pink and restive and his eye-glass flashed defensively. "I hold by the swallows," he repeated. "If you can't see my point about that I don't know what else I can say."

He began with the fact and reverted to the fact that there were no swallows to be seen in Utopia, and there were no swallows to be seen in Utopia because there were no gnats nor midges. There had been an enormous deliberate reduction of insect life in Utopia, and that had seriously affected every sort of creature that was directly or indirectly dependent upon insect life. So soon as the new state of affairs was securely established in Utopia and the educational state working, the attention of the Utopian community had been given to the long-cherished idea of a systematic extermination of tiresome and mischievous species. A careful inquiry was made into the harmfulness and the possibility of eliminating the house-fly for example, wasps and hornets, various species of mice and rats, rabbits, stinging nettles. Ten thousand species, from disease-germ to rhinoceros and hyena, were put upon their trial. Every species found was given an advocate. Of each it was asked: What good is it? What harm does it do? How can it be extirpated? What else may go with it if it goes? Is it worthwhile wiping it out of existence? Or can it be mitigated and retained? And even when the verdict was death final and complete, Utopia set about the business of extermination with great caution. A reserve would be kept and was in many cases still being kept, in some secure isolation, of every species condemned.

Most infectious and contagious fevers had been completely stamped out; some had gone very easily; some had only been driven out of human life by proclaiming a war and subjecting the whole population to discipline. Many internal and external parasites of man and animals had also been got rid of completely. And further, there had been a great cleansing of the world from noxious insects, from weeds and vermin and hostile beasts. The mosquito had gone, the house-fly, the blow-fly, and indeed a great multitude of flies had gone; they had been driven out of life by campaigns involving an immense effort and extending over many generations. It had been infinitely easier to get rid of such big annoyances as the hyena and the wolf than to abolish these smaller pests. The attack upon the flies had involved the virtual rebuilding of a large proportion of Utopian houses and a minute cleansing of them all throughout the planet.

The question of what else would go if a certain species went was one of the most subtle that Utopia had to face. Certain insects, for example, were destructive and offensive grubs in the opening stage of their lives, were evil as caterpillar or pupa and then became either beautiful in themselves or necessary to the fertilization of some useful or exquisite flowers. Others offensive in themselves were a necessary irreplaceable food to pleasant and desirable creatures. It was not true that swallows had gone from Utopia, but they had become extremely rare; and rare too were a number of little insectivorous birds, the fly-catcher for example, that harlequin of the air. But they had not died out altogether; the extermination of insects had not gone to that length; sufficient species had remained to make some districts still habitable for these delightful birds.

Many otherwise obnoxious plants were a convenient source of chemically complex substances that were still costly or tedious to make synthetically, and so had kept a restricted place in life. Plants and flowers, always simpler and more plastic in the hands of the breeder and hybridizer than animals, had been enormously changed in Utopia. Our Earthlings were to find a hundred sorts of foliage and of graceful and scented blossoms that were altogether strange to them. Plants, Mr. Barnstaple learnt, had been trained and bred to make new and unprecedented secretions, waxes, gums, essential oils and the like, of the most desirable quality.

There had been much befriending and taming of big animals; the larger carnivora, combed and cleaned, reduced to a milk dietary, emasculated in spirit and altogether be-catted, were pets and ornaments in Utopia. The almost extinct elephant had increased again and Utopia had saved her giraffes. The brown bear had always been disposed to sweets and vegetarianism and had greatly improved in intelligence. The dog had given up barking and was comparatively rare. Sporting dogs were not used nor small pet animals.

Horses Mr. Barnstaple did not see, but as he was a very modern urban type he did not miss them very much and he did not ask any questions about them while he was actually in Utopia. He never found out whether they had or had not become extinct.

As he heard on his first afternoon in that world of this revision and editing, this weeding and cultivation of the kingdoms of nature by mankind, it seemed to him to be the most natural and necessary phase in human history. "After all," he said to himself, "it was a good invention to say that man was created a gardener."

And now man was weeding and cultivating his own strain....

The Utopians told of eugenic beginnings, of a new and surer decision in the choice of parents, of an increasing certainty in the science of heredity; and as Mr. Barnstaple contrasted the firm clear beauty of face and limb that every Utopian displayed with the carelessly assembled features and bodily disproportions of his earthly associates, he realized that already, with but three thousand years or so of advantage, these Utopians were passing beyond man towards a nobler humanity. They were becoming different in kind.

THE WERE DIFFERENT IN KIND.

As the questions and explanations and exchanges of that afternoon went on, it became more and more evident to Mr. Barnstaple that the difference of their bodies was as nothing to the differences of their minds. Innately better to begin with, the minds of these children of light had grown up uninjured by any such tremendous frictions, concealments, ambiguities and ignorances as cripple the growing mind of an Earthling. They were clear and frank and direct. They had never developed that defensive suspicion of the teacher, that resistance to instruction, which is the natural response to teaching that is half aggression. They were beautifully unwary in their communications. The ironies, concealments, insincerities, vanities and pretensions of earthly conversation seemed unknown to them. Mr. Barnstaple found this mental nakedness of theirs as sweet and refreshing as the mountain air he was breathing. It amazed him that they could be so patient and lucid with beings so underbred.

Underbred was the word he used in his mind. Himself, he felt the most underbred of all; he was afraid of these Utopians; snobbish and abject before them, he was like a mannerless earthy lout in a drawing-room, and he was bitterly ashamed of his own abjection. All the other Earthlings except Mr. Burleigh and Lady Stella betrayed the defensive spite of consciously inferior creatures struggling against that consciousness.

Like Father Amerton, Mr. Burleigh's chauffeur was evidently greatly shocked and disturbed by the unclothed condition of the Utopians; his feelings expressed themselves by gestures, grimaces and an occasional sarcastic comment such as "I *don't* think!" or "What O!" These he addressed for the most part to Mr. Barnstaple, for whom, as the owner of a very little old car, he evidently mingled feelings of profound contempt and social fellowship. He would also direct Mr. Barnstaple's attention to anything that he considered remarkable in bearing or gesture, by means of a peculiar stare and grimace combined with raised eyebrows. He had a way of pointing with his mouth and nose that Mr. Barnstaple under more normal circumstances might have found entertaining.

Lady Stella, who had impressed Mr. Barnstaple at first as a very great lady of the modern type, he was now beginning to feel was on her defence and becoming rather too ladylike. Mr. Burleigh however retained a certain aristocratic sublimity. He had been a great man on earth for all his life and it was evident that he saw no reason why he should not be accepted as a great man in Utopia. On earth he had done little and had been intelligently receptive with the happiest results. That alert, questioning mind of his, free of all persuasions, convictions or revolutionary desires, fell with the utmost ease into the pose of a distinguished person inspecting, in a sympathetic but entirely non-committal manner, the institutions of an alien state. "Tell me," that engaging phrase, laced his conversation.

The evening was drawing on; the clear Utopian sky was glowing with the gold of sunset and a towering mass of cloud above the lake was fading from pink to a dark purple, when Mr. Rupert Catskill imposed himself upon Mr. Barnstaple's attention. He was fretting in his place. "I have something to say," he said. "I have something to say."

Presently he jumped up and walked to the centre of the semi-circle from which Mr. Burleigh had spoken earlier in the afternoon. "Mr. Serpentine," he said. "Mr. Burleigh. There are a few things I should be glad to say —if you can give me this opportunity of saying them."

HE TOOK OFF HIS GREY TOP HAT, WENT BACK AND PLACED IT ON HIS seat and returned to the centre of the apse. He put back his coat tails, rested his hands on his hips, thrust his head forward, regarded his audience for a moment with an expression half cunning, half defiant, muttered something inaudible and began.

His opening was not prepossessing. There was some slight impediment in his speech, the little brother of a lisp, against which his voice beat gutturally. His first few sentences had an effect of being jerked out by unsteady efforts. Then it became evident to Mr. Barnstaple that Mr. Catskill was expressing a very definite point of view, he was offering a reasoned and intelligible view of Utopia. Mr. Barnstaple disagreed with that criticism, indeed he disagreed with it violently, but he had to recognize that it expressed an understandable attitude of mind.

Mr. Catskill began with a sweeping admission of the beauty and order of Utopia. He praised the "glowing health" he saw "on every cheek," the wealth, tranquillity and comfort of Utopian life. They had "tamed the forces of nature and subjugated them altogether to one sole end, to the material comfort of the race."

"But Arden and Greenlake?" murmured Mr. Barnstaple.

Mr. Catskill did not hear or heed the interruption. "The first effect, Mr. Speaker—Mr. Serpentine, I *should* say—the first effect upon an earthly mind is overwhelming. Is it any wonder"—he glanced at Mr. Burleigh and Mr. Barnstaple—"is it any wonder that admiration has carried some of us off our feet? Is it any wonder that for a time your almost magic beauty has charmed us into forgetting much that is in our own natures—into forgetting deep and mysterious impulses, cravings, necessities, so that we have been ready to say, 'Here at last is Lotus Land. Here let us abide, let us adapt ourselves to this planned and ordered splendour and live our lives out here and die.' I, too, Mr.—Mr. Serpentine, succumbed to that magic for a time. But only for a time. Already, Sir, I find myself full of questionings.".....

His bright, headlong mind had seized upon the fact that every phase in the weeding and cleansing of Utopia from pests and parasites and diseases had been accompanied by the possibility of collateral limitations and losses; or perhaps it would be more just to say that that fact had seized upon his mind. He ignored the deliberation and precautions that had accompanied every step in the process of making a world securely healthy and wholesome for human activity. He assumed there had been losses with every gain, he went on to exaggerate these losses and ran on glibly to the inevitable metaphor of throwing away the baby with its bath—inevitable, that is, for a British parliamentarian. The Utopians, he declared, were living lives of extraordinary ease, safety and "may I say so—indulgence" ("They work," said Mr. Barnstaple), but with a thousand annoyances and disagreeables gone had not something else greater and more precious gone also? Life on earth was, he admitted, insecure, full of pains and anxieties, full indeed of miseries and distresses and anguish, but also, and indeed by reason of these very things, it had moments of intensity, hopes, joyful surprises, escapes, attainments, such as the ordered life of Utopia could not possibly afford. "You have been getting away from conflicts and distresses. Have you not also been getting away from the living and quivering realities of life?"

He launched out upon a eulogy of earthly life. He extolled the vitality of life upon earth as though there were no signs of vitality in the high splendour about him. He spoke of the "thunder of our crowded cities," of the "urge of our teeming millions," of the "broad tides of commerce and industrial effort and warfare," that "swayed and came and went in the hives and harbours of our race."

He had the knack of the plausible phrase and that imaginative touch which makes for eloquence. Mr. Barnstaple forgot that slight impediment and the thickness of the voice that said these things. Mr. Catskill boldly admitted all the earthly evils and dangers that Mr. Burleigh had retailed. Everything that Mr. Burleigh had said was true. All that he had said fell indeed far short of the truth. Famine we knew, and pestilence. We suffered from a thousand diseases that Utopia had eliminated. We were afflicted by a thousand afflictions that were known to Utopia now only by ancient tradition. "The rats gnaw and the summer flies persecute and madden. At times life reeks and stinks. I admit it, Sir, I admit it. We go down far below your extremest experiences into discomforts and miseries, anxieties and anguish of soul and body, into bitterness, terror and despair. Yea. But do we not also go higher? I challenge you with that. What can you know in this immense safety of the intensity, the frantic, terror-driven intensity, of many of our efforts? What can you know of reprieves and interludes and escapes? Think of our many happinesses beyond your ken! What do you know here of the sweet early days of convalescence? Of going for a holiday out of disagreeable surroundings? Of taking some great risk to body or fortune and bringing it off? Of winning a bet against enormous odds? Of coming out of prison? And, Sir, it has been said that there are those in our world who have found a fascination even in pain itself. Because our life is dreadfuller, Sir, it has, and it must have, moments that are infinitely brighter than yours. It is titanic, Sir, where this is merely tidy. And we are inured to it and hardened by it. We are tempered to a finer edge. That is the point to which I am coming. Ask us to give up our earthly disorder, our miseries and distresses, our high death-rates and our hideous diseases, and at the first question every man and woman in the world would say, 'Yes! Willingly, Yes!' At the first question, Sir!"

Mr. Catskill held his audience for a moment on his extended finger.

"And then we should begin to take thought. We should ask, as you say your naturalists asked about your flies and such-like offensive small game, we should ask, 'What goes with it? What is the price?' And when we learnt that the price was to surrender that intensity of life, that tormented energy, that pickled and experienced toughness, that rat-like, wolf-like toughness our perpetual struggle engenders, we should hesitate. We should hesitate. In the end, Sir, I believe, I hope and believe, indeed I pray and believe, we should say, 'No!' We should say, 'No!'"

Mr. Catskill was now in a state of great cerebral exaltation. He was making short thrusting gestures with his clenched fist. His voice rose and fell and boomed; he swayed and turned about, glanced for the approval of his fellow Earthlings, flung stray smiles at Mr. Burleigh.

This idea that our poor wrangling, nerveless, chance-driven world was really a fierce and close-knit system of powerful reactions in contrast with the evening serenities of a made and finished Utopia, had taken complete possession of his mind. "Never before, Sir, have I realized, as I realize now, the high, the terrible and adventurous destinies of our earthly race. I look upon this Golden Lotus Land of yours, this divine perfected land from which all conflict has been banished—"

Mr. Barnstaple caught a faint smile on the face of the woman who had reminded him of the *Delphic Sibyl.*

"—and I admit and admire its order and beauty as some dusty and resolute pilgrim might pause, on his exalted and mysterious quest, and admit and admire the order and beauty of the pleasant gardens of some prosperous Sybarite. And like that pilgrim I may beg leave, Sir, to question the wisdom of your way of living. For I take it, Sir, that it is now a proven thing that life and all the energy and beauty of life are begotten by struggle and competition and conflict; we were moulded and wrought in hardship, and so, Sir, were you. And yet you dream here that you have eliminated conflict forever. Your economic state, I gather, is some form of socialism; you have abolished competition in all the businesses of peace. Your political state is one universal unity; you have altogether cut out the bracing and ennobling threat and the purging and terrifying experience of war. Everything is ordered and provided for. Everything is secure. Everything is secure, Sir, except for one thing....

"I grieve to trouble your tranquillity, Sir, but I must breathe the name of that one forgotten thing—*degeneration*! What is there here to prevent degeneration? Are you preventing degeneration?

"What penalties are there any longer for indolence? What rewards for exceptional energy and effort? What is there to keep men industrious, what watchful, when there is no personal danger and no personal loss but only some remote danger or injury to the community? For a time by a sort of inertia you may keep going. You may seem to be making a success of things. I admit it, you *do* seem to be making a success of things. Autumnal glory! Sunset splendour! *While about you in universes parallel to yours, parallel races still toil, still suffer, still compete and eliminate and gather strength and energy!*"

Mr. Catskill flourished his hand at the Utopians in rhetorical triumph.

"I would not have you think, Sir, that these criticisms of your world are offered in a hostile spirit. They are offered in the most amiable and helpful spirit. I am the skeleton, but the most friendly and apologetic skeleton, at your feast. I ask my searching and disagreeable question because I must. Is it indeed the wise way that you have chosen? You have sweetness and light —and leisure. Granted. But if there is all this multitude of Universes, of which you have told us, Mr. Serpentine, so clearly and illuminatingly, and if one may suddenly open into another as ours has done into yours, I would ask you most earnestly how safe is your sweetness, your light and your leisure? We talk here, separated by we know not how flimsy a partition from innumerable worlds. And at that thought, Sir, it seems to me that as I stand here in the great golden calm of this place I can almost hear the trampling of hungry myriads as fierce and persistent as rats or wolves, the snarling voices of races inured to every pain and cruelty, the threat of terrible heroisms and pitiless aggressions...."

He brought his discourse to an abrupt end. He smiled faintly; it seemed to Mr. Barnstaple that he triumphed over Utopia. He stood with hands on his hips and, as if he bent his body by that method, bowed stiffly. "Sir," he said with that ghost of a lisp of his, his eye on Mr. Burleigh, "I have said my say."

He turned about and regarded Mr. Barnstaple for a moment with his face screwed up almost to the appearance of a wink. He nodded his head, as if he tapped a nail with a hammer, jerked himself into activity, and returned to his proper place.

Urthred did not so much answer Mr. Catskill as sit, elbow on knee and chin on hand, thinking audibly about him.

"The gnawing vigour of the rat," he mused, "the craving pursuit of the wolf, the mechanical persistence of wasp and fly and disease-germ, have gone out of our world. That is true. We have obliterated that much of life's devouring forces. And lost nothing worth having. Pain, filth, indignity for ourselves—or any creatures; they have gone or they go. But it is not true that competition has gone from our world. Why does he say it has? Everyone here works to his or her utmost—for service and distinction. None may cheat himself out of toil or duty as men did in the Age of Confusion, when the mean and acquisitive lived and bred in luxury upon the heedlessness of more generous types. Why does he say we degenerate? He has been told better already. The indolent and inferior do not procreate here. And why should he threaten us with fancies of irruptions from other, fiercer, more barbaric worlds? It is we who can open the doors into such other universes or close them as we choose. Because we know. We can go to them—when we know enough we shall—but they cannot come to us. There is no way but knowledge out of the cages of life.... What is the matter with the mind of this man?

"These Earthlings are only in the beginnings of science. They are still for all practical ends in that phase of fear and taboos that came also in the development of Utopia before confidence and understanding. Out of which phase our own world struggled during the Last Age of Confusion. The minds of these Earthlings are full of fears and prohibitions, and though it has dawned upon them that they may possibly control their universe, the thought is too terrible yet for them to face. They avert their minds from it. They still want to go on thinking, as their fathers did before them, that the universe is being managed for them better than they can control it for themselves. Because if that is so, they are free to obey their own violent little individual motives. Leave things to God, they cry, or leave them to Competition."

"Evolution was our blessed word," said Mr. Barnstaple, deeply interested.

"It is all the same thing—God, or Evolution, or what you will —so long as you mean a Power beyond your own which excuses you from your duty. Utopia says, 'Do not leave things at all. Take hold.' But these Earthlings still lack the habit of looking at reality—undraped. This man with the white linen fetter round his neck is afraid even to look upon men and women as they are. He is disgustingly excited by the common human body. This man with the glass lens before his left eye struggles to believe that there is a wise old Mother Nature behind the appearances of things, keeping a Balance. It was fantastic to hear about his Balance of Nature. Cannot he with two eyes and a lens see better than that? This last man who spoke so impressively, thinks that this old Beldame Nature is a limitless source of will and energy if only we submit to her freaks and cruelties and imitate her most savage moods, if only we sufficiently thrust and kill and rob and ravish one another.... He too preaches the old fatalism and believes it is the teaching of science....

"These Earthlings do not yet dare to see what our Mother Nature is. At the back of their minds is still the desire to abandon themselves to her. They do not see that except for our eyes and wills, she is purposeless and blind. She is not awful, she is horrible. She takes no heed to our standards, nor to any standards of excellence. She made us by accident; all her children are bastards—undesired; she will cherish or expose them, pet or starve or torment without rhyme or reason. She does not heed, she does not care. She will lift us up to power and intelligence, or debase us to the mean feebleness of the rabbit or the slimy white filthiness of a thousand of her parasitic inventions. There must be good in her because she made all that is good in us —but also there is endless evil. Do not you Earthlings see the dirt of her, the cruelty, the insane indignity of much of her work?"

"Phew! Worse than 'Nature red in tooth and claw,'" murmured Mr. Freddy Mush.

"These things are plain," mused Urthred. "If they dared to see.

"Half the species of life in our planet also, half and more than half of all the things alive, were ugly or obnoxious, inane, miserable, wretched, with elaborate diseases, helplessly ill-adjusted to Nature's continually fluctuating conditions, when first we took this old Hag, our Mother, in hand. We have, after centuries of struggle, suppressed her nastier fancies, and washed her and combed her and taught her to respect and heed the last child of her wantonings—Man. With Man came Logos, the Word and the Will into our universe, to watch it and fear it, to learn it and cease to fear it, to know it and comprehend it and master it. So that we of Utopia are no longer the beaten and starved children of Nature, but her free and adolescent sons. We have taken over the Old Lady's Estate. Every day we learn a little better how to master this little planet. Every day our thoughts go out more surely to our inheritance, the stars. And the deeps beyond and beneath the stars."

"You have reached the stars?" cried Mr. Barnstaple.

"Not yet. Not even the other planets. But very plainly the time draws near when those great distances will cease to restrain us...."

He paused. "Many of us will have to go out into the deeps of space.... And never return.... Giving their lives...."

"And into these new spaces—countless brave men...."

Urthred turned towards Mr. Catskill. "We find your frankly expressed thoughts particularly interesting to-day. You help us to understand the past of our own world. You help us to deal with an urgent problem that we will presently explain to you. There are thoughts and ideas like yours in our ancient literature of two or three thousand years ago, the same preaching of selfish violence as though it was a virtue. Even then intelligent men knew better, and you yourself might know better if you were not wilfully set in wrong opinions. But it is plain to see from your manner and bearing that you are very wilful indeed in your opinions.

"You are not, you must realize, a very beautiful person, and probably you are not very beautiful in your pleasures and proceedings. But you have superabundant energy, and so it is natural for you to turn to the excitements of risk and escape, to think that the best thing in life is the sensation of conflict and winning. Also in the economic confusion of such a world as yours there is an intolerable amount of toil that must be done, toil so disagreeable that it makes everyone of spirit anxious to thrust away as much of it as possible and to claim exemption from it on account of nobility, gallantry or good fortune. People in your world no doubt persuade themselves very easily that they are justifiably exempted, and you are under that persuasion. You live in a world of classes. Your badly trained mind has been under no necessity to invent its own excuses; the class into which you were born had all its excuses ready for you. So it is you take the best of everything without scruple and you adventure with life, chiefly at the expense of other people, with a mind trained by all its circumstances to resist the idea that there is any possible way of human living that can be steadfast and disciplined and at the same time vigorous and happy. You have argued against that persuasion all your life as though it were your personal enemy. It is your personal enemy; it condemns your way of life altogether, it damns you utterly for your adventures.

"Confronted now with an ordered and achieved beauty of living you still resist; you resist to escape dismay; you argue that this world of ours is unromantic, wanting in intensity, decadent, feeble. Now—in the matter of physical strength, grip hands with that young man who sits beside you."

Mr. Catskill glanced at the extended hand and shook his head knowingly. "You go on talking," he said.

"Yet when I tell you that neither our wills nor our bodies are as feeble as yours, your mind resists obstinately. You will not believe it. If for a moment your mind admits it, afterwards it recoils to the system of persuasions that protect your self-esteem. Only one of you accepts our world at all, and he does so rather because he is weary of yours than willing for ours. So I suppose it has to be. Yours are Age of Confusion minds, trained to conflict, trained to insecurity and secret self-seeking. In that fashion Nature and your state have taught you to live and so you must needs live until you die. Such lessons are to be unlearnt only in ten thousand generations, by the slow education of three thousand years.

"And we are puzzled by the question, what are we to do with you? We will try our utmost to deal fairly and friendly with you if you will respect our laws and ways.

"But it will be very difficult, we know, for you. You do not realize yet how difficult your habits and preconceptions will make it for you. Your party so far has behaved very reasonably and properly, in act if not in thought. But we have had another experience of Earthling ways to-day of a much more tragic kind. Your talk of fiercer, barbaric worlds breaking in upon us has had its grotesque parallel in reality to-day. It is true; there is something fierce and ratlike and dangerous about Earthly men. You are not the only Earthlings who came into Utopia through this gate that swung open for a moment to-day. There are others—"

276

"Of course!" said Mr. Barnstaple. "I should have guessed it! That third lot!"

"There is yet another of these queer locomotive machines of yours in Utopia."

"The grey car!" said Mr. Barnstaple to Mr. Burleigh. "It wasn't a hundred yards ahead of you."

"Raced us from Hounslow," said Mr. Burleigh's driver. "Real hot stuff."

Mr. Burleigh turned to Mr. Freddy Mush. "I think you said you recognised some one?"

"Lord Barralonga, Sir, almost to a certainty, and I *think* Miss Greeta Grey."

"There were two other men," said Mr. Barnstaple.

"They will complicate things," said Mr. Burleigh.

"They do complicate things," said Urthred. "They have killed a man."

"A Utopian?"

"These other people—there are five of them—whose names you seem to know, came into Utopia just in front of your two vehicles. Instead of stopping as you did when they found themselves on a new strange road, they seem to have quickened their pace very considerably. They passed some men and women and they made extraordinary gestures to them and abominable noises produced by an instrument specially designed for that purpose. Further on they encountered a silver cheetah and charged at it and ran right over it, breaking its back. They do not seem to have paused to see what became of it. A young man named Gold came out into the road to ask them to stop. But their machine is made in the most fantastic way, very complex and very foolish. It is quite unable to stop short suddenly. It is not driven by a single engine that is completely controlled. It has a complicated internal conflict. It has a sort of engine that drives it forward by a complex cogged gear on the axle of the hind wheels and it has various clumsy stopping contrivances by means of friction at certain points. You can apparently drive the engine at the utmost speed and at the same time jam the wheels to prevent them going round. When this young man stepped forward in front of them, they were quite unable to stop. They may have tried to do so. They say they did. Their machine swerved dangerously and struck him with its side."

"And killed him?"

"And killed him instantly. His body was horribly injured.... But they did not stop even for that. They slowed down and had a hasty consultation, and then seeing that people were coming they set their machine in motion again and made off. They seem to have been seized with a panic fear of restraint and punishment. Their motives are very difficult to understand. At any rate they went on. They rode on and on into our country for some hours. An aeroplane was presently set to follow them and another to clear the road in front of them. It was very difficult to clear the road because neither our people nor our animals understand such vehicles as theirs— nor such behaviour. In the afternoon they got among mountains and evidently found our roads much too smooth and difficult for their machine. It made extraordinary noises as though it was gritting its teeth, and emitted a blue vapour with an offensive smell. At one corner where it should have stopped short, it skated about and slid suddenly sideways and rolled over a cliff and fell for perhaps twice the height of a man into a torrent."

"And they were killed?" asked Mr. Burleigh, with, as it seemed to Mr. Barnstaple, a touch of eagerness in his voice.

"Not one of them."

"Oh!" said Mr. Burleigh, "then what happened?"

"One of them has a broken arm and another is badly cut about the face. The other two men and the woman are uninjured except for fright and shock. When our people came up to them the four men held their hands above their heads. Apparently they feared they would be killed at once and did this as an appeal for mercy."

"And what are you doing with them?"

"We are bringing them here. It is better, we think, to keep all you Earthlings together. At present we cannot imagine what must be done to you. We want to learn from you and we want to be friendly with you if it is possible. It has been suggested that you should be returned to your world. In the end that may be the best thing to do. But at present we do not know enough to do this certainly. Arden and Greenlake, when they made the attempt to rotate a part of our matter through the F dimension, believed that they would rotate it in empty space in that dimension. The fact that you were there and were caught into our universe, is the most unexpected thing that has happened in Utopia for a thousand years."

7

The Bringing in of Lord Barralonga's Party

~

THE CONFERENCE BROKE UP UPON THIS ANNOUNCEMENT, BUT LORD Barralonga and his party were not brought to the Conference Gardens until long after dark. No effort was made to restrain or control the movements of the Earthlings. Mr. Burleigh walked down to the lake with Lady Stella and the psychologist whose name was Lion, asking and answering questions. Mr. Burleigh's chauffeur wandered rather disconsolately, keeping within hail of his employer. Mr. Rupert Catskill took Mr. Mush off by the arm as if to give him instructions.

Mr. Barnstaple wanted to walk about alone to recall and digest the astounding realisations of the afternoon and to accustom himself to the wonder of this beautiful world, so beautiful and now in the twilight so mysterious also, with its trees and flowers becoming dim and shapeless notes of pallor and blackness and with the clear forms and gracious proportions of its buildings melting into a twilight indistinctness.

The earthliness of his companions intervened between him and this world into which he felt he might otherwise have been accepted and absorbed. He was in it, but in it only as a strange and discordant intruder. Yet he loved it already and desired it and was passionately anxious to become a part of it. He had a vague but very powerful feeling that if only he could get away from his companions, if only in some way he could cast off his earthly clothing and everything upon him that marked him as earthly and linked him to earth, he would by the very act of casting that off become himself native to Utopia, and then that this tormenting sense, this bleak distressing strangeness would vanish out of his mind. He would suddenly find himself a Utopian in nature and reality, and it was Earth that would become the incredible dream, a dream that would fade at last completely out of his mind.

For a time, however, Father Amerton's need of a hearer prevented any such detachment from earthly thoughts and things. He stuck close to Mr. Barnstaple and maintained a stream of questions and comments that threw over this Utopian scene the quality of some Earl's Court exhibition that the two of them were visiting and criticizing together. It was evidently so provisional, so disputable and unreal to him, that at any moment Mr. Barnstaple felt he would express no astonishment if a rift in the scenery suddenly let in the clatter of the Earl's Court railway station or gave a glimpse of the conventional Gothic spire of St. Barnabas in the West.

At first Father Amerton's mind was busy chiefly with the fact that on the morrow he was to be "dealt with" on account of the scene in the conference. "How *can* they deal with me?" he said for the fourth time.

"I beg your pardon," said Mr. Barnstaple. Every time Mr. Amerton began speaking Mr. Barnstaple said, "I beg your pardon," in order to convey to him that he was interrupting a train of thought. But every time Mr. Barnstaple said, "I beg your pardon," Mr. Amerton would merely remark, "You ought to consult some one about your hearing," and then go on with what he had to say.

"How can I be *dealt with*?" he asked of Mr. Barnstaple and the circumambient dusk. "How can I be dealt with?"

"Oh! psycho-analysis or something of that sort," said Mr. Barnstaple.

"It takes two to play at that game," said Father Amerton, but it seemed to Mr. Barnstaple with a slight flavour of relief in his tone. "Whatever they ask me, whatever they suggest to me, I will not fail—I will bear my witness."

"I have no doubt they will find it hard to suppress you," said Mr. Barnstaple bitterly....

For a time they walked among the tall sweet-smelling, white-flowered shrubs in silence. Now and then Mr. Barnstaple would quicken or slacken his pace with the idea of increasing his distance from Father Amerton but quite mechanically Father Amerton responded to these efforts.

"Promiscuity," he began again presently. "What other word could you use?"

"I really beg your pardon," said Mr. Barnstaple.

"What other word could I have used *but* 'promiscuity'? What else could one expect—with people running about in this amazing want of costume, but the morals of the monkeys' cage? They admit that our institution of marriage is practically unknown to them!"

"It's a different world," said Mr. Barnstaple irritably. "A different world."

"The Laws of Morality hold good for every conceivable world."

"But in a world in which people propagated by fission and there was no sex?"

"Morality would be simpler but it would be the same morality."

Presently Mr. Barnstaple was begging his pardon again.

"I was saying that this is a lost world."

"It doesn't *look* lost," said Mr. Barnstaple.

"It has rejected and forgotten Salvation."

Mr. Barnstaple put his hands in his pockets and began to whistle the barcarolle from *The Tales of Hoffman*, very softly to himself. Would Father Amerton never leave him? Could nothing be done with Father Amerton? At the old shows at Earl's Court there used to be wire baskets for waste paper and cigarette ends and bores generally. If one could only tip Father Amerton suddenly into some such receptacle!

"Salvation has been offered them, and they have rejected it and well-nigh forgotten it. And that is why we have been sent to them. We have been sent to them to recall them to the One Thing that Matters, to the One Forgotten Thing. Once more we have to raise the healing symbol as Moses raised it in the Wilderness. Ours is no light mission. We have been sent into this Hell of sensuous materialism—"

"Oh, *Lord*!" said Mr. Barnstaple, and relapsed into the barcarolle....

"I *beg* your pardon," he exclaimed again presently.

"Where is the Pole Star? What has happened to the Wain?"

Mr. Barnstaple looked up.

He had not thought of the stars before, and he looked up prepared in this fresh Universe to see the strangest constellations. But just as the life and size of the planet they were on ran closely parallel to the earth's, so he beheld above him a starry vault of familiar forms. And just as the Utopian world failed to be altogether parallel to its sister universe, so did these constellations seem to be a little out in their drawing. Orion, he thought, straddled wider and with a great unfamiliar nebula at one corner, and it was true—the Wain was flattened out and the pointers pointed to a great void in the heavens.

"Their Pole Star gone! The Pointers, the Wain askew! It is symbolical," said Father Amerton.

It was only too obviously going to be symbolical. Mr. Barnstaple realized that a fresh storm of eloquence was imminent from Father Amerton. At any cost he felt this nuisance must be abated.

~

ON EARTH MR. BARNSTAPLE HAD BEEN A PASSIVE VICTIM TO BORES OF all sorts, delicately and painfully considerate of the mental limitations that made their insensitive pressure possible. But the free air of Utopia had already mounted to his head and released initiatives that his excessively deferential recognition of others had hitherto restrained. He had had enough of Father Amerton; it was necessary to turn off Father Amerton, and he now proceeded to do so with a simple directness that surprised himself.

"Father Amerton," he said, "I have a confession to make to you."

"Ah!" cried Father Amerton. "Please—anything?"

"You have been walking about with me and shouting at my ears until I am strongly impelled to murder you."

"If what I have said has struck home—"

"It hasn't struck home. It has been a tiresome, silly, deafening jabbering in my ears. It wearies me indescribably. It prevents my attending to the marvellous things about us. I see exactly what you mean when you say that there is no Pole Star here and that that is symbolical. Before you begin I appreciate the symbol, and a very obvious, weak and ultimately inaccurate symbol it is. But you are one of those obstinate spirits who believes in spite of all evidence that the eternal hills are still eternal and the fixed stars fixed forever. I want you to understand that I am entirely out of sympathy with all this stuff of yours. You seem to embody all that is wrong and ugly and impossible in Catholic teaching. I agree with these Utopians that there is something wrong with your mind about sex, in all probability a nasty twist given to it in early life, and that what you keep saying and hinting about sexual life here is horrible and outrageous. And I am equally hostile to you and exasperated and repelled by you when you speak of religion proper. You make religion disgusting just as you make sex disgusting. You are a dirty priest. What *you* call Christianity is a black and ugly superstition, a mere excuse for malignity and persecution. It is an outrage upon Christ. If you are a Christian, then most passionately I declare myself *not* a Christian. But there are other meanings for Christianity than those you put upon it, and in another sense this Utopia here is Christian beyond all dreaming. Utterly beyond your understanding. We have come into this glorious world, which, compared to our world, is like a bowl of crystal compared to an old tin can, and you have the insufferable impudence to say that we have been sent hither as missionaries to teach them—God knows what!"

"God *does* know what," said Father Amerton a little taken aback, but coming up very pluckily.

"Oh!" cried Mr. Barnstaple, and was for a moment speechless.

"Listen to me, my Friend," said Father Amerton, catching at his sleeve.

"Not for my life!" cried Mr. Barnstaple, recoiling. "See! Down that vista, away there on the shore of the lake, those black figures are Mr. Burleigh, Mr. Mush and Lady Stella. They brought you here. They belong to your party and you belong to them. If they had not wanted your company you would not have been in their car. Go to them. I will not have you with me any longer. I refuse you and reject you. That is your way. This, by this little building, is mine. Don't follow me, or I will lay hands on you and bring in these Utopians to interfere between us.... Forgive my plainness, Mr. Amerton. But get away from me! Get away from me!"

Mr. Barnstaple turned, and seeing that Father Amerton stood hesitating at the parting of the ways, took to his heels and ran from him.

He fled along an alley behind tall hedges, turned sharply to the right and then to the left, passed over a high bridge that crossed in front of a cascade that flung a dash of spray in his face, blundered by two couples of lovers who whispered softly in the darkling, ran deviously across flower-studded turf, and at last threw himself down breathless upon the steps that led up to a terrace that looked towards lake and mountains, and was adorned, it seemed in the dim light, with squat stone figures of seated vigilant animals and men.

"Ye merciful stars!" cried Mr. Barnstaple. "At last I am alone."

He sat on these steps for a long time with his eyes upon the scene about him, drinking in the satisfying realisation that for a brief interval at any rate, with no earthly presence to intervene, he and Utopia were face to face.

~

HE COULD NOT CALL THIS WORLD THE WORLD OF HIS DREAMS BECAUSE he had never dared to dream of any world so closely shaped to the desires and imaginations of his heart. But surely this world it was, or a world the very fellow of it, that had lain deep beneath the thoughts and dreams of thousands of sane and troubled men and women in the world of disorder from which he had come. It was no world of empty peace, no such golden decadence of indulgence as Mr. Catskill tried to imagine it; it was a world, Mr. Barnstaple perceived, intensely militant, conquering and to conquer, prevailing over the obduracy of force and matter, over the lifeless separations of empty space and all the antagonistic mysteries of being.

In Utopia in the past, obscured by the superficial exploits of statesmen like Burleigh and Catskill and the competition of traders and exploiters every whit as vile and vulgar as their earthly compeers, the work of quiet and patient thinkers and teachers had gone on and the foundations which sustained this serene intensity of activity had been laid. How few of these pioneers had ever felt more than a transitory gleam of the righteous loveliness of the world their lives made possible!

And yet even in the hate and turmoil and distresses of the Days of Confusion there must have been earnest enough of the exquisite and glorious possibilities of life. Over the foulest slums the sunset called to the imaginations of men, and from mountain ridges, across great valleys, from cliffs and hill-sides and by the uncertain and terrible splendours of the sea, men must have had glimpses of the conceivable and attainable magnificence of being. Every flower petal, every sunlit leaf, the vitality of young things, the happy moments of the human mind transcending itself in art, all these things must have been material for hope, incentive to effort. And now at last—this world!

Mr. Barnstaple lifted up his hands like one who worships to the friendly multitude of the stars above him.

"I have seen," he whispered. "I have seen."

Little lights and soft glows of illumination were coming out here and there over this great park of flowerlike buildings and garden spaces that sloped down towards the lake. A circling aeroplane, itself a star, hummed softly overhead.

A slender girl came past him down the steps and paused at the sight of him.

"Are you one of the Earthlings?" came the question, and a beam of soft light shone momentarily upon Mr. Barnstaple from the bracelet on her arm.

"I came to-day," said Mr. Barnstaple, peering up at her.

"You are the man who came alone in a little machine of tin, with rubber air-bags round the wheels, very rusty underneath, and painted yellow. I have been looking at it."

"It is not a bad little car," said Mr. Barnstaple.

"At first we thought the priest came in it with you."

"He is no friend of mine."

"There were priests like that in Utopia many years ago. They caused much mischief among the people."

"He was with the other lot," said Mr. Barnstaple. "For their week-end party I should think him—rather a mistake."

She sat down a step or so above him.

"It is wonderful that you should come here out of your world to us. Do you find this world of ours very wonderful? I suppose many things that seem quite commonplace to me because I have been born among them seem wonderful to you."

"You are not very old?"

"I am eleven. I am learning the history of the Ages of Confusion, and they say your world is still in an Age of Confusion. It is just as though you came to us out of the past—out of history. I was in the Conference and I was watching your face. You love this present world of ours—at least you love it much more than your other people do."

"I want to live all the rest of my life in it."

"I wonder if that is possible?"

"Why should it not be possible? It will be easier than sending me back. I should not be very much in the way. I should only be here for twenty or thirty years at the most, and I would learn everything I could and do everything I was told."

"But isn't there work that you have to do in your own world?"

Mr. Barnstaple made no answer to that. He did not seem to hear it. It was the girl who presently broke the silence.

"They say that when we Utopians are young, before our minds and characters are fully formed and matured, we are very like the men and women of the Age of Confusion. We are more egotistical then, they tell us; life about us is still so unknown, that we are adventurous and romantic. I suppose I am egotistical yet—and adventurous. And it does still seem to me that in spite of many terrible and dreadful things there was much that must have been wildly exciting and desirable in that past—which is still so like your present. What can it have been like to have been a general entering a conquered city? Or a prince being crowned? Or to be rich and able to astonish people by acts of power and benevolence? Or to be a martyr led out to die for some splendid misunderstood cause?"

"These things sound better in stories and histories than in reality," said Mr. Barnstaple after due consideration. "Did you hear Mr. Rupert Catskill, the last of the Earthlings to make a speech?"

"He thought romantically—but he did not look romantic."

"He has lived most romantically. He has fought bravely in wars. He has been a prisoner and escaped wonderfully from prison. His violent imaginations have caused the deaths of thousands of people. And presently we shall see another romantic adventurer in this Lord Barralonga they are bringing hither. He is enormously rich and he tries to astonish people with his wealth—just as you have dreamt of astonishing people."

"Are they not astonished?"

"Romance is not reality," said Mr. Barnstaple. "He is one of a number of floundering, corrupting rich men who are a weariness to themselves and an intolerable nuisance to the rest of our world. They want to do vulgar showy things. This man Barralonga was an assistant to a photographer and something of an actor when a certain invention called moving pictures came into our world. He became a great prospector in the business of showing these pictures, partly by accident, partly by the unscrupulous cheating of various inventors. Then he launched out into speculations in shipping and in a trade we carry on in our world in frozen meat brought from great distances. He made food costly for many people and impossible for some, and so he grew rich. For in our world men grow wealthy by intercepting rather than by serving. And having become ignobly rich, certain of our politicians, for whom he did some timely services, ennobled him by giving him the title of Lord. Do you understand the things I am saying? Was your Age of Confusion so like ours? *You did not know it was so ugly*. Forgive me if I disillusion you about the Age of Confusion and its romantic possibilities. But I have just stepped out of the dust and disorder and noise of its indiscipline, out of limitation, cruelties and distresses, out of a weariness in which hope dies.... Perhaps if my world attracts you, you may yet have an opportunity of adventuring out of all this into its disorders.... That will be an adventure indeed.... Who knows what may happen between our worlds?... But you will not like it, I am afraid. You cannot imagine how dirty our world is.... Dirt and disease, these are in the trailing skirts of all romance...."

A silence fell between them; he followed his own thoughts and the girl sat and wondered over him.

At length he spoke again.

"Shall I tell you what I was thinking of when you spoke to me?"

"Yes?"

"Your world is the consummation of a million ancient dreams. It is wonderful! It is wonder, high as heaven. But it is a great grief to me that two dear friends of mine cannot be here with me to see what I am seeing. It is queer how strong the thought of them is in my mind. One has passed now beyond all the universes, alas!—but the other is still in my world. You are a student, my dear; everyone of your world, I suppose, is a student here, but in our world students are a class apart. We three were happy together because we were students and not yet caught into the mills of senseless toil, and we were none the less happy perhaps because we were miserably poor and often hungry together. We used to talk and dispute together and in our students' debating society, discussing the disorders of our world and how some day they might be bettered. Was there, in your Age of Confusion, that sort of eager, hopeful, poverty-struck student life?"

"Go on," said the girl with her eyes intent on his dim profile. "In old novels I have read of just that hungry dreaming student world."

"We three agreed that the supreme need of our time was education. We agreed that was the highest service we could join. We all set about it in our various ways, I the least useful of the three. My friends and I drifted a little apart. They edited a great monthly periodical that helped to keep the world of science together, and my friend, serving a careful and grudging firm of publishers, edited school books for them, conducted an educational paper, and also inspected schools for our university. He was too heedless of pay and profit ever to become even passably well off though these publishers profited greatly by his work; his whole life was a continual service of toil for teaching; he did not take as much as a month's holiday in any year in his life. While he lived I thought little of the work he was doing, but since he died I have heard from teachers whose schools he inspected, and from book writers whom he advised, of the incessant high quality of his toil and the patience and sympathy of his work. On such lives as his this Utopia in which your sweet life is opening is founded; on such lives our world of earth will yet build its Utopia. But the life of this friend of mine ended abruptly in a way that tore my heart. He worked too hard and too long through a crisis in which it was inconvenient for him to take a holiday. His nervous system broke down with shocking suddenness, his mind gave way, he passed into a phase of acute melancholia and—died. For it is perfectly true, old Nature has neither righteousness nor pity. This happened a few weeks ago. That other old friend and I, with his wife, who had been his tireless helper, were chief among the mourners at his funeral. To-night the memory of that comes back to me with extraordinary vividness. I do not know how you dispose of your dead here, but on earth the dead are mostly buried in the earth."

"We are burnt," said the girl.

"Those who are liberal-minded in our world burn also. Our friend was burnt, and we stood and took our part in a service according to the rites of our ancient religion in which we no longer believed, and presently we saw his coffin, covered with wreaths of flowers, slide from before us out of our sight through the gates that led to the furnaces of the crematorium, and as it went, taking with it so much of my youth, I saw that my other dear old friend was sobbing, and I too was wrung to the pitch of tears to think that so valiant and devoted and industrious a life should end, as it seemed, so miserably and thanklessly. The priest had been reading a long contentious discourse by a theological writer named Paul, full of bad arguments by analogy and weak assertions. I wished that instead of the ideas of this ingenious ancient we could have had some discourse upon the real nobility of our friend, on the pride and intensity of his work and on his scorn for mercenary things. All his life he had worked with unlimited devotion for such a world as this, and yet I doubt if he had ever had any realisation of the clearer, nobler life for man that his life of toil and the toil of such lives as his, were making sure and certain in the days to come. He lived by faith. He lived too much by faith. There was not enough sunlight in his life. If I could have him here now—and that other dear friend who grieved for him so bitterly; if I could have them both here; if I could give up my place here to them so that they could see, as I see, the real greatness of their lives reflected in these great consequences of such lives as theirs—then, then I could rejoice in Utopia indeed.... But I feel now as if I had taken my old friend's savings and was spending them on myself...."

Mr. Barnstaple suddenly remembered the youth of his hearer. "Forgive me, my dear child, for running on in this fashion. But your voice was kind."

The girl's answer was to bend down and brush his extended hand with her soft lips.

Then suddenly she sprang to her feet. "Look at that light," she said, "among the stars!"

Mr. Barnstaple stood up beside her.

"That is the aeroplane bringing Lord Barralonga and his party; Lord Barralonga who killed a man to-day! Is he a very big, strong man—ungovernable and wonderful?"

Mr. Barnstaple, struck by a sudden doubt, looked sharply at the sweet upturned face beside him.

"I have never seen him. But I believe he is a youngish, baldish, under-sized man, who suffers very gravely from a disordered liver and kidneys. This has prevented the dissipation of his energies upon youthful sports and pleasures and enabled him to concentrate upon the acquisition of property. And so he was able to buy the noble title that touches your imagination. Come with me and look at him."

The girl stood still and met his eyes. She was eleven years old and she was as tall as he was.

"But was there no romance in the past?"

"Only in the hearts of the young. And it died."

"But is there no romance?"

"Endless romance—and it has all to come. It comes for you."

THE BRINGING IN OF LORD BARRALONGA AND HIS PARTY WAS something of an anti-climax to Mr. Barnstaple's wonderful day. He was tired and, quite unreasonably, he resented the invasion of Utopia by these people.

The two parties of Earthlings were brought together in a brightly lit hall near the lawn upon which the Barralonga aeroplane had come down. The newcomers came in in a group together, blinking, travel-worn and weary-looking. But it was evident they were greatly relieved to encounter other Earthlings in what was to them a still intensely puzzling experience. For they had had nothing to compare with the calm and lucid discussion of the Conference Place. Their lapse into this strange world was still an incomprehensible riddle for them.

Lord Barralonga was the owner of the gnome-like face that had looked out at Mr. Barnstaple when the large grey car had passed him on the Maidenhead Road. His skull was very low and broad above his brows so that he reminded Mr. Barnstaple of the flat stopper of a glass bottle. He looked hot and tired, he was considerably dishevelled as if from a struggle, and one arm was in a sling; his little brown eyes were as alert and wary as those of a wicked urchin in the hands of a policeman. Sticking close to him like a familiar spirit was a small, almost jockey-like chauffeur, whom he addressed as "Ridley." Ridley's face also was marked by the stern determination of a man in a difficult position not in any manner to give himself away. His left cheek and ear had been cut in the automobile smash and were liberally adorned with sticking-plaster. Miss Greeta Grey, the lady of the party, was a frankly blonde beauty in a white flannel tailor-made suit. She was extraordinarily unruffled by the circumstances in which she found herself; it was as if she had no sense whatever of their strangeness. She carried herself with the habitual hauteur of a beautiful girl almost professionally exposed to the risk of unworthy advances. Anywhere.

The other two people of the party were a grey-faced, grey-clad American, also very wary-eyed, who was, Mr. Barnstaple learnt from Mr. Mush, Hunker, the Cinema King, and a thoroughly ruffled-looking Frenchman, a dark, smartly dressed man, with an imperfect command of English, who seemed rather to have fallen into Lord Barralonga's party than to have belonged to it properly. Mr. Barnstaple's mind leapt to the conclusion, and nothing occurred afterwards to change his opinion, that some interest in the cinematograph had brought this gentleman within range of Lord Barralonga's hospitality and that he had been caught, as a foreigner may so easily be caught, into the embrace of a thoroughly uncongenial week-end expedition.

As Lord Barralonga and Mr. Hunker came forward to greet Mr. Burleigh and Mr. Catskill, this Frenchman addressed himself to Mr. Barnstaple with the inquiry whether he spoke French.

"I cannot understand," he said. "We were to have gone to Viltshire—Wiltshire, and then one 'orrible thing has happen after another. What is it we have come to and what sort of people are all these people who speak most excellent French? Is it a joke of Lord Barralonga, or a dream, or what has happen to us?"

Mr. Barnstaple attempted some explanation.

"Another dimension," said the Frenchman, "another worl'. That is all very well. But I have my business to attend to in London. I have no need to be brought back in this way to France, some sort of France, some other France in some other worl'. It is too much of a joke altogether."

Mr. Barnstaple attempted some further exposition. It was clear from his interlocutor's puzzled face that the phrases he used were too difficult.

He turned helplessly to Lady Stella and found her ready to undertake the task. "This lady," he said, "will be able to make things plain to you. Lady Stella, this is Monsieur—"

"Emile Dupont," the Frenchman bowed. "I am what you call a journalist and publicist. I am interested in the cinematograph from the point of view of education and propaganda. It is why I am here with his Lordship Barralonga."

French conversation was Lady Stella's chief accomplishment. She sailed into it now very readily. She took over the elucidation of M. Dupont, and only interrupted it to tell Miss Greeta Grey how pleasant it was to have another woman with her in this strange world.

Relieved of M. Dupont, Mr. Barnstaple stood back and surveyed the little group of Earthlings in the centre of the hall and the circle of tall, watchful Utopians about them and rather aloof from them. Mr. Burleigh was being distantly cordial to Lord Barralonga, and Mr. Hunker was saying what a great pleasure it was to him to meet "Britain's foremost statesman." Mr. Catskill stood in the most friendly manner beside Barralonga; they knew each other well; and Father Amerton exchanged comments with Mr. Mush. Ridley and Penk, after some moments of austere regard, had gone apart to discuss the technicalities of the day's experience in undertones. Nobody paid any attention to Mr. Barnstaple.

It was like a meeting at a railway station. It was like a reception. It was utterly incredible and altogether commonplace. He was weary. He was saturated and exhausted by wonder.

"Oh, I am going to my bed!" he yawned suddenly. "I am going to my little bed."

He made his way through the friendly-eyed Utopians out into the calm starlight. He nodded to the strange nebula at the corner of Orion as a weary parent might nod to importunate offspring. He would consider it again in the morning. He staggered drowsily through the gardens to his own particular retreat.

He disrobed and went to sleep as immediately and profoundly as a tired child.

8

Early Morning in Utopia

~

Mr. Barnstaple awakened slowly out of profound slumber.

He had a vague feeling that a very delightful and wonderful dream was slipping from him. He tried to keep on with the dream and not to open his eyes. It was about a great world of beautiful people who had freed themselves from a thousand earthly troubles. But it dissolved and faded from his mind. It was not often nowadays that dreams came to Mr. Barnstaple. He lay very still with his eyes closed, reluctantly coming awake to the affairs of every day.

The cares and worries of the last fortnight resumed their sway. Would he ever be able to get away for a holiday by himself? Then he remembered that he had already got his valise stowed away in the Yellow Peril. But surely that was not last night; that was the night before last, and he had started—he remembered now starting and the little thrill of getting through the gate before Mrs. Barnstaple suspected anything. He opened his eyes and fixed them on a white ceiling, trying to recall that journey. He remembered turning into the Camberwell New Road and the bright exhilaration of the morning, Vauxhall Bridge and that nasty tangle of traffic at Hyde Park Corner. He always maintained that the west of London was far more difficult for motoring than the east. Then —had he gone to

Uxbridge? No. He recalled the road to Slough and then came a blank in his mind.

What a very good ceiling this was! Not a crack nor a stain!

But how had he spent the rest of the day? He must have got somewhere because here he was in a thoroughly comfortable bed—an excellent bed. With a thrush singing. He had always maintained that a good thrush could knock spots off a nightingale, but this thrush was a perfect Caruso. And another answering it! In July! Pangbourne and Caversham were wonderful places for nightingales. In June. But this was July—and thrushes.... Across these drowsy thought-phantoms came the figure of Mr. Rupert Catskill, hands on hips, face and head thrust forward speaking, saying astonishing things. To a naked seated figure with a grave intent face. And other figures. One with a face like the *Delphic Sibyl*. Mr. Barnstaple began to remember that in some way he had got himself mixed up with a week-end party at Taplow Court. Now had this speech been given at Taplow Court? At Taplow Court they wear clothes. But perhaps the aristocracy in retirement and privacy—?

Utopia?... But was it possible?

Mr. Barnstaple sat up in his bed in a state of extreme amazement. "Impossible!" he said. He was lying in a little loggia half open to the air. Between the slender pillars of fluted glass he saw a range of snow-topped mountains, and in the foreground a great cluster of tall spikes bearing deep red flowers. The bird was still singing—a glorified thrush, in a glorified world. Now he remembered everything. Now it was all clear. The sudden twisting of the car, the sound like the snapping of a fiddle string and—Utopia! Now he had it all, from the sight of sweet dead Greenlake to the bringing in of Lord Barralonga under the strange unfamiliar stars. It was no dream. He looked at his hand on the exquisitely fine coverlet. He felt his rough chin. It was a world real enough for shaving—and for a very definite readiness for breakfast. Very—for he had missed his supper. And as if in answer to his thought a smiling girl appeared ascending the steps to his sleeping-place and bearing a little tray. After all, there was much to be said for Mr. Burleigh. To his swift statesmanship it was that Mr. Barnstaple owed this morning cup of tea.

"Good morning," said Mr. Barnstaple.

"Why not?" said the young Utopian, and put down his tea and smiled at him in a motherly fashion and departed.

"Why not a good morning, I suppose," said Mr. Barnstaple and meditated for a moment, chin on knees, and then gave his attention to the bread-and-butter and tea.

~

THE LITTLE DRESSING-ROOM IN WHICH HE FOUND HIS CLOTHES LYING just as he had dumped them overnight, was at once extraordinarily simple and extraordinarily full of interest for Mr. Barnstaple. He paddled about it humming as he examined it.

The bath was much shallower than an ordinary earthly bath; apparently the Utopians did not believe in lying down and stewing. And the forms of everything were different, simpler and more graceful. On earth, he reflected, art was largely wit. The artist had a certain limited selection of obdurate materials and certain needs, and his work was a clever reconciliation of the obduracy and the necessity and of the idiosyncrasy of the substance to the aesthetic preconceptions of the human mind. How delightful, for example, was the earthly carpenter dealing cleverly with the grain and character of this wood or that. But here the artist had a limitless control of material, and that element of witty adaptation had gone out of his work. His data were the human mind and body. Everything in this little room was unobtrusively but perfectly convenient—and difficult to misuse. If you splashed too much a thoughtful outer rim tidied things up for you.

In a tray by the bath was a very big fine sponge. So either Utopians still dived for sponges or they grew them or trained them (who could tell?) to come up of their own accord.

As he set out his toilet things a tumbler was pushed off a glass shelf on to the floor and did not break. Mr. Barnstaple in an experimental mood dropped it again and still it did not break.

He could not find taps at first though there was a big washing basin as well as a bath. Then he perceived a number of studs on the walls with black marks that might be Utopian writing. He experimented. He found very hot water and then very cold water filling his bath, a fountain of probably soapy warm water, and other fluids—one with an odour of pine and one with a subdued odour of chlorine. The Utopian characters on these studs set him musing for a time; they were the first writing he had seen; they appeared to be word characters, but whether they represented sounds or were greatly simplified hieroglyphics he could not imagine. Then his mind went off at a tangent in another direction because the only metal apparent in this dressing-room was gold. There was, he noted, an extraordinary lot of gold in the room. It was set and inlaid in gold. The soft yellow lines gleamed and glittered. Gold evidently was cheap in Utopia. Perhaps they knew how to make it.

He roused himself to the business of his toilet. There was no looking-glass in the room, but when he tried what he thought was the handle of a cupboard door, he found himself opening a triple full-length mirror. Afterwards he was to discover that there were no displayed mirrors in Utopia; Utopians, he was to learn, thought it indecent to be reminded of themselves in that way. The Utopian method was to scrutinize oneself, see that one was all right and then forget oneself for the rest of the day. He stood now surveying his pyjamaed and unshaven self with extreme disfavour. Why do respectable citizens favour such ugly pink-striped pyjamas? When he unpacked his nail-brush and tooth-brush, shaving-brush and washing-glove, they seemed to him to have the coarseness of a popular burlesque. His tooth-brush was a particularly ignoble instrument. He wished now he had bought a new one at the chemist's shop near Victoria Station.

And what nasty queer things his clothes were!

He had a fantastic idea of adopting Utopian ideas of costume, but a reflective moment before his mirror restrained him. Then he remembered that he had packed a silk tennis shirt and flannels. Suppose he wore those, without a collar stud or tie—and went bare-footed?

He surveyed his feet. As feet went on earth they were not unsightly feet. But on earth they had been just wasted.

A PARTICULARLY CLEAN AND RADIANT MR. BARNSTAPLE, WHITE-CLAD, bare-necked and bare-footed, presently emerged into the Utopian sunrise. He smiled, stretched his arms and took a deep breath of the sweet air. Then suddenly his face became hard and resolute.

From another little sleeping house not two hundred yards away Father Amerton was emerging. Intuitively Mr. Barnstaple knew he meant either to forgive or be forgiven for the overnight quarrel. It would be a matter of chance whether he would select the rôle of offender or victim; what was certain was that he would smear a dreary mess of emotional personal relationship over the jewel-like clearness and brightness of the scene. A little to the right of Mr. Barnstaple and in front of him were wide steps leading down towards the lake. Three strides and he was going down these steps two at a time. It may have been his hectic fancy, but it seemed to him that he heard the voice of Father Amerton, "Mr. *Barn*—staple," in pursuit.

Mr. Barnstaple doubled and doubled again and crossed a bridge across an avalanche gully, a bridge with huge masonry in back and roof and with delicate pillars of prismatic glass towards the lake. The sunlight entangled in these pillars broke into splashes of red and blue and golden light. Then at a turfy corner gay with blue gentians, he narrowly escaped a collision with Mr. Rupert Catskill. Mr. Catskill was in the same costume that he had worn on the previous day except that he was without his grey top hat. He walked with his hands clasped behind him.

"Hullo!" he said. "What's the hurry? We seem to be the first people up."

"I saw Father Amerton—"

"That accounts for it. You were afraid of being caught up in a service, Matins or Prime or whatever he calls it. Wise man to run. He shall pray for the lot of us. Me too."

He did not wait for any endorsement from Mr. Barnstaple, but went on talking.

"You have slept well? What did you think of the old fellow's answer to my speech, eh? Evasive cliches. When in doubt, abuse the plaintiff's attorney. We don't agree with him because we have bad hearts."

"What old fellow do you mean?"

"The worthy gentleman who spoke after me."

"Urthred! But he's not forty."

"He's seventy-three. He told us afterwards. They live long here, a lingering business. Our lives are a fitful hectic fever from their point of view. But as Tennyson said, 'Better fifty years of Europe than a cycle of Cathay!' H'm? He evaded my points. This is Lotus Land, Sunset Land; we shan't be thanked for disturbing its slumbers."

"I doubt their slumbers."

"Perhaps the Socialist bug has bit you too. Yes—I see it has! Believe me this is the most complete demonstration of decadence it would be possible to imagine. Complete. And we *shall* disturb their slumbers, never fear. Nature, you will see, is on our side—in a way no one has thought of yet."

"But I don't see the decadence," said Mr. Barnstaple.

"None so blind as those who won't see. It's everywhere. Their large flushed pseudo-health. Like fatted cattle. And their treatment of Barralonga. They don't know how to treat him. They don't even arrest him.

They've never arrested any one for a thousand years. He careers through their land, killing and slaying and frightening and disturbing and they're flabbergasted, Sir, simply flabbergasted. It's like a dog running amuck in a world full of sheep. If he hadn't had a side-slip I believe he would be hooting and snorting and careering along now—killing people. They've lost the instinct of social defence."

"I wonder."

"A very good attitude of mind. If indulged in, in moderation. But when your wondering is over, you will begin to see that I am right. H'm? Ah! There on that terrace! Isn't that my Lord Barralonga and his French acquaintance? It is. Inhaling the morning air. I think with your permission I will go on and have a word with them. Which way did you say Father Amerton was? I don't want to disturb his devotions. This way? Then if I go to the right—"

He grimaced amiably over his shoulder.

Mr. Barnstaple came upon two Utopians gardening. They had two light silvery wheelbarrows, and they were cutting out old wood and overblown clusters from a line of thickets that sprawled over a rough-heaped ridge of rock and foamed with crimson and deep red roses. These gardeners had great leather gauntlets and aprons of tanned skin, and they carried hooks and knives.

Mr. Barnstaple had never before seen such roses as they were tending here; their fragrance filled the air. He did not know that double roses could be got in mountains; bright red single sorts he had seen high up in Switzerland, but not such huge loose-flowered monsters as these. They dwarfed their leaves. Their wood was in long, thorny, snaky-red streaked stems that writhed wide and climbed to the rocky lumps over which they grew. Their great petals fell like red snow and like drifting moths and like blood upon the soft soil that sheltered amidst the brown rocks.

"You are the first Utopians I have actually seen at work," he said.

"This isn't our work," smiled the nearer of the two, a fair-haired, freck-led, blue-eyed youth. "But as we are for these roses we have to keep them in order."

"Are they your roses?"

"Many people think these double mountain roses too much trouble and a nuisance with their thorns and sprawling branches, and many people think only the single sorts of roses ought to be grown in these high places and that this lovely sort ought to be left to die out up here. Are you for our roses?"

"Such roses as these?" said Mr. Barnstaple. "Altogether."

"Good! Then just bring me up my barrow closer for all this litter. We're responsible for the good behaviour of all this thicket reaching right down there almost to the water."

"And you have to see to it yourselves?"

"Who else?"

"But couldn't you get someone—pay someone to see to it for you?"

"Oh, hoary relic from the ancient past!" the young man replied. "Oh, fossil ignoramus from a barbaric universe! Don't you realize that there is no working class in Utopia? It died out fifteen hundred years or so ago. Wages-slavery, pimping and so forth are done with. We read about them in books. Who loves the rose must serve the rose—himself."

"But you work."

"Not for wages. Not because any one else loves or desires something else and is too lazy to serve it or get it himself. We work, part of the brain, part of the will, of Utopia."

"May I ask at what?"

"I explore the interior of our planet. I study high-pressure chemistry. And my friend—"

He interrogated his friend, whose dark face and brown eyes appeared suddenly over a foam of blossom. "I do Food."

"A cook?"

"Of sorts. Just now I am seeing to your Earthling dietary. It's most interesting and curious—but I should think rather destructive. I plan your meals.... I see you look anxious, but I saw to your breakfast last night." He glanced at a minute wrist-watch under the gauntlet of his gardening glove. "It will be ready in about an hour. How was the early tea?"

"Excellent," said Mr. Barnstaple.

"Good," said the dark young man. "I did my best. I hope the breakfast will be as satisfactory. I had to fly two hundred kilometres for a pig last night and kill it and cut it up myself, and find out how to cure it. Eating bacon has gone out of fashion in Utopia. I hope you will find my rashers satisfactory."

"It seems very rapid curing—for a rasher," said Mr. Barnstaple. "We could have done without it."

"Your spokesman made such a point of it."

The fair young man struggled out of the thicket and wheeled his barrow away. Mr. Barnstaple wished the dark young man "Good morning."

"Why shouldn't it be?" asked the dark young man.

HE DISCOVERED RIDLEY AND PENK APPROACHING HIM. RIDLEY'S FACE and ear were still adorned with sticking-plaster and his bearing was eager and anxious. Penk followed a little way behind him, holding one hand to the side of his face. Both were in their professional dress, white-topped caps, square-cut leather coats and black gaiters; they had made no concessions to Utopian laxity.

Ridley began to speak as soon as he judged Mr. Barnstaple was within earshot.

"You don't 'appen to know, Mister, where these 'ere decadents shoved our car?"

"I thought your car was all smashed up."

"Not a Rolls-Royce—not like that. Wind-screen, mud-guards and the on-footboard perhaps. We went over sideways. I want to 'ave a look at it. And I didn't turn the petrol off. The carburettor was leaking a bit. My fault. I 'adn't been careful enough with the strainer. If she runs out of petrol, where's one to get more of it in this blasted Elysium? I ain't seen a sign anywhere. I know if I don't get that car into running form before Lord Barralonga wants it there's going to be trouble."

Mr. Barnstaple had no idea where the cars were.

"'Aven't you a car of your own?" asked Ridley reproachfully.

"I have. But I've never given it a thought since I got out of it."

"Owner-driver," said Ridley bitterly.

"Anyhow, I can't help you find your cars. Have you asked any of the Utopians?"

"Not us. We don't like the style of 'em," said Ridley.

"They'll tell you."

"And watch us—whatever we do to our cars. They don't get a chance of looking into a Rolls-Royce every day in the year. Next thing we shall have them driving off in 'em. I don't like the place, and I don't like these people. They're queer. They ain't decent. His lordship says they're a lot of degenerates, and it seems to me his lordship is about right. I ain't a Puritan, but all this running about without clothes is a bit too thick for me. I wish I knew where they'd stowed those cars."

Mr. Barnstaple was considering Penk. "You haven't hurt your face?" he asked.

"Nothing to speak of," said Penk. "I suppose we ought to be getting on."

Ridley looked at Penk and then at Mr. Barnstaple. "He's had a bit of a contoosion," he remarked, a faint smile breaking through his sourness.

"We better be getting on if we're going to find those cars," said Penk.

A grin of intense enjoyment appeared upon Ridley's face. "'E's bumped against something."

"Oh—*shut it*!" said Penk.

But the thing was too good to keep back. "One of these girls 'it 'im."

"What do you mean?" said Mr. Barnstaple. "You haven't been taking liberties—?"

"I 'ave *not*," said Penk. "But as Mr. Ridley's been so obliging as to start the topic I suppose I got to tell wot 'appened. It jest illustrates the uncertainties of being among a lot of arf-savage, arf-crazy people, like we got among."

Ridley smiled and winked at Mr. Barnstaple. "Regular 'ard clout she gave 'im. Knocked him over. 'E put 'is 'and on 'er shoulder and *clop*! over 'e went. Never saw anything like it."

"Rather unfortunate," said Mr. Barnstaple.

"It all 'appened in a second like."

"It's a pity it happened."

"Don't you go making any mistake about it, Mister, and don't you go running off with any false ideas about it," said Penk. "I don't want the story to get about—it might do me a lot of 'arm with Mr. Burleigh. Pity Mr. Ridley couldn't 'old 'is tongue. What provoked her I do not know. She came into my room as I was getting up, and she wasn't what you might call wearing anything, and she looked a bit saucy, to my way of thinking, and—well, something come into my head to say to her, something—well, just the least little bit sporty, so to speak. One can't always control one's thoughts—can one? A man's a man. If a man's expected to be civil in his private thoughts to girls without a stitch, so to speak—*well*! I dunno. I really do not know. It's against nature. I never said it, whatever it was I thought of. Mr. Ridley 'ere will bear me out. I never said a word to her. I 'adn't opened my lips when she hit me. Knocked me over, she did—like a ninepin. Didn't even seem angry about it. A 'ook-'it—sideways. It was surprise as much as anything floored me."

"But Ridley says you touched her."

"Laid me 'and on 'er shoulder perhaps, in a sort of fatherly way. As she was turning to go—not being sure whether I wasn't going to speak to her, I admit. And there you are! If I'm to get into trouble because I was wantonly 'it—"

Penk conveyed despair of the world by an eloquent gesture.

Mr. Barnstaple considered. "I shan't make trouble," he said. "But all the same I think we must all be very careful with these Utopians. Their ways are not our ways."

"Thank God!" said Ridley. "The sooner I get out of this world back to Old England, the better I shall like it."

He turned to go.

"You should 'ear 'is lordship," said Ridley over his shoulder. "'E says it's just a world of bally degenerates—rotten degenerates—in fact, if you'll excuse me—@*@*!*!*$*$*! degenerates. Eh? That about gets 'em."

"The young woman's arm doesn't seem to have been very degenerate," said Mr. Barnstaple, standing the shock bravely.

"Don't it?" said Ridley bitterly. "That's all *you* know. Why! if there's one sign more sure than another about degeneration it's when women take to knocking men about. It's against instink. In any respectable decent world such a thing couldn't possibly 'ave 'appened. No 'ow!"

"No—'ow," echoed Penk.

"In *our* world, such a girl would jolly soon 'ave 'er lesson. Jolly soon. See?"

But Mr. Barnstaple's roving eye had suddenly discovered Father Amerton approaching very rapidly across a wide space of lawn and making arresting gestures. Mr. Barnstaple perceived he must act at once.

"Now here's someone who will certainly be able to help you find your cars, if he cares to do so. He's a most helpful man—Father Amerton. And the sort of views he has about women are the sort of views you have. You are bound to get on together. If you will stop him and put the whole case to him—plainly and clearly."

He set off at a brisk pace towards the lake shore.

He could not be far now from the little summer-house that ran out over the water against which the gaily coloured boats were moored.

If he were to get into one of these and pull out into the lake he would have Father Amerton at a very serious disadvantage. Even if that good man followed suit. One cannot have a really eloquent emotional scene when one is pulling hard in pursuit of another boat.

~

As Mr. Barnstaple untied the bright white canoe with the big blue eye painted at its prow that he had chosen, Lady Stella appeared on the landing-stage. She came out of the pavilion that stood over the water, and something in her quick movement as she emerged suggested to Mr. Barnstaple's mind that she had been hiding there. She glanced about her and spoke very eagerly. "Are you going to row out upon the lake, Mr. Bastaple? May I come?"

She was attired, he noted, in a compromise between the Earthly and the Utopian style. She was wearing what might have been either a very simple custard-coloured tea-robe or a very sophisticated bath-wrap; it left her slender, pretty arms bare and free except for a bracelet of amber and gold, and on her bare feet—and they were unusually shapely feet—were sandals. Her head was bare, and her dark hair very simply done with a little black and gold fillet round it that suited her intelligent face. Mr. Barnstaple was an ignoramus about feminine costume, but he appreciated the fact that she had been clever in catching the Utopian note.

He helped her into the canoe. "We will paddle right out—a good way," she said with another glance over her shoulder, and sat down.

For a time Mr. Barnstaple paddled straight out so that he had nothing before him but sunlit water and sky, the low hills that closed in the lake towards the great plain, the huge pillars of the distant dam, and Lady Stella. She affected to be overcome by the beauty of the Conference garden slope with its houses and terraces behind him, but he could see that she was not really looking at the scene as a whole, but searching it restlessly for some particular object or person.

She made conversational efforts, on the loveliness of the morning and on the fact that birds were singing—"in July."

"But here it is not necessarily July," said Mr. Barnstaple.

"How stupid of me! Of course not."

"We seem to be in a fine May."

"It is probably very early," she said. "I forgot to wind my watch."

"Oddly enough we seem to be at about the same hours in our two worlds," said Mr. Barnstaple. "My wrist-watch says seven."

"No," said Lady Stella, answering her own thoughts and with her eyes on the distant gardens. "That is a Utopian girl. Have you met any others— of our party—this morning?"

Mr. Barnstaple brought the canoe round so that he too could look at the shore. From here they could see how perfectly the huge terraces and avalanche walls and gullies mingled and interwove with the projecting ribs and cliffs of the mountain masses behind. The shrub tangles passed up into hanging pinewoods; the torrents and cascades from the snowfield above were caught and distributed amidst the emerald slopes and gardens of the Conference Park. The terraces that retained the soil and held the whole design spread out on either hand to a great distance and were continued up into the mountain substance; they were built of a material that ranged through a wide variety of colours from a deep red to a purple-veined white, and they were diversified by great arches over torrents and rock gullies, by huge round openings that spouted water and by cascades of steps. The buildings of the place were distributed over these terraces and over the grassy slopes they contained, singly or in groups and clusters, buildings of purple and blue and white as light and delicate as the Alpine flowers about them. For some moments Mr. Barnstaple was held silent by this scene, and then he attended to Lady Stella's question. "I met Mr. Rupert Catskill and the two chauffeurs," he said, "and I saw Father Amerton and Lord Barralonga and M. Dupont in the distance. I've seen nothing of Mr. Mush or Mr. Burleigh."

"Mr. Cecil won't be about for hours yet. He will lie in bed until ten or eleven. He always takes a good rest in the morning when there is any great mental exertion before him."

The lady hesitated and then asked: "I suppose you haven't seen Miss Greeta Grey?"

"No," said Mr. Barnstaple. "I wasn't looking for our people. I was just strolling about—and avoiding somebody."

"The censor of manners and costumes?"

"Yes…. That, in fact, is why I took to this canoe."

The lady reflected and decided on a confidence.

"I was running away from some one too."

"Not the preacher?"

"Miss Grey!"

Lady Stella apparently went off at a tangent. "This is going to be a very difficult world to stay in. These people have very delicate taste. We may easily offend them."

"They are intelligent enough to understand."

"Do people who understand necessarily forgive? I've always doubted that proverb."

Mr. Barnstaple did not wish the conversation to drift away into generalities, so he paddled and said nothing.

"You see Miss Grey used to play Phryne in a Revue."

"I seem to remember something about it. There was a fuss in the newspapers."

"That perhaps gave her a bias."

Three long sweeps with the paddle.

"But this morning she came to me and told me that she was going to wear complete Utopian costume."

"Meaning?"

"A little rouge and face powder. It doesn't suit her the least little bit, Mr. Bastaple. It's a faux pas. It's indecent. But she's running about the gardens—. She might meet any one. It's lucky Mr. Cecil isn't up. If she meets Father Amerton—! But it's best not to think of that. You see, Mr. Bastaple, these Utopians and their sun-brown bodies—and everything, are in the picture. They don't embarrass me. But Miss Grey—. An earthly civilised woman taken out of her clothes *looks* taken out of her clothes. Peeled. A sort of *bleached* white. That nice woman who seems to hover round us, Lychnis, when she advised me what to wear, never for one moment suggested anything of the sort.... But, of course, I don't know Miss Grey well enough to talk to her and besides, one never knows how a woman of that sort is going to take a thing...."

Mr. Barnstaple stared shoreward. Nothing was to be seen of an excessively visible Miss Greeta Grey. Then he had a conviction. "Lychnis will take care of her," he said.

"I hope she will. Perhaps, if we stay out here for a time—"

"She will be looked after," said Mr. Barnstaple. "But I think Miss Grey and Lord Barralonga's party generally are going to make trouble for us. I wish they hadn't come through with us."

"Mr. Cecil thinks that," said Lady Stella.

"Naturally we shall all be thrown very much together and judged in a lump."

"Naturally," Lady Stella echoed.

She said no more for a little while. But it was evident that she had more to say. Mr. Barnstaple paddled slowly.

"Mr. Bastaple," she began presently.

Mr. Barnstaple's paddle became still.

"Mr. Bastaple—are you *afraid?*"

Mr. Barnstaple judged himself. "I have been too full of wonder to be afraid."

Lady Stella decided to confess. "I *am* afraid," she said. "I wasn't at first. Everything seemed to go so easily and simply. But in the night I woke up —horribly afraid."

"No," considered Mr. Barnstaple. "No. It hasn't taken me like that— yet.... Perhaps it will."

Lady Stella leant forward and spoke confidentially, watching the effect of her words on Mr. Barnstaple. "These Utopians—I thought at first they were just simple, healthy human beings, artistic and innocent. But they are not, Mr. Bastaple. There is something hard and complicated about them, something that goes beyond us and that we don't understand. And they don't care for us. They look at us with heartless eyes. Lychnis is kind, but hardly any of the others are the least bit kind. And I think they find us inconvenient."

Mr. Barnstaple thought it over. "Perhaps they do. I have been so preoccupied with admiration—so much of this is fine beyond dreaming — that I have not thought very much how we affected them. But—yes—they seem to be busy about other things and not very attentive to us. Except the ones who have evidently been assigned to watch and study us. And Lord Barralonga's headlong rush through the country must certainly have been inconvenient."

"He killed a man."

"I know."

They remained thoughtfully silent for some moments.

"And there are other things," Lady Stella resumed. "They think quite differently from our way of thinking. I believe they despise us already. I noted something.... Last evening you were not with us by the lake when Mr. Cecil asked them about their philosophy. He told them things about Hegel and Bergson and Lord Haldane and his own wonderful scepticism. He opened out —unusually. It was very interesting—to me. But I was watching Urthred and Lion and in the midst of it I saw—I am convinced—they were talking to each other in that silent way they have, about something quite different. They were just *shamming* attention. And when Freddy Mush tried to interest them in Neo-Georgian poetry and the effect of the war upon literature, and how he hoped that they had something *half* as beautiful as the *Iliad* in Utopia, though he confessed he couldn't believe they had, they didn't even pretend to listen. They did not answer him at all.... Our minds don't matter a bit to them."

"In these subjects. They are three thousand years further on. But we might be interesting as learners."

"Would it have been interesting to have taken a Hottentot about London explaining things to him—after one had got over the first fun of showing off his ignorance? Perhaps it would. But I don't think they want us here very much and I don't think they are going to like us very much, and I don't know what they are likely to do to us if we give too much trouble. And so I am afraid."

She broke out in a new place. "In the night I was reminded of my sister Mrs. Kelling's monkeys.

"It's a mania with her. They run about the gardens and come into the house and the poor things are always in trouble. They don't quite know what they may do and what they may not do; they all look frightfully worried and they get slapped and carried to the door and thrown out and all sorts of things like that. They spoil things and make her guests uneasy. You never seem to know what a monkey's going to do. And everybody hates to have them about except my sister. And she keeps on scolding them. 'Come *down*, Jacko! Put that *down*, Sadie'!"

Mr. Barnstaple laughed. "It isn't going to be quite so bad as that with us, Lady Stella. We are not monkeys."

She laughed too. "Perhaps it isn't. But all the same—in the night—I felt it might be. We are inferior creatures. One has to admit it...."

She knitted her brows. Her pretty face expressed great intellectual effort. "Do you realize how we are cut off?... Perhaps you will think it silly of me, Mr. Bastaple, but last night before I went to bed I sat down to write my sister a letter and tell her all about things while they were fresh in my mind. And suddenly realized I might as well write—to Julius Caesar."

Mr. Barnstaple hadn't thought of that.

"That's a thing I can't get out of my head, Mr. Bastaple—no letters, no telegrams, no newspapers, no Bradshaw in Utopia. All the things we care for really—All the people we live for. Cut off! I don't know for how long. But completely cut off.... How long are they likely to keep us here?"

Mr. Barnstaple's face became speculative.

"Are you *sure* they can ever send us back?" the lady asked.

"There seems to be some doubt. But they are astonishingly clever people."

"It seemed so easy coming here—just as if one walked round a corner —but, of course, properly speaking we are out of space and time.... More out of it even than dead people.... The North Pole or Central Africa is a whole universe nearer home than we are.... It's hard to grasp that. In this sunlight it all seems so bright and familiar.... Yet last night there were moments when I wanted to scream...."

She stopped short and scanned the shore. Then very deliberately she sniffed.

Mr. Barnstaple became aware of a peculiarly sharp and appetizing smell drifting across the water to him.

"Yes," he said.

"It's breakfast bacon!" cried Lady Stella with a squeak in her voice.

"Exactly as Mr. Burleigh told them," said Mr. Barnstaple mechanically turning the canoe shoreward.

"Breakfast bacon! That's the most reassuring thing that has happened yet.... Perhaps after all it was silly to feel frightened. And there they are signalling to us!" She waved her arm.

"Greeta in a white robe—as you prophesied—and Mr. Mush in a sort of toga talking to her.... Where could he have got that toga?"

A faint sound of voices calling reached them.

"Com—*ing*!" cried Lady Stella.

"I hope I haven't been pessimistic," said Lady Stella. "But I felt *horrid* in the night."

BOOK THE SECOND

Quarantine Crag

1

The Epidemic

~

THE SHADOW OF THE GREAT EPIDEMIC IN UTOPIA FELL UPON OUR LITTLE band of Earthlings in the second day after their irruption. For more than twenty centuries the Utopians had had the completest freedom from infectious and contagious disease of all sorts. Not only had the graver epidemic fevers and all sorts of skin diseases gone out of the lives of animals and men, but all the minor infections of colds, coughs, influenzas and the like had also been mastered and ended. By isolation, by the control of carriers, and so forth, the fatal germs had been cornered and obliged to die out.

And there had followed a corresponding change in the Utopian physiology. Secretions and reactions that had given the body resisting power to infection had diminished; the energy that produced them had been withdrawn to other more serviceable applications. The Utopian physiology, relieved of these merely defensive necessities, had simplified itself and become more direct and efficient. This cleaning up of infections was such ancient history in Utopia that only those who specialized in the history of pathology understood anything of the miseries mankind had suffered under from this source, and even these specialists do not seem to have had any idea of how far the race had lost its former resistance to infection. The first person to think of this lost resisting power seems to have been

Mr. Rupert Catskill. Mr. Barnstaple recalled that when they had met early on the first morning of their stay in the Conference Gardens, he had been hinting that Nature was in some unexplained way on the side of the Earthlings.

If making them obnoxious was being on their side then certainly Nature was on their side. By the evening of the second day after their arrival nearly everybody who had been in contact with the Earthlings, with the exception of Lychnis, Serpentine and three or four others who had retained something of their ancestral antitoxins, was in a fever with cough, sore throat, aching bones, headache and such physical depression and misery as Utopia had not known for twenty centuries. The first inhabitant of Utopia to die was that leopard which had sniffed at Mr. Rupert Catskill on his first arrival. It was found unaccountably dead on the second morning after that encounter. In the afternoon of the same day one of the girls who had helped Lady Stella to unpack her bags sickened suddenly and died....

Utopia was even less prepared for the coming of these disease-germs than for the coming of the Earthlings who brought them. The monstrous multitude of general and fever hospitals, doctors, drug shops, and so forth that had existed in the Last Age of Confusion had long since passed out of memory; there was a surgical service for accidents and a watch kept upon the health of the young, and there were places of rest at which those who were extremely old were assisted, but there remained scarcely anything of the hygienic organization that had formerly struggled against disease. Abruptly the Utopian intelligence had to take up again a tangle of problems long since solved and set aside, to improvise forgotten apparatus and organizations for disinfection and treatment, and to return to all the disciplines of the war against diseases that had marked an epoch in its history twenty centuries before. In one respect indeed that war had left Utopia with certain permanent advantages. Nearly all the insect disease carriers had been exterminated, and rats and mice and the untidier sorts of small bird had passed out of the problem of sanitation. That set very definite limits to the spread of the new infections and to the nature of the infections that could be spread. It enabled the Earthlings only to communicate such ailments as could be breathed across an interval, or conveyed by a contaminating touch. Though not one of them was ailing at all, it became clear that some one among them had brought latent measles into the Utopian universe, and that three or four of them had liberated a long suppressed influenza. Themselves too tough to suffer, they remained at the focus of these two epidemics, while their victims coughed and sneezed and kissed and whispered them about the Utopian planet. It was not until the afternoon of the second day after the irruption that Utopia realized what had happened, and set itself to deal with this relapse into barbaric solicitudes.

~

MR. BARNSTAPLE WAS PROBABLY THE LAST OF THE EARTHLINGS TO HEAR of the epidemic. He was away from the rest of the party upon an expedition of his own.

It was early clear to him that the Utopians did not intend to devote any considerable amount of time or energy to the edification of their Earthling visitors. After the *éclaircissement* of the afternoon of the irruption there were no further attempts to lecture to the visitors upon the constitution and methods of Utopia and only some very brief questioning upon the earthly state of affairs. The Earthlings were left very much together to talk things out among themselves. Several Utopians were evidently entrusted with their comfort and well-being, but they did not seem to think that their functions extended to edification. Mr. Barnstaple found much to irritate him in the ideas and comments of several of his associates, and so he obeyed his natural inclination to explore Utopia for himself. There was something that stirred his imagination in the vast plain below the lake that he had glimpsed before his aeroplane descended into the valley of the Conference, and on his second morning he had taken a little boat and rowed out across the lake to examine the dam that retained its waters and to get a view of the great plain from the parapet of the dam.

The lake was much wider than he had thought it and the dam much larger. The water was crystalline clear and very cold, and there were but few fish in it. He had come out immediately after his breakfast, but it was near midday before he had got to the parapet of the great dam and could look down the lower valley to the great plain.

The dam was built of huge blocks of red and gold-veined rock, but steps at intervals gave access to the roadway along its crest. The great seated figures which brooded over the distant plain had been put there, it would seem, in a mood of artistic light-heartedness. They sat as if they watched or thought, vast rude shapes, half mountainous, half human. Mr. Barnstaple guessed them to be perhaps two hundred feet high; by pacing the distance between two of them and afterwards counting the number of them, he came to the conclusion that the dam was between seven and ten miles long. On the far side it dropped sheerly for perhaps five hundred feet, and it was sustained by a series of enormous buttresses that passed almost insensibly into native rock. In the bays between these buttresses hummed great batteries of water turbines, and then, its first task done, the water dropped foaming and dishevelled and gathered in another broad lake retained by a second great dam two miles or so away and perhaps a thousand feet lower. Far away was a third lake and a third dam and then the plain. Only three or four minute-looking Utopians were visible amidst all this Titanic engineering.

Mr. Barnstaple stood, the smallest of objects, in the shadow of a brooding Colossus, and peered over these nearer things at the hazy levels of the plain beyond.

What sort of life was going on there? The relationship of plain to mountain reminded him very strongly of the Alps and the great plain of Northern Italy, down into which he had walked as the climax of many a summer holiday in his youth. In Italy he knew that those distant levels would be covered with clustering towns and villages and carefully irrigated and closely cultivated fields. A dense population would be toiling with an ant-like industry in the production of food; for ever increasing its numbers until those inevitable consequences of overcrowding, disease and pestilence, established a sort of balance between the area of the land and the number of families scraping at it for nourishment. As a toiling man can grow more food than he can actually eat, and as virtuous women can bear more children than the land can possibly employ, a surplus of landless population would be gathered in wen-like towns and cities, engaged there in legal and financial operations against the agriculturalist or in the manufacture of just plausible articles for sale.

Ninety-nine out of every hundred of this population would be concentrated from childhood to old age upon the difficult task which is known as "getting a living." Amidst it, sustained by a pretence of magical propitiations, would rise shrines and temples, supporting a parasitic host of priests and monks and nuns. Eating and breeding, the simple routines of the common life since human societies began, complications of food-getting, elaborations of acquisitiveness and a tribute paid to fear; such would be the spectacle that any warm and fertile stretch of earth would still display. There would be gleams of laughter and humour there, brief interludes of holiday, flashes of youth before its extinction in adult toil; but a driven labour, the spite and hates of overcrowding, the eternal uncertainty of destitution, would dominate the scene. Decrepitude would come by sixty; women would be old and worn out by forty. But this Utopian plain below, sunlit and fertile though it was, was under another law. Here that common life of mankind, its ancient traditions, its hoary jests and tales repeated generation after generation, its seasonal festivals, its pious fears and spasmodic indulgences, its limited yet incessant and pitifully childish hoping, and its abounding misery and tragic futility, had come to an end. It had passed for ever out of this older world. That high tide of common living had receded and vanished while the soil was still productive and the sun still shone.

It was with something like awe that Mr. Barnstaple realized how clean a sweep had been made of the common life in a mere score of centuries, how boldly and dreadfully the mind of man had taken hold, soul and body and destiny, of the life and destiny of the race. He knew himself now for the creature of transition he was, so deep in the habits of the old, so sympathetic with the idea of the new that has still but scarcely dawned on earth. For long he had known how intensely he loathed and despised that reeking peasant life which is our past; he realized now for the first time how profoundly he feared the high austere Utopian life which lies before us. This world he looked out upon seemed very clean and dreadful to him. What were they doing upon those distant plains? What daily life did they lead there?

He knew enough of Utopia now to know that the whole land would be like a garden, with every natural tendency to beauty seized upon and developed and every innate ugliness corrected and overcome. These people could work and struggle for loveliness, he knew, for his two rose growers had taught him as much. And to and fro the food folk and the housing people and those who ordered the general life went, keeping the economic machine running so smoothly that one heard nothing of the jangling and jarring and internal breakages that constitute the dominant melody in our Earth's affairs. The ages of economic disputes and experiments had come to an end; the right way to do things had been found. And the population of this Utopia, which had shrunken at one time to only two hundred million, was now increasing again to keep pace with the constant increase in human resources. Having freed itself from a thousand evils that would otherwise have grown with its growth, the race could grow indeed.

And down there under the blue haze of the great plain almost all those who were not engaged in the affairs of food and architecture, health, education and the correlation of activities, were busied upon creative work; they were continually exploring the world without or the world within, through scientific research and artistic creation. They were continually adding to their collective power over life or to the realized worth of life.

Mr. Barnstaple was accustomed to think of our own world as a wild rush of inventions and knowledge, but all the progress of earth for a hundred years could not compare, he knew, with the forward swing of these millions of associated intelligences in one single year. Knowledge swept forward here and darkness passed as the shadow of a cloud passes on a windy day. Down there they were assaying the minerals that lie in the heart of their planet, and weaving a web to capture the sun and the stars. Life marched here; it was terrifying to think with what strides. Terrifying —because at the back of Mr. Barnstaple's mind, as at the back of so many intelligent minds in our world still, had been the persuasion that presently everything would be known and the scientific process come to an end. And then we should be happy for ever after.

He was not really acclimatized to progress. He had always thought of Utopia as a tranquillity with everything settled for good. Even to-day it seemed tranquil under that level haze, but he knew that this quiet was the steadiness of a mill race, which seems almost motionless in its quiet onrush until a bubble or a fleck of foam or some stick or leaf shoots along it and reveals its velocity.

And how did it feel to be living in Utopia? The lives of the people must be like the lives of very successful artists or scientific workers in this world, a continual refreshing discovery of new things, a constant adventure into the unknown and untried. For recreation they went about their planet, and there was much love and laughter and friendship in Utopia and an abundant easy informal social life. Games that did not involve bodily exercise, those substitutes of the half-witted for research and mental effort, had gone entirely out of life, but many active games were played for the sake of fun and bodily vigour.... It must be a good life for those who had been educated to live it, indeed a most enviable life.

And pervading it all must be the happy sense that it mattered; it went on to endless consequences. And they loved no doubt—subtly and deliciously—but perhaps a little hardly. Perhaps in those distant plains there was not much pity nor tenderness. Bright and lovely beings they were—in no way pitiful. There would be no need for those qualities....

Yet the woman Lychnis looked kind....

Did they keep faith or need to keep faith as earthly lovers do? What was love like in Utopia? Lovers still whispered in the dusk.... What was the essence of love? A preference, a sweet pride, a delightful gift won, the most exquisite reassurance of body and mind.

What could it be like to love and be loved by one of these Utopian women?—to have her glowing face close to one's own—to be quickened into life by her kiss?...

Mr. Barnstaple sat in his flannels, bare-footed, in the shadow of a stone Colossus. He felt like some minute stray insect perched upon the big dam. It seemed to him that it was impossible that this triumphant Utopian race could ever fall back again from its magnificent attack upon the dominion of all things. High and tremendously this world had clambered and was still clambering. Surely it was safe now in its attainment. Yet all this stupendous security and mastery of nature had come about in the little space of three thousand years....

The race could not have altered fundamentally in that brief interval. Essentially it was still a stone-age race, it was not twenty thousand years away from the days when it knew nothing of metals and could not read nor write. Deep in its nature, arrested and undeveloped, there still lay the seeds of anger and fear and dissension. There must still be many uneasy and insubordinate spirits in this Utopia. Eugenics had scarcely begun here. He remembered the keen sweet face of the young girl who had spoken to him in the starlight on the night of his arrival, and the note of romantic eagerness in her voice when she had asked if Lord Barralonga was not a very vigorous and cruel man.

Did the romantic spirit still trouble imaginations here? Possibly only adolescent imaginations.

Might not some great shock or some phase of confusion still be possible to this immense order? Might not its system of education become wearied by its task of discipline and fall a prey to the experimental spirit? Might not the unforeseen be still lying in wait for this race? Suppose there should prove to be an infection in Father Amerton's religious fervour or Rupert Catskill's incurable craving for fantastic enterprises!

No! It was inconceivable. The achievement of this world was too calmly great and assured.

Mr. Barnstaple stood up and made his way down the steps of the great dam to where, far below, his little skiff floated like a minute flower petal upon the clear water.

He became aware of a considerable commotion in the Conference places.

There were more than thirty aeroplanes circling in the air and descending and ascending from the park, and a great number of big white vehicles were coming and going by the pass road. Also people seemed to be moving briskly among the houses, but it was too far off to distinguish what they were doing. He stared for a time and then got into his little boat.

He could not watch what was going on as he returned across the lake because his back was towards the slopes, but once an aeroplane came down very close to him, and he saw its occupant looking at him as he rowed. And once when he rested from rowing and sat round to look he saw what he thought was a litter carried by two men.

As he drew near the shore a boat put off to meet him. He was astonished to see that its occupants were wearing what looked like helmets of glass with white pointed visors. He was enormously astonished and puzzled.

As they approached their message resonated into his mind. "Quarantine. You have to go into quarantine. You Earthlings have started an epidemic and it is necessary to put you into quarantine."

Then these glass helmets must be a sort of gas-mask!

When they came alongside him he saw that this was so. They were made of highly flexible and perfectly translucent material....

Mr. Barnstaple was taken past some sleeping loggias where Utopians were lying in beds, while others who wore gas-masks waited upon them. He found that all the Earthlings and all their possessions, except their cars, were assembled in the hall of the first day's Conference. He was told that the whole party were to be removed to a new place where they could be isolated and treated.

The only Utopians with the party were two who wore gas masks and lounged in the open portico in attitudes disagreeably suggestive of sentries or custodians.

The Earthlings sat about in little groups among the seats, except for

Mr. Rupert Catskill, who was walking up and down in the apse talking. He was hatless, flushed and excited, with his hair in some disorder.

"It's what I foresaw would happen all along," he repeated. "Didn't I tell you Nature was on our side? Didn't I say it?"

Mr. Burleigh was shocked and argumentative. "For the life of me I can't see the logic of it," he declared. "Here are we—absolutely the only perfectly immune people here—and we—*we* are to be isolated."

"They say they catch things from us," said Lady Stella.

"Very well," said Mr. Burleigh, making his point with his long white hand. "Very well, then let *them* be isolated! This is—Chinese; this is topsy-turvy. I'm disappointed in them."

"I suppose it's their world," said Mr. Hunker, "and we've got to do things their way."

Mr. Catskill concentrated upon Lord Barralonga and the two chauffeurs. "I welcome this treatment. I welcome it."

"What's your idea, Rupert?" said his lordship. "We lose our freedom of action."

"Not at all," said Mr. Catskill. "Not at all. We gain it. We are to be isolated. We are to be put by ourselves in some island or mountain. Well and good. Well and good. This is only the beginning of our adventures. We shall see what we shall see."

"But how?"

"Wait a little. Until we can speak more freely.... These are panic measures. This pestilence is only in its opening stage. Everything is just beginning. Trust me."

Mr. Barnstaple sat sulkily by his valise, avoiding the challenge of Mr. Catskill's eye.

2

The Castle on the Crag

~

The quarantine place to which the Earthlings were taken must have been at a very considerable distance from the place of the Conference, because they were nearly six hours upon their journey, and all the time they were flying high and very swiftly. They were all together in one flying ship; it was roomy and comfortable and could have held perhaps four times as many passengers. They were accompanied by about thirty Utopians in gas-masks, among whom were two women. The aviators wore dresses of a white fleecy substance that aroused the interest and envy of both Miss Grey and Lady Stella. The flying ship passed down the valley and over the great plain and across a narrow sea and another land with a rocky coast and dense forests, and across a great space of empty sea. There was scarcely any shipping to be seen upon this sea at all; it seemed to Mr. Barnstaple that no earthly ocean would be so untravelled; only once or twice did he see very big drifting vessels quite unlike any earthly ships, huge rafts or platforms they seemed to be rather than ships, and once or twice he saw what was evidently a cargo boat—one with rigged masts and sails. And the air was hardly more frequented. After he was out of sight of land he saw only three aeroplanes until the final landfall.

They crossed a rather thickly inhabited, very delightful-looking coastal belt and came over what was evidently a rainless desert country, given over to mining and to vast engineering operations. Far away were very high snowy mountains, but the aeroplane descended before it came to these. For a time the Earthlings were flying over enormous heaps of slaggy accumulations, great mountains of them, that seemed to be derived from a huge well-like excavation that went down into the earth to an unknown depth. A tremendous thunder of machinery came out of this pit and much smoke. Here there were crowds of workers and they seemed to be living in camps among the debris. Evidently the workers came to this place merely for spells of work; there were no signs of homes. The aeroplane of the Earthlings skirted this region and flew on over a rocky and almost treeless desert deeply cut by steep gorges of the canyon type. Few people were to be seen, but there were abundant signs of engineering activity. Every torrent, every cataract was working a turbine, and great cables followed the cliffs of the gorges and were carried across the desert spaces. In the wider places of the gorges there were pine woods and a fairly abundant vegetation.

The high crag which was their destination stood out, an almost completely isolated headland, in the fork between two convergent canyons. It towered up to a height of perhaps two thousand feet above the foaming clash of the torrents below, a great mass of pale greenish and purple rocks, jagged and buttressed and cleft deeply by joint planes and white crystalline veins. The gorge on one side of it was much steeper than that on the other, it was so overhung indeed as to be darkened like a tunnel, and here within a hundred feet or so of the brow a slender metallic bridge had been flung across the gulf. Some yards above it were projections that might have been the remains of an earlier bridge of stone. Behind, the crag fell steeply for some hundreds of feet to a long slope covered with a sparse vegetation which rose again to the main masses of the mountain, a wall of cliffs with a level top.

It was on this slope that the aeroplane came down alongside of three or four smaller machines. The crag was surmounted by the tall ruins of an ancient castle, within the circle of whose walls clustered a number of buildings which had recently harboured a group of chemical students. Their researches, which had been upon some question of atomic structure quite incomprehensible to Mr. Barnstaple, were finished now and the place had become vacant. Their laboratory was still stocked with apparatus and material; and water and power were supplied to it from higher up the gorge by means of pipes and cables. There was also an abundant store of provisions. A number of Utopians were busily adapting the place to its new purpose of isolation and disinfection when the Earthlings arrived.

Serpentine appeared in the company of a man in a gas mask whose name was Cedar. This Cedar was a cytologist, and he was in charge of the arrangements for this improvised sanatorium.

Serpentine explained that he himself had flown to the crag in advance, because he understood the equipment of the place and the research that had been going on there, and because his knowledge of the Earthlings and his comparative immunity to their infections made him able to act as an intermediary between them and the medical men who would now take charge of their case. He made these explanations to Mr. Burleigh, Mr. Barnstaple, Lord Barralonga and Mr. Hunker. The other Earthlings stood about in small groups beside the aeroplane from which they had alighted, regarding the castellated summit of the crag, the scrubby bushes of the bleak upland about them and the towering cliffs of the adjacent canyons with no very favourable expressions.

Mr. Catskill had gone apart nearly to the edge of the great canyon, and was standing with his hands behind his back in an attitude almost Napoleonic, lost in thought, gazing down into those sunless depths. The roar of the unseen waters below, now loud, now nearly inaudible, quivered in the air.

Miss Greeta Grey had suddenly produced a Kodak camera; she had been reminded of its existence when packing for this last journey, and she was taking a snapshot of the entire party.

Cedar said that he would explain the method of treatment he proposed to follow, and Lord Barralonga called "Rupert!" to bring Mr. Catskill into the group of Cedar's hearers.

Cedar was as explicit and concise as Urthred had been. It was evident, he said, that the Earthlings were the hosts of a variety of infectious organisms which were kept in check in their bodies by immunizing counter substances, but against which the Utopians had no defences ready and could hope to secure immunity only after a painful and disastrous epidemic. The only way to prevent this epidemic devastating their whole planet indeed, was firstly to gather together and cure all the cases affected, which was being done by converting the Conference Park into a big hospital, and next to take the Earthlings in hand and isolate them absolutely from the Utopians until they could be cleaned of their infections. It was, he confessed, an inhospitable thing to do to the Earthlings, but it seemed the only possible thing to do, to bring them into this peculiarly high and dry desert air and there to devise methods for their complete physical cleansing. If that was possible it would be done, and then the Earthlings would again be free to go and come as they pleased in Utopia.

"But suppose it is not possible?" said Mr. Catskill abruptly.

"I think it will be."

"But if you fail?"

Cedar smiled at Serpentine. "Physical research is taking up the work in which Arden and Greenlake were foremost, and it will not be long before we are able to repeat their experiment. And then to reverse it."

"With us as your raw material?"

"Not until we are fairly sure of a safe landing for you."

"You mean," said Mr. Mush, who had joined the circle about Cedar and Serpentine, "that you are going to send us back?"

"If we cannot keep you," said Cedar, smiling.

"Delightful prospect!" said Mr. Mush unpleasantly. "To be shot across space in a gun. Experimentally."

"And may I ask," came the voice of Father Amerton, "may I ask the nature of this *treatment* of yours, these experiments of which we are to be the—guinea pigs, so to speak. Is it to be anything in the nature of vaccination?"

"Injections," explained Mr. Barnstaple.

"I have hardly decided yet," said Cedar. "The problem raises questions this world has forgotten for ages."

"I may say at once that I am a confirmed anti-vaccinationist," said Father Amerton. "Absolutely. Vaccination is an outrage on nature. If I had any doubts before I came into this world of—of *vitiation*, I have no doubts now. Not a doubt! If God had meant us to have these serums and ferments in our bodies he would have provided more natural and dignified means of getting them there than a squirt."

Cedar did not discuss the point. He went on to further apologies. For a time he must ask the Earthlings to keep within certain limits, to confine themselves to the crag and the slopes below it as far as the mountain cliffs. And further, it was impossible to set young people to attend to them as had hitherto been done. They must cook for themselves and see to themselves generally. The appliances were all to be found above upon the crest of the crag and he and Serpentine would make any explanations that were needful. They would find there was ample provision for them.

"Then are we to be left alone here?" asked M. Catskill.

"For a time. When we have our problem clearer we will come again and tell you what we mean to do."

"Good," said Mr. Catskill. "Good."

"I wish I hadn't sent my maid by train," said Lady Stella.

"I have come to my last clean collar," said M. Dupont with a little humorous grimace. "It is no joke this week-end with Lord Barralonga."

Lord Barralonga turned suddenly to his particular minion. "I believe that Ridley has the makings of a very good cook."

"I don't mind trying my hand," said Ridley. "I've done most things— and once I used to look after a steam car."

"A man who can keep one of those—those things in order can do anything," said Mr. Penk with unusual emotion. "I've no objection to being a temporary general utility along of Mr. Ridley. I began my career in the pantry and I ain't ashamed to own it."

"If this gentleman will show us the gadgets," said Mr. Ridley, indicating Serpentine.

"Exactly," said Mr. Penk.

"And if all of us give as little trouble as possible," said Miss Greeta bravely.

"I think we shall be able to manage," said Mr. Burleigh to Cedar. "If at first you can spare us a little advice and help."

CEDAR AND SERPENTINE REMAINED WITH THE EARTHLINGS UPON Quarantine Crag until late in the afternoon. They helped to prepare a supper and set it out in the courtyard of the castle. They departed with a promise to return on the morrow, and the Earthlings watched them and their accompanying aeroplanes soar up into the sky.

Mr. Barnstaple was surprised to find himself distressed at their going. He had a feeling that mischief was brewing amongst his companions and that the withdrawal of these Utopians removed a check upon this mischief. He had helped Lady Stella in the preparation of an omelette; he had to carry back a dish and a frying-pan to the kitchen after it was served, so that he was the last to seat himself at the supper-table. He found the mischief he dreaded well afoot.

Mr. Catskill had finished his supper already and was standing with his foot upon a bench orating to the rest of the company.

"I ask you, Ladies and Gentlemen," Mr. Catskill was saying; "I ask you:

Is not Destiny writ large upon this day's adventure? Not for nothing was this place a fortress in ancient times. Here it is ready to be a fortress again. M'm—a fortress.... In such an adventure as will make the stories of Cortez and Pizarro pale their ineffectual fires!"

"My dear Rupert!" cried Mr. Burleigh. "What have you got in that head of yours now?"

Mr. Catskill waved two fingers dramatically. "The conquest of a world!"

"Good God!" cried Mr. Barnstaple. "Are you mad?"

"As Clive," said Mr. Catskill, "or Sultan Baber when he marched to Panipat."

"It's a tall proposition," said Mr. Hunker, who seemed to have had his mind already prepared for these suggestions, "but I'm inclined to give it a hearing. The alternative so far as I can figure it out is to be scoured and white-washed inside and out and then fired back into our own world—with a chance of hitting something hard on the way. You tell them, Mr. Catskill."

"Tell them," said Lord Barralonga, who had also been prepared. "It's a gamble, I admit. But there's situations when one has to gamble—or be gambled with. I'm all for the active voice."

"It's a gamble—certainly," said Mr. Catskill. "But upon this narrow peninsula, upon this square mile or so of territory, the fate, Sir, of two universes awaits decision. This is no time for the faint heart and the paralyzing touch of discretion. Plan swiftly—act swiftly...."

"This is simply *thrilling*!" cried Miss Greeta Grey clasping her hands about her knees and smiling radiantly at Mr. Mush.

"These people," Mr. Barnstaple interrupted, "are three thousand years ahead of us. We are like a handful of Hottentots in a showman's van at Earl's Court, planning the conquest of London."

Mr. Catskill, hands on hips, turned with extraordinary good humour upon Mr. Barnstaple. "Three thousand years away from us—*yes*! Three thousand years ahead of us—*no*! That is where you and I join issue. You say these people are super-men. M'm—super-men.... I say they are degenerate men. Let me call your attention to my reasons for this belief—in spite of their beauty, their very considerable material and intellectual achievements and so forth. Ideal people, I admit.... What then?... My case is that they have reached a summit—and passed it, that they are going on by inertia and that they have lost the power not only of resistance to disease —that weakness we shall see develop more and more—but also of meeting strange and distressing emergencies. They are gentle. Altogether too gentle. They are ineffectual. They do not know what to do. Here is Father Amerton. He disturbed that first meeting in the most insulting way. (You know you did, Father Amerton. I'm not blaming you. You are morally—sensitive. And there were things to outrage you.) He was threatened—as a little boy is threatened by a feeble old woman. Something was to be done to him. Has anything been done to him?"

"A man and a woman came and talked to me," said Father Amerton.

"And what did you do?"

"Simply confuted them. Lifted up my voice and confuted them."

"What did they say?"

"What *could* they say?"

"We all thought tremendous things were going to be done to poor Father Amerton. Well, and now take a graver case. Our friend Lord Barralonga ran amuck with his car—and killed a man. M'm. Even at home they'd have endorsed your licence you know. And fined your man. But here?... The thing has scarcely been mentioned since. Why? Because they don't know what to say about it or do about it. And now they have put us here and begged us to be good. Until they are ready to come and try experiments upon us and inject things into us and I don't know what. And if we submit, Sir, if we submit, we lose one of our greatest powers over these people, our power of at once giving and resisting malaise, and in addition, I know not what powers of initiative that may very well be associated with that physiological toughness of which we are to be robbed. They may trifle with our ductless glands. But science tells us that these very glands secrete our personalities. Mentally, morally we shall be dissolved. If we submit, Sir—if we submit. But suppose we do not submit; what then?"

"Well," said Lord Barralonga, "what then?"

"They will not know what to do. Do not be deceived by any outward shows of beauty and prosperity. These people are living, as the ancient Peruvians were living in the time of Pizarro, in an enervating dream. They have drunken the debilitating draught of Socialism and, as in ancient Peru, there is no health nor power of will left in them any more. A handful of resolute men and women who can dare—may not only dare but triumph in the face of such a world. And thus it is I lay my plans before you."

"You mean to jump this entire Utopian planet?" said Mr. Hunker.

"Big order," said Lord Barralonga.

"I mean, Sir, to assert the rights of a more vigorous form of social life over a less vigorous form of social life. Here we are—in a fortress. It is a real fortress and quite defensible. While you others have been unpacking, Barralonga and Hunker and I have been seeing to that. There is a sheltered well so that if need arises we can get water from the canyon below. The rock is excavated into chambers and shelters; the wall on the land side is sound and high, glazed so that it cannot be scaled. This great archway can easily be barricaded when the need arises. Steps go down through the rock to that little bridge which can if necessary be cut away. We have not yet explored all the excavations. In Mr. Hunker we have a chemist—he was a chemist before the movie picture claimed him as its master—and he says there is ample material in the laboratory for a store of bombs. This party, I find, can muster five revolvers with ammunition. I scarcely dared hope for that. We have food for many days."

"Oh! This is ridiculous!" cried Mr. Barnstaple standing up and then sitting down again. "This is preposterous! To turn on these friendly people! But they can blow this little headland to smithereens whenever they want to."

"Ah!" said Mr. Catskill and held him with his outstretched finger. "We've thought of that. But we can take a leaf from the book of Cortez—who, in the very centre of Mexico, held Montezuma as his prisoner and hostage. We too will have our hostage. Before we lift a finger—. First our hostage...."

"Aerial bombs!"

"Is there such a thing in Utopia? Or such an idea? And again—we must have our hostage."

"Somebody of importance," said Mr. Hunker.

"Cedar and Serpentine are both important people," said Mr. Burleigh in tones of disinterested observation.

"But surely, Sir, you do not countenance this schoolboy's dream of piracy!" cried Mr. Barnstaple, sincerely shocked.

"Schoolboys!" cried Father Amerton. "A cabinet minister, a peer and a great entrepreneur!"

"My dear Sir," said Mr. Burleigh, "we are, after all, only envisaging eventualities. For the life of me, I do not see why we should not thresh out these possibilities. Though I pray to Heaven we may never have to realize them. You were saying, Rupert—?"

"We have to establish ourselves here and assert our independence and make ourselves *felt* by these Utopians."

"'Ear, 'ear!" said Mr. Ridley cordially. "One or two I'd like to make feel personally."

"We have to turn this prison into a capitol, into the first foothold of mankind in this world. It is like a foot thrust into a reluctant door that must never more close upon our race."

"It is closed," said Mr. Barnstaple. "Except by the mercy of these Utopians we shall never see our world again. And even with their mercy, it is doubtful."

"That's been keeping me awake nights," said Mr. Hunker.

"It's an idea that must have occurred to all of us," said Mr. Burleigh.

"And it's an idea that's so thundering disagreeable that one hasn't cared to talk about it," said Lord Barralonga.

"I never 'ad it until this moment," said Penk. "You don't reely mean to say, Sir, *we can't get back?*"

"Things will be as they will be," said Mr. Burleigh. "That is why I am anxious to hear Mr. Catskill's ideas."

Mr. Catskill rested his hands on his hips and his manner became very solemn. "For once," he said, "I am in agreement with Mr. Barnaby. I believe that the chances are *against* our ever seeing the dear cities of our world again."

"I felt that," said Lady Stella, with white lips. "I *knew* that two days ago."

"And so behold my week-end expand to an eternity!" said M. Dupont, and for a time no one said another word.

"It's as if—" Penk said at last. "Why! One might be dead!"

"But I *murst* be back," Miss Greeta Grey broke out abruptly, as one who sets aside a foolish idea. "It's absurd. I have to go on at the Alhambra on September the 2nd. It's imperative. We came here quite easily; it's ridiculous to say I can't go back in the same way."

Lord Barralonga regarded her with affectionate malignity. "You wait," he said.

"But I murst!" she sang.

"There's such things as impossibilities—even for Miss Greeta Grey."

"Charter a special aeroplane!" she said. "Anything."

He regarded her with an elfin grin and shook his head.

"My dear man," she said, "you've only seen me in a holiday mood, so far. Work is serious."

"My dear girl, that Alhambra of yours is about as far from us now as the Court of King Nebuchadnezzar.... It can't be done."

"But it *murst*," she said in her queenly way. "And that's all about it."

Mr. Barnstaple got up from the table and walked apart to where a gap in the castle wall gave upon the darkling wilderness without. He sat down there. His eyes went from the little group talking around the supper-table to the sunlit crest of the cliffs across the canyon and to the wild and lonely mountain slopes below the headland. In this world he might have to live out the remainder of his days.

And those days might not be very numerous if Mr. Catskill had his way. Sydenham, and his wife and the boys were indeed as far—"as the Court of King Nebuchadnezzar."

He had scarcely given his family a thought since he had posted his letter at Victoria. Now he felt a queer twinge of desire to send them some word or token—if only he could. Queer that they would never hear from him or of him again! How would they get on without him? Would there be any difficulty about the account at the bank? Or about the insurance money? He had always intended to have a joint and several account with his wife at the bank, and he had never quite liked to do it. Joint and several.... A thing every man ought to do.... His attention came back to Mr. Catskill unfolding his plans.

"We have to make up our minds to what may be a prolonged, a very prolonged stay here. Do not let us deceive ourselves upon that score. It may last for years—it may last for generations."

Something struck Penk in that. "I don't 'ardly see," he said, "how that can be—*generations?*"

"I am coming to that," said Mr. Catskill.

"Un'appily," said Mr. Penk, and became profoundly restrained and thoughtful with his eyes on Lady Stella.

"We have to remain, a little alien community, in this world until we dominate it, as the Romans dominated the Greeks, and until we master its science and subdue it to our purpose. That may mean a long struggle. It may mean a very long struggle indeed. And meanwhile we must maintain ourselves as a community; we must consider ourselves a colony, a garrison, until that day of reunion comes. We must hold our hostages, Sir, and not only our hostages. It may be necessary for our purpose, and if it is necessary for our purpose, so be it—to get in others of these Utopians, to catch them young, before this so-called education of theirs unfits them for our purpose, to train them in the great traditions of our Empire and our race."

Mr. Hunker seemed on the point of saying something but refrained.

M. Dupont got up sharply from the table, walked four paces away, returned and stood still, watching Mr. Catskill.

"Generations?" said Mr. Penk.

"Yes," said Mr. Catskill. "Generations. For here we are strangers—strangers, like that other little band of adventurers who established their citadel five-and-twenty centuries ago upon the Capitol beside the rushing Tiber. This is our Capitol. A greater Capitol—of a greater Rome—in a vaster world. And like that band of Roman adventurers we too may have to reinforce our scanty numbers at the expense of the Sabines about us, and take to ourselves servants and helpers and—*mates*! No sacrifice is too great for the high possibilities of this adventure."

M. Dupont seemed to nerve himself for the sacrifice.

"Duly married," injected Father Amerton.

"Duly married," said Mr. Catskill in parenthesis. "And so, Sir, we will hold out here and maintain ourselves and dominate this desert country-side and spread our prestige and our influence and our spirit into the inert body of this decadent Utopian world. Until at last we are able to master the secret that Arden and Greenlake were seeking and recover the way back to our own people, opening to the crowded millions of our Empire—"

~

"Just a moment," said Mr. Hunker. "Just a moment! About this empire —!"

"Exactly," said M. Dupont, recalled abruptly from some romantic day-dream. "About your Empire—!"

Mr. Catskill regarded them thoughtfully and defensively. "When I say Empire I mean it in the most general sense."

"Exactly," snapped M. Dupont.

"I was thinking generally of our—Atlantic civilisation."

"Before, Sir, you go on to talk of Anglo-Saxon unity and the English-speaking race," said M. Dupont, with a rising note of bitterness in his voice, "permit me to remind you, Sir, of one very important fact that you seem to be overlooking. The language of Utopia, Sir, is French. I want to remind you of that. I want to recall it to your mind. I will lay no stress here on the sacrifices and martyrdoms that France has endured in the cause of Civilisation—"

The voice of Mr. Burleigh interrupted. "A very natural misconception.

But, if you will pardon the correction, the language of Utopia is *not* French."

Of course, Mr. Barnstaple reflected, M. Dupont had not heard the explanation of the language difficulty.

"Permit me, Sir, to believe the evidence of my own ears," the Frenchman replied with dignified politeness. "These Utopians, I can assure you, speak French and nothing but French—and very excellent French it is."

"They speak no language at all," said Mr. Burleigh.

"Not even English?" sneered M. Dupont.

"Not even English."

"Not League of Nations, perhaps? But—Bah! Why do I argue? They speak French. Not even a Bosch would deny it. It needs an Englishman—"

A beautiful wrangle, thought Mr. Barnstaple. There was no Utopian present to undeceive M. Dupont and he stuck to his belief magnificently. With a mixture of pity and derision and anger, Mr. Barnstaple listened to this little band of lost human beings, in the twilight of a vast, strange and possibly inimical world, growing more and more fierce and keen in a dispute over the claims of their three nations to "dominate" Utopia, claims based entirely upon greeds and misconceptions. Their voices rose to shouts and sank to passionate intensity as their life-long habits of national egotism reasserted themselves. Mr. Hunker would hear nothing of any "Empire"; M. Dupont would hear of nothing but the supreme claim of France. Mr. Catskill twisted and turned. To Mr. Barnstaple this conflict of patriotic prepossessions seemed like a dog-fight on a sinking ship. But at last Mr. Catskill, persistent and ingenious, made headway against his two antagonists.

He stood at the end of the table explaining that he had used the word Empire loosely, apologizing for using it, explaining that when he said Empire he had all Western Civilisation in mind. "When I said it," he said, turning to Mr. Hunker, "I meant a common brotherhood of understanding." He faced towards M. Dupont. "I meant our tried and imperishable Entente."

"There are at least no Russians here," said M. Dupont. "And no Germans."

"True," said Lord Barralonga. "We start ahead of the Hun here, and we can keep ahead."

"And I take it," said Mr. Hunker, "that Japanese are barred."

"No reason why we shouldn't start clean with a complete colour bar," reflected Lord Barralonga. "This seems to me a White Man's World."

"At the same time," said M. Dupont, coldly and insistently, "you will forgive me if I ask you for some clearer definition of our present relationship and for some guarantee, some effective guarantee, that the immense sacrifices France has made and still makes in the cause of civilised life, will receive their proper recognition and their due reward in this adventure....

"I ask only for justice," said M. Dupont.

~

INDIGNATION MADE MR. BARNSTAPLE BOLD. HE GOT DOWN FROM HIS perch upon the wall and came up to the table.

"Are you mad," he said, "or am I?

"This squabble over flags and countries and fanciful rights and deserts —it is hopeless folly. Do you not realize even now the position we are in?"

His breath failed him for a moment and then he resumed.

"Are you incapable of thinking of human affairs except in terms of flags and fighting and conquest and robbery? Cannot you realize the proportion of things and the quality of this world into which we have fallen? As I have said already, we are like some band of savages in a show at Earl's Court, plotting the subjugation of London. We are like suppressed cannibals in the heart of a great city dreaming of a revival of our ancient and forgotten filthiness. What are our chances in this fantastic struggle?"

Mr. Ridley spoke reprovingly. "You're forgetting everythink you just been told. Everythink. 'Arf their population is laid out with flu and measles. And there's no such thing as a 'ealthy fighting will left in all Utopia."

"Precisely," said Mr. Catskill.

"Well, suppose you have chances? If that makes your scheme the more hopeful, it also makes it the more horrible. Here we are lifted up out of the troubles of our time to a vision, to a reality of civilisation such as our own world can only hope to climb to in scores of centuries! Here is a world at peace, splendid, happy, full of wisdom and hope! If our puny strength and base cunning can contrive it, we are to shatter it all! We are proposing to wreck a world! I tell you it is not an adventure. It is a crime. It is an abomination. I will have no part in it. I am against you in this attempt."

Father Amerton would have spoken but Mr. Burleigh arrested him by a gesture.

"What would *you* have us do?" asked Mr. Burleigh.

"Submit to their science. Learn what we can from them. In a little while we may be cured of our inherent poisons and we may be permitted to return from this outlying desert of mines and turbines and rock, to those gardens of habitation we have as yet scarcely seen. There we too may learn something of civilisation.... In the end we may even go back to our own disordered world—with knowledge, with hope and help, missionaries of a new order."

"But why——?" began Father Amerton.

Again Mr. Burleigh took the word. "Everything you say," he remarked, "rests on unproven assumptions. You choose to see this Utopia through rose-tinted glasses. We others—for it is"—he counted—"eleven to one against you—see things without such favourable preconceptions."

"And may I ask, Sir," said Father Amerton, springing to his feet and hitting the table a blow that set all the glasses talking. "May I ask, who *you* are, to set yourself up as a judge and censor of the common opinion of mankind? For I tell you, Sir, that here in this lonely and wicked and strange world, we here, we twelve, do represent mankind. We are the advance guard, the pioneers—in the new world that God has given us, even as He gave Canaan to Israel His chosen, three thousand years ago. Who are *you*——"

"Exactly," said Penk. "Who are you?"

And Mr. Ridley reinforced him with a shout: "Oo the 'ell are *you*?"

Mr. Barnstaple had no platform skill to meet so direct an attack. He stood helpless. Astonishingly Lady Stella came to his rescue.

"That isn't fair, Father Amerton," she said. "Mr. Bastaple, whoever he is, has a perfect right to express his own opinion."

"And having expressed it," said Mr. Catskill, who had been walking up and down on the other side of the table to that on which Mr. Barnstaple stood, "M'm, having expressed it, to allow us to proceed with the business in hand. I suppose it was inevitable that we should find the conscientious objector in our midst—even in Utopia. The rest of us, I take it, are very much of one mind about our situation."

"We are," said Mr. Mush, regarding Mr. Barnstaple with a malevolent expression.

"Very well. Then I suppose we must follow the precedents established for such cases. We will not ask Mr.—Mr. Bastaple to share the dangers—

and the honours—of a combatant. We will ask him merely to do civilian work of a helpful nature—"

Mr. Barnstaple held up his hand. "No," he said. "I am not disposed to be helpful. I do not recognize the analogy of the situation to the needs of the Great War, and, anyhow, I am entirely opposed to this project—this brigandage of a civilisation. You cannot call me a conscientious objector to fighting, because I do not object to fighting in a just cause. But this adventure of yours is not a just cause.... I implore you, Mr. Burleigh, you who are not merely a politician, but a man of culture and a philosopher, to reconsider what it is we are being urged towards—towards acts of violence and mischief from which there will be no drawing back!"

"Mr. Barnstaple," said Mr. Burleigh with grave dignity and something like a note of reproach in his voice, "I *have* considered. But I think I may venture to say that I am a man of some experience, some traditional experience, in human affairs. I may not altogether agree with my friend Mr. Catskill. Nay! I will go further and say that in many respects I do *not* agree with him. If I were the autocrat here I would say that we have to offer these Utopians resistance—for our self-respect—but not to offer them the violent and aggressive resistance that he contemplates. I think we could be far more subtle, far more elaborate, and far more successful than Mr. Catskill is likely to be. But that is my own opinion. Neither Mr. Hunker nor Lord Barralonga, nor Mr. Mush, nor M. Dupont shares it. Nor do Mr. —our friends, the ah!—technical engineers here share it. And what I do perceive to be imperative upon our little band of Earthlings, lost here in a strange universe, is *unity of action*. Whatever else betide, dissension must not betray us. We must hold together and act together as one body. Discuss if you will, when there is any time for discussion, but in the end *decide*. And having decided abide loyally by the decision. Upon the need of securing a hostage or two I have no manner of doubt whatever. Mr. Catskill is right."

Mr. Barnstaple was a bad debater. "But these Utopians are as human as we are," he said. "All that is most sane and civilised in ourselves is with them."

Mr. Ridley interrupted in a voice designedly rough. "Oh Lord!" he said. "We can't go on jawing 'ere for ever. It's sunset, and Mr.—this gentleman 'as 'ad 'is say, and more than 'is say. We ought to have our places and know what is expected of us before night. May I propose that we elect Mr. Catskill our Captain with full military powers?"

"I second that," said Mr. Burleigh with grave humility.

"Perhaps M. Dupont," said Mr. Catskill, "will act with me as associated Captain, representing our glorious ally, his own great country."

"In the absence of a more worthy representative," acquiesced M. Dupont, "and to see that French interests are duly respected."

"And if Mr. Hunker would act as my lieutenant?... Lord Barralonga will be our quartermaster and Father Amerton our chaplain and censor. Mr. Burleigh, it goes without saying, will be our civil head."

Mr. Hunker coughed. He frowned with the expression of one who makes a difficult explanation. "I won't be exactly lieutenant," he said. "I'll take no official position. I've a sort of distaste for—foreign entanglements. I'll be a looker-on—who helps. But I think you will find you can count on me, Gentlemen—when help is needed."

Mr. Catskill seated himself at the head of the table and indicated the chair next to his for M. Dupont. Miss Greeta Grey seated herself on his other hand between him and Mr. Hunker. Mr. Burleigh remained in his place, a chair or so from Mr. Hunker. The rest came and stood round the Captain except Lady Stella and Mr. Barnstaple.

Almost ostentatiously Mr. Barnstaple turned his back on the new command. Lady Stella, he saw, remained seated far down the table, looking dubiously at the little crowd of people at the end. Then her eyes went to the desolate mountain crest beyond.

She shivered violently and stood up. "It's going to be very cold here after sunset," she said, with nobody heeding her. "I shall go and unpack a wrap."

She walked slowly to her quarters and did not reappear.

MR. BARNSTAPLE DID NOT WANT TO SEEM TO LISTEN TO THIS COUNCIL of War. He walked to the wall of the old castle and up a flight of stone steps and along the rampart to the peak of the headland. Here the shattering and beating sound of the waters in the two convergent canyons was very loud.

There was still a bright upper rim of sunlit rock on the mountain face behind, but all the rest of the world was now in a deepening blue shadow, and a fleecy white mist was gathering in the canyons below and hiding the noisy torrents. It drifted up almost to the level of the little bridge that spanned the narrower canyon to a railed step way from the crest on the further side. For the first time since he had arrived in Utopia Mr. Barnstaple felt a chill in the air. And loneliness like a pain.

Up the broader of the two meeting canyons some sort of engineering work was going on and periodic flashes lit the drifting mist. Far away over the mountains a solitary aeroplane, very high, caught the sun's rays ever and again and sent down quivering flashes of dazzling golden light, and then, as it wheeled about, vanished again in the deepening blue.

He looked down into the great courtyard of the ancient castle below him. The modern buildings in the twilight looked like phantom pavilions amidst the archaic masonry. Some one had brought a light, and Captain Rupert Catskill, the new Cortez, was writing orders, while his Commando stood about him.

The light shone on the face and shoulders and arms of Miss Greeta Grey; she was peering over the Captain's arm to see what he was writing. And as Mr. Barnstaple looked he saw her raise her hand suddenly to conceal an involuntary yawn.

3

Mr. Barnstaple as a Traitor to Mankind

⁓

MR. BARNSTAPLE SPENT A LARGE PART OF THE NIGHT SITTING UPON HIS bed and brooding over the incalculable elements of the situation in which he found himself.

What could he do? What ought he to do? Where did his loyalty lie? The dark traditions and infections of the Earth had turned this wonderful encounter into an ugly and dangerous antagonism far too swiftly for him to adjust his mind to the new situation. Before him now only two possibilities seemed open. Either the Utopians would prove themselves altogether the stronger and the wiser and he and all his fellow pirates would be crushed and killed like vermin, or the desperate ambitions of Mr. Catskill would be realized and they would become a spreading sore in the fair body of this noble civilisation, a band of robbers and destroyers, dragging Utopia year by year and age by age back to terrestrial conditions. There seemed only one escape from the dilemma; to get away from this fastness to the Utopians, to reveal the whole scheme of the Earthlings to them, and to throw himself and his associates upon their mercy. But this must be done soon, before the hostages were seized and bloodshed began.

But in the first place it might be very difficult now to get away from the Earthling band. Mr. Catskill would already have organised watchers and sentinels, and the peculiar position of the crag exposed every avenue of escape. And in the next place Mr. Barnstaple had a life-long habit of mind which predisposed him against tale-bearing and dissentient action. His school training had moulded him into subservience to any group or gang in which he found himself; his form, his side, his house, his school, his club, his party and so forth. Yet his intelligence and his limitless curiosities had always been opposed to these narrow conspiracies against the world at large. His spirit had made him an uncomfortable rebel throughout his whole earthly existence. He loathed political parties and political leaders, he despised and rejected nationalism and imperialism and all the tawdry loyalties associated with them; the aggressive conqueror, the grabbing financier, the shoving business man, he hated as he hated wasps, rats, hyenas, sharks, fleas, nettles and the like: all his life he had been a citizen of Utopia exiled upon Earth. After his fashion he had sought to serve Utopia. Why should he not serve Utopia now? Because his band was a little and desperate band, that was no reason why he should serve the things he hated. If they were a desperate crew, the fact remained that they were also, as a whole, an evil crew. There is no reason why liberalism should degenerate into a morbid passion for minorities....

Only two persons among the Earthlings, Lady Stella and Mr. Burleigh, held any of his sympathy. And he had his doubts about Mr. Burleigh. Mr. Burleigh was one of those strange people who seem to understand everything and feel nothing. He impressed Mr. Barnstaple as being intelligently irresponsible. Wasn't that really more evil than being unintelligently adventurous like Hunker or Barralonga?

Mr. Barnstaple's mind returned from a long excursion in ethics to the realities about him. To-morrow he would survey the position and make his plans, and perhaps in the twilight he would slip away.

It was entirely in his character to defer action in this way for the better part of the day. His life had been one of deferred action almost from the beginning.

~

But events could not wait for Mr. Barnstaple.

He was called at dawn by Penk, who told him that henceforth the garrison would be aroused every morning by an electric hooter he and Ridley had contrived. As Penk spoke a devastating howl from this contrivance inaugurated the new era. He handed Mr. Barnstaple a slip of paper torn from a note-book on which Mr. Catskill had written:—

"Non-comb. Barnaby. To assist Ridley prepare breakfast, lunch and dinner, times and menu on mess-room wall, clear away and wash up smartly and at other times to be at disposal of Lt. Hunker, in chemical laboratory for experimenting and bomb-making. Keep laboratory clean."

"That's your job," said Penk. "Ridley's waitin' for you."

"Well," said Mr. Barnstaple, and got up. It was no use precipitating a quarrel if he was to escape. So he went to the scarred and bandaged Ridley, and they produced a very good imitation of a British military kitchen in that great raw year, 1914.

Everyone was turned out to breakfast at half-past six by a second solo on the hooter. The men were paraded and inspected by Mr. Catskill, with M. Dupont standing beside him; Mr. Hunker stood parallel with these two and a few yards away; all the other men fell in except Mr. Burleigh, who was to be civil commander in Utopia, and was, in that capacity, in bed, and Mr. Barnstaple the non-combatant. Miss Greeta Grey and Lady Stella sat in a sunny corner of the courtyard sewing at a flag. It was to be a blue flag with a white star, a design sufficiently unlike any existing national flag to avoid wounding the patriotic susceptibilities of any of the party. It was to represent the Earthling League of Nations.

After the parade the little garrison dispersed to its various posts and duties, M. Dupont assumed the chief command, and Mr. Catskill, who had watched all night, went to lie down. He had the Napoleonic quality of going off to sleep for an hour or so at any time in the day.

Mr. Penk went up to the top of the castle, where the hooter was installed, to keep a look out.

There were some moments to be snatched between the time when Mr. Barnstaple had finished with Ridley and the time when Hunker would discover his help was available, and this time he devoted to an inspection of the castle wall on the side of the slopes. While he was standing on the old rampart weighing his chances of slipping away that evening in the twilight, an aeroplane appeared above the crag and came down upon the nearer slope. Two Utopians descended, talked with their aviator for a time, and then turned their faces towards the fastness of the Earthlings.

A single note of the hooter brought out Mr. Catskill upon the rampart beside Mr. Barnstaple. He produced a field-glass and surveyed the approaching figures.

"Serpentine and Cedar," he said, lowering his field-glass. "And they come alone. Good."

He turned round and signalled with his hand to Penk, who responded with two short whoops of his instrument. This was the signal for a general assembly.

Down below in the courtyard appeared the rest of the Allied force and Mr. Hunker and fell in with a reasonable imitation of discipline.

Mr. Catskill passed Mr. Barnstaple without taking any notice of him, joined M. Dupont, Mr. Hunker and their subordinates below and proceeded to instruct them in his plans for the forthcoming crisis. Mr. Barnstaple could not hear what was said. He noted with sardonic disapproval that each man, as Mr. Catskill finished with him, clicked his heels together and saluted. Then at a word of command they dispersed to their posts.

There was a partly ruined flight of steps leading down from the general level of the courtyard through this great archway in the wall that gave access to and from the slopes below. Ridley and Mush went down to the right of these steps and placed themselves below a projecting mass of masonry so as to be hidden from any one approaching from below. Father Amerton and Mr. Hunker concealed themselves similarly to the left. Father Amerton, Mr. Barnstaple noted, had been given a coil of rope, and then his roving eye discovered Mr. Mush glancing at a pistol in his hand and then replacing it in his pocket. Lord Barralonga took up a position for himself some steps above Mr. Mush and produced a revolver which he held in his one efficient hand. Mr. Catskill remained at the head of the stairs. He also was holding a revolver. He turned to the citadel, considered the case of Penk for a moment, and then motioned him down to join the others. M. Dupont, armed with a stout table leg, placed himself at Mr. Catskill's right hand.

For a time Mr. Barnstaple watched these dispositions without any realisation of their significance. Then his eyes went from the crouching figures within the castle to the two unsuspecting Utopians who were coming up towards them, and he realized that in a couple of minutes Serpentine and Cedar would be struggling in the grip of their captors....

He perceived he had to act. And his had been a contemplative, critical life with no habit of decision.

He found himself trembling violently.

He still desired some mediatory intervention even in these fatal last moments. He raised an arm and cried "Hi!" as much to the Earthlings below as to the Utopians without. No one noticed either his gesture or his feeble cry.

Then his will seemed to break through a tangle of obstacles to one simple idea. Serpentine and Cedar must not be seized. He was amazed and indignant at his own vacillation. Of course they must not be seized! This foolery must be thwarted forthwith. In four strides he was on the wall above the archway and now he was shouting loud and clear. "Danger!" he shouted. "Danger!" and again "Danger!"

He heard Catskill's cry of astonishment and then a pistol bullet whipped through the air close to him.

Serpentine stopped short and looked up, touched Cedar's arm and pointed.

"These Earthlings want to imprison you. Don't come here! Danger!" yelled Mr. Barnstaple waving his arms and "*pat, pat, pat*," Mr. Catskill experienced the disappointments of revolver shooting.

Serpentine and Cedar were turning back—but slowly and hesitatingly.

For a moment Mr. Catskill knew not what to do. Then he flung himself down the steps, crying, "After them! Stop them! Come on!"

"Go back!" cried Mr. Barnstaple to the Utopians. "Go back! Quickly! Quickly!"

Came a clatter of feet from below and then the eight men who constituted the combatant strength of the Earthling forces in Utopia emerged from under the archway running towards the two astonished Utopians. Mr. Mush led, with Ridley at his heels; he was pointing his revolver and shouting. Next came M. Dupont zealous and active. Father Amerton brought up the rear with the rope.

"Go back!" screamed Mr. Barnstaple, with his voice breaking.

Then he stopped shouting and watched—with his hands clenched.

The aviator was running down the slope from his machine to the assistance of Serpentine and Cedar. And above out of the blue two other aeroplanes had appeared.

The two Utopians disdained to hurry and in a few seconds their pursuers had come up with them. Hunker, Ridley and Mush led the attack. M. Dupont, flourishing his stick, was abreast with them but running out to the right as though he intended to get between them and the aviator. Mr. Catskill and Penk were a little behind the leading three; the one-armed Barralonga was perhaps ten yards behind and Father Amerton had halted to re-coil his rope more conveniently.

There seemed to be a moment's parley and then Serpentine had moved quickly as if to seize Hunker. A pistol cracked and then another went off rapidly three times. "Oh God!" cried Mr. Barnstaple. "Oh God!" as he saw Serpentine throw up his arms and fall backward, and then Cedar had grasped and lifted up Mush and hurled him at Mr. Catskill and Penk, bowling both of them over into one indistinguishable heap. With a wild cry M. Dupont closed in on Cedar but not quickly enough. His club shot into the air as Cedar parried his blow, and then the Utopian stooped, caught him by a leg, overthrew him, lifted him and whirled him round as one might whirl a rabbit, to inflict a stunning blow on Mr. Hunker.

Lord Barralonga ran back some paces and began shooting at the approaching aviator.

The confusion of legs and arms on the ground became three separate people again. Mr. Catskill shouting directions, made for Cedar, followed by Penk and Mush and, a moment after by Hunker and Dupont. They clung to Cedar as hounds will cling to a boar. Time after time he flung them off him. Father Amerton hovered unhelpfully with his rope.

For some moments Mr. Barnstaple's attention was concentrated upon this swaying and staggering attempt to overpower Cedar, and then he became aware of other Utopians running down the slope to join the fray.... The other two aeroplanes had landed.

Mr. Catskill realized the coming of these reinforcements almost as soon as Mr. Barnstaple. His shouts of "Back! Back to the castle!" reached Mr. Barnstaple's ears. The Earthlings scattered away from the tall dishevelled figure, hesitated, and began to walk and then run back towards the castle.

And then Ridley turned and very deliberately shot Cedar, who clutched at his breast and fell into a sitting position.

The Earthlings retreated to the foot of the steps that led up through the archway into the castle, and stood there in a panting, bruised and ruffled group. Fifty yards away Serpentine lay still, the aviator whom Barralonga had shot writhed and moaned, and Cedar sat up with blood upon his chest trying to feel his back. Five other Utopians came hurrying to their assistance.

"What is all this firing?" said Lady Stella, suddenly at Mr. Barnstaple's elbow.

"Have they caught their hostages?" asked Miss Greeta Grey.

"For the life of me!" said Mr. Burleigh, who had come out upon the wall a yard or so away, "this ought never to have happened. How did this get—*muffed*, Lady Stella?"

"I called out to them," said Mr. Barnstaple.

"*You*—called—out to them!" said Mr. Burleigh incredulous.

"Treason I did not calculate upon," came the wrathful voice of Mr. Catskill ascending out of the archway.

FOR SOME MOMENTS MR. BARNSTAPLE MADE NO ATTEMPT TO ESCAPE the danger that closed in upon him. He had always lived a life of very great security and with him, as with so many highly civilised types, the power of apprehending personal danger was very largely atrophied. He was a spectator by temperament and training alike. He stood now as if he looked at himself, the central figure of a great and hopeless tragedy. The idea of flight came belatedly, in a reluctant and apologetic manner into his mind.

"Shot as a traitor," he said aloud. "Shot as a traitor."

There was that bridge over the narrow gorge. He might still get over that, if he went for it at once. If he was quick—quicker than they were. He was too intelligent to dash off for it; that would certainly have set the others running. He walked along the wall in a leisurely fashion past Mr. Burleigh, himself too civilised to intervene. In a quickening stroll he gained the steps that led to the citadel. Then he stood still for a moment to survey the situation. Catskill was busy setting sentinels at the gate. Perhaps he had not thought yet of the little bridge and imagined that Mr. Barnstaple was at his disposal at any time that suited him. Up the slope the Utopians were carrying off the dead or wounded men.

Mr. Barnstaple ascended the steps as if buried in thought and stood on the citadel for some seconds, his hands in his trouser pockets, as if he surveyed the view. Then he turned to the winding staircase that went down to a sort of guard room below. As soon as he was surely out of sight he began to think and move very quickly.

The guard-room was perplexing. It had five doors, any one of which except the one by which he had just entered the room, might lead down to the staircase. Against one, however, stood a pile of neat packing-cases. That left three to choose from. He ran from one to the other leaving each door open. In each case stone steps ran down to a landing and a turning place. He stood hesitating at the third and noted that a cold draught came blowing up from it. Surely that meant that this went down to the cliff face, or whence came the air? Surely this was it!

Should he shut the doors he had opened? No! Leave them all open.

He heard a clatter coming down the staircase from the citadel. Softly and swiftly he ran down the steps and halted for a second at the corner landing. He was compelled to stop and listen to the movements of his pursuers. "This is the door to the bridge, Sir!" he heard Ridley cry, and then he heard Catskill say, "The Tarpeian Rock," and Barralonga, "Exactly! Why should we waste a cartridge? Are you sure this goes to the bridge, Ridley?"

The footsteps pattered across the guard room and passed—down one of the other staircases.

"A reprieve!" whispered Mr. Barnstaple and then stopped aghast.

He was trapped! The staircase they were on was the staircase to the bridge!

They would go down as far as the bridge and as soon as they got to it they would see that he was neither on it nor on the steps on the opposite side of the gorge and that therefore he could not possibly have escaped. They would certainly bar that way either by closing and fastening any door there might be or, failing such a barrier, by setting a sentinel, and then they would come back and hunt for him at their leisure.

What was it Catskill had been saying? The Tarpeian Rock?...

Horrible!

They mustn't take him alive....

He must fight like a rat in a corner and oblige them to shoot him....

He went on down the staircase. It became very dark and then grew light again. It ended in an ordinary big cellar, which may once have been a gun-pit or magazine. It was fairly well lit by two unglazed windows cut in the rock. It now contained a store of provisions. Along one side stood an array of the flask-like bottles that were used for wine in Utopia; along the other was a miscellany of packing-cases and cubes wrapped in gold-leaf. He lifted one of the glass flasks by its neck. It would make an effective club. Suppose he made a sort of barrier of the packing-cases across the entrance and stood beside it and clubbed the pursuers as they came in! Glass and wine would smash over their skulls.... It would take time to make the barrier.... He chose and carried three of the larger flasks to the doorway where they would be handy for him. Then he had an inspiration and looked at the window.

He listened at the door of the staircase for a time. Not a sound came from above. He went to the window and lay down in the deep embrasure and wriggled forward until he could see out and up and down. The cliff below fell sheer; he could have spat on to the brawling torrent fifteen hundred feet perhaps below. The crag here was made up of almost vertical strata which projected and receded; a big buttress hid almost all of the bridge except the far end which seemed to be about twenty or thirty yards lower than the opening from which Mr. Barnstaple was looking. Mr. Catskill appeared upon this bridge, very small and distant, scrutinizing the rocky stairway beyond the bridge. Mr. Barnstaple withdrew his head hastily. Then very discreetly he peeped again. Mr. Catskill was no longer to be seen. He was coming back.

To business! There was not much time.

In his earlier days before the Great War had made travel dear and uncomfortable Mr. Barnstaple had done some rock climbing in Switzerland and he had also had some experience in Cumberland and Wales. He surveyed now the rocks close at hand with an intelligent expertness. They were cut by almost horizontal joint planes into which there had been a considerable infiltration chiefly of white crystalline material. This stuff, which he guessed was calcite, had weathered more rapidly than the general material of the rock, leaving a series of irregular horizontal grooves. With luck it might be possible to work along the cliff face, turn the buttress and scramble to the bridge.

And then came an even more hopeful idea. He could easily get along the cliff face to the first recess, flatten himself there and remain until the Earthlings had searched his cellar. After they had searched he might creep back to the cellar. Even if they looked out of the window they would not see him and even if he left finger marks and so forth in the embrasure, they would be likely to conclude that he had either jumped or fallen down the crag into the gorge below. But at first it might be slow work negotiating the cliff face.... And this would cut him off from his weapons, the flasks....

But the idea of hiding in the recess had taken a strong hold upon his imagination. Very cautiously he got out of the window, found a handhold, got his feet on to his ledge and began to work his way along towards his niche.

But there were unexpected difficulties, a gap of nearly five yards in the handhold—nothing. He had to flatten himself and trust to his feet and for a time he remained quite still in that position.

Further on was a rotten lump of the vein mineral and it broke away under him very disconcertingly, but happily his fingers had a grip and the other foot was firm. The detached crystals slithered down the rock face for a moment and then made no further sound. They had dropped into the void. For a time he was paralyzed.

"I'm not in good form," whispered Mr. Barnstaple. "I'm not in good form."

He clung motionless and prayed.

With an effort he resumed his traverse.

He was at the very corner of the recess when some faint noise drew his eyes to the window from which he had emerged. Ridley's face was poked out slowly and cautiously, his eye red and fierce among his white bandages.

HE DID NOT AT FIRST SEE MR. BARNSTAPLE. "GAWD!" HE SAID WHEN HE did so and withdrew his head hastily.

Came a sound of voices saying indistinguishable things.

Some inappropriate instinct kept Mr. Barnstaple quite still, though he could have got into cover in the recess quite easily before Mr. Catskill looked out revolver in hand.

For some moments they stared at each other in silence.

"Come back or I shoot," said Mr. Catskill unconvincingly.

"Shoot!" said Mr. Barnstaple after a moment's reflection.

Mr. Catskill craned his head out and stared down into the shadowy blue depths of the canyon. "It isn't necessary," he answered. "We have to save cartridges."

"You haven't the guts," said Mr. Barnstaple.

"It's not quite that," said Mr. Catskill.

"No," said Mr. Barnstaple, "it isn't. You are fundamentally a civilised man."

Mr. Catskill scowled at him without hostility.

"You have a very good imagination," Mr. Barnstaple reflected. "The trouble is that you have been so damnably educated. What is the trouble with you? You are be-Kiplinged. Empire and Anglo-Saxon and boy-scout and sleuth are the stuff in your mind. If I had gone to Eton I might have been the same as you are, I suppose."

"Harrow," corrected Mr. Catskill.

"A perfectly *beastly* public school. Suburban place where the boys wear chignons and straw haloes. I might have guessed Harrow. But it's queer I bear you no malice. Given decent ideas you might have been very different from what you are. If I had been your schoolmaster—But it's too late now."

"It is," said Mr. Rupert Catskill smiling genially and cocked his eye down into the canyon.

Mr. Barnstaple began to feel for his ledge round the corner with one foot.

"Don't go for a minute," said Mr. Catskill. "I'm not going to shoot."

A voice from within, probably Lord Barralonga's, said something about heaving a rock at Mr. Barnstaple. Some one else, probably Ridley, approved ferociously.

"Not without due form of trial," said Mr. Catskill over his shoulder. His face was inscrutable, but a fantastic idea began to run about in Mr. Barnstaple's mind that Mr. Catskill did not want to have him killed. He had thought about things and he wanted him now to escape—to the Utopians and perhaps rig up some sort of settlement with them.

"We intend to try you, Sir," said Mr. Catskill. "We intend to try you. We cite you to appear."

Mr. Catskill moistened his lips and considered. "The court will sit almost at once." His little bright brown eyes estimated the chances of Mr. Barnstaple's position very rapidly. He craned towards the bridge. "We shall not waste time over our procedure," he said. "And I have little doubt of our verdict. We shall condemn you to death. So—there you are, Sir. I doubt if we shall be more than a quarter of an hour before your fate is legally settled."

He glanced up trying to see the crest of the crag. "We shall probably throw rocks," he said.

"*Moriturus te saluo*," said Mr. Barnstaple with an air of making a witty remark. "If you will forgive me I will go on now to find a more comfortable position."

Mr. Catskill remained looking hard at him.

"I've never borne you any ill-will," said Mr. Barnstaple. "Had I been your schoolmaster everything might have been different. Thanks for the quarter of an hour more you give me. And if by any chance—"

"Exactly," said Mr. Catskill.

They understood one another.

When Mr. Barnstaple stepped round the bend into the recess Mr. Catskill was still looking out and Lord Barralonga was faintly audible advocating the immediate heaving of rocks.

~

THE WAYS OF THE HUMAN MIND ARE PAST FINDING OUT. FROM desperation Mr. Barnstaple's mood had passed to exhilaration. His first sick horror of climbing above this immense height had given place now to an almost boyish assurance. His sense of immediate death had gone. He was appreciating this adventure, indeed he was enjoying it, with an entire disregard now of how it was to end.

He made fairly good time until he got to the angle of the buttress, though his arms began to ache rather badly, and then he had a shock. He had now a full view of the bridge and up the narrow gorge. The ledge he was working along did not run to the bridge at all. It ran a good thirty feet below it. And what was worse, between himself and the bridge were two gullies and chimneys of uncertain depth. At this discovery he regretted for the first time that he had not stayed in the cellar and made a fight for it there.

He had some minutes of indecision—with the ache in his arms increasing.

He was roused from his inaction by what he thought at first was the shadow of a swift-flying bird on the rock. Presently it returned. He hoped he was not to be assailed by birds. He had read a story—but never mind that now.

Then came a loud crack overhead, and he glanced up to see a lump of rock which had just struck a little bulge above him fly to fragments. From which incident he gathered firstly that the court had delivered an adverse verdict rather in advance of Mr. Catskill's time, and secondly that he was visible from above. He resumed his traverse towards the shelter of the gully with feverish energy.

The gully was better than he expected, a chimney; difficult, he thought, to ascend, but quite practicable downward. It was completely overhung. And perhaps a hundred feet below there was a sort of step in it that gave a quite broad recess, sheltered from above and with room enough for a man to sprawl on it if he wanted to do so. There would be rest for Mr. Barnstaple's arms, and without any needless delay he clambered down to it and abandoned himself to the delightful sensation of not holding on to anything. He was out of sight and out of reach of his Earthling pursuers.

In the back of the recess was a trickle of water. He drank and began to think of food and to regret that he had not brought some provision with him from the store in the cellar. He might have opened one of those gold-leaf-covered cubes or pocketed a small flask of wine. Wine would be very heartening just now. But it did not do to think of that. He stayed for a long time, as it seemed to him, on this precious shelf, scrutinizing the chimney below very carefully. It seemed quite practicable for a long way down. The sides became very smooth, but they seemed close enough together to get down with his back against one side and his feet against the other.

He looked at his wrist-watch. It was still not nine o'clock in the morning—it was about ten minutes to nine. He had been called by Ridley before half-past five. At half-past six he had been handing out breakfast in the courtyard. Serpentine and Cedar must have appeared about eight o'clock. In about ten minutes Serpentine had been murdered. Then the flight and the pursuit. How quickly things had happened!...

He had all day before him. He would resume his descent at half-past nine. Until then he would rest.... It was absurd to feel hungry yet....

He was climbing again before half-past nine. For perhaps a hundred feet it was easy. Then by imperceptible degrees the gully broadened. He only realized it when he found himself slipping. He slipped, struggling furiously, for perhaps twenty feet, and then fell outright another ten and struck a rock and was held by a second shelf much broader than the one above. He came down on it with a jarring concussion and rolled—happily he rolled inward. He was bruised, but not seriously hurt. "My luck," he said. "My luck holds good."

He rested for a time, and then, confident that things would be all right, set himself to inspect the next stage of his descent. It was with a sort of incredulity that he discovered the chimney below his shelf was absolutely unclimbable. It was just a straight, smooth rock on either side for twenty yards at least and six feet wide. He might as well fling himself over at once as try to get down that. Then he saw that it was equally impossible to retrace his steps. He could not believe it; it seemed too silly. He laughed as one might laugh if one found one's own mother refusing to recognize one after a day's absence.

Then abruptly he stopped laughing.

He repeated every point in his examination. He fingered the smooth rocks about him. "But this is absurd," he said breaking out into a cold perspiration. There was no way out of this corner into which he had so painfully and laboriously got himself. He could neither go on nor go back. He was caught. His luck had given out.

~

AT MIDDAY BY HIS WRIST-WATCH MR. BARNSTAPLE WAS SITTING IN HIS recess as a weary invalid suffering from some incurable disease might sit up in an arm-chair during a temporary respite from pain, with nothing to do and no hope before him. There was not one chance in ten thousand that anything could happen to release him from this trap into which he had clambered. There was a trickle of water at the back but no food, not even a grass blade to nibble. Unless he saw fit to pitch himself over into the gorge, he must starve to death.... It would perhaps be cold at nights but not cold enough to kill him.

To this end he had come then out of the worried journalism of London and the domesticities of Sydenham.

Queer journey it was that he and the Yellow Peril had made!— Camberwell, Victoria, Hounslow, Slough, Utopia, the mountain paradise, a hundred fascinating and tantalizing glimpses of a world of real happiness and order, that long, long aeroplane flight half round a world.... And now —death.

The idea of abbreviating his sufferings by jumping over had no appeal for him. He would stay here and suffer such suffering as there might be before the end. And three hundred yards away or so were his fellow Earthlings, also awaiting their fate.... It was amazing. It was prosaic....

After all to this or something like this most humanity had to come.

Sooner or later people had to lie and suffer, they had to think and then think feverishly and then weakly, and so fade to a final cessation of thought.

On the whole, he thought, it was preferable to die in this fashion, preferable to a sudden death, it was worthwhile to look death in the face for a time, have leisure to write *finis* in one's mind, to think over life and such living as one had done and think it over with a detachment, an independence, that only an entire inability to alter one jot of it now could give.

At present his mind was clear and calm; a bleak serenity like a clear winter sky possessed him. There was suffering ahead, he knew, but he did not believe it would be intolerable suffering. If it proved intolerable the canyon yawned below. In that respect this shelf or rock was a better death bed than most, a more convenient death bed. Your sick bed presented pain with a wide margin, set it up for your too complete examination. But to starve was not so very dreadful, he had read; hunger and pain there would be, most distressful about the third day, and after that one became feeble and did not feel so much. It would not be like the torture of many cancer cases or the agony of brain fever; it would not be one tithe as bad as that. Lonely it would be. But is one much less lonely on a death bed at home? They come and say, "There! there!" and do little serviceable things —but are there any other interchanges?... You go your solitary way, speech and movement and the desire to speak or move passing from you, and their voices fade.... Everywhere death is a very solitary act, a going apart....

A younger man would probably have found this loneliness in the gorge very terrible, but Mr. Barnstaple had outlived the more intense delusions of companionship. He would have liked a last talk with his boys and to have put his wife into a good frame of mind, but even these desires were perhaps more sentimental than real. When it came to talks with his boys he was apt to feel shy. As they had come to have personalities of their own and to grow through adolescence, he had felt more and more that talking intimately to them was an invasion of their right to grow up along their own lines. And they too he felt were shy with him, defensively shy. Perhaps later on sons came back to a man—that was a later on that he would never know now. But he wished he could have let them know what had happened to him. That troubled him. It would set him right in their eyes, it would perhaps be better for their characters, if they did not think—as they were almost bound to think—that he had run away from them or lapsed mentally or even fallen into bad company and been made away with. As it was they might be worried and ashamed, needlessly, or put to expense to find out where he was, and that would be a pity.

One had to die. Many men had died as he was going to die, fallen into strange places, lost in dark caverns, marooned on desert islands, astray in the Australian bush, imprisoned and left to perish. It was good to die without great anguish or insult. He thought of the myriads of men who had been crucified by the Romans—was it eight thousand or was it ten thousand of the army of Spartacus that they killed in that fashion along the Appian Way?—of negroes hung in chains to starve, and of an endless variety of such deaths. Shocking to young imaginations such things were and more fearful in thought than in reality. It is all a matter of a little more pain or a little less pain—but God will not have any great waste of pain. Cross, wheel, electric chair or bed of suffering—the thing is, *you die and have done.*

It was pleasant to find that one could think stoutly of these things. It was good to be caught and to find that one was not frantic. And Mr. Barnstaple was surprised to find how little he cared, now that he faced the issue closely, whether he was immortal or whether he was not. He was quite prepared to find himself immortal or at least not ending with death, in whole or in part. It was ridiculous to be dogmatic and say that a part, an impression, of his conscience and even of his willing life might not go on in some fashion. But he found it impossible to imagine how that could be. It was unimaginable. It was not to be anticipated. He had no fear of that continuation. He had no thought nor fear of the possibility of punishment or cruelty. The universe had at times seemed to him to be very carelessly put together, but he had never believed that it was the work of a malignant imbecile. It impressed him as immensely careless but not as dominatingly cruel. He had been what he had been, weak and limited and sometimes silly, but the punishment of these defects lay in the defects themselves.

He ceased to think about his own death. He began to think of life generally, its present lowliness, its valiant aspiration. He found himself regretting bitterly that he was not to see more of this Utopian world, which was in so many respects so near an intimation of what our own world may become. It had been very heartening to see human dreams and human ideals vindicated by realisation, but it was distressing to have had the vision snatched away while he was still only beginning to examine it. He found himself asking questions that had no answers for him, about economics, about love and struggle. Anyhow, he was glad to have seen as much as he had. It was good to have been purged by this vision and altogether lifted out of the dreary hopelessness of Mr. Peeve, to have got life into perspective again.

The passions and conflicts and discomforts of A.D. 1921 were the discomforts of the fever of an uninoculated world. The Age of Confusion on the Earth also would, in its own time, work itself out, thanks to a certain obscure and indomitable righteousness in the blood of the human type. Squatting in a hole in the cliff of the great crag, with unclimbable heights and depths above him and below, chilly, hungry and uncomfortable, this thought was a profound comfort to the strangely constituted mind of Mr. Barnstaple.

But how miserably had he and his companions failed to rise to the great occasions of Utopia! No one had raised an effectual hand to restrain the puerile imaginations of Mr. Catskill and the mere brutal aggressiveness of his companions. How invincibly had Father Amerton headed for the rôle of the ranting, hating, persecuting, quarrel-making priest. How pitifully weak and dishonest Mr. Burleigh—and himself scarcely better!

disapproving always and always in ineffective opposition. What an unintelligent beauty-cow that woman Greeta Grey was, receptive, acquisitive, impenetrable to any idea but the idea of what was due to her as a yielding female! Lady Stella was of finer clay, but fired to no service. Women, he thought, had not been well represented in this chance expedition, just one waster and one ineffective. Was that a fair sample of Earth's womankind?

All the use these Earthlings had had for Utopia was to turn it back as speedily as possible to the aggressions, subjugations, cruelties and disorders of the Age of Confusion to which they belonged. Serpentine and Cedar, the man of scientific power and the man of healing, they had sought to make hostages to disorder, and failing that they had killed or sought to kill them.

They had tried to bring back Utopia to the state of Earth, and indeed but for the folly, malice and weakness of men Earth was now Utopia. Old Earth was Utopia now, a garden and a glory, the Earthly Paradise, except that it was trampled to dust and ruin by its Catskills, Hunkers, Barralongas, Ridleys, Duponts and their kind. Against their hasty trampling folly nothing was pitted, it seemed, in the whole wide world at present but the whinings of the Peeves, the acquiescent disapproval of the Burleighs and such immeasurable ineffectiveness as his own protest. And a few writers and teachers who produced results at present untraceable.

Once more Mr. Barnstaple found himself thinking of his old friend, the school inspector and school-book writer, who had worked so steadfastly and broken down and died so pitifully. He had worked for Utopia all his days. Were there hundreds or thousands of such Utopians yet on earth? What magic upheld them?

"I wish I could get some message through to them," said Mr. Barnstaple, "to hearten them."

For it was true, though he himself had to starve and die like a beast fallen into a pit, nevertheless Utopia triumphed and would triumph. The grabbers and fighters, the persecutors and patriots, the lynchers and boycotters and all the riff-raff of short-sighted human violence, crowded on to final defeat. Even in their lives they know no happiness, they drive from excitement to excitement and from gratification to exhaustion. Their enterprises and successes, their wars and glories, flare and pass. Only the true thing grows, the truth, the clear idea, year by year and age by age, slowly and invincibly as a diamond grows amidst the darkness and pressures of the earth, or as the dawn grows amidst the guttering lights of some belated orgy.

What would be the end of those poor little people up above there? Their hold on life was even more precarious than his own, for he might lie and starve here slowly for weeks before his mind gave its last flicker. But they had openly pitted themselves against the might and wisdom of Utopia, and even now the ordered power of that world must be closing in upon them. He still had a faint irrational remorse for his betrayal of Catskill's ambush. He smiled now at the passionate conviction he had felt at the time that if once Catskill could capture his hostages, Earth might prevail over Utopia. That conviction had rushed him into action. His weak cries had seemed to be all that was left to avert this monstrous disaster. But suppose he had not been there at all, or suppose he had obeyed the lingering instinct of fellowship that urged him to fight with the others; what then?

When he recalled the sight of Cedar throwing Mush about as one might throw a lap-dog about, and the height and shape of Serpentine, he doubted whether even upon the stairs in the archway it would have been possible for the Earthlings to have overpowered these two. The revolvers would have come into use just as they had come into use upon the slope, and Catskill would have got no hostages but only two murdered men.

How unutterably silly the whole scheme of Catskill had been! But it was no sillier than the behaviour of Catskill, Burleigh and the rest of the world's statesmen had been on earth, during the last few years. At times during the world agony of the Great War it had seemed that Utopia drew near to earth. The black clouds and smoke of these dark years had been shot with the light of strange hopes, with the promise of a world reborn. But the nationalists, financiers, priests and patriots had brought all those hopes to nothing. They had trusted to old poisons and infections and to the weak resistances of the civilised spirit. They had counted their weapons and set their ambushes and kept their women busy sewing flags of discord....

For a time they had killed hope, but only for a time. For Hope, the redeemer of mankind, there is perpetual resurrection.

"Utopia will win," said Mr. Barnstaple and for a time he sat listening to a sound he had heard before without heeding it very greatly, a purring throb in the rocks about him, like the running of some great machine. It grew louder and then faded down to the imperceptible again.

His thoughts came back to his erstwhile companions. He hoped they were not too miserable or afraid up there. He was particularly desirous that something should happen to keep up Lady Stella's courage. He worried affectionately about Lady Stella. For the rest it would be as well if they remained actively combative to the end. Possibly they were all toiling at some preposterous and wildly hopeful defensive scheme of Catskill's. Except Mr. Burleigh who would be resting—convinced that for him at least there would still be a gentlemanly way out. And probably not much afraid if there wasn't. Amerton and possibly Mush might lapse into a religious revival—that would irritate the others a little, or possibly even provide a mental opiate for Lady Stella and Miss Greeta Grey. Then for Penk there was wine in the cellar....

They would follow the laws of their being, they would do the things that nature and habit would require of them. What else was possible?

Mr. Barnstaple plunged into a metaphysical gulf....

Presently he caught himself looking at his wrist-watch. It was twenty minutes past twelve. He was looking at his watch more and more frequently or time was going more slowly.... Should he wind his watch or let it run down? He was already feeling very hungry. That could not be real hunger yet; it must be his imagination getting out of control.

●4

The End of Quarantine Crag

∽

MR. BARNSTAPLE AWOKE SLOWLY AND RELUCTANTLY FROM A DREAM about cookery. He was Soyer, the celebrated chef of the Reform Club, and he was inventing and tasting new dishes. But in the pleasant way of dreamland he was not only Soyer, but at the same time he was a very clever Utopian biologist and also God Almighty. So that he could not only make new dishes, but also make new vegetables and meats to go into them. He was particularly interested in a new sort of fowl, the Chateaubriand breed of fowls, which was to combine the rich quality of very good beefsteak with the size and delicacy of a fowl's breast. And he wanted to stuff it with a blend of pimento, onion and mushroom—except that the mushroom wasn't quite the thing. The mushrooms—he tasted them—indeed just the least little modification. And into the dream came an assistant cook, several assistant cooks, all naked as Utopians, bearing fowls from the pantry and saying that they had not kept, they had gone "high" and they were going higher. In order to illustrate this idea of their going higher these assistant cooks lifted the fowls above their heads and then began to climb the walls of the kitchen, which were rocky and for a kitchen remarkably close together. Their figures became dark. They were thrown up in black outline against the luminous steam arising from a cauldron of boiling soup. It was boiling soup, and yet it was cold soup and cold steam.

Mr. Barnstaple was awake.

In the place of luminous steam there was mist, brightly moonlit mist, filling the gorge. It threw up the figures of the two Utopians in black silhouette....

What Utopians?

His mind struggled between dreaming and waking. He started up rigidly attentive. They moved with easy gestures, quite unaware of his presence so close to them. They had already got a thin rope ladder fixed to some point overhead, but how they had managed to do this he did not know. One still stood on the shelf, the other swayed above him stretched across the gully clinging to the rope with his feet against the rock. The head of a third figure appeared above the edge of the shelf. It swayed from side to side. He was evidently coming up by a second rope ladder. Some sort of discussion was in progress. It was borne in upon Mr. Barnstaple that this last comer thought that he and his companions had clambered high enough, but that the uppermost man insisted they should go higher. In a few moments the matter was settled.

The uppermost Utopian became very active, lunged upward, swung out and vanished by jerks out of Mr. Barnstaple's field of view. His companions followed him and one after the other was lost to sight, leaving nothing visible but the convulsively agitated rope ladder and a dangling rope that they seemed to be dragging up the crag with them.

Mr. Barnstaple's taut muscles relaxed. He yawned silently, stretched his painful limbs and stood up very cautiously. He peered up the gully. The Utopians seemed to have reached the shelf above and to be busy there. The rope that had dangled became taut. They were hauling up something from below. It was a large bundle, possibly of tools or weapons or material wrapped in something that deadened its impacts against the rock. It jumped into view, hung spinning for a moment and was then snatched upward as the Utopians took in a fresh reef of rope. A period of silence followed.

He heard a metallic clang and then, thud, thud, a dull intermittent hammering. Then he jumped back as the end of a thin rope, apparently running over a pulley, dropped past him. The sounds from above now were like filing and then some bits of rock fell past him into the void.

HE DID NOT KNOW WHAT TO DO. HE WAS AFRAID TO CALL TO THESE Utopians and make his presence known to them. After the murder of Serpentine he was very doubtful how a Utopian would behave to an Earthling found hiding in a dark corner.

He examined the rope ladder that had brought these Utopians to his level. It was held by a long spike the end of which was buried in the rock at the side of the gully. Possibly this spike had been fired at the rock from below while he was asleep. The ladder was made up of straight lengths and rings at intervals of perhaps two feet. It was of such light material that he would have doubted its capacity to bear a man if he had not seen the Utopians upon it. It occurred to him that he might descend by this now and take his chances with any Utopians who might be below. He could not very well bring himself to the attention of these three Utopians above except by some sudden and startling action which might provoke sudden and unpleasant responses, but if he appeared first clambering slowly from above any Utopians beneath would have time to realize and consider the fact of his proximity before they dealt with him. And also he was excessively eager to get down from this dreary ledge.

He gripped a ring, thrust a leg backwards over the edge of the shelf, listened for some moments to the little noises of the three workers above him, and then began his descent.

It was an enormous descent. Presently he found himself regretting that he had not begun counting the rings of the ladder. He must already have handed himself down hundreds. And still when he craned his neck to look down, the dark gulf yawned below. It had become very dark now. The moonlight did not cut down very deeply into the canyon and the faint reflection from the thin mists above was all there was to break the blackness. And even overhead the moonlight seemed to be passing.

Now he was near the rock, now it fell away and the rope ladder seemed to fall plumb into lightless bottomless space. He had to feel for each ring, and his bare feet and hands were already chafed and painful. And a new and disagreeable idea had come into his head—that some Utopian might presently come rushing up the ladder. But he would get notice of that because the rope would tighten and quiver, and he would be able to cry out, "I am an Earthling coming down. I am a harmless Earthling."

He began to cry out these words experimentally. The gorge re-echoed them, and there was no answering sound.

He became silent again, descending grimly and as steadily as possible, because now an intense desire to get off this infernal rope ladder and rest his hot hands and feet was overmastering every other motive.

Clang, clang and a flash of green light.

He became rigid peering into the depths of the canyon. Came the green flash again. It revealed the depths of the gorge, still as it seemed an immense distance below him. And up the gorge—something; he could not grasp what it was during that momentary revelation. At first he thought it was a huge serpent writhing its way down the gorge, and then he concluded it must be a big cable that was being brought along the gorge by a handful of Utopians. But how the three or four figures he had indistinctly seen could move this colossal rope he could not imagine. The head of this cable serpent seemed to be lifting itself obliquely up the cliff. Perhaps it was being dragged up by ropes he had not observed. He waited for a third flash, but none came. He listened. He could hear nothing but a throbbing sound he had already noted before, like the throbbing of an engine running very smoothly.

He resumed his descent.

When at last he reached a standing place it took him by surprise. The rope ladder fell past it for some yards and ended. He was swaying more and more and beginning to realize that the rope ladder came to an end, when he perceived the dim indication of a nearly horizontal gallery cut along the rock face. He put out a foot and felt an edge and swung away out from it. He was now so weary and exhausted that for a time he could not relinquish his grip on the rope ladder and get a footing on the shelf. At last he perceived how this could be done. He released his feet and gave himself a push away from the rock with them. He swung back into a convenient position for getting a foothold. He repeated this twice, and then had enough confidence to abandon his ladder and drop on to the shelf. The ladder dangled away from him into the darkness and then came wriggling back to tap him playfully and startlingly on the shoulder blade.

The gallery he found himself in seemed to follow a great vein of crystalline material, along the cliff face. Borings as high as a man ran into the rock. He peered and felt his way along the gallery for a time. Manifestly if this was a mine there would be some way of ascending to it and descending from it into the gorge. The sound of the torrent was much louder now, and he judged he had perhaps come down two-thirds of the height of the crag. He was inclined to wait for daylight. The illuminated dial of his wrist-watch told him it was now four o'clock. It would not be long before dawn. He found a comfortable face of rock for his back and squatted down.

Dawn seemed to come very quickly, but in reality he dozed away the interval. When he glanced at his watch again it was half-past five.

He went to the edge of the gallery and peered up the gorge to where he had seen the cable. Things were pale and dim and very black and white, but perfectly clear. The walls of the canyon seemed to go up for ever and vanish at last in cloud. He had a glimpse of a Utopian below, who was presently hidden by the curve of the gorge. He guessed that the great cable must have been brought so close up to the Quarantine Crag as to be invisible to him.

He could find no down-going steps from the gallery, but some thirty or forty yards off were five or six cable ways running at a steep angle from the gallery to the opposite side of the gorge. They looked very black and distinct. He went along to them. Each was a carrier cable on which ran a small carrier trolley with a big hook below. Three of the carrier cables were empty, but on two the trolley was hauled up. Mr. Barnstaple examined the trolleys and found a catch retained them. He turned over one of these catches and the trolley ran away promptly, nearly dropping him into the gulf. He saved himself by clutching the carrier cable. He watched the trolley swoop down like a bird to a broad stretch of sandy beach on the other side of the torrent and come to rest there. It seemed all right. Trembling violently, he turned to the remaining trolley.

His nerves and will were so exhausted now that it was a long time before he could bring himself to trust to the hook of the remaining trolley and to release its catch. Then smoothly and swiftly he swept across the gorge to the beach below. There were big heaps of crystalline mineral on this beach and a cable—evidently for raising it—came down out of the mists above from some invisible crane, but not a Utopian was in sight. He relinquished his hold and dropped safely on his feet. The beach broadened down-stream and he walked along it close to the edge of the torrent.

The light grew stronger as he went. The world ceased to be a world of greys and blacks; colour came back to things. Everything was heavily bedewed. And he was hungry and almost intolerably weary. The sand changed in its nature and became soft and heavy for his feet. He felt he could walk no further. He must wait for help. He sat down on a rock and looked up towards Quarantine Crag towering overhead.

Sheer and high the great headland rose like the prow of some gigantic ship behind the two deep blue canyons; a few wisps and layers of mist still hid from Mr. Barnstaple its crest and the little bridge across the narrower gorge. The sky above between the streaks of mist was now an intense blue. And even as he gazed the mists swirled and dissolved, the rays of the rising sun smote the old castle to blinding gold, and the fastness of the Earthlings stood out clear and bright.

The bridge and the castle were very remote and all that part of the crag was like a little cap on the figure of a tall upstanding soldier. Round beneath the level of the bridge at about the height at which the three Utopians had worked or were still working ran something dark, a rope-like band. He jumped to the conclusion that this must be the cable he had seen lit up by those green flashes in the night. Then he noted a peculiar body upon the crest of the more open of the two gorges. It was an enormous vertical coil, a coil flattened into a disc, which had appeared on the edge of the cliff opposite to Coronation Crag. Less plainly seen because of a projecting mass of rock was a similar coil in the narrower canyon close to the steps that led up from the little bridge. Two or three Utopians, looking very small because they were so high and very squat because they were so foreshortened, were moving along the cliff edge and handling something that apparently had to do with these coils.

Mr. Barnstaple stared at these arrangements with much the same uncomprehending stare as that with which some savage who had never heard a shot fired in anger might watch the loading of a gun.

Came a familiar sound, faint and little. It was the hooter of Quarantine Castle sounding the reveille. And almost simultaneously the little Napoleonic figure of Mr. Rupert Catskill emerged against the blue. The head and shoulders of Penk rose and halted and stood at attention behind him. The captain of the Earthlings produced his field glasses and surveyed the coils through them.

"I wonder what he makes of them," said Mr. Barnstaple.

Mr. Catskill turned and gave some direction to Penk, who saluted and vanished.

A click from the nearer gorge jerked his attention back to the little bridge. It had gone. His eye dropped and caught it up within a few yards of the water. He saw the water splash and the metal framework crumple up and dance two steps and lie still, and then a moment later the crash and clatter of the fall reached his ears.

"Now who did that?" asked Mr. Barnstaple and Mr. Catskill answered his question by going hastily to that corner of the castle and staring down. Manifestly he was surprised. Manifestly therefore it was the Utopians who had cut the bridge.

Mr. Catskill was joined almost immediately by Mr. Hunker and Lord Barralonga. Their gestures suggested an animated discussion.

The sunlight was creeping by imperceptible degrees down the front of Quarantine Crag. It had now got down to the cable that encircled the crest; in the light this shone with a coppery sheen. The three Utopians who had awakened Mr. Barnstaple in the night became visible descending the rope ladder very rapidly. And once more Mr. Barnstaple was aware of that humming sound he had heard ever and again during the night, but now it was much louder and it sounded everywhere about him, in the air, in the water, in the rocks and in his bones.

Abruptly something black and spear-shaped appeared beside the little group of Earthlings above. It seemed to jump up beside them, it paused and jumped again half the height of a man and jumped again. It was a flag being hauled up a flag staff, that Mr. Barnstaple had not hitherto observed. It reached the top of the staff and hung limp.

Then some eddy in the air caught it. It flapped out for a moment, displayed a white star on a blue ground and dropped again.

This was the flag of Earth—this was the flag of the crusade to restore the blessings of competition, conflict and warfare to Utopia. Beneath it appeared the head of Mr. Burleigh, examining the Utopian coils through his glasses.

THE THROBBING AND HUMMING IN MR. BARNSTAPLE'S EARS GREW rapidly louder and rose acutely to an extreme intensity. Suddenly great flashes of violet light leapt across from coil to coil, passing through Quarantine Castle as though it was not there.

For a moment longer it *was* there.

The flag flared out madly and was torn from its staff. Mr. Burleigh lost his hat. A half length of Mr. Catskill became visible struggling with his coat tails which had blown up and enveloped his head. At the same time Mr. Barnstaple saw the castle rotating upon the lower part of the crag, exactly as though some invisible giant had seized the upper tenth of the headland and was twisting it round.

And then it vanished.

As it did so, a great column of dust poured up into its place; the waters in the gorge sprung into the air in tall fountains and were splashed to spray, and a deafening thud smote Mr. Barnstaple's ears. Aerial powers picked him up and tossed him a dozen yards and he fell amidst a rain of dust and stones and water. He was bruised and stunned.

"My God!" he cried, "My God," and struggled to his knees, feeling violently sick.

He had a glimpse of the crest of Quarantine Crag, truncated as neatly as though it had been cheese cut with a sharp knife. And then fatigue and exhaustion had their way with him and he sprawled forward and lay insensible.

BOOK THE THIRD

A Neophyte in Utopia

1

The Peaceful Hills Beside the River

~

"GOD HAS MADE MORE UNIVERSES THAN THERE ARE PAGES IN ALL THE libraries of earth; man may learn and grow for ever amidst the multitude of His worlds."

Mr. Barnstaple had a sense of floating from star to star and from plane to plane, through an incessant variety and wonder of existences. He passed over the edge of being; he drifted for ages down the faces of immeasurable cliffs; he travelled from everlasting to everlasting in a stream of innumerable little stars. At last came a phase of profound restfulness. There was a sky of level clouds, warmed by the light of a declining sun, and a skyline of gently undulating hills, golden grassy upon their crests and carrying dark purple woods and thickets and patches of pale yellow like ripening corn upon their billowing slopes. Here and there were domed buildings and terraces, flowering gardens and little villas and great tanks of gleaming water.

There were many trees like the eucalyptus—only that they had darker leaves—upon the slopes immediately below and round and about him; and all the land fell at last towards a very broad valley down which a shining river wound leisurely in great semi-circular bends until it became invisible in evening haze.

A slight movement turned his eyes to discover Lychnis seated beside him. She smiled at him and put her finger on her lips. He had a vague desire to address her, and smiled faintly and moved his head. She got up and slipped away from him past the head of his couch. He was too feeble and incurious to raise his head and look to see where she had gone. But he saw that she had been sitting at a white table on which was a silver bowl full of intensely blue flowers, and the colour of the flowers held him and diverted his first faint impulse of curiosity.

He wondered whether colours were really brighter in this Utopian world or whether something in the air quickened and clarified his apprehension.

Beyond the table were the white pillars of the loggia. A branch of one of these eucalyptus-like trees, with leaves bronze black, came very close outside.

And there was music. It was a little trickle of sound, that dripped and ran, a mere unobtrusive rivulet of little clear notes upon the margin of his consciousness, the song of some fairyland Debussy.

Peace....

~

HE WAS AWAKE AGAIN.

He tried hard to remember.

He had been knocked over and stunned in some manner too big and violent for his mind to hold as yet.

Then people had stood about him and talked about him. He remembered their feet. He must have been lying on his face with his face very close to the ground. Then they had turned him over, and the light of the rising sun had been blinding in his eyes.

Two gentle goddesses had given him some restorative in a gorge at the foot of high cliffs. He had been carried in a woman's arms as a child is carried. After that there were cloudy and dissolving memories of a long journey, a long flight through the air. There was something next to this, a vision of huge complicated machinery that did not join on to anything else. For a time his mind held this up in an interrogative fashion and then dropped it wearily. There had been voices in consultation, the prick of an injection and some gas that he had had to inhale. And sleep—or sleeps, spells of sleep interspersed with dreams....

Now with regard to that gorge; how had he got there?

The gorge—in another light, a greenish light—with Utopians who struggled with a great cable.

Suddenly hard and clear came the vision of the headland of Coronation Crag towering up against the bright blue morning sky, and then the crest of it grinding round, with its fluttering flags and its dishevelled figures, passing slowly and steadily, as some great ship passes out of a dock, with its flags and passengers into the invisible and unknown. All the wonder of his great adventure returned to Mr. Barnstaple's mind.

He sat up in a state of interrogation and Lychnis reappeared at his elbow.

She seated herself on his bed close to him, shook up some pillows behind him and persuaded him to lie back upon them. She conveyed to him that he was cured of some illness and no longer infectious, but that he was still very weak. Of what illness? he asked himself. More of the immediate past became clear to him.

"There was an epidemic," he said. "A sort of mixed epidemic—of all our infections."

She smiled reassuringly. It was over. The science and organization of Utopia had taken the danger by the throat and banished it. Lychnis, however, had had nothing to do with the preventive and cleansing work that had ended the career of these invading microbes so speedily; her work had been the help and care of the sick. Something came through to the intelligence of Mr. Barnstaple that made him think that she was faintly sorry that this work of pity was no longer necessary. He looked up into her beautiful kindly eyes and met her affectionate solicitude. She was not sorry Utopia was cured again; that was incredible; but it seemed to him that she was sorry that she could no longer spend herself in help and that she was glad that he at least was still in need of assistance.

"What became of those people on the rock?" he asked. "What became of the other Earthlings?"

She did not know. They had been cast out of Utopia, she thought.

"Back to earth?"

She did not think they had gone back to earth. They had perhaps gone into yet another universe. But she did not know. She was one of those who had no mathematical aptitudes, and physico-chemical science and the complex theories of dimensions that interested so many people in Utopia were outside her circle of ideas. She believed that the crest of Coronation Crag had been swung out of the Utopian universe altogether. A great number of people were now intensely interested in this experimental work upon the unexplored dimensions into which physical processes might he swung, but these matters terrified her. Her mind recoiled from them as one recoils from the edge of a cliff. She did not want to think where the Earthlings had gone, what deeps they had reeled over, what immensities they had seen and swept down into. Such thoughts opened dark gulfs beneath her feet where she had thought everything fixed and secure. She was a conservative in Utopia. She loved life as it was and as it had been. She had given herself to the care of Mr. Barnstaple when she had found that he had escaped the fate of the other Earthlings and she had not troubled very greatly about the particulars of that fate. She had avoided thinking about it.

"But where are they? Where have they gone?"

She did not know.

She conveyed to him haltingly and imperfectly her own halting and unsympathetic ideas of these new discoveries that had inflamed the Utopian imagination. The crucial moment had been the experiment of Arden and Greenlake that had brought the Earthlings into Utopia. That had been the first rupture of the hitherto invincible barriers that had held their universe in three spatial dimensions. That had opened these abysses. That had been the moment of release for all the new work that now filled Utopia. That had been the first achievement of practical results from an intricate network of theory and deduction. It sent Mr. Barnstaple's mind back to the humbler discoveries of earth, to Franklin snapping the captive lightning from his kite and Galvani, with his dancing frog's legs, puzzling over the miracle that brought electricity into the service of men. But it had taken a century and a half for electricity to make any sensible changes in human life because the earthly workers were so few and the ways of the world so obstructive and slow and spiteful. In Utopia to make a novel discovery was to light an intellectual conflagration. Hundreds of thousands of experimentalists in free and open co-operation were now working along the fruitful lines that Arden and Greenlake had made manifest. Every day, every hour now, new and hitherto fantastic possibilities of inter-spatial relationship were being made plain to the Utopians.

Mr. Barnstaple rubbed his head and eyes with both hands and then lay back, blinking at the great valley below him, growing slowly golden as the sun sank. He felt himself to be the most secure and stable of beings at the very centre of a sphere of glowing serenity. And that effect of an immense tranquillity was a delusion; that still evening peace, was woven of incredible billions of hurrying and clashing atoms.

All the peace and fixity that man has ever known or will ever know is but the smoothness of the face of a torrent that flies along with incredible speed from cataract to cataract. Time was when men could talk of ever-lasting hills. To-day a schoolboy knows that they dissolve under the frost and wind and rain and pour seaward, day by day and hour by hour. Time was when men could speak of Terra Firma and feel the earth fixed, adamantine beneath their feet. Now they know that it whirls through space eddying about a spinning, blindly driven sun amidst a sheeplike drift of stars. And this fair curtain of appearance before the eyes of Mr. Barnstaple, this still and level flush of sunset and the great cloth of starry space that hung behind the blue; that too was now to be pierced and torn and rent asunder....

The extended fingers of his mind closed on the things that concerned him most.

"But where are my people?" he asked. "Where are their bodies? Is it just possible they are still alive?"

She could not tell him.

He lay thinking.... It was natural that he should be given into the charge of a rather backward-minded woman. The active-minded here had no more use for him in their lives than active-minded people on earth have for pet animals. She did not want to think about these spatial relations at all; the subject was too difficult for her; she was one of Utopia's educational failures. She sat beside him with a divine sweetness and tranquillity upon her face, and he felt his own judgment upon her like a committed treachery. Yet he wanted to know very badly the answer to his question.

He supposed the crest of Coronation Crag had been twisted round and flung off into some outer space. It was unlikely that this time the Earthlings would strike a convenient planet again. In all probability they had been turned off into the void, into the interstellar space of some unknown universe....

What would happen then? They would freeze. The air would instantly diffuse right out of them. Their own gravitation would flatten them out, crush them together, collapse them! At least they would have no time to suffer. A gasp, like some one flung into ice-cold water....

He contemplated these possibilities.

"Flung out!" he said aloud. "Like a cageful of mice thrown over the side of a ship!"

"I don't understand," said Lychnis, turning to him.

He appealed to her. "And now—tell me. What is to become of me?"

FOR A TIME LYCHNIS GAVE HIM NO ANSWER. SHE SAT WITH HER SOFT eyes upon the blue haze into which the great river valley had now dissolved. Then she turned to him with a question:

"You want to stay in this world?"

"Surely any Earthling would want to stay in this world. My body has been purified. Why should I not stay?"

"It seems a good world to you?"

"Loveliness, order, health, energy and wonder; it has all the good things for which my world groans and travails."

"And yet our world is not content."

"I could be contented."

"You are tired and weak still."

"In this air I could grow strong and vigorous. I could almost grow young in this world. In years, as you count them here, I am still a young man."

Again she was silent for a time. The mighty lap of the landscape was filled now with indistinguishable blue, and beyond the black silhouettes of the trees upon the hillside only the skyline of the hills was visible against the yellow green and pale yellow of the evening sky. Never had Mr. Barnstaple seen so peaceful a nightfall. But her words denied that peace. "Here," she said, "there is no rest. Every day men and women awake and say: What new thing shall we do to-day? What shall we change?"

"They have changed a wild planet of disease and disorder into a sphere of beauty and safety. They have made the wilderness of human motives bear union and knowledge and power."

"And research never rests, and curiosity and the desire for more power and still more power consumes all our world."

"A healthy appetite. I am tired now, as weak and weary and soft as though I had just been born; but presently when I have grown stronger I too may share in that curiosity and take a part in these great discoveries that now set Utopia astir. Who knows?"

He smiled at her kind eyes.

"You will have much to learn," she said.

She seemed to measure her own failure as she said these words.

Some sense of the profound differences that three thousand years of progress might have made in the fundamental ideas and ways of thinking of the race dawned upon Mr. Barnstaple's mind. He remembered that in Utopia he heard only the things he could understand, and that all that found no place in his terrestrial circle of ideas was inaudible to his mind. The gulfs of misunderstanding might be wider and deeper than he was assuming. A totally illiterate Gold Coast negro trying to master thermo-electricity would have set himself a far more hopeful task.

"After all it is not the new discoveries that I want to share," he said; "quite possibly they are altogether beyond me; it is this perfect, beautiful daily life, this life of all the dreams of my own time come true, that I want. I just want to be alive here. That will be enough for me."

"You are weak and tired yet," said Lychnis. "When you are stronger you may face other ideas."

"But what other ideas—?"

"Your mind may turn back to your own world and your own life."

"Go back to Earth!"

Lychnis looked out at the twilight again for a while before she turned to him with, "You are an Earthling born and made. What else can you be?"

"What else can I be?" Mr. Barnstaple's mind rested upon that, and he lay feeling rather than thinking amidst its implications as the pin-point lights of Utopia pricked the darkling blue below and ran into chains and groups and coalesced into nebulous patches.

He resisted the truth below her words. This glorious world of Utopia, perfect and assured, poised ready for tremendous adventures amidst untravelled universes, was a world of sweet giants and uncompanionable beauty, a world of enterprises in which a poor muddy-witted, weak-willed Earthling might neither help nor share. They had plundered their planet as one empties a purse; they thrust out their power amidst the stars.... They were kind. They were very kind.... But they were different....

2

A Loiterer in a Living World

~

IN A FEW DAYS MR. BARNSTAPLE HAD RECOVERED STRENGTH OF BODY
and mind. He no longer lay in bed in a loggia, filled with self-pity and the
beauty of a world subdued; he went about freely and was soon walking
long distances over the Utopian countryside, seeking acquaintances and
learning more and more of this wonderland of accomplished human
desires.

For that is how it most impressed him. Nearly all the greater evils of
human life had been conquered; war, pestilence and malaise, famine and
poverty had been swept out of human experience. The dreams of artists,
of perfected and lovely bodies and of a world transfigured to harmony and
beauty had been realized; the spirits of order and organization ruled
triumphant. Every aspect of human life had been changed by these
achievements.

The climate of this Valley of Rest was bland and sunny like the climate
of South Europe, but nearly everything characteristic of the Italian or
Spanish scene had gone. Here were no bent and aged crones carrying
burthens, no chattering pursuit by beggars, no ragged workers lowering by
the wayside. The puny terracing, the distressing accumulations of hand
cultivation, the gnarled olives, hacked vines, the little patches of grain or
fruit, and the grudged litigious irrigation of those primitive conditions,

gave place to sweeping schemes of conservation, to a broad and subtle handling of slope and soil and sunshine. No meagre goats nor sheep, child-tended, cropped among the stones, no tethered cattle ate their apportioned circles of herbage and no more. There were no hovels by the wayside, no shrines with tortured, blood-oozing images, no slinking misbegotten curs nor beaten beasts sweating and panting between their overloaded paniers at the steeper places of rutted, rock-strewn and dung-strewn roads. Instead the great smooth indestructible ways swept in easy gradients through the land, leaping gorges and crossing valleys upon wide-arched viaducts, piercing cathedral-like aisles through the hillsides, throwing off bastions to command some special splendour of the land. Here were resting places and shelters, stairways clambering to pleasant arbours and summer-houses where friends might talk and lovers shelter and rejoice. Here were groves and avenues of such trees as he had never seen before. For on earth as yet there is scarcely such a thing as an altogether healthy fully grown tree, nearly all our trees are bored and consumed by parasites, rotten and tumorous with fungi, more gnarled and crippled and disease-twisted even than mankind.

The landscape had absorbed the patient design of five-and-twenty centuries. In one place Mr. Barnstaple found great works in progress; a bridge was being replaced, not because it was outworn, but because someone had produced a bolder, more delightful design.

For a time he did not observe the absence of telephonic or telegraphic communication; the posts and wires that mark a modern countryside had disappeared. The reasons for that difference he was to learn later. Nor did he at first miss the railway, the railway station and the wayside inn. He perceived that the frequent buildings must have specific functions, that people came and went from them with an appearance of interest and preoccupation, that from some of them seemed to come a hum and whir of activity; work of many sorts was certainly in progress; but his ideas of the mechanical organization of this new world were too vague and tentative as yet for him to attempt to fix any significance to this sort of place or that. He walked agape like a savage in a garden.

He never came to nor saw any towns. The reason for any such close accumulations of human beings had largely disappeared. In certain places, he learnt, there were gatherings of people for studies, mutual stimulation, or other convenient exchanges, in great series of communicating buildings; but he never visited any of these centres.

And about this world went the tall people of Utopia, fair and wonderful, smiling or making some friendly gesture as they passed him but giving him little chance for questions or intercourse. They travelled swiftly in machines upon the high road or walked, and ever and again the shadow of a silent soaring aeroplane would pass over him. He went a little in awe of these people and felt himself a queer creature when he met their eyes. For like the gods of Greece and Rome theirs was a cleansed and perfected humanity, and it seemed to him that they were gods. Even the great tame beasts that walked freely about this world had a certain divinity that checked the expression of Mr. Barnstaple's friendliness.

PRESENTLY HE FOUND A COMPANION FOR HIS RAMBLES, A BOY OF thirteen, a cousin of Lychnis, named Crystal. He was a curly-headed youngster, brown-eyed as she was; and he was reading history in a holiday stage of his education.

So far as Mr. Barnstaple could gather the more serious part of his intellectual training was in mathematical work interrelated to physical and chemical science, but all that was beyond an Earthling's range of ideas. Much of this work seemed to be done in co-operation with other boys, and to be what we should call research on earth. Nor could Mr. Barnstaple master the nature of some other sort of study which seemed to turn upon refinements of expression. But the history brought them together. The boy was just learning about the growth of the Utopian social system out of the efforts and experiences of the Ages of Confusion. His imagination was alive with the tragic struggles upon which the present order of Utopia was founded, he had a hundred questions for Mr. Barnstaple, and he was full of explicit information which was destined presently to sink down and become part of the foundations of his adult mind. Mr. Barnstaple was as good as a book to him, and he was as good as a guide to Mr. Barnstaple. They went about together talking upon a footing of the completest equality, this rather exceptionally intelligent Earthling and this Utopian stripling, who topped him by perhaps an inch when they stood side by side.

The boy had the broad facts of Utopian history at his fingers' ends. He could explain and find an interest in explaining how artificial and upheld the peace and beauty of Utopia still were. Utopians were in essence, he said, very much what their ancestors had been in the beginnings of the newer stone-age, fifteen thousand or twenty thousand years ago. They were still very much what Earthlings had been in the corresponding period. Since then there had been only six hundred or seven hundred generations and no time for any very fundamental changes in the race. There had not been even a general admixture of races. On Utopia as on earth there had been dusky and brown peoples, and they remained distinct. The various races mingled socially but did not interbreed very much; rather they purified and intensified their racial gifts and beauties. There was often very passionate love between people of contrasted race, but rarely did such love come to procreation. There had been a certain deliberate elimination of ugly, malignant, narrow, stupid and gloomy types during the past dozen centuries or so; but except for the fuller realisation of his latent possibilities, the common man in Utopia was very little different from the ordinary energetic and able people of a later stone-age or early bronze-age community. They were infinitely better nourished, trained and educated, and mentally and physically their condition was clean and fit, but they were the same flesh and nature as we are.

"But," said Mr. Barnstaple, and struggled with that idea for a time. "Do you mean to tell me that half the babies born on earth to-day might grow to be such gods as these people I meet?"

"Given our air, given our atmosphere."

"Given your heritage."

"Given our freedom."

In the past of Utopia, in the Age of Confusion, Mr. Barnstaple had to remember, everyone had grown up with a crippled or a thwarted will, hampered by vain restrictions or misled by plausible delusions. Utopia still bore it in mind that human nature was fundamentally animal and savage and had to be adapted to social needs, but Utopia had learnt the better methods of adaptation—after endless failures of compulsion, cruelty and deception. "On Earth we tame our animals with hot irons and our fellow men by violence and fraud," said Mr. Barnstaple, and described the schools and books, newspapers and public discussions of the early twentieth century to his incredulous companion. "You cannot imagine how beaten and fearful even decent people are upon Earth. You learn of the Age of Confusion in your histories but you do not know what the realities of a bad mental atmosphere, an atmosphere of feeble laws, hates and superstitions, are. As night goes round the Earth always there are hundreds of thousands of people who should be sleeping, lying awake, fearing a bully, fearing a cruel competition, dreading lest they cannot make good, ill of some illness they cannot comprehend, distressed by some irrational quarrel, maddened by some thwarted instinct or some suppressed and perverted desire."...

Crystal admitted that it was hard to think now of the Age of Confusion in terms of misery. Much of the every-day misery of Earth was now inconceivable. Very slowly Utopia had evolved its present harmony of law and custom and education. Man was no longer crippled and compelled; it was recognised that he was fundamentally an animal and that his daily life must follow the round of appetites satisfied and instincts released. The daily texture of Utopian life was woven of various and interesting foods and drinks, of free and entertaining exercise and work, of sweet sleep and of the interest and happiness of fearless and spiteless love-making. Inhibition was at a minimum. But where the power of Utopian education began was after the animal had been satisfied and disposed of. The jewel on the reptile's head that had brought Utopia out of the confusions of human life, was curiosity, the play impulse, prolonged and expanded in adult life into an insatiable appetite for knowledge and an habitual creative urgency. All Utopians had become as little children, learners and makers.

It was strange to hear this boy speaking so plainly and clearly of the educational process to which he was being subjected, and particularly to find he could talk so frankly of love.

An earthly bashfulness almost prevented Mr. Barnstaple from asking, "But you—You do not make Love?"

"I have had curiosities," said the boy, evidently saying what he had been taught to say. "But it is not necessary nor becoming to make love too early in life nor to let desire take hold of one. It weakens youth to become too early possessed by desire—which often will not leave one again. It spoils and cripples the imagination. I want to do good work as my father has done before me."

Mr. Barnstaple glanced at the beautiful young profile at his side and was suddenly troubled by memories of a certain study number four at school, and of some ugly phases of his adolescence, the stuffy, secret room, the hot and ugly fact. He felt a beastlier Earthling than ever. "Heigho!" he sighed. "But this world of yours is as clean as starlight and as sweet as cold water on a dusty day."

"Many people I love," said the boy, "but not with passion. Some day that will come. But one must not be too eager and anxious to meet passionate love or one might make-believe and give or snatch at a sham.... There is no hurry. No one will prevent me when my time comes. All good things come to one in this world in their own good time."

But work one does not wait for; one's work, since it concerns one's own self only, one goes to meet. Crystal thought very much about the work that he might do. It seemed to Mr. Barnstaple that work, in the sense of uncongenial toil, had almost disappeared from Utopia. Yet all Utopia was working. Everyone was doing work that fitted natural aptitudes and appealed to the imagination of the worker. Everyone worked happily and eagerly—as those people we call geniuses do on our Earth.

For suddenly Mr. Barnstaple found himself telling Crystal of the happiness of the true artist, of the true scientific worker, of the original man even on earth as it is to-day. They, too, like the Utopians, do work that concerns themselves and is in their own nature for great ends. Of all Earthlings they are the most enviable.

"If such men are not happy on earth," said Mr. Barnstaple, "it is because they are touched with vulgarity and still heed the soiled successes and honours and satisfactions of vulgar men, still feel neglect and limitation that should concern them no more. But to him who has seen the sun shine in Utopia surely the utmost honour and glory of earth can signify no more and be no more desirable than the complimentary spittle of the chieftain and a string of barbaric beads."

CRYSTAL WAS STILL OF AN AGE TO BE PROUD OF HIS *SAVOIR FAIRE*. HE showed Mr. Barnstaple his books and told him of his tutors and exercises.

Utopia still made use of printed books; books were still the simplest, clearest way of bringing statement before a tranquil mind. Crystal's books were very beautifully bound in flexible leather that his mother had tooled for him very prettily, and they were made of hand-made paper. The lettering was some fluent phonetic script that Mr. Barnstaple could not understand. It reminded him of Arabic; and frequent sketches, outline maps and diagrams were interpolated. Crystal was advised in his holiday reading by a tutor for whom he prepared a sort of exercise report, and he supplemented his reading by visits to museums; but there was no educational museum convenient in the Valley of Peace for Mr. Barnstaple to visit.

Crystal had passed out of the opening stage of education which was carried on, he said, upon large educational estates given up wholly to the lives of children. Education up to eleven or twelve seemed to be much more carefully watched and guarded and taken care of in Utopia than upon earth. Shocks to the imagination, fear and evil suggestions were warded off as carefully as were infection and physical disaster; by eight or nine the foundations of a Utopian character were surely laid, habits of cleanliness, truth, candour and helpfulness, confidence in the world, fearlessness and a sense of belonging to the great purpose of the race.

Only after nine or ten did the child go outside the garden of its early growth and begin to see the ordinary ways of the world. Until that age the care of the children was largely in the hands of nurses and teachers, but after that time the parents became more of a factor than they had been in a youngster's life. It was always a custom for the parents of a child to be near and to see that child in its nursery days, but just when earthly parents tended to separate from their children as they went away to school or went into business, Utopian parentage grew to be something closer. There was an idea in Utopia that between parent and child there was a necessary temperamental sympathy; children looked forward to the friendship and company of their parents, and parents looked forward to the interest of their children's adolescence, and though a parent had practically no power over a son or daughter, he or she took naturally the position of advocate, adviser and sympathetic friend. The friendship was all the franker and closer because of that lack of power, and all the easier because age for age the Utopians were so much younger and fresher-minded than Earthlings. Crystal it seemed had a very great passion for his mother. He was very proud of his father, who was a wonderful painter and designer; but it was his mother who possessed the boy's heart.

On his second walk with Mr. Barnstaple he said he was going to hear from his mother, and Mr. Barnstaple was shown the equivalent of correspondence in Utopia. Crystal carried a little bundle of wires and light rods; and presently coming to a place where a pillar stood in the midst of a lawn he spread this affair out like a long cat's cradle and tapped a little stud in the pillar with a key that he carried on a light gold chain about his neck. Then he took up a receiver attached to his apparatus, and spoke aloud and listened and presently heard a voice.

It was a very pleasant woman's voice; it talked to Crystal for a time without interruption, and then Crystal talked back, and afterwards there were other voices, some of which Crystal answered and some which he heard without replying. Then he gathered up his apparatus again.

This Mr. Barnstaple learnt was the Utopian equivalent of letter and telephone. For in Utopia, except by previous arrangement, people do not talk together on the telephone. A message is sent to the station of the district in which the recipient is known to be, and there it waits until he chooses to tap his accumulated messages. And any that one wishes to repeat can be repeated. Then he talks back to the senders and dispatches any other messages he wishes. The transmission is wireless. The little pillars supply electric power for transmission or for any other purpose the Utopians require. For example, the gardeners resort to them to run their mowers and diggers and rakes and rollers.

Far away across the valley Crystal pointed out the district station at which this correspondence gathered and was dispersed. Only a few people were on duty there; almost all the connexions were automatic. The messages came and went from any part of the planet.

This set Mr. Barnstaple going upon a long string of questions.

He discovered for the first time that the message organization of Utopia had a complete knowledge of the whereabouts of every soul upon the planet. It had a record of every living person and it knew in what message district he was. Everyone was indexed and noted.

To Mr. Barnstaple, accustomed to the crudities and dishonesties of earthly governments, this was an almost terrifying discovery. "On earth that would be the means of unending blackmail and tyranny," he said. "Everyone would lie open to espionage. We had a fellow at Scotland Yard. If he had been in your communication department he would have made life in Utopia intolerable in a week. You cannot imagine the nuisance he was."…

Mr. Barnstaple had to explain to Crystal what blackmail meant. It was like that in Utopia to begin with, Crystal said. Just as on earth so in Utopia there was the same natural disposition to use knowledge and power to the disadvantage of one's fellows, and the same jealousy of having one's personal facts known. In the stone age in Utopia men kept their true names secret and could only be spoken of by nicknames. They feared magic abuses. "Some savages still do that on earth," said Mr. Barnstaple. It was only very slowly that Utopians came to trust doctors and dentists and only very slowly that doctors and dentists became trustworthy. It was a matter of scores of centuries before the chief abuses of the confidences and trusts necessary to a modern social organization could be effectively corrected.

Every young Utopian had to learn the Five Principles of Liberty, without which civilisation is impossible. The first was the Principle of Privacy. This is that all individual personal facts are private between the citizen and the public organization to which he entrusts them, and can be used only for his convenience and with his sanction. Of course all such facts are available for statistical uses, but not as individual personal facts. And the second principle is the Principle of Free Movement. A citizen, subject to the due discharge of his public obligations, may go without permission or explanation to any part of the Utopian planet. All the means of transport are freely at his service. Every Utopian may change his surroundings, his climate and his social atmosphere as he will. The third principle is the Principle of Unlimited Knowledge. All that is known in Utopia, except individual personal facts about living people, is on record and as easily available as a perfected series of indices, libraries, museums and inquiry offices can make it. Whatever the Utopian desires to know he may know with the utmost clearness, exactness and facility so far as his powers of knowing and his industry go. Nothing is kept from him and nothing is misrepresented to him. And that brought Mr. Barnstaple to the fourth Principle of Liberty, which was that Lying is the Blackest Crime.

Crystal's definition of Lying was a sweeping one; the inexact statement of facts, even the suppression of a material fact, was lying.

"Where there are lies there cannot be freedom."

Mr. Barnstaple was mightily taken by this idea. It seemed at once quite fresh to him and one that he had always unconsciously entertained. Half the difference between Utopia and our world he asserted lay in this, that our atmosphere was dense and poisonous with lies and shams.

"When one comes to think of it," said Mr. Barnstaple, and began to expatiate to Crystal upon all the falsehoods of human life. The fundamental assumptions of earthly associations were still largely lies, false assumptions of necessary and unavoidable differences in flags and nationality, pretences of function and power in monarchy; impostures of organised learning, religious and moral dogmas and shams. And one must live in it; one is a part of it. You are restrained, taxed, distressed and killed by these insane unrealities. "Lying the Primary Crime! How simple that is! how true and necessary it is! That dogma is the fundamental distinction of the scientific world-state from all preceding states." And going on from that Mr. Barnstaple launched out into a long and loud tirade against the suppression and falsifications of earthly newspapers.

It was a question very near his heart. The London newspapers had ceased to be impartial vehicles of news; they omitted, they mutilated, they misstated. They were no better than propaganda rags. Rags! Nature, within its field, was shiningly accurate and full, but that was a purely scientific paper; it did not touch the every-day news. The Press, he held, was the only possible salt of contemporary life, and if the salt had lost its savour—!

The poor man was orating as though he was back at his Sydenham breakfast-table after a bad morning's paper.

"Once upon a time Utopia was in just such a tangle," said Crystal consolingly. "But there is a proverb, 'Truth comes back where once she has visited.' You need not trouble so much as you do. Some day even your press may grow clear."

"How do *you* manage about newspapers and criticism?" said Mr. Barnstaple.

Crystal explained that there was a complete distinction between news and discussion in Utopia. There were houses—one was in sight—which were used as reading-rooms. One went to these places to learn the news. Thither went the reports of all the things that were happening on the planet, things found, things discovered, things done. The reports were made as they were needed; there were no advertisement contracts to demand the same bulk of news every day. For some time Crystal said the reports had been very full and amusing about the Earthlings, but he had not been reading the paper for many days because of the interest in history the Earthling affair had aroused in him. There was always news of fresh scientific discoveries that stirred the imagination. One frequent item of public interest and excitement was the laying out of some wide scheme of research. The new spatial work that Arden and Greenlake had died for was producing much news. And when people died in Utopia it was the custom to tell the story of their lives. Crystal promised to take Mr. Barnstaple to a news place and entertain him by reading him some of the Utopian descriptions of earthly life which had been derived from the Earthlings, and Mr. Barnstaple asked that when this was done he might also hear about Arden and Greenlake, who had been not only great discoverers, but great lovers, and of Serpentine and Cedar, for whom he had conceived an intense admiration. Utopian news lacked of course the high spice of an earthly newspaper; the intriguing murders and amusing misbehaviours, the entertaining and exciting consequences of sexual ignorance and sexual blunderings, the libel cases and detected swindles, the great processional movements of Royalty across the general traffic, and the romantic fluctuations of the stock exchange and sport. But where the news of Utopia lacked liveliness, the liveliness of discussion made up for it. For the Fifth Principle of Liberty in Utopia was Free Discussion and Criticism.

Any Utopian was free to criticize and discuss anything in the whole universe provided he told no lies about it directly or indirectly; he could be as respectful or disrespectful as he pleased; he could propose anything however subversive. He could break into poetry or fiction as he chose. He could express himself in any literary form he liked or by sketch or caricature as the mood took him. Only he must refrain from lying; that was the one rigid rule of controversy. He could get what he had to say printed and distributed to the news rooms. There it was read or neglected as the visitors chanced to approve of it or not. Often if they liked what they read they would carry off a copy with them. Crystal had some new fantastic fiction about the exploration of space among his books; imaginative stories that boys were reading very eagerly; they were pamphlets of thirty or forty pages printed on a beautiful paper that he said was made directly from flax and certain reeds. The librarians noted what books and papers were read and taken away, and these they replaced with fresh copies. The piles that went unread were presently reduced to one or two copies and the rest went back to the pulping mills. But many of the poets and philosophers, and story-tellers whose imaginations found no wide popularity were nevertheless treasured and their memories kept alive by a few devoted admirers.

"I AM NOT AT ALL CLEAR IN MY MIND ABOUT ONE THING," SAID MR. Barnstaple. "I have seen no coins and nothing like money passing in this world. By all outward appearance this might be a Communism such as was figured in a book we used to value on Earth, a book called *News from Nowhere* by an Earthling named William Morris. It was a graceful impossible book. In that dream everyone worked for the joy of working and took what he needed. But I have never believed in Communism because I recognize, as here in Utopia you seem to recognize, the natural fierceness and greediness of the untutored man. There is joy in creation for others to use, but no natural joy in unrequited service. The sense of justice to himself is greater in man than the sense of service. Somehow here you must balance the work any one does for Utopia against what he destroys or consumes. How do you do it?"

Crystal considered. "There were Communists in Utopia in the Last Age of Confusion. In some parts of our planet they tried to abolish money suddenly and violently and brought about great economic confusion and want and misery. To step straight to Communism failed—very tragically. And yet Utopia to-day is practically a Communism, and except by way of curiosity I have never had a coin in my hand in all my life."

In Utopia just as upon earth, he explained, money came as a great discovery; as a method of freedom. Hitherto, before the invention of money, all service between man and man had been done through bondage or barter. Life was a thing of slavery and narrow choice. But money opened up the possibility of giving a worker a free choice in his reward. It took Utopia three thousand years and more to realize that possibility. The idea of money abounded in pitfalls and was easily corruptible; Utopia floundered its way to economic lucidity through long centuries of credit and debt, false and debased money; extravagant usury and every possibility of speculative abuse. In the matter of money more than in any other human concern, human cunning has set itself most vilely and treacherously to prey upon human necessity. Utopia once carried, as earth carries now, a load of parasitic souls, speculators, forestallers, gamblers and bargain-pressing Shylocks, exacting every conceivable advantage out of the weaknesses of the monetary system; she had needed centuries of economic sanitation. It was only when Utopia had got to the beginnings of world-wide political unity and when there were sufficiently full statistics of world resources and world production, that human society could at last give the individual worker the assurance of a coin of steadfast significance, a coin that would mean for him to-day or to-morrow or at any time the certainty of a set quantity of elemental values. And with peace throughout the planet and increasing social stability, interest, which is the measure of danger and uncertainty, dwindled at last to nothing. Banking became a public service perforce, because it no longer offered profit to the individual banker. "Rentier classes," Crystal conveyed, "are not a permanent element in any community. They mark a phase of transition between a period of insecurity and high interest and a period of complete security and no interest. They are a dawn phenomenon."

Mr. Barnstaple digested this statement after an interval of incredulity. He satisfied himself by a few questions that young Utopia really had some idea of what a rentier class was, what its moral and imaginative limitations were likely to be and the role it may have played in the intellectual development of the world by providing a class of independent minds.

"Life is intolerant of all independent classes," said Crystal, evidently repeating an axiom. "Either you must earn or you must rob.... We have got rid of robbing."

The youngster still speaking by his book went on to explain how the gradual disuse of money came about. It was an outcome of the general progressive organization of the economic system, the substitution of collective enterprises for competitive enterprises and of wholesale for retail dealing. There had been a time in Utopia when money changed hands at each little transaction and service. One paid money if one wanted a newspaper or a match or a bunch of flowers or a ride on a street conveyance. Everybody went about the world with pockets full of small coins paying on every slight occasion. Then as economic science became more stable and exact the methods of the club and the covering subscription extended. People were able to buy passes that carried them by all the available means of transport for a year or for ten years or for life. The State learnt from clubs and hotels to provide matches, newspapers, stationery and transport for a fixed annual charge. The same inclusive system spread from small and incidental things great and essential matters, to housing and food and even clothing. The State postal system knew where every Utopian citizen was, was presently able in conjunction with the public banking system to guarantee his credit in any part of the world. People ceased to draw coin for their work; the various departments of service, and of economic, educational and scientific activity would credit the individual with his earnings in the public bank and debit him with his customary charges for all the normal services of life.

"Something of this sort is going on on earth even now," said Mr. Barnstaple. "We use money in the last resort, but a vast volume of our business is already a matter of book-keeping."

Centuries of unity and energy had given Utopia very complete control of many fountains of natural energy upon the planet, and this was the heritage of every child born therein. He was credited at his birth with a sum sufficient to educate and maintain him up to four- or five-and-twenty, and then he was expected to choose some occupation to replenish his account.

"But if he doesn't?" said Mr. Barnstaple.

"Everyone does."

"But if he didn't?"

"He'd be miserable and uncomfortable. I've never heard of such a case. I suppose he'd be discussed. Psychologists might examine him.... But one must do something."

"But suppose Utopia had no work for him to do?"

Crystal could not imagine that. "There is always something to be done."

"But in Utopia once, in the old times, you had unemployment?"

"That was part of the Confusion. There was a sort of hypertrophy of debt; it had become paralysis. Why, when they had unemployment at that same time there was neither enough houses nor food nor clothing. They had unemployment and shortage at one and the same time. It is incredible."

"Does everyone earn about the same amount of pay?"

"Energetic and creative people are often given big grants if they seem to need the help of others or a command of natural resources.... And artists sometimes grow rich if their work is much desired."

"Such a gold chain as yours you had to buy?"

"From the maker in his shop. My mother bought it."

"Then there are shops?"

"You shall see some. Places where people go to see new and delightful things."

"And if an artist grows rich, what can he do with his money?"

"Take time and material to make some surpassingly beautiful thing to leave the world. Or collect and help with the work of other artists. Or do whatever else he pleases to teach and fine the common sense of beauty in Utopia. Or just do nothing.... Utopia can afford it—if he can."

"Cedar and Lion," said Mr. Barnstaple, "explained to the rest of us how it is that your government is as it were broken up and dispersed among the people who have special knowledge of the matters involved. The balance between interests, we gathered, was maintained by those who studied the general psychology and the educational organization of Utopia. At first it was very strange to our earthly minds that there should be nowhere a pretended omniscience and a practical omnipotence, that is to say a sovereign thing, a person or an assembly whose *fiat* was final. Mr. Burleigh and Mr. Catskill thought that such a thing was absolutely necessary, and so, less surely, did I. 'Who will decide?' was their riddle. They expected to be taken to see the President or the Supreme Council of Utopia. I suppose it seems to you the most natural of things that there should be nothing of the sort, and that a question should go simply and naturally to the man who knows best about it."

"Subject to free criticism," said Crystal.

"Subject to the same process that has made him eminent and responsible. But don't people thrust themselves forward even here—out of vanity? And don't people get thrust forward in front of the best—out of spite?"

"There is plenty of spite and vanity in every Utopian soul," said Crystal. "But people speak very plainly and criticism is very searching and free. So that we learn to search our motives before we praise or question."

"What you say and do shows up here plainly at its true value," said Mr. Barnstaple. "You cannot throw mud in the noise and darkness unchallenged or get a false claim acknowledged in the disorder."

"Some years ago there was a man, an artist, who made a great trouble about the work of my father. Often artistic criticism is very bitter here, but he was bitter beyond measure. He caricatured my father and abused him incessantly. He followed him from place to place. He tried to prevent the allocation of material to him. He was quite ineffective. Some people answered him, but for the most part he was disregarded...."

The boy stopped short.

"Well?"

"He killed himself. He could not escape from his own foolishness. Everyone knew what he had said and done...."

"But in the past there were kings and councils and conferences in Utopia," said Mr. Barnstaple, returning to the main point.

"My books teach me that our state could have grown up in no other way. We had to have these general dealers in human relationship, politicians and lawyers, as a necessary stage in political and social development. Just as we had to have soldiers and policemen to save people from mutual violence. It was only very slowly that politicians and lawyers came to admit the need for special knowledge in the things they had to do. Politicians would draw boundaries without any proper knowledge of ethnology or economic geography, and lawyers decide about will and purpose with the crudest knowledge of psychology. They produced the most preposterous and unworkable arrangements in the gravest fashion."

"Like Tristram Shandy's parish bull—which set about begetting the peace of the world at Versailles," said Mr. Barnstaple.

Crystal looked puzzled.

"A complicated allusion to a purely earthly matter," said Mr. Barnstaple. "This complete diffusion of the business of politics and law among the people with knowledge, is one of the most interesting things of all to me in this world. Such a diffusion is beginning upon earth. The people who understand world-health for instance are dead against political and legal methods, and so are many of our best economists. And most people never go into a law court, and wouldn't dream of doing so upon business of their own, from their cradles to their graves. What became of your politicians and lawyers? Was there a struggle?"

"As light grew and intelligence spread they became more and more evidently unnecessary. They met at last only to appoint men of knowledge as assessors and so forth, and after a time even these appointments became foregone conclusions. Their activities melted into the general body of criticism and discussion. In places there are still old buildings that used to be council chambers and law courts. The last politician to be elected to a legislative assembly died in Utopia about a thousand years ago. He was an eccentric and garrulous old gentleman; he was the only candidate and one man voted for him, and he insisted upon assembling in solitary state and having all his speeches and proceedings taken down in shorthand. Boys and girls who were learning stenography used to go to report him. Finally he was dealt with as a mental case."

"And the last judge?"

"I have not learnt about the last judge," said Crystal. "I must ask my tutor. I suppose there was one, but I suppose nobody asked him to judge anything. So he probably got something more respectable to do."

"I begin to apprehend the daily life of this world," said Mr. Barnstaple. "It is a life of demi-gods, very free, strongly individualized, each following an individual bent, each contributing to great racial ends. It is not only cleanly naked and sweet and lovely but full of personal dignity. It is, I see, a practical communism, planned and led up to through long centuries of education and discipline and collectivist preparation. I had never thought before that socialism could exalt and ennoble the individual and individualism degrade him, but now I see plainly that here the thing is proved. In this fortunate world—it is indeed the crown of all its health and happiness —there is no Crowd. The old world, the world to which I belong, was and in my universe alas still is, the world of the Crowd, the world of that detestable crawling mass of un-featured, infected human beings.

"You have never seen a Crowd, Crystal; and in all your happy life you never will. You have never seen a Crowd going to a football match or a race meeting or a bull-fight or a public execution or the like crowd joy; you have never watched a Crowd wedge and stick in a narrow place or hoot or howl in a crisis. You have never watched it stream sluggishly along the streets to gape at a King, or yell for a war, or yell quite equally for a peace. And you have never seen the Crowd, struck by some Panic breeze, change from Crowd proper to Mob and begin to smash and hunt. All the Crowd celebrations have gone out of this world; all the Crowd's gods, there is no Turf here, no Sport, no war demonstrations, no Coronations and Public Funerals, no great shows, but only your little theatres.... Happy Crystal! who will never see a Crowd!"

"But I have seen Crowds," said Crystal.

"Where?"

"I have seen cinematograph films of Crowds, photographed thirty centuries ago and more. They are shown in our history museums. I have seen Crowds streaming over downs after a great race meeting, photographed from an aeroplane, and Crowds rioting in some public square and being dispersed by the police. Thousands and thousands of swarming people. But it is true what you say. There are no more Crowds in Utopia. Crowds and the crowd-mind have gone forever."

WHEN AFTER SOME DAYS CRYSTAL HAD TO RETURN TO HIS mathematical studies, his departure left Mr. Barnstaple very lonely. He found no other companion. Lychnis seemed always near him and ready to be with him, but her want of active intellectual interests, so remarkable in this world of vast intellectual activities, estranged him from her. Other Utopians came and went, friendly, amused, polite, but intent upon their own business. They would question him curiously, attend perhaps to a question or so of his own, and depart with an air of being called away.

Lychnis, he began to realize, was one of Utopia's failures. She was a lingering romantic type and she cherished a great sorrow in her heart. She had had two children whom she had loved passionately. They were adorably fearless, and out of foolish pride she had urged them to swim out to sea and they had been taken by a current and drowned. Their father had been drowned in attempting their rescue and Lychnis had very nearly shared their fate. She had been rescued. But her emotional life had stopped short at that point, had, as it were, struck an attitude and remained in it. Tragedy possessed her. She turned her back on laughter and gladness and looked for distress. She had rediscovered the lost passion of pity, first pity for herself and then a desire to pity others. She took no interest any more in vigorous and complete people, but her mind concentrated upon the consolation to be found in consoling pain and distress in others. She sought her healing in healing them. She did not want to talk to Mr. Barnstaple of the brightness of Utopia; she wanted him to talk to her of the miseries of earth and of his own miseries. That she might sympathize. But he would not tell her of his own miseries because indeed, such was his temperament, he had none; he had only exasperations and regrets.

She dreamt, he perceived, of being able to come to earth and give her beauty and tenderness to the sick and poor. Her heart went out to the spectacle of human suffering and weakness. It went out to these things hungrily and desirously....

Before he detected the drift of her mind he told her many things about human sickness and poverty. But he spoke of these matters not with pity but indignation, as things that ought not to be. And when he perceived how she feasted on these things he spoke of them hardly and cheerfully as things that would presently be swept away. "But they will still have suffered," she said....

Since she was always close at hand, she filled for him perhaps more than her legitimate space in the Utopian spectacle. She lay across it like a shadow. He thought very frequently about her and about the pity and resentment against life and vigour that she embodied. In a world of fear, weakness, infection, darkness and confusion, pity, the act of charity, the alms and the refuge, the deed of stark devotion, might show indeed like sweet and gracious presences; but in this world of health and brave enterprises, pity betrayed itself a vicious desire. Crystal, Utopian youth, was as hard as his name. When he had slipped one day on some rocks and twisted and torn his ankle, he had limped but he had laughed. When Mr. Barnstaple was winded on a steep staircase Crystal was polite rather than sympathetic. So Lychnis had found no confederate in the dedication of her life to sorrow; even from Mr. Barnstaple she could win no sympathy. He perceived that indeed so far as temperament went he was a better Utopian than she was. To him as to Utopia it seemed rather an occasion for gladness than sorrow that her man and her children had met death fearlessly. They were dead; a brave stark death; the waters still glittered and the sun still shone. But her loss had revealed some underlying racial taint in her, something very ancient in the species, something that Utopia was still breeding out only very slowly, the dark sacrificial disposition that bows and responds to the shadow. It was strange and yet perhaps it was inevitable that Mr. Barnstaple should meet again in Utopia that spirit which Earth knows so well, the spirit that turns from the Kingdom of Heaven to worship the thorns and the nails, which delights to represent its God not as the Resurrection and the Life but as a woeful and defeated cadaver.

She would talk to him of his sons as if she envied him because of the loss of her own, but all she said reminded him of the educational disadvantages and narrow prospects of his boys and how much stouter and finer and happier their lives would have been in Utopia. He would have risked drowning them a dozen times to have saved them from being clerks and employees of other men. Even by earthly standards he felt now that he had not done his best by them; he had let many things drift in their lives and in the lives of himself and his wife that he now felt he ought to have controlled. Could he have his time over again he felt that he would see to it that his sons took a livelier interest in politics and science and were not so completely engulfed in the trivialities of suburban life, in tennis playing, amateur theatricals, inane flirtations and the like. They were good boys in substance he felt, but he had left them to their mother; and he had left their mother too much to herself instead of battling with her for the sake of his own ideas. They were living trivially in the shadow of one great catastrophe and with no security against another; they were living in a world of weak waste and shabby insufficiency. And his own life also had been— weak waste.

His life at Sydenham began to haunt him. "I criticized everything but I altered nothing," he said. "I was as bad as Peeve. Was I any more use in that world than I am in this? But on Earth we are all wasters...."

He avoided Lychnis for a day or so and wandered about the valley alone. He went into a great reading-room and fingered books he could not read; he was suffered to stand in a workshop, and he watched an artist make a naked girl of gold more lovely than any earthly statuette and melt her again dissatisfied; here he came upon men building, and here was work upon the fields, here was a great shaft in the hillside and something deep in the hill that flashed and scintillated strangely; they would not let him go in to it; he saw a thousand things he could not understand. He began to feel as perhaps a very intelligent dog must sometimes feel in the world of men, only that he had no master and no instincts that could find a consolation in canine abjection. The Utopians went about their business in the day-time, they passed him smiling and they filled him with intolerable envy. They knew what to do. They belonged. They went by in twos and threes in the evening, communing together and sometimes singing together. Lovers would pass him, their sweetly smiling faces close together, and his loneliness became an agony of hopeless desires.

Because, though he fought hard to keep it below the threshold of his consciousness, Mr. Barnstaple desired greatly to love and be loved in Utopia. The realisation that no one of these people could ever conceive of any such intimacy of body or spirit with him was a humiliation more fundamental even than his uselessness. The loveliness of the Utopian girls and women who glanced at him curiously or passed him with a serene indifference, crushed down his self-respect and made the Utopian world altogether intolerable to him. Mutely, unconsciously, these Utopian goddesses concentrated upon him the uttermost abasement of caste and race inferiority. He could not keep his thoughts from love where everyone it seemed had a lover, and in this Utopian world love for him was a thing grotesque and inconceivable....

Then one night as he lay awake distressed beyond measure by the thought of such things, an idea came to him whereby it seemed to him he might restore his self-respect and win a sort of citizenship in Utopia.

So that they might even speak of him and remember him with interest and sympathy.

The Service of the Earthling

THE MAN TO WHOM MR. BARNSTAPLE, AFTER DUE INQUIRIES, WENT TO talk was named Sungold. He was probably very old, because there were lines of age about his eyes and over his fine brow. He was a ruddy man, bearded with an auburn beard that had streaks of white, and his eyes were brown and nimble under his thick eyebrows. His hair had thinned but little and flowed back like a mane, but its copper-red colour had gone. He sat at a table with papers spread before him, making manuscript notes. He smiled at Mr. Barnstaple, for he had been expecting him, and indicated a seat for him with his stout and freckled hand. Then he waited smilingly for Mr. Barnstaple to begin.

"This world is one triumph of the desire for order and beauty in men's minds," said Mr. Barnstaple. "But it will not tolerate one useless soul in it. Everyone is happily active. Everyone but myself.... I belong nowhere. I have nothing to do. And no one—is related to me."

Sungold moved his head slightly to show that he understood.

"It is hard for an Earthling, with an earthly want of training, to fall into any place here. Into any usual work or any usual relationship. One is—a stranger.... But it is still harder to have no place at all. In the new work, of which I am told you know most of any one and are indeed the centre and regulator, it has occurred to me that I might be of some use, that I might indeed be as good as a Utopian.... If so, I want to be of use. You may want some one just to risk death—to take the danger of going into some strange place—some one who desires to serve Utopia—and who need not have skill or knowledge—or be a beautiful or able person?"

Mr. Barnstaple stopped short.

Sungold conveyed the completest understanding of all that was in Mr. Barnstaple's mind.

Mr. Barnstaple sat interrogative while for a time Sungold thought.

Then words and phrases began to string themselves together in Mr. Barnstaple's mind.

Sungold wondered if Mr. Barnstaple understood either the extent or the limitations of the great discoveries that were now being made in Utopia. Utopia, he said, was passing into a phase of intense intellectual exaltation. New powers and possibilities intoxicated the imagination of the race, and it was indeed inconceivable that an unteachable and perplexed Earthling could be anything but distressed and uncomfortable amidst the vast strange activities that must now begin. Even many of their own people, the more backward Utopians, were disturbed. For centuries Utopian philosophers and experimentalists had been criticizing, revising and reconstructing their former instinctive and traditional ideas of space and time, of form and substance, and now very rapidly the new ways of thinking were becoming clear and simple and bearing fruit in surprising practical applications. The limitations of space which had seemed for ever insurmountable were breaking down; they were breaking down in a strange and perplexing way but they were breaking down. It was now theoretically possible, it was rapidly becoming practicably possible, to pass from the planet Utopia to which the race had hitherto been confined, to other points in its universe of origin, that is to say to remote planets and distant stars.... That was the gist of the present situation.

"I cannot imagine that," said Mr. Barnstaple.

"You cannot imagine it," Sungold agreed, quite cordially. "But it is so. A hundred years ago it was inconceivable—here."

"Do you get there by some sort of backstairs in another dimension?" said Mr. Barnstaple.

Sungold considered this guess. It was a grotesque image, he said, but from the point of view of an Earthling it would serve. That conveyed something of its quality. But it was so much more wonderful....

"A new and astounding phase has begun for life here. We learnt long ago the chief secrets of happiness upon this planet. Life is good in this world. You find it good?... For thousands of years yet it will be our fastness and our home. But the wind of a new adventure blows through our life. All this world is in a mood like striking camp in the winter quarters when spring approaches."

He leant over his papers towards Mr. Barnstaple, and held up a finger and spoke audible words as if to make his meaning plainer. It seemed to Mr. Barnstaple that each word translated itself into English as he spoke it. At any rate Mr. Barnstaple understood. "The collision of our planet Utopia with your planet Earth was a very curious accident, but an unimportant accident, in this story. I want you to understand that. Your universe and ours are two out of a great number of gravitation-time universes, which are translated together through the inexhaustible infinitude of God. They are similar throughout, but they are identical in nothing. Your planet and ours happen to be side by side, so to speak, but they are not travelling at exactly the same pace nor in a strictly parallel direction. They will drift apart again and follow their several destinies. When Arden and Greenlake made their experiment the chances of their hitting anything in your universe were infinitely remote. They had disregarded it, they were merely rotating some of our matter out of and then back into our universe. You fell into us—as amazingly for us as for you. The importance of our discoveries for us lies in our own universe and not in yours. We do not want to come into your universe nor have more of your world come into ours. You are too like us, and you are too dark and troubled and diseased—you are too contagious—and we, we cannot help you yet because we are not gods but men."

Mr. Barnstaple nodded.

"What could Utopians do with the men of Earth? We have no strong instinct in us to teach or dominate other adults. That has been bred out of us by long centuries of equality and free co-operation. And you would be too numerous for us to teach and much of your population would be grown up and set in bad habits. Your stupidities would get in our way, your quarrels and jealousies and traditions, your flags and religions and all your embodied spites and suppressions, would hamper us in everything we should want to do. We should be impatient with you, unjust, overbearing. You are too like us for us to be patient with your failures. It would be hard to remember constantly how ill-bred you were. In Utopia we found out long ago that no race of human beings was sufficiently great, subtle and powerful to think and act for any other race. Perhaps already you are finding out the same thing on Earth as your races come into closer contact. And much more would this be true between Utopia and Earth. From what I know of your people and their ignorance and obstinacies it is clear our people would despise you; and contempt is the cause of all injustice. We might end by exterminating you.... But why should we make that possible?... We must leave you alone. We cannot trust ourselves with you.... Believe me this is the only reasonable course for us."

Mr. Barnstaple assented silently.

"You and I—two individuals—can be friends and understand."

"What you say is true," said Mr. Barnstaple. "It is true. But it grieves me it is true.... Greatly.... Nevertheless, I gather, I at least may be of service in Utopia?"

"You can."

"How?"

"By returning to your own world."

Mr. Barnstaple thought for some moments. It was what he had feared. But he had offered himself. "I will do that."

"By attempting to return, I should say. There is risk. You may be killed."

"I must take that."

"We want to verify all the data we have of the relations of our universe to yours. We want to reverse the experiment of Arden and Greenlake and see if we can return a living being to your world. We are almost certain now that we can do so. And that human being must care for us enough and care for his own world enough to go back and give us a sign that he has got there."

Mr. Barnstaple spoke huskily. "I can do that," he said.

"We can put you into that machine of yours and into the clothes you wore. You can be made again exactly as you left your world."

"Exactly. I understand."

"And because your world is vile and contentious and yet has some strangely able brains in it, here and there, we do not want your people to know of us, living so close to you—for we shall be close to you yet for some hundreds of years at least—we do not want them to know for fear that they should come here presently, led by some poor silly genius of a scientific man, come in their greedy, foolish, breeding swarms, hammering at our doors, threatening our lives, and spoiling our high adventures, and so have to be beaten off and killed like an invasion of rats or parasites."

"Yes," said Mr. Barnstaple. "Before men can come to Utopia, they must learn the way here. Utopia, I see, is only a home for those who have learnt the way."

He paused and answered some of his own thoughts. "When I have returned," he said, "shall I begin to forget Utopia?"

Sungold smiled and said nothing.

"All my days the nostalgia of Utopia will distress me."

"And uphold you."

"I shall take up my earthly life at the point where I laid it down, but—on Earth—I shall be a Utopian. For I feel that having offered my service and had it accepted, that I am no longer an outcast in Utopia. I belong...."

"Remember you may be killed. You may die in the trial."

"As it may happen."

"Well—Brother!"

The friendly paw took Mr. Barnstaple's and pressed it and the deep eyes smiled.

"After you have returned and given us your sign, several of the other Earthlings may also be sent back."

Mr. Barnstaple sat up. "*But*!" he gasped. His voice rose high in amazement. "I thought they were hurled into the blank space of some outer universe and altogether destroyed!"

"Several were killed. They killed themselves by rushing down the side of the old fortress in the outer darkness as the crag rotated. The men in leather. The man you call Long Barrow—"

"Barralonga?"

"Yes. And the man who shrugged his shoulders and said, 'What would you?' The others came back as the rotation was completed late in the day —asphyxiated and frozen but not dead. They have been restored to life, and we are puzzled now how to dispose of them.... They are of no use whatever in this world. They encumber us."

"It is only too manifest," said Mr. Barnstaple.

"The man you call Burleigh seems to be of some importance in your earthly affairs. We have searched his mind. His powers of belief are very small. He believes in very little but the life of a cultivated wealthy gentleman who holds a position of modest distinction in the councils of a largely fictitious empire. It is doubtful if he will believe in the reality of any of this experience. We will make sure anyhow that he thinks it has been an imaginative dream. He will consider it too fantastic to talk about because it is plain he is already very afraid of his imagination. He will find himself back in your world a few days after you reach it and he will make his way to his own home unobtrusively. He will come next after you. You will see him reappear in political affairs. Perhaps a little wiser."

"It might well be," said Mr. Barnstaple.

"And—what are the sounds of his name?—Rupert Catskill; he too will return. Your world would miss him."

"Nothing will make *him* wiser," said Mr. Barnstaple with conviction.

"Lady Stella will come."

"I am glad she has escaped. She will say nothing about Utopia. She is very discreet."

"The priest is mad. His behaviour became offensive and obscene and he is under restraint."

"What did he do?"

"He made a number of aprons of black silk and set out with them to attack our young people in an undignified manner."

"You can send him back," said Mr. Barnstaple after reflection.

"But will your world allow that sort of thing?"

"*We* call that sort of thing Purity," said Mr. Barnstaple. "But of course if you like to keep him...."

"He shall come back," said Sungold.

"The others you can keep," said Mr. Barnstaple. "In fact you will have to keep them. Nobody on Earth will trouble about them very much. In our world there are so many people that always a few are getting lost. As it is, returning even the few you propose to do may excite attention. Local people may begin to notice all these wanderers coming from nowhere in particular and asking their way home upon the Maidenhead Road. They might give way under questions.... You cannot send any more. Put the rest on an island. Or something of that sort. I wish I could advise you to keep the priest also. But many people would miss him. They would suffer from suppressed Purity and begin to behave queerly. The pulpit of St. Barnabas satisfies a recognised craving. And it will be quite easy to persuade him that Utopia is a dream and delusion. All priests believe that naturally of all Utopias. He will think of it, if he thinks of it at all, as—what would he call it—as a moral nightmare."

THEIR BUSINESS WAS FINISHED, BUT MR. BARNSTAPLE WAS LOTH TO GO.

He looked Sungold in the eye and found something kindly there.

"You have told me all that I have to do," he said, "and it is fully time that I went away from you, for any moment in your life is more precious than a day of mine. Yet because I am to go so soon and so obediently out of this vast and splendid world of yours back to my native disorders, I could find it in my heart to ask you to unbend if you could, to come down to me a little, and to tell me simply and plainly of the greater days and greater achievements that are now dawning upon this planet. You speak of your being able presently to go out of this Utopia to remote parts in your universe. That perplexes my mind. Probably I am unfitted to grasp that idea, but it is very important to me. It has been a belief in our world that at last there must be an end to life because our sun and planets are cooling, and there seems no hope of escape from the little world upon which we have arisen. We were born with it and we must die with it. That robbed many of us of hope and energy: for why should we work for progress in a world that must freeze and die?"

Sungold laughed. "Your philosophers concluded too soon."

He sprawled over the table towards his hearer and looked him earnestly in the face.

"Your Earthly science has been going on for how long?"

"Two hundred—three hundred years."

Sungold held up two fingers. "And men? How many men?"

"A few hundred who mattered in each generation."

"We have gone on for three thousand years now, and a hundred million good brains have been put like grapes into the wine-press of science. And we know to-day—how little we know. There is never an observation made but a hundred observations are missed in the making of it; there is never a measurement but some impish truth mocks us and gets away from us in the margin of error. I know something of where your scientific men are, all power to the poor savages! because I have studied the beginnings of our own science in the long past of Utopia. How can I express our distances? Since those days we have examined and tested and tried and retried a score of new ways of thinking about space, of which time is only a specialized form. We have forms of expression that we cannot get over to you so that things that used to seem difficult and paradoxical to us—that probably seem hopelessly difficult and paradoxical to you, lose all their difficulty in our minds. It is hard to convey to you. We think in terms of a space in which the space and time system, in terms of which you think, is only a specialized case. So far as our feelings and instincts and daily habits go we too live in another such system as you do—but not so far as our knowledge goes, not so far as our powers go. Our minds have exceeded our lives—as yours will. We are still flesh and blood, still hope and desire, we go to and fro and look up and down, but things that seemed remote are brought near, things that were inaccessible bow down, things that were insurmountable lie under the hollows of our hands."

"And you do not think your race nor, for the matter of that, ours, need ever perish?"

"Perish! We have hardly begun!"

The old man spoke very earnestly. Unconsciously he parodied Newton. "We are like little children who have been brought to the shores of a limitless ocean. All the knowledge we have gathered yet in the few score generations since first we began to gather knowledge, is like a small handful of pebbles gathered upon the shore of that limitless sea.

"Before us lies knowledge, endlessly, and we may take and take, and as we take, grow. We grow in power, we grow in courage. We renew our youth. For mark what I say, our worlds grow younger. The old generations of apes and sub-men before us had aged minds; their narrow reluctant wisdom was the meagre profit, hoarded and stale and sour, of innumerable lives. They dreaded new things; so bitterly did they value the bitterly won old. But to learn is, at length, to become young again, to be released, to begin afresh. Your world, compared with ours, is a world of unteachable encrusted souls, of bent and droning traditions, of hates and injuries and such-like unforgettable things. But some day you too will become again like little children, and it will be you who will find your way through to us —to us, who will be waiting for you. Two universes will meet and embrace, to beget a yet greater universe.... You Earthlings do not begin to realize yet the significance of life. Nor we Utopians—scarcely more.... Life is still only a promise, still waits to be born, out of such poor stirrings in the dust as we....

"Some day here and everywhere, Life of which you and I are but anticipatory atoms and eddies, Life will awaken indeed, one and whole and marvellous, like a child awaking to conscious life. It will open its drowsy eyes and stretch itself and smile, looking the mystery of God in the face as one meets the morning sun. We shall be there then, all that matters of us, you and I....

"And it will be no more than a beginning, no more than a beginning...."

4

The Return of the Earthling

~

TOO SOON THE MORNING CAME WHEN MR. BARNSTAPLE WAS TO LOOK his last upon the fair hills of Utopia and face the great experiment to which he had given himself. He had been loth to sleep and he had slept little that night, and in the early dawn he was abroad, wearing for the last time the sandals and the light white robe that had become his Utopian costume. Presently he would have to struggle into socks and boots and trousers and collar; the strangest gear. It would choke him he felt, and he stretched his bare arms to the sky and yawned and breathed his lungs full. The valley below still drowsed beneath a coverlet of fleecy mists; he turned his face uphill, the sooner to meet the sun.

Never before had he been out among the Utopian flowers at such an early hour; it was amusing to see how some of the great trumpets still drooped asleep and how many of the larger blossoms were furled and hung. Many of the leaves too were wrapped up, as limp as new-hatched moths. The gossamer spiders had been busy and everything was very wet with dew. A great tiger came upon him suddenly out of a side path and stared hard at him for some moments with round yellow eyes. Perhaps it was trying to remember the forgotten instincts of its breed.

Some way up the road he passed under a vermilion archway and went up a flight of stone stairs that promised to bring him earlier to the crest.

A number of friendly little birds, very gaily coloured, flew about him for a time and one perched impudently upon his shoulder, but when he put up his hand to caress it it evaded him and flew away. He was still ascending the staircase when the sun rose. It was as if the hillside slipped off a veil of grey and blue and bared the golden beauty of its body.

Mr. Barnstaple came to a landing place upon the staircase and stopped, and stood very still watching the sunrise search and quicken the brooding deeps of the valley below.

Far away, like an arrow shot from east to west, appeared a line of dazzling brightness on the sea.

~

"Serenity," he murmured. "Beauty. All the works of men—in perfect harmony....minds brought to harmony...."

According to his journalistic habit he tried over phrases. "An energetic peace.... confusions dispersed.... A world of spirits, crystal clear...."

What was the use of words?

For a time he stood quite still listening, for from some slope above a lark had gone heavenward, spraying sweet notes. He tried to see that little speck of song and was blinded by the brightening blue of the sky.

Presently the lark came down and ceased. Utopia was silent, except for a burst of childish laughter somewhere on the hillside below.

It dawned upon Mr. Barnstaple how peaceful was the Utopian air in comparison with the tormented atmosphere of Earth. Here was no yelping and howling of tired or irritated dogs, no braying, bellowing, squealing and distressful outcries of uneasy beasts, no farmyard clamour, no shouts of anger, no barking and coughing, no sounds of hammering, beating, sawing, grinding, mechanical hooting, whistling, screaming and the like, no clattering of distant trains, clanking of automobiles or other ill-contrived mechanisms; the tiresome and ugly noises of many an unpleasant creature were heard no more. In Utopia the ear like the eye was at peace. The air which had once been a mud of felted noises was now—a purified silence. Such sounds as one heard lay upon it like beautiful printing on a generous sheet of fine paper.

His eyes returned to the landscape below as the last fleecy vestiges of mist dissolved away. Water-tanks, roads, bridges, buildings, embankments, colonnades, groves, gardens, channels, cascades and fountains grew multitudinously clear, framed under a branch of dark foliage from a white-stemmed tree that gripped a hold among the rocks at his side.

"Three thousand years ago this was a world like ours.... Think of it—in a hundred generations.... In three thousand years we might make our poor waste of an Earth, jungle and desert, slag-heap and slum, into another such heaven of beauty and power....

"Worlds they are—similar, but not the same....

"If I could tell them what I have seen!...

"Suppose all men could have this vision of Utopia....

"They would not believe it if I told them. No....

"They would bray like asses at me and bark like dogs!... They will have no world but their own world. It hurts them to think of any world but their own. Nothing can be done that has not been done already. To think otherwise would be humiliation.... Death, torture, futility—anything but humiliation! So they must sit among their weeds and excrement, scratching and nodding sagely at one another, hoping for a good dog-fight and to gloat upon pain and effort they do not share, sure that mankind stank, stinks and must always stink, that stinking is very pleasant indeed, and that there is nothing new under the sun...."

His thoughts were diverted by two young girls who came running one after the other up the staircase. One was dark even to duskiness and her hands were full of blue flowers; the other who pursued her was a year or so younger and golden fair. They were full of the limitless excitement of young animals at play. The former one was so intent upon the other that she discovered Mr. Barnstaple with a squeak of surprise after she had got to his landing. She stared at him with a quick glance of inquiry, flashed into impudent roguery, flung two blue flowers in his face and was off up the steps above. Her companion, intent on capture, flew by. They flickered up the staircase like two butterflies of buff and pink; halted far above and came together for a momentary consultation about the stranger, waved hands to him and vanished.

Mr. Barnstaple returned their greeting and remained cheered.

THE VIEW-POINT TO WHICH LYCHNIS HAD DIRECTED MR. BARNSTAPLE stood out on the ridge between the great valley in which he had spent the last few days and a wild and steep glen down which ran a torrent that was destined after some hundred miles of windings to reach the river of the plain. The view-point was on the crest of a crag, it bad been built out upon great brackets so that it hung sheer over a bend in the torrent below; on the one hand was mountainous scenery and a rich and picturesque foam of green vegetation in the depths, on the other spread the broad garden spaces of a perfected landscape. For a time Mr. Barnstaple scrutinized this glen into which he looked for the first time. Five hundred feet or so below him, so that he felt that he could have dropped a pebble upon its outstretched wings, a bustard was soaring.

Many of the trees below he thought must be fruit trees, but they were too far off to see distinctly. Here and there he could distinguish a footpath winding up among the trees and rocks, and among the green masses were little pavilions in which he knew the wayfarer might rest and make tea for himself and find biscuits and such-like refreshment and possibly a couch and a book. The whole world, he knew, was full of such summer-houses and kindly shelters....

After a time he went back to the side of this view place up which he had come, and regarded the great valley that went out towards the sea. The word Pisgah floated through his mind. For indeed below him was the Promised Land of human desires. Here at last, established and secure, were peace, power, health, happy activity, length of days and beauty. All that we seek was found here and every dream was realized.

How long would it be yet—how many centuries or thousands of years —before a man would be able to stand upon some high place on earth also and see mankind triumphant and wholly and forever at peace?...

He folded his arms under him upon the parapet and mused profoundly.

There was no knowledge in this Utopia of which Earth had not the germs, there was no power used here that Earthlings might not use. Here, but for ignorance and darkness and the spites and malice they permit, was Earth to-day....

Towards such a world as this Utopia Mr. Barnstaple had been striving weakly all his life. If the experiment before him succeeded, if presently he found himself alive again on Earth, it would still be towards Utopia that his life would be directed. And he would not be alone. On Earth there must be thousands, tens of thousands, perhaps hundreds of thousands, who were also struggling in their minds and acts to find a way of escape for themselves and for their children from the disorders and indignities of the Age of Confusion, hundreds of thousands who wanted to put an end to wars and waste, to heal and educate and restore, to set the banner of Utopia over the shams and divisions that waste mankind.

"Yes, but we fail," said Mr. Barnstaple and walked fretfully to and fro. "Tens and hundreds of thousands of men and women! And we achieve so little! Perhaps every young man and every young woman has had some dream at least of serving and bettering the world. And we are scattered and wasted, and the old things and the foul things, customs, delusions, habits, tolerated treasons, base immediacies, triumph over us!"

He went to the parapet again and stood with his foot on a seat, his elbow on his knee and his chin in his hand, staring at the loveliness of this world he was to leave so soon....

"We could do it."

And suddenly it was borne in upon Mr. Barnstaple that he belonged now soul and body to the Revolution, to the Great Revolution that is afoot on Earth; that marches and will never desist nor rest again until old Earth is one city and Utopia set up therein. He knew clearly that this Revolution is life, and that all other living is a trafficking of life with death. And as this crystallized out in his mind he knew instantly that so presently it would crystallize out in the minds of countless others of those hundreds of thousands of men and women on Earth whom minds are set towards Utopia.

He stood up. He began walking to and fro. "We shall do it," he said.

Earthly thought was barely awakened as yet to the task and possibilities before mankind. All human history so far had been no more than the stirring of a sleeper, a gathering discontent, a rebellion against the limitations set upon life, the unintelligent protest of thwarted imaginations. All the conflicts and insurrections and revolutions that had ever been on Earth were but indistinct preludes of the revolution that has still to come. When he had started out upon this fantastic holiday Mr. Barnstaple realized he had been in a mood of depression; earthly affairs had seemed utterly confused and hopeless to him; but now from the view-point of Utopia achieved, and with his health renewed, he could see plainly enough how steadily men on earth were feeling their way now, failure after failure, towards the opening drive of the final revolution. He could see how men in his own lifetime had been struggling out of such entanglements as the lie of monarchy, the lies of dogmatic religion and dogmatic morality towards public self-respect and cleanness of mind and body. They struggled now also towards international charity and the liberation of their common economic life from a network of pretences, dishonesties and impostures. There is confusion in all struggles; retractions and defeats; but the whole effect seen from the calm height of Utopia was one of steadfast advance....

There were blunders, there were set-backs, because the forces of revolution still worked in the twilight. The great effort and the great failure of the socialist movement to create a new state in the world had been contemporaneous with Mr. Barnstaple's life; socialism had been the gospel of his boyhood; he had participated in its hopes, its doubts, its bitter internal conflicts. He had seen the movement losing sweetness and gathering force in the narrowness of the Marxist formulae. He had seen it sacrifice its constructive power for militant intensity. In Russia he had marked its ability to overthrow and its inability to plan or build. Like every liberal spirit in the world he had shared the chill of Bolshevik presumption and Bolshevik failure, and for a time it had seemed to him that this open bankruptcy of a great creative impulse was no less and no more than a victory for reaction, that it gave renewed life to all the shams, impostures, corruptions, traditional anarchies and ascendancies that restrain and cripple human life.... But now from this high view-point in Utopia he saw clearly that the Phoenix of Revolution flames down to ashes only to be born again. While the noose is fitted round the Teacher's neck the youths are reading his teaching. Revolutions arise and die; the Great Revolution comes incessantly and inevitably.

The time was near—and in what life was left to him, he himself might help to bring it nearer—when the forces of that last and real revolution would work no longer in the twilight but in the dawn, and a thousand sorts of men and women now far apart and unorganised and mutually antagonistic would be drawn together by the growth of a common vision of the world desired. The Marxist had wasted the forces of revolution for fifty years; he had had no vision; he had had only a condemnation for established things. He had estranged all scientific and able men by his pompous affectation of the scientific; he had terrified them by his intolerant orthodoxy; his delusion that all ideas are begotten by material circumstances had made him negligent of education and criticism. He had attempted to build social unity on hate and rejected every other driving force for the bitterness of a class war. But now, in its days of doubt and exhaustion, vision was returning to Socialism, and the dreary spectacle of a proletarian dictatorship gave way once more to Utopia, to the demand for a world fairly and righteously at peace, its resources husbanded and exploited for the common good, its every citizen freed not only from servitude but from ignorance, and its surplus energies directed steadfastly to the increase of knowledge and beauty. The attainment of that vision by more and more minds was a thing now no longer to be prevented. Earth would tread the path Utopia had trod. She too would weave law, duty and education into a larger sanity than man has ever known. Men also would presently laugh at the things they had feared, and brush aside the impostures that had overawed them and the absurdities that had tormented and crippled their lives. And as this great revolution was achieved and earth wheeled into daylight, the burthen of human miseries would lift, and courage oust sorrow from the hearts of men. Earth, which was now no more than a wilderness, sometimes horrible and at best picturesque, a wilderness interspersed with weedy scratchings for food and with hovels and slums and slag-heaps, Earth too would grow rich with loveliness and fair as this great land was fair. The sons of Earth also, purified from disease, sweet-minded and strong and beautiful, would go proudly about their conquered planet and lift their daring to the stars.

"Given the will," said Mr. Barnstaple. "Given only the will."...

FROM SOME DISTANT PLACE CAME THE SOUND OF A SWEET-TONED BELL striking the hour.

The time for the service to which he was dedicated was drawing near. He must descend, and be taken to the place where the experiment was to be made.

He took one last look at the glen and then went back to the broad prospect of the great valley, with its lakes and tanks and terraces, its groves and pavilions, its busy buildings and high viaducts, its wide slopes of sunlit cultivation, its universal gracious amenity. "Farewell Utopia," he said, and was astonished to discover how deeply his emotions were stirred.

"Dear Dream of Hope and Loveliness, Farewell!"

He stood quite still in a mood of sorrowful deprivation too deep for tears.

It seemed to him that the spirit of Utopia bent down over him like a goddess, friendly, adorable—and inaccessible.

His very mind stood still.

"Never," he whispered at last, "for me.... Except to serve.... No...."

Presently he began to descend the steps that wound down from the view-point. For a time he noted little of the things immediately about him.

Then the scent of roses invaded his attention, and he found himself walking down a slanting pergola covered with great white roses and very active with little green birds. He stopped short and stood looking up at the leaves, light-saturated, against the sky. He put up his hands and drew down one of the great blossoms until it touched his cheek.

§ 5

They took Mr. Barnstaple back by aeroplane to the point upon the glassy road where he had first come into Utopia. Lychnis came with him and Crystal, who was curious to see what would be done.

A group of twenty or thirty people, including Sungold, awaited him. The ruined laboratory of Arden and Greenlake had been replaced by fresh buildings, and there were additional erections on the further side of the road; but Mr. Barnstaple could recognize quite clearly the place where Mr. Catskill had faced the leopard and where Mr. Burleigh had accosted him. Several new kinds of flowers were now out, but the blue blossoms that had charmed him on arrival still prevailed. His old car, the Yellow Peril, looking now the clumsiest piece of ironmongery conceivable, stood in the road. He went and examined it. It seemed to be in perfect order; it had been carefully oiled and the petrol tank was full.

In a little pavilion were his bag and all his earthly clothes. They were very clean and they had been folded and pressed, and he put them on. His shirt seemed tight across his chest and his collar decidedly tight, and his coat cut him a little under the arms. Perhaps these garments had shrunken when they were disinfected. He packed his bag and Crystal put it in the car for him.

Sungold explained very simply all that Mr. Barnstaple had to do. Across the road, close by the restored laboratory, stretched a line as thin as gossamer. "Steer your car to that and break it," he said. "That is all you have to do. Then take this red flower and put it down exactly where your wheel tracks show you have entered your own world."

Mr. Barnstaple was left beside the car. The Utopians went back twenty or thirty yards and stood in a circle about him. For a few moments everyone was still.

MR. BARNSTAPLE GOT INTO HIS CAR, STARTED HIS ENGINE, LET IT THROB for a minute and then put in the clutch. The yellow car began to move towards the line of gossamer. He made a gesture with one hand which

Lychnis answered. Sungold and others of the Utopians also made friendly movements. But Crystal was watching too intently for any gesture.

"Good-bye, Crystal!" cried Mr. Barnstaple, and the boy responded with a start.

Mr. Barnstaple accelerated, set his teeth and, in spite of his will to keep them open, shut his eyes as he touched the gossamer line. Came that sense again of unendurable tension and that sound like the snapping of a bow-string. He had an irresistible impulse to stop—go back. He took his foot from the accelerator, and the car seemed to fall a foot or so and stopped so heavily and suddenly that he was jerked forward against the steering wheel. The oppression lifted. He opened his eyes and looked about him.

The car was standing in a field from which the hay had recently been carried. He was tilted on one side because of a roll in the ground. A hedge in which there was an open black gate separated this hay-field from the high road. Close at hand was a board advertisement of some Maidenhead hotel. On the far side of the road were level fields against a background of low wooded hills. Away to the left was a little inn. He turned his head and saw Windsor Castle in the remote distance rising above poplar-studded meadows. It was not, as his Utopians had promised him, the exact spot of his departure from our Earth, but it was certainly less than a hundred yards away.

He sat still for some moments, mentally rehearsing what he had to do. Then he started the Yellow Peril again and drove it close up to the black gate.

He got out and stood with the red flower in his hand. He had to go back to the exact spot at which he had re-entered this universe and put that flower down there. It would be quite easy to determine that point by the track the car had made in the stubble. But he felt an extraordinary reluctance to obey these instructions. He wanted to keep this flower. It was the last thing, the only thing, he had now from that golden world. That and the sweet savour on his hands.

It was extraordinary that he had brought no more than this with him. Why had he not brought a lot of flowers? Why had they given him nothing, no little thing, out of all their wealth of beauty? He wanted intensely to keep this flower. He was moved to substitute a spray of honeysuckle from the hedge close at hand. But then he remembered that that would be infected stuff for them. He must do as he was told. He walked back along the track of his car to its beginning, stood for a moment hesitating, tore a single petal from that glowing bloom, and then laid down the rest of the great flower carefully in the very centre of his track. The petal he put in his pocket. Then with a heavy heart he went back slowly to his car and stood beside it, watching that star of almost luminous red.

His grief and emotion were very great. He was bitterly sorrowful now at having left Utopia.

It was evident the great drought was still going on, for the field and the hedges were more parched and brown than he had ever seen an English field before. Along the road lay a thin cloud of dust that passing cars continually renewed. This old world seemed to him to be full of unlovely sights and sounds and odours already half forgotten. There was the honking of distant cars, the uproar of a train, a thirsty cow mourning its discomfort; there was the irritation of dust in his nostrils and the smell of sweltering tar; there was barbed wire in the hedge nearby and along the top of the black gate, and horse-dung and scraps of dirty paper at his feet. The lovely world from which he had been driven had shrunken now to a spot of shining scarlet.

Something happened very quickly. It was as if a hand appeared for a moment and took the flower. In a moment it had gone. A little eddy of dust swirled and drifted and sank....

It was the end.

At the thought of the traffic on the main road Mr. Barnstaple stooped down so as to hide his face from the passers-by. For some minutes he was unable to regain his self-control. He stood with his arm covering his face, leaning against the shabby brown hood of his car....

At last this gust of sorrow came to an end and he could get in again, start up the engine and steer into the main road.

He turned eastward haphazard. He left the black gate open behind him. He went along very slowly for as yet he had formed no idea of whither he was going. He began to think that probably in this old world of ours he was being sought for as a person who had mysteriously disap-peared. Some one might discover him and he would become the focus of a thousand impossible questions. That would be very tiresome and disagree-able. He had not thought of this in Utopia. In Utopia it had seemed quite possible that he could come back into Earth unobserved. Now on earth that confidence seemed foolish. He saw ahead of him the board of a modest tea-room. It occurred that he might alight there, see a newspaper, ask a discreet question or so, and find out what had been happening to the world and whether he had indeed been missed.

He found a table already laid for tea under the window. In the centre of the room a larger table bore an aspidistra in a big green pot and a selection of papers, chiefly out-of-date illustrated papers. But there was also a copy of the morning's *Daily Express*.

He seized upon this eagerly, fearful that he would find it full of the mysterious disappearance of Mr. Burleigh, Lord Barralonga, Mr. Rupert Catskill, Mr. Hunker, Father Amerton and Lady Stella, not to mention the lesser lights.... Gradually as he turned it over his fears vanished. There was not a word about any of them!

"But surely," he protested to himself, now clinging to his idea, "their friends must have missed them!"

He read through the whole paper. Of one only did he find mention and that was the last name he would have expected to find—Mr. Freddy Mush. The Princess de Modena-Frascati (*nee* Higgisbottom) Prize for English literature had been given away to nobody in particular by Mr. Graceful Gloss owing to "the unavoidable absence of Mr. Freddy Mush abroad."

The problem of why there had been no hue and cry for the others opened a vast field of worldly speculation to Mr. Barnstaple in which he wandered for a time. His mind went back to that bright red blossom lying among the cut stems of the grass in the mown field and to the hand that had seemed to take it. With that the door that had opened so marvellously between that strange and beautiful world and our own had closed again.

Wonder took possession of Mr. Barnstaple's mind. That dear world of honesty and health was beyond the utmost boundaries of our space, utterly inaccessible to him now for evermore; and yet, as he had been told, it was but one of countless universes that move together in time, that lie against one another, endlessly like the leaves of a book. And all of them are as nothing in the endless multitudes of systems and dimensions that surround them. "Could I but rotate my arm out of the limits set to it," one of the Utopians had said to him; "I could thrust it into a thousand universes."...

A waitress with his teapot recalled him to mundane things.

The meal served to him seemed tasteless and unclean. He drank the queer brew of the tea because he was thirsty but he ate scarcely a mouthful.

Presently he chanced to put his hand in his pocket and touched something soft. He drew out the petal he had torn from the red flower. It had lost its glowing red, and as he held it out in the stuffy air of the room it seemed to writhe as it shrivelled and blackened; its delicate scent gave place to a mawkish odour.

"Manifestly," he said. "I should have expected this."

He dropped the lump of decay on his plate, then picked it up again and thrust it into the soil in the pot of the aspidistra.

He took up the *Daily Express* again and turned it over, trying to recover his sense of this world's affairs.

FOR A LONG TIME MR. BARNSTAPLE MEDITATED OVER THE *DAILY Express* in the tea-room at Colnebrook. His thoughts went far so that presently the newspaper slipped to the ground unheeded. He roused himself with a sigh and called for his bill. Paying, he became aware of a pocket-book still full of pound notes. "This will be the cheapest holiday I have ever had," he thought. "I've spent no money at all." He inquired for the post-office, because he had a telegram to send.

Two hours later he stopped outside the gate of his little villa at Sydenham. He set it open—the customary bit of stick with which he did this was in its usual place—and steered the Yellow Peril with the dexterity of use and went past the curved flower-bed to the door of his shed. Mrs. Barnstaple appeared in the porch.

"Alfred! You're back at last?"

"Yes, I'm back. You got my telegram?"

"Ten minutes ago. Where have you been all this time? It's more than a month."

"Oh! just drifting about and dreaming. I've had a wonderful time."

"You ought to have written. You really ought to have written.... You *did*, Alfred...."

"I didn't bother. The doctor said I wasn't to bother. I told you. Is there any tea going? Where are the boys?"

"The boys are out. Let me make you some fresh tea." She did so and came and sat down in the cane chair in front of him and the tea-table. "I'm glad to have you back. Though I could scold you....

"You're looking wonderfully well," she said. "I've never seen your skin so clear and brown."

"I've been in good air all the time."

"Did you get to the Lakes?"

"Not quite. But it's been good air everywhere. Healthy air."

"You never got lost?"

"Never."

"I had ideas of you getting lost—losing your memory. Such things happen. You didn't?"

"My memory's as bright as a jewel."

"But where did you go?"

"I just wandered and dreamt. Lost in a day-dream. Often I didn't ask the name of the place where I was staying. I stayed in one place and then in another. I never asked their names. I left my mind passive. Quite passive. I've had a tremendous rest—from everything. I've hardly given a thought to politics or money or social questions—at least, the sort of thing *we* call social questions—or any of these worries, since I started.... Is that this week's *Liberal?*"

He took it, turned it over, and at last tossed it on to the sofa. "Poor old Peeve," he said. "Of course I must leave that paper. He's like wall-paper on a damp wall. Just blotches and rustles and fails to stick.... Gives me mental rheumatics."

Mrs. Barnstaple stared at him doubtfully. "But I always thought that the *Liberal* was such a safe job."

"I don't want a safe job now. I can do better. There's other work before me.... Don't you worry. I can take hold of things surely enough after this rest.... How are the boys?"

"I'm a little anxious about Frankie."

Mr. Barnstaple had picked up the *Times*. An odd advertisement in the Agony column had caught his eye. It ran: "Cecil. Your absence exciting remark. Would like to know what you wish us to tell people. Write fully Scotch address. Di. ill with worry. All instructions will be followed."

"I beg your pardon, my dear?" he said putting the paper aside.

"I was saying that he doesn't seem to be settling down to business. He doesn't like it. I wish you could have a good talk to him. He's fretting because he doesn't *know* enough. He says he wants to be a science student at the Polytechnic and go on learning things."

"Well, he can. Sensible boy! I didn't think he had it in him. I meant to have a talk to him. But this meets me half-way. Certainly he shall study science."

"But the boy has to earn a living."

"That will come. If he wants to study science he shall."

Mr. Barnstaple spoke in a tone that was altogether new to Mrs. Barnstaple, a tone of immediate, quiet, and assured determination. It surprised her still more that he should use this tone without seeming to be aware that he had used it.

He bit his slice of bread-and-butter, and she could see that something in the taste surprised and displeased him. He glanced doubtfully at the remnant of the slice in his hand. "Of course," he said. "London butter. Three days' wear. Left about. Funny how quickly one's taste alters."

He picked up the *Times* again and ran his eye over its columns.

"This world is really very childish," he said. "Very. I had forgotten. Imaginary Bolshevik plots. Sinn Fein proclamations. The Prince. Poland. Obvious lies about the Chinese. Obvious lies about Egypt. People pulling Wickham Steed's leg. Sham-pious article about Trinity-Sunday. The Hitchin murder.... H'm!—rather a nasty one.... The Pomfort Rembrandt.... Insurance.... Letter from indignant peer about Death Duties.... Dreary Sport. Boating, Tennis, Schoolboy cricket. Collapse of Harrow! As though such things were of the slightest importance!... How silly it is—all of it! It's like coming back to the quarrels of servants and the chatter of children."

He found Mrs. Barnstaple regarding him intently. "I haven't seen a paper from the day I started until this morning," he explained.

He put down the paper and stood up. For some minutes Mrs. Barnstaple had been doubting whether she was not the victim of an absurd hallucination. Now she realized that she was in the presence of the most amazing fact she had ever observed.

"Yes," she said. "It is so. Don't move! Keep like that. I know it sounds ridiculous, Alfred, but you have grown taller. It's not simply that your stoop has gone. You have grown oh!—two or three inches."

Mr. Barnstaple stared at her, and then held out his arm. Certainly he was showing an unusual length of wrist. He tried to judge whether his trousers had also the same grown-out-of look.

Mrs. Barnstaple came up to him almost respectfully. She stood beside him and put her shoulder against his arm. "Your shoulder used to be exactly level with mine," she said. "See where we are now!"

She looked up into his eyes. As though she was very glad indeed to have him back with her.

But Mr. Barnstaple remained lost in thought. "It must be the extreme freshness of the air. I have been in some wonderful air.... Wonderful!... But at my age! To have grown! And I *feel* as though I'd grown, inside and out, mind and body."...

Mrs. Barnstaple presently began to put the tea-things together for removal.

"You seem to have avoided the big towns."

"I did."

"And kept to the country roads and lanes."

"Practically.... It was all new country to me.... Beautiful.... Wonderful...."

His wife still watched him.

"You must take *me* there some day," she said. "I can see that it has done you a world of good."

AFTERWORD

H.G. Wells: Dystopias, Utopias, and Cheating

When I was asked to write a foreword to a volume of stories by H.G. Wells, I readily and cheerfully agreed. After all, how hard could it be? I write science fiction. He wrote science fiction.

Oh, any number of famous volumes, most of which I've read:

The War of the Worlds. Still to this day—probably until the end of days—the classic tale of alien invasion and attempted conquest of the Earth.

The Time Machine. Possibly the first—I'm not sure about that, but I think it is—novel about time travel. Certainly, the one that set the basic parameters for that branch of science fiction.

The Island of Doctor Moreau. A novel which has second billing in the "mad scientist creates a monster" category only because it was preceded by Mary Shelley's *Frankenstein*. And, at least for my money, one that exceeds Shelley's tale in terms of the madness of the mad scientist involved. Poor Frankenstein was a victim of his own recklessness and lack of caution, not someone guilty of depraved insanity.

The War in the Air. The foundation novel of military science fiction.

The Invisible Man. Not simply one of the first explorations of optical manipulation but a story that, even more than the tales of Edgar Allan Poe, crosses science fiction with crime. As a piece of fiction, it's not really the equal of Alfred Bester's *The Demolished Man*, but it created the framework for it.

Right up my alley. A foreword I could practically write in my sleep.

And then the organizers of this project sprung the trap on me.

"We want you to write a foreword discussing H.G. Wells's lesser-known novels, *The Sleeper Awakes* and *Men Like Gods*."

Uh... excuse me?

I had at least read *The Sleeper Awakes*, although that was decades ago in that period of fearless youth when a person will read anything. I even remembered it, vaguely. A story about how good intentions go sour when the people overseeing the good intentions become corrupted by the privileges and power that oversight provides them. The "sleeper" of the title is a wealthy man who falls into a coma for two centuries. When he awakes, he discovers that his continually accumulating wealth has been used by his trustees to create a gigantic political and economic world order—of which they have made themselves the beneficiaries. He leads a revolution, which is triumphant, but at the end of which he dies in battle.

This novel is almost invariably called a "dystopia," but it isn't one. The mere fact that a story begins with a very bad situation does not make it a dystopia. As I will explain in a moment, almost *all* stories (of necessity) begin with a situation which is bad to one degree or another. Some are worse than others, of course. In one story, two would-be lovers fall afoul of (frequently preposterous) crossed signals which cause them a degree of angst before true love wins out. In others, someone is being hunted for sport and barely manages to outwit his would-be murderers. But, either way, in the end, the Right and Good prevail.

Which is exactly what happens in *The Sleeper Awakes*. In the final scene in the novel, just ten short paragraphs from the end, the hero Graham exults: "They win," he shouted to the empty air; "the people win!"

Sadly, in the very last paragraph he realizes his plane is about to crash and he is doomed. But that's just a personal misfortune. The so-called "dystopia" has been *corrected*. Which means it was no dystopia at all.

No, no, no. A *true* dystopia is distinguished above all else by the fact that by the end of the story, the hero or heroine's travails have achieved nothing. The terrible situation remains just as it was—maybe even worse.

George Orwell's *1984* is a dystopia. So is Aldous Huxley's *Brave New World*.

The Sleeper Awakes is not a dystopia—and don't let anyone tell you otherwise. Very few stories are. The reason is simple: Reading a dystopia may be good for your philosophical growth. I'm not at all sure that it is, but you can make a case for the proposition. That said, very few people read a dystopia a second time.

There are a few stories that are hard to categorize. Technically speaking, George Orwell's *Animal Farm* is a dystopia. But I've read it at least three times in the course of my life, which calls its dystopic reputation into question. The problem is that it's a wickedly funny satire, not the usual oh-so-dreary tale of hopelessness and misery.

And what of Franz Kafka's "The Metamorphosis"? From the standpoint of the protagonist Gregor Samsa, who wakes up one morning to discover he's become a huge insect, a situation about as dystopian as it gets—and, sure enough, he winds up dying of starvation. But from the standpoint of his family, his death is a blessing. His pretty young sister Grete no longer has to take care of him and is free to find a husband.

Speaking personally, there's a certain irony in my being asked to write a foreword discussing an H.G. Wells novel that's usually considered a dystopia. As it happens, some years ago I wrote a novel titled *Rats, Bats & Vats* which depicts a very dystopian setting which I based partly on H.G. Wells's own brand of socialism, the school of thought known as Fabian Socialism. George Bernard Shaw, another famous author, was also part of the group.

It was an odd variety of "socialism," based very much in England's upper crust and reflecting their views of the world. The end result is a political and economic order that isn't too different from the one Wells depicts in *The Sleeper Awakes*.

I know I'd read *The Sleeper Awakes* before I wrote my novel. Long before, in fact. Was I subconsciously influenced by it? It's possible.

In any event, I hasten to add that *Rats, Bats & Vats* is certainly not a dystopia. Yes, the situation at the start is wretched: A smug and well-situated ruling caste presides over a world in which uplifted rats and bats and vat-grown orphans must "earn" their place in society, and do so in an economic framework that makes that effectively impossible.

But—just as in *The Sleeper Awakes*—a revolution erupts! (This one's led by rats, bats, and vats, though, not the richest man in the world.) And by the end, while the situation is far from perfect, it's clear that the rotten bastards at the top are getting their just desserts and things are looking a lot brighter for the ones on the bottom. (And my hero and heroine survive, dammit, they don't die in the last sentence. What was Wells *thinking*?)

I have never written a dystopia, properly so-named. I can say with absolute confidence that I never will. The damn things are depressing and dreary, which means for the author who has to spend months writing the story—this author, anyway—they are boring.

And now we come to *Men Like Gods*. Which, God help me, is a *utopia*.

What author in their right mind would write a utopia? A utopian story violates the fundamental rule of all storytelling. It begins by jettisoning the Seven Essential Words that stand at the center of any story worth hearing or reading.

If you don't know the Seven Essential Words, here they are:

Oh, no! What do I/we do now?

That's what a story is. That's *all* it is.

We begin with the critical setting: *Oh, no!*

Translation: *Something is wrong.*

It could be anything. Aliens are invading. Locusts are invading. Bad guys are invading. There's an earthquake or a volcano or a skyscraper on fire or an airplane is about to crash. Your girlfriend/boyfriend is dumping you.

But no matter what it is, something is *wrong*.

There has to be something wrong. If there isn't, there's no story to tell.

This is not rocket science. The story that unfolds beginning from *Oh, no!* is, of course, *what do I (or we) do now?* But if you don't have an "oh, no!" then there's nothing that needs to be done.

This is the quandary—no, the Great Fallacy—of writing a utopia. The Seven Pointless Words of which are: *Yes, indeed. Everything is fine and dandy.*

Where do you go from there?

What H.G. Wells did with his novel *Men Like Gods*—I don't know any polite way to says this—is that he *cheated*. What he did was tell a story in which people from our oh-so-very-not-utopian world travel into the future and then—

This is cheating, pure and simple!

—they try to *overthrow* utopia.

I admit, it's a clever trick. It'd be like Dante's plot of the *Paradiso* revolving around Satan's attempted invasion and overthrow of Heaven. But cheating is cheating, no matter how you try to pretty it up.

Mind you, I don't blame Wells. If I were foolish enough to try to write a utopia, I'd cheat, too. How else can you possibly make the story interesting?

I've gone on long enough. I will leave you with this one thought, should you now or at any time in the future be tempted to read a utopia:

For every thousand people who've read Dante's *Inferno*, not more than a handful have ever read the *Paradiso*. And probably only one—maybe two—of them remembers any of it.

There's a reason for that. Storytellers don't call them the Seven Essential Words for nothing.

ERIC FLINT

PUBLISHER'S NOTE

This book was produced as part of the Publishing master's degree program at Western Colorado University, Graduate Program in Creative Writing. The students worked cooperatively to produce these fine new editions of worthy public-domain works. The intent is to bring literary classics to a new readership. For the enjoyment of a modern audience, some minor revisions to archaic terms or punctuation may have been made.

Because these works were written in a different time, some attitudes and phrasing may seem outdated to a modern audience. After careful consideration, rather than revising the author's work, we have chosen to preserve the original wording and intent.

COLOPHON

The Sleeper Awakes serialized in *The Graphic* & *Harper's Weekly* Jan 1899–May1899 as *When the Sleeper Awakes*, first book edition, Harper & Brothers London & New York 1899, revised by H.G. Wells in 1910 & re-released as *The Sleeper Awakes*. 1921, published by Collins & Sons of London.

Men Like Gods, serialized in *The Westminster Gazette*, Dec 1922–Feb 1923, first book edition, Cassell & Co., London, 1923, first US edition, The Macmillan Company, New York, 1923

ABOUT THE AUTHOR

Herbert George Wells is referred to as the Father of Science Fiction because of his groundbreaking works in establishing the genre. His most influential pieces include: *The Time Machine*, *The War of the Worlds*, *The Invisible Man*, and *The Island of Doctor Moreau*.

The youngest of four children, he was born in Kent, England on September 21, 1866, to former domestic servants. Wells fell in love with reading in his childhood while mending a broken leg and during his failed early career paths still read extensively from the house library where his mother had returned to working as a servant. He became a teacher at Midhurst Grammar school and was known for his abilities in Latin and science. He later won a scholarship to study science at what became the Royal College of Science in London. He joined the Debating Society there and sparked an interest in philosophers and the reformation of society—specifically, the concept of socialism. He wrote for the school journal and published his first serialized fiction story soon after. He continued his teaching career, studies, and writing—eventually teaching such renowned pupils as A.A. Milne. Many of his shorter articles and early writings remain unattributed to him. Wells was a diabetic and helped found The Diabetic Association in the UK. He married in 1891 but separated in 1894 after an affair with one of his students, Amy Catherine Robbins (called

Jane), whom he wed in 1895 and fathered two sons with. Wells had numerous affairs, frequently with much younger women, and even had a daughter with writer Amber Reeves, a son with feminist Rebecca West, and a list of mistresses that included Margaret Sanger, Odette Keun, and Moura Budberg (Countess Benckendorf).

His writings were fairly prolific, and he dabbled in nearly every genre, but science was his true love and science fiction became his most renowned mistress. He was a four-time nominee for the Nobel Prize in Literature (1921,1932,1935, and 1946). Wells is accredited with foreseeing the invention of tanks, nuclear weaponry, aircraft, and even the nebulous concept of the internet. He became a beloved patriarch in popular culture thanks to his contributions to science fiction – even being reimagined in television shows such as *Warehouse 13* and Sir Ridley Scott's *Prophets of Science Fiction*. He died at the age of 79 in his home at Regent's Park on August 13th, 1946.

OTHER WORDFIRE PRESS TITLES BY H.G. WELLS

Kipps: The Story of a Simple Man

The Complete War of the Worlds

The War in the Air

Our list of other WordFire Press authors and titles is always growing. To find out more and to shop our selection of titles, visit us at:
wordfirepress.com

 facebook.com/WordfireIncWordfirePress
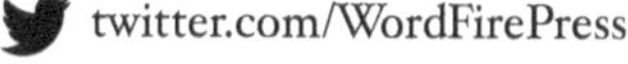 twitter.com/WordFirePress
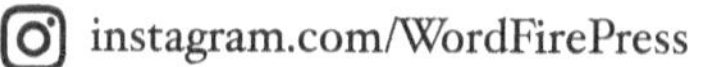 instagram.com/WordFirePress
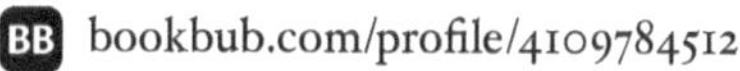 bookbub.com/profile/4109784512

9 781680 572094